Thomas Allen Jenckes, United States Congress

The Civil Service

report of Mr. Jenckes, of Rhode Island, from the Joint Select Committee on

Retrenchment, made to the House of Representatives of the United States, May

14, 1868

Thomas Allen Jenckes, United States Congress

The Civil Service
report of Mr. Jenckes, of Rhode Island, from the Joint Select Committee on Retrenchment,
made to the House of Representatives of the United States, May 14, 1868

ISBN/EAN: 9783337380564

Printed in Europe, USA, Canada, Australia, Japan

Cover: Foto ©Andreas Hilbeck / pixelio.de

More available books at **www.hansebooks.com**

THE CIVIL SERVICE.

REPORT

OF

MR. JENCKES, OF RHODE ISLAND,

FROM THE

JOINT SELECT COMMITTEE ON RETRENCHMENT,

MADE TO THE

HOUSE OF REPRESENTATIVES OF THE UNITED STATES, MAY 14, 1868.

WASHINGTON:
GOVERNMENT PRINTING OFFICE.
1868.

INDEX.

APPENDIX C—Continued:

CIVIL SERVICE OF THE UNITED STATES.

[To accompany bill H. R. No. 948.]

MAY 25, 1868.—Ordered to be printed.

Mr. JENCKES, from the Joint Select Committee on Retrenchment, submitted the following

REPORT.

The Joint Select Committee on Retrenchment, who were by a concurrent resolution of the two houses instructed to "consider the expediency of so amending the law under which appointments to the public service are now made, as to provide for the selection of subordinate officers after due examination by proper boards, their continuance in office during specified terms, unless dismissed upon charges preferred and sustained before tribunals designated for that purpose, and for withdrawing the public service from being used as an instrument of political or party patronage," beg leave to submit the following report:

Prior to the adoption of the Constitution of the United States, the civil service of the government included no other officers than those appointed by the Congress of the confederation. The entire civil administration was committed to the governments of the States and officials appointed by them. There were no government revenue laws, and no government revenue offices; nor were there any executive departments, with their chiefs and staff of clerks and force of employés. Upon the adoption of the Constitution, the power to create offices and to appoint officers of the United States, independent of those of the States, and superior to them, for the purposes of the general government, first came into being. This power was exercised at first cautiously and with great discrimination. Upon the organization of the government under the Constitution, the only civil officers recognized were those created by the Constitution, and the necessary officers for the transaction of the business of the first Congress. The first attempt to enlarge the number of civil officers in the exercise of the powers granted by the Constitution, was by the passage of "An act establishing an executive department to be denominated the Department of Foreign Affairs," passed July 27, 1789; and this act merely provided for the appointment of the head of that department, and a chief clerk. These two officers were then believed to be sufficient to transact all the business of the foreign relations of this government.

On the 31st of July, 1789, an act was passed "to regulate the collection of duties," which provided for a number of customs officers in the several districts which were declared to be ports of entry and ports of delivery, but the number of offices created by this act was less than 200.

The next act authorizing the appointment of civil officers is that establishing the Department of War, passed on the 7th of August, 1789, and this provided for two principal officers, and the possible appointment or employment of other subordinates. The acts "establishing light-houses" and "making provision for the coasting trade, and for the registering and clearing of vessels," implied the employment of additional officers, and in fact admitted into the service of the United States all those who had been employed under the authority of the several States, for the purposes and in the capacities named in the acts of Congress.

The act establishing the Treasury Department, passed September 2, 1789, made provision for a Secretary of the Treasury, a Comptroller, an Auditor, a Treasurer, a Register, and an assistant to the Secretary of the Treasury; and the act immediately following it, of the 11th of September, 1789, authorized the heads of departments to "appoint such clerks therein, respectively, as they shall find necessary," but limited the salary of each of said clerks to the sum of $500 per annum.

These were the small beginnings of the civil service of the United States. Under the administration of President Washington, the whole number of employés in the departments of the civil service was said by him to be "a mere handful," and the manner in which they were appointed, the great care which he took in the selection, and the personal supervision which he gave, as it was possible for a President then to do to all his appointees, will be referred to and shown by quotations from his correspondence and messages.

By the acts "establishing duties on distilled spirits, on carriages, on selling wines by retail, on properties sold at auction, on stamps, on snuff, and on other articles," and by the act of March 2, 1799, "regulating the collection of duties on imports and tonnage," the number of these offices was increased; but we have no authentic record of the number appointed and employed in each department until "the roll of the persons having appointment under the United States" was transmitted by President Jefferson to Congress on the 16th of February, 1802. So far as the committee have been able to ascertain, the small volume containing this "roll" is the first authentic publication of the names of the persons in the employment of the government of the United States. From this volume it appears that the total number of officers in the customs, or, as then called, "the external revenue," was 713, (less than the present force of the New York custom-house,) and their annual compensation amounted to $439,567; the number of officers in the internal revenue was 493, and their compensation was $113,000; the number of officers connected with the land office 8, and their annual compensation $4,765 26; the number of postmasters, 994, with an annual compensation of $69,900; while in all other departments of the civil establishment, including the officers at the seat of government and in the diplomatic service, there were 414 receiving annually a total of $445,000.

These were the small beginnings of a service which now numbers more than 53,000 persons, and whose annual compensation amounts to about thirty millions of dollars.

No other authentic record of the persons employed in the civil service was published until after the second war with Great Britain. On the 27th of April, 1816, Congress passed a joint resolution requiring the Secretary of State to compile and print once in every two years a register of all officers and agents, civil, military, and naval, in the service of the United States; and the first attempt to comply with the requisitions of this joint resolution was published in the same year in a small octavo volume of 175 printed pages, which includes the names of all persons employed in the civil, postal, military, and naval departments of the United States. From that date we have registers published regularly in every second year, which have swollen from the small octavo volume of 190 pages published in 1817, containing 5,608 names, (including 3,502 deputy postmasters and 154 assistants or clerks in post offices,) to the Blue Book of 1867, which contains 878 large octavo pages and over 60,000 names.

By the Constitution and the acts of Congress passed in pursuance of the authority granted by the Constitution, the appointment of all these officers is vested in the President of the United States or in the heads of departments, or in the courts of law. The number actually authorized to be appointed by the courts of law is very few, extending no further than to the officers of the several courts.

No person charged with the duty of making executive appointments was ever more careful in the selection of officers than President Washington. He was as solicitous about the character and qualifications of a person to be appointed in any of the custom-houses of the United States as if he was to be employed in his own household. He never inquired into the political opinions of any candidate for executive appointment. Private friendship was not only no recommendation to his favor, but was actually an obstacle to the appointment of any person claiming his favor for that reason. He was incapable of being swayed by political or private motives.

"My friend ———," he says in one of his letters, "I receive with cordial welcome to my house and welcome to my heart; but with all his good qualities he is not a man of business. His opponent, with all his politics so hostile to me, *is* a man of business. My private feelings have nothing to do with the case. I am not George Washington, *but* President of the United States. As George Washington, I would do this man any kindness in my power. As President of the United States, I can do nothing."

Persons appointed to office by a superior acting upon this principle were not considered subject to removal except for misconduct. During the eight years' administration of President Washington he removed but nine persons from office—six unimportant collectors, one district surveyor, one vice-consul, and one foreign minister. The last was Mr Pinckney, who was recalled from Paris, not for any misconduct of his own, but because his principles and conduct were offensive to the then government of France—the Directory. "All the other dismissals were for cause." Under the administration of President Adams nine subordinate officers were removed, but none for political opinion's sake. One head of a department was removed for cause.

On the advent of President Jefferson to power, which was not only a change of administration but a change of party, and after one of the most violent and embittered political contests ever known, it was feared that he might use the power with which he was clothed to remove the subordinate officers of the government on account of their opposition to his election, and for political reasons alone. But he took an early opportunity to set himself right on this question before the country; and in a letter to Dr. Rush, written from Washington on the 24th of March, 1801, twenty days after his inauguration, he says, speaking of the obstacles which might "check the confidence" of the people in his administration:

The great stumbling block will be removals, which, though made on those just principles only on which my predecessors ought to have removed the same persons, will nevertheless be ascribed to removal on party principles.

Then, after describing the classes of persons over whom the power of removal might be exercised, he says:

Of the thousands of officers, therefore, in the United States, a very few individuals only, probably not twenty, will be removed, and those only for doing what they ought not to have done.

I know that in stopping thus short in the career of removal I shall give great offence to many of my friends. That torrent has been pressing me heavily, and will require all my force to bear up against; but my maxim is *fiat justitia, ruat cælum.*

In a letter written a few days after to General Knox, President Jefferson says:

I am aware of the necessity of a few removals for legal oppressions, delinquencies, and other malversations may be misconstrued as done for political opinions, would produce hesitation in the coalition so much to be desired; but the extent of these will be too limited to make permanent impressions.

And in his celebrated letter to the merchants of New Haven, dated July 12, 1801, he concludes by saying:

The only questions concerning a candidate shall be, is he honest? is he capable? is he faithful to the Constitution?

In the whole course of his administration, acting on the principles which he declared in his letter to Dr. Rush, President Jefferson removed but 39 persons; and he himself repeatedly and solemnly declared, and it has never been gainsaid, that not one of them was removed because he belonged to the party opposed to his own The "thousands" of officers then in the civil service were less than *five*, and they now exceed *fifty*.

Mr. Madison made five removals; Mr. Monroe nine; Mr. John Quincy Adams two. Of course these removals were among the class of officers which required confirmation by the Senate; but if we should inquire concerning the inferior officers who are within the scope of the bill herewith reported, we should find that the number of removals was even less in proportion to the whole. These officers were selected with great care and for their fitness to discharge the duties required of them, and retained their places although their chiefs might be removed. The committee have inquired from the sources of information accessible, but have not learned of a single removal among this class of inferior officers, except for cause, from the commencement of the administration of President Washington to the accession of President Jackson.

The present system of appointment to office, which the proposed bill is an attempt to reform, commenced in the first month of the presidency of General Jackson. Down to this time all the offices in the civil service of the government had been considered to be held by the tenure 'of good behavior. No removals were made except for cause satisfactorily proved to the officer having the power of appointment. The following extract from a letter of General Dearborn, collector of the port of Boston, to Hon. W. H. Crawford, Secretary of the Treasury, in the year 1822, is an example of the care with which subordinate officers of the customs were selected and appointed, and an illustration of their fidelity and industry.

I have employed no more clerks than I found indispensably necessary to the prompt and correct discharge of the duties of the office. Their duties are constant and arduous, and every moment of their time is employed; in fact there has been so much labor for them that if motives of the most rigid economy had not governed, my feelings would have prompted me to increase the number. The duties of some are complicated, and of the highest responsibility, requiring clear heads, industrious habits, and the most honest exactness in the discharge of their duties. It is difficult to obtain characters well qualified for such stations, and the duties are so complicated and various, that it requires a long time to render them ready and useful.

The following description of the duties of General Dearborn's cashier is written by a person who has personally an accurate knowledge of the Boston custom-house:

The bond and debenture clerks were at that time paid the highest salaries. Among this number of competent and hard-working employés was Mr Robert Farley, jr., the cashier, whose pay was but $800 per annum. Mr. F. received his appointment in 1819, when quite young, being not more than 18, and for five years, besides receiving and paying out on an average about four millions of dollars yearly, he acted as book-keeper, the duties of the two positions involving a great amount of labor. In addition to this, an important portion of the accounts since 1815 had been neglected, the sum of $2,800 in the impost had not been accounted for, and it devolved on him to journalize, post, and balance them for the four years previous to his appointment. It was a most laborious task, performed out of office hours, and taking him five long and weary years to accomplish it. He worked not only in the hours of daylight, but often far into the night, and confesses, that although he was fond of going to church, his practice was almost invariably to attend the afternoon service only, giving the forenoon of each Sunday to making up these back accounts.

From among the many descriptions received by the committee of the present condition of the custom-house service, we select the following, which we believe to be applicable to more than one of those institutions:

The revenue department of this government has been most shamefully maltreated, and by all political parties, as they have successively come into power. Its various institutions, instead of subserving the public interests as they should, have been converted into hospitals, alms-houses, political fortresses, and places of refuge, (if not refuse.) Instead of capable officers, honest, respectable and faithful, brawling politicians, broken-down hacks, and imbecile persons have filled the places, through favoritism, nepotism, or corruption of some kind. The government has lavished its funds, and for the purpose of having its business faithfully transacted it has appropriated an ample amount for that object; but intrigue and favoritism have almost neutralized its legitimate and intended effects in several ways. Incompetent and inefficient men are foisted in; they constitute the corps of loafers, whose time hangs idle on their hands, and who are continually hovering about the industrious, and are serious obstacles to these. By means of personal influence, and plenty of time to wield it, they generally secure the fattest salaries, especially at a season when salaries are raised. Dishonest persons are another corps, embezzlers, peculators, corrupt or venal; these insinuate themselves into all branches as furtively as Ulysses managed to elude the searching bands of Polyphemus. Intemperate people also use the public fund, not for their families, but to distress and tantalize them. Partisans steeped in the elixir of ignorance disgrace the public books with their scrawling chirography, their blundering arithmetic, their dislocated orthography, and their downright assassination of grammar. The services of such seem to be venerated, and, therefore, they are very apt to sit in the highest places, and to be most richly remunerated for their actual impositions upon their great almoner, their direct employer. Nor is this all; they are generally the most strongly fortified in their positions, while the well qualified, quiet, faithful, unobtrusive incumbent is often the first to be removed—for what? To make room for a green hand, of course inexperienced, and perhaps unable to make good the vacancy at any time or by any discipline of training. This makes the official business limp, and perhaps inflicts serious damage upon it. Nor has the industrious, competent, faithful victim been removed from an easy and lucrative but from a decidedly laborious and meagerly paid station; and if it be too difficult for his inexperienced successor, the business will be diminished, or he will be provided with an assistant, or another will be appointed his substitute, while he is transferred to an easier, and very likely more lucrative, post.

But let me not weary you with my observations, which could be protracted almost *ad infinitum.* Suffice it to say that the government appropriates enough money to pay for the *aggregate* services rendered to it, but the appropriation is so unequally and unjustly distributed that they who do the most work and the best qualified get scanty salaries, while the sinecure, semi-sinecure, and ill-qualified drones realize large and altogether disproportionate compensation. It is so—truly so, incontrovertibly so, lamentably so. Very few do the work, and are poorly paid; they work in and out of hours, closely and incessantly; salaries small. Others have most of the day for yawning, gadding, spinning yarns to the annoyance of others, snapping beans or corn, and reading newspapers, or writing for them, to while away the official interval. Soon as the hour of three arrives they are off quick as a flock of ducks at the discharge of a gun. They reap largely at the month's end, while the workers, who have been employed during their neighbor's ennui, and who have been left behind, still plod on their drudgery, and at the end of the month receive but an unjust, a shameful pittance. Talk about injustice to factory operatives; the custom-house clerk who does the work of others that really receive the pay is as unjustly treated as the operative. There are two iniquities: the work is unequally distributed, and the pay is unequally distributed.

The change which commenced with the Presidency of General Jackson is too well known to need description, which is summed up in a single phrase, " to the victors belong the spoils." This means that the entire force of the civil service of the United States may be changed for mere political opinion, without any regard whatever to the qualifications or the meritorious services of the person in office or the person seeking office. The manner in which this change of policy was announced, in which it was received, and its effect upon the public service are well described, if not altogether impartially, in a recent biography of President Jackson, which is quoted in an appendix to this report, marked A.

From that time to the present, nearly forty years, the partisan obligations of the candidate for office have been held to be of more consequence than his qualifications for the place for which he is a candidate, and every administrative department of the government has been " used as an instrument of political or party patronage," the discontinuance of which system was one of the objects in view in the appointment of this committee.

The evil effects of this custom of discharging well-trained officers, and of appointing unskilled persons in their places, has been well described by the present head of the Treasury Department. Secretary McCulloch says:

The importance of *retaining tried and experienced clerks* can hardly be overrated, and the estimation in which such are held by business men is too often exemplified by their withdrawal from the department under the inducement of salaries offered them much greater than existing laws permit them to receive from the government. There have been 531 resignations since January, 1866, many of them by persons competent and of considerable experience in their respective duties. Could ample salaries be paid and permanence of employment assured, independent of political questions, there could be no difficulty in organizing the department on a basis greatly superior in point of efficiency than any private establishment. *A single experienced clerk can often perform with ease duties that could be but indifferently discharged by several inexperienced persons.*

The assistant secretaries and heads of bureaus, charged by law with duties and responsibilities of the highest importance, are less *favored in respect to salary than bank-tellers and book-keepers in many private business houses.* The clerks, particularly those holding prominent positions, as chiefs of divisions, many of them directing the operations of numerous others, *receive at present little more than half the salary their services would command from private parties employing them in situations of like importance.* This is especially true in regard to the clerks in the Secretary's office, upon whose experience, judgment, and integrity the Secretary must necessarily in a great measure rely for aid in the performance of his multifarious duties.

For the cost of the present system in the internal revenue department, and of the change of an assessor, the committee refer to the report of the special commissioner of the revenue.

The committee, under the resolution directing their appointment, have made inquiries into the present condition of the administrative departments of the government and considered the remedies for the evil complained of, and present the bill herewith reported as best calculated to produce the desired result. The remedy proposed by this bill is not based upon conjecture, or inference, or concurrence of opinion; but upon the direct and positive testimony of the greater number of the chief officers in the civil service. The committee prepared a circular letter, embracing 37 questions, addressed to the principal officers in the civil service of the grade required to be confirmed by the Senate, who have under them subordinates of the class within the scope of this bill, and they have received answers to these questions from more than 450 of these superior officers. The circular letter propounding these questions is hereto annexed, marked Appendix B.

Abstracts from these reports, showing the present condition of the greater portion of the civil service, as represented by its chief officers, will be found in Appendix C to this report.

The adverse report of John M. Connell, assessor 12th district, Ohio, is given in full.

The opinions of the earlier Presidents and others upon the principles which should govern appointments to office, are given in extracts from their writings, Appendix D.

Abstracts of civil service in other countries:

China...Appendix F.
Prussia..Appendix G.
England...Appendix H.
France...Appendix I.

Also portions of a report made in the 39th Congress, Appendix K.

The committee also acknowledge the encouragement granted by the press to the advancement of this measure, and they submit extracts from articles in the North American Review, the National Quarterly Review, the Round Table, the Nation, the Chicago Tribune, the New York Tribune, the New York World, the Post and Advertiser of Boston, the New York Evening Post, and other papers and periodicals, Appendix E.

They also acknowledge the services of Mr. Julius Bing, in his co-operation with the committee in their researches into the systems of other countries, and in digesting the reports received from the officers of our own service, and for his efficient assistance in many other matters connected with the performance of their duties.

The phrase, "the civil service," is popularly used to designate all those persons in the employment of the government who are not in the military or naval service, and by whose labors the executive and administrative business of the country is carried on. This service now includes more than 50,000 officers, exclusive of that class which are required by law and by the Constitution to be confirmed by the Senate, and is more numerous than the whole force of the army and navy combined, as authorized by existing laws. About 30,000 of these are in the postal department, and the remainder—about 20,000—are within the scope of the proposed bill. They are employed in the various public offices in discharge of the public business throughout the United States.

This service is divided into several branches and subdivided into numerous grades. The great proportion of offices under the control of the Department of State are those which require confirmation of the appointees by the Senate, and the number of clerks and others employed in the proper duties of the department in Washington is insignificant. In the Department of the Treasury the number of officers is greater than in all the other departments combined: These officers are employed in a great diversity of duties; some in the collection of revenues from customs, some in the assessment and collection of the internal revenue, some in the care and keeping of light-houses, some in the coast survey, some in the office of the Treasurer of the United States, some in the office of the Register of the Treasury, many in the offices of the Auditors and Comptrollers of the Treasury, some in the Loan department, some in the office of the Comptroller of the Currency and the Bureau of Internal Revenue, the Bureau of Statistics, in the printing and issuing of the currency, in the revenue cutter service, in the inspection of steamboats and steam-boilers, in the special agencies, and as police and detectives, and as special agents in the Bureau of the Commissioner of Customs.

In the Department of the Interior there are also a variety of duties. In addition to the general staff of that department, there are in the General Land Office a large number of officers who have charge of the public business relating to the public lands; in the Patent Office, a number of persons skilled in technology, who decide upon the granting of patents for inventions; in the Indian Office, a large number of persons who transact the business connected with the various Indian tribes; in the Pension Office, those who attend to the granting of pensions to invalid soldiers and to the widows and children of those who have lost their lives in the service.

In the War Department there are all those who are employed in the Quartermasters' Department, the Subsistence Department, the Pay Department, the Surgeon General's Office, the Ordnance Office, the Freedmen's Bureau, the Adjutant General's Office, the Engineer's Office, and the bureaus who have charge of the Washington aqueduct and the public buildings. In the Navy Department there are all the clerks at Washington and those attached to the bureaus and commissions and employed at the navy yards throughout the country. In the Post Office Department are all the clerks at Washington and also in the principal post offices throughout the country.

The bill proposes to establish a board of commissioners who shall ascertain and determine the standard of qualification required for a candidate for each class and grade of these inferior offices, and provides that every such candidate shall pass a satisfactory examination in such manner as the board of commissioners shall require before being appointed to any of these places, and shall serve satisfactorily during the period of probation, the limit and conditions of which shall also be fixed by the board before he shall be entitled to a permanent place in the service. It is an attempt to require a certain degree of fitness in every candidate for the office which he wishes to hold, and to permit no one that does not possess the requisite qualifications to enter into the public service. Ample powers are given to the commissioners to establish rules and regulations which shall govern the examinations and probations, and the admission of all candidates to the public service, and to eject from that service all who may be found deficient in these qualifications, or who may be inefficient or incompetent from any other cause.

APPENDIX A.

EXTRACT FROM PARTON'S LIFE OF JACKSON, VOL. III., PAGES 209-225.

Up to the hour of the delivery of General Jackson's inaugural address, it was supposed that the new President would act upon the principles of his predecessors. In his Monroe letters he had taken strong ground against partisan appointments, and when he resigned his seat in the Senate he had advocated two amendments to the Constitution designed to limit and purify the exercise of the appointing power. One of these proposed amendments forbade the re-election of a President, and the other the appointment of members of Congress to any office not judicial.

The sun had not gone down upon the day of his inauguration before it was known in all official circles in Washington that the "reforms" alluded to in the inaugural address meant a removal from office of all who had conspicuously opposed, and an appointment to office of those who had conspicuously aided, the election of the new President. The work was promptly begun. Figures are not important here, and the figures relating to this matter have been disputed. Some have declared that during the first year of the presidency of General Jackson 2,000 persons in the civil employment of the government were removed from office, and 2,000 partisans of the President appointed in their stead. This statement has been denied. It cannot be denied that in the first month of this administration more removals were made than had occurred from the foundation of the government to that time. It cannot be denied that the principle was now acted upon that partisan services should be rewarded by public office, though it involved the removal from office of competent and faithful incumbents. Colonel Benton will not be suspected of overstating the facts respecting the removals, but he admits that their number, during the year 1829, was 690. He expresses himself on this subject with less than his usual directness. His estimate of 690 does not include the little army of clerks and others who were at the disposal of some of the 690. The estimate of 2,000 includes all who lost their places in consequence of General Jackson's accession to power; and, though the exact number cannot be ascertained, I presume it was not less than 2,000. Colonel Benton says that of the 8,000 postmasters, only 491 were removed; but he does not add, as he might have added, that the 491 vacated places comprised nearly all in the department that were worth having. Nor does he mention that the removal of the postmasters of half a dozen great cities was equivalent to the removal of many hundreds of clerks, book-keepers, and carriers.

General Harrison, who had courteously censured General Jackson's course in the Seminole war, who had warmly defended his friend Henry Clay against the charge of bargain and corruption, was recalled from Colombia just four days after General Jackson had acquired the power to recall him. General Harrison had only resided in Colombia a few weeks when he received the news of his recall. A Kentuckian, who was particularly inimical to Mr. Clay, was sent out to take his place.

The appointment of a soldier so distinguished as General Harrison to represent the United States in the infant republic of Colombia was regarded by the Colombians as a great honor done them, and an emphatic recognition of their disputed claim to a place among the nations. A purer patriot, a worthier gentleman, than General William Henry Harrison has not adorned the public service of his country. His singular merits as a scholar, as a man of honor, as a soldier, and as a statesman, were only obscured by the calumny and eulogium incident to a presidential campaign My studies of the Indian affairs of the country have given me the highest idea of his valor, skill, and humanity.

Samuel Swartwout was among the expectants at Washington—an easy, good-natured man, most inexact, and even reckless, in the management of business; the last man in the whole world to be intrusted with millions. He had hopes of the collectorship of New York. On the 14th of March he wrote to his friend Jesse Hoyt, to let him know how he was getting on, and to give Hoyt the benefit of his observations, Hoyt himself being a seeker.

I hold to your doctrine fully, (wrote Swartwout,) that no d——d rascal who made use of his office or its profits for the purpose of keeping Mr. Adams in and General Jackson out of power is entitled to the least lenity or mercy, save that of hanging. So we think both alike on that head. Whether or not I shall get anything, in the general scramble for plunder, remains to be proven; but I rather guess I shall. What it will he is not yet so certain; perhaps keeper of the Bergen light-house. I rather think Massa Pomp stands a smart chance of going somewhere, perhaps to the place you have named, or to the devil. Your man, if you want a place, is Colonel Hamilton, he being now the second officer in the government of the Union, and in all probability our next President. Make your suit to him, then, and you will get what you want. I know Mr. Ingham slightly, and would recommend you to push like a devil if you expect anything from that quarter. I can do you no good in any quarter of the world, having mighty little influence beyond Hoboken. The great goers are the new men, the old troopers being all spavined and ring-boned from previous hard travel. I've got the bots, the fetlock, hip-joint, gravel, halt, and founders, and I assure you if I can only keep my own legs I shall do well; but I'm darned if I can carry any weight with me. When I left home I thought my nag sound and strong, but the beast is rather broken down here. I'll tell you more about it when I see you in New York. In seriousness, my dear sir, your support must come from Mr. Van Buren and Mr. Colonel Hamilton. I could not help you any more than your clerk.

The President, distracted with the number of applications for the New York collectorship, and extremely fond of the man who had "pushed like a devil" a quarter of a century before at Richmond, gave Swartwout the place. Upon his return to New York his proverbial good-nature was put to a severe test, for the applicants for posts in the custom-house met him at every turn, crowded his office, invaded his house, and stuffed his letter-box. There was a general dismission of Adams men from the New York custom-house, and the new appointments were made solely on the ground that the applicants had aided the election of General Jackson.

Henry Lee was appointed to a remote foreign consulship, a place which he deemed beneath his talents, and an inadequate reward for his services. He would have probably obtained a better place but for the fear that the Senate would reject the nomination. The Senate did reject his nomination even to the consulship, and by such a decided majority that nothing could be done for him. Even Colonel Benton voted against him. Lee, I may add, died soon after in Paris, where he wrote part of a history of the Emperor Napoleon.

Terror, meanwhile, reigned in Washington. No man knew what the rule was upon which removals were made. No man knew what offences were reckoned causes of removal, nor whether he had or had not committed the unpardonable sin. The great body of officials awaited their fate in silent horror, glad when the office hours expired at having escaped another day.

The gloom of suspicion (says Mr. Stansbury, himself an office-holder) pervaded the face of society. No man deemed it safe and prudent to trust his neighbor, and the interior of the department presented a fearful scene of guarded silence, secret intrigue, espionage, and talebearing. A casual remark dropped in the street would, within an hour, be repeated at headquarters; and many a man received unceremonious dismission who could not, for his life, conceive or conjecture wherein he had offended.

At that period, it must be remembered, to be removed from office in the city of Washington was like being driven from the solitary spring in a wide expanse of desert. The public treasury was almost the sole source of emolument. Salaries were small, the expenses of living high, and a few of the officials had made provision for engaging in private business, or even for removing their families to another city. No one had anticipated a necessity of removal. Clerks, appointed by the early Presidents, had grown gray in the service of the government, and were so habituated to the routine of their places that, if removed, they were beggared and helpless.

An old friend of General Jackson was in Washington this summer. He wrote on the 4th of July to a friend :

I have seen the President, and have dined with him, but have had no free communication or conversation with him. The reign of this administration—I wish another word could be used—is in very strong contrast with the mild and lenient sway of Madison, Monroe, and Adams. To me it feels harsh ; it seems to have had an unhappy effect on the free thoughts and unrestrained speech which have heretofore prevailed. I question whether the ferreting out treasury rats and the correction of abuses are sufficient to compensate for the reign of terror which appears to have commenced. It would be well enough if it were confined to evil-doers, but it spreads abroad like a contagion : spies, informers, denunciations—the fecula of despotism. Where there are listeners there will be tale-bearers. A stranger is warned by his friend on his first arrival to be careful how he expresses himself in relation to any one or anything which touches the administration. I had hoped that this would be a national administration, but it is not even an administration of a party. Our republic henceforth will be governed by factions, and the struggle will be who shall get the offices and their emoluments—a struggle embittered by the most base and sordid passions of the human heart.

So numerous were the removals in the city of Washington that the business of the place seemed paralyzed. In July, a Washington paper said :

Thirty-three houses which were to have been built this year have, we learn, been stopped in consequence of the unsettled and uncertain state of things now existing here ; and the merchant cannot sell his goods or collect his debts from the same cause. We have never known the city to be in a state like this before, though we have known it for many years. The individual distress, too, produced in many cases by the removal of the destitute officers is harrowing and painful to all who possess the ordinary sympathies of our nature, without regard to party feeling. No man, not absolutely brutal, can be pleased to see his personal friend or neighbor suddenly stripped of the means of support, and cast upon the cold charity of the world without a shelter or a home. Frigid and insensible must be the heart of that man, who could witness some of the scenes that have lately been exhibited here, without a tear of compassion or a throb of sympathy. But what is still more to be regretted is that this system, having been once introduced, must necessarily be kept up at the commencement of every presidential term ; and he who goes into office, knowing its limited and uncertain tenure, feels no disposition to make permanent improvements or to form for himself a permanent residence. He therefore takes care to lay up what he can during his brief official existence, to carry off to some more congenial spot, where he means to spend his life or re-enter into business. All, therefore, that he might have expended in city improvements is withdrawn, and the revenue of the corporation, as well as the trade of the city, is so far lessened and decreased. It is obviously a most injurious policy as it respects the interests of our city. Many of the oldest and most respectable citizens of Washington, those who have adhered to its fortunes through all their vicissitudes, who have "grown with its growth and strengthened with its strength," have been cast off to make room for strangers, who feel no interest in the prosperity of our infant metropolis, and who care not whether it advances or retrogrades.

As an illustration of the state of things in Washington at this time, I will here transcribe the story of Colonel T. L. McKinney, for many years the honest and capable Superintendent of Indian Affairs, appointed to that office by Mr. Monroe.

Some time after General Jackson had been inaugurated, the Secretary of War, Major Eaton, inquired of me *if I had been to see the President?* I said I had not. "Had you not better go over ?" "Why, sir ?" I asked. "I have had no official business to call me there, nor have I now ; why should I go ?" "You know, in these times," replied the Secretary, "it is well to cultivate those personal relations which will go far toward securing the good will of one in power"—and he wound up by more than intimating that the President had heard some things in disparagement of me ; when I determined forthwith to go and see him, and ascertain what they were. On arriving at the door of the President's House, I was answered by the doorkeeper that the President was in, and having gone to report me, returned, saying the President would see me. On arriving at the door, it having been thrown open by the doorkeeper, I saw the President very busily engaged writing, and with great earnestness ; so much so, indeed, that I stood for some time before he took his eyes off the paper, fearing to interrupt him, and not wishing to seem intrusive. Presently he raised his eyes from the paper, and at the same time his spectacles from his nose, and, looking at me, said : "Come in, sir, come in." "You are engaged, sir ?" "No more so than I always am, and always expect to be," drawing a long breath, and giving signs of great uneasiness.

I had just said, "I am here, sir, at the instance of the Secretary of War," when the door was thrown open, and three members of Congress entered. They were received with great courtesy. I rose, saying : "You are engaged, sir ; I will call when you are more at leisure ;" and bowed myself out. On returning to my office, I addressed a note to the President of the following import : "Colonel McKinney's respects to the President of the United

States, and requests to be informed when it will suit his convenience to see him?" to which Major Donelson replied: "The President will see Colonel McKinney to-day, at 12 o'clock." I was punctual, and found the President alone. I commenced by repeating what I had said at my first visit, that I was there at the instance of the Secretary of War, who had more than intimated to me that impressions of an unfavorable sort had been made upon him with regard to me; and that I was desirous of knowing what the circumstances were that had produced them. "It is true, sir," said the President, "I have been told things that are highly discreditable to you, and which have come to me from such sources as to satisfy me of their truth." "Very well, sir, will you do me the justice to let me know what these things are that you have heard from such respectable sources?" "You know, Colonel McKinney, I am a candid man"— "I beg pardon, sir," I remarked, interrupting him, "but I am not here to question that, but to hear charges, which it appears have been made to you, affecting my character, either as an officer of the government or a man." "Well, sir," he resumed, "I will frankly tell you what these charges are, and, sir, they are of a character which I can never respect." "No doubt of that, sir; but what are they?" "Why, sir, I am told, and on the best authority, that you were one of the promoters of that vile paper, *We the People*, as a contributor toward establishing it, and as a writer afterwards, in which my wife Rachel was so shamefully abused. I am told, further, on authority no less respectable, that you took an active part in distributing, under the frank of your office, the '*coffin handbills*;' and that, in your recent travels, you largely and widely circulated the militia pamphlet." Here he paused, crossed his legs, shook his foot, and clasped his hands around the upper knee, and looked at me as though he had actually convicted me and prostrated me; when, after a moment's pause, I asked: "Well, sir, what else?" "Why, sir," he answered, "I think such conduct highly unbecoming in one who fills a place in the government such as you fill, and very derogatory to you, as it would be to any one who should be guilty of such practices." "All this," I replied, "may be well enough; but I request to know if this is all you have heard, and whether there are any more charges." "Why, yes, sir, there is one more: I am told your office is not in the condition in which it should be." "Well, sir, what more?" "Nothing, sir; but these are all serious charges, sir." "Then, sir, these comprise all?" "They do, sir." "Well, general," I answered, "I am not going to reply to all this, or to any part of it, with any view to retaining my office; nor do I intend to reply to it at all, *except under the solemnity of an oath;*" when I threw up my hand toward heaven, saying, "*The answers I am about to give to these allegations I solemnly swear shall be the truth, the whole truth, and nothing but the truth.* My oath, sir, is taken, and is, no doubt, recorded." He interrupted me, by saying, "You are making quite a serious affair of it." "It is, sir, what I mean to do," I answered.

"Now, sir, in regard to the paper called '*We the People*,' I never did, directly or indirectly, either by my money or by my pen, contribute toward its establishment or its continuance. I never circulated one copy of it, more or less; nor did I subscribe for a copy of it, more or less; nor have I ever, to the best of my knowledge and belief, handled a copy of it; nor have I ever seen but two copies, and these were on the table of a friend, among other newspapers. So much for that charge.

"In regard to the '*coffin handbills*,' I never circulated any, either under the frank of my office or otherwise, and never saw but two, and am not certain that I ever saw but one, and that some fool sent me, under cover, from Richmond, in Virginia, and which I found on my desk, among other papers, on going to my office; and which, on seeing what it was, I tore up and threw aside among the waste paper, to be swept out by my messenger. The other, which I took to be one of these bills, but which might have been an account of the hanging of some convict, I saw some time ago pendent from a man's finger and thumb, he having a roll under his arm as he crossed Broadway, in New York. So much for the coffin handbills.

"As to the 'militia pamphlet,' I have seen reference made to it in the newspapers, it is true, but I have never handled it, have never read it, or circulated a copy or copies of it, directly or indirectly.

"And now, sir, as to my office: That is my monument; its records are its inscriptions. Let it be examined; and I invite a commission for that purpose. Nor will I return to it to put a paper in its place, should it be out of place, or in any other way prepare it for the ordeal; and if there is a single flaw in it, or any just ground for complaint, either on the part of the white or the red man, implicating my capacity, my diligence, or want of due regard to the interests of all having business with it, including the government, then, sir, you shall have my free consent to put any mark upon me you may think proper, or subject me to as much opprobrium as shall gratify those who have thus abused your confidence by their secret attempts to injure me."

"Colonel McKinney," said the general, who had kept his eyes upon me during the whole of my reply, "I believe every word you have said, and am satisfied that those who communicated to me those allegations were mistaken." "I thank you, sir," I replied, "for your confidence; but I am not satisfied. I request to have my accusers brought up, and that I may be allowed to confront them in your presence." "No, no, sir," he answered; "I am satisfied. Why then push the matter any further?" when, rising from his chair, he took my arm, and said: "Come, sir; come down, and allow me to introduce you to my family." I accompanied him, and was introduced to Mrs. Donaldson, Major Donaldson, and some others who were present, partook of the offering of a glass of wine, and retired.

The next morning, I believe it was, or, if not the next, some morning not far off, a Mr. R-b-s-n, a very worthy, gentlemanly fellow, and well known to me, came into my office. "You are busy, colonel," he said, as he entered. "No, sir; not very," I replied. "Come in; I have learned to write and talk, too, at the same time. Come in; sit down; I am glad to see you." Looking round the office, the entire walls of which I had covered with portraits of Indians, he asked, pointing to the one that hung over my desk: "Who is that?" "Red Jacket," I answered. "And that?" "Shin-guab-O'Wassin," I replied; and so he continued. He then asked: "Who wrote the treaties with the Indians, and gave instructions to commissions, and, in general, carried on the correspondence of the office?" "These are within the circle of my duties, the whole being under a general supervision of the Secretary of War," I answered. "Well, then," after a pause, he said, "the office will not suit me." "What office?" I asked. "This," he replied. "General Jackson told me, this morning, it was at my service; but before seeing the Secretary of War, I thought I would come and have a little chat with you first." I rose from my chair, saying: "Take it, my dear sir, take it. The sword of Damocles has been hanging over my head long enough." "No," said he, "it is not the sort of place for me; I prefer an Auditor's office. where forms are established." This worthy citizen had, in the fulness of his heart, doubtless, and out of pure affection for General Jackson, made that distinguished personage a present of the pair of pistols which General Washington had carried during the war of the Revolution.

Colonel McKinney retained his office some time longer, because the Secretary of War assured the President that its duties were complex and numerous, and could not be discharged by a person inexperienced in Indian affairs. He tells us, however, that he was kept in constant suspense, and had occasionally an ominous warning:

My chief clerk, Mr. Hambleton, came into my room one morning, soon after I had taken my seat at my table, and putting his hands upon it, leaned over. I looked up, and saw his eyes were full of tears! To my question, "Is anything the matter, Mr. Hambleton?" "Yes, sir; I am pained to inform you that you are to be displaced to-day! We all feel it. Our connection has been one of unbroken harmony, and we are grieved at the thought of a separation. The President has appointed General Thompson, a member of Congress, of Georgia. He boards at my mother's, and I have it from himself. He says I shall remain, but the rest of the clerks he shall dismiss, to make room for some of the President's friends." "Well, Mr. H.," I replied, "it is what I have been constantly looking for. Your annunciation does not at all surprise me; indeed, it puts an end to my suspense, and, apart from the pain of leaving you all, and the thought that others are to be cut adrift as well as myself, I feel relieved." He walked a few times across my room, and then retired to his, which joined mine. Two hours after I heard walking and earnest talking in the passage; they continued for half an hour. When they ceased, Mr. Hambleton came into my room, his face all dressed in smiles, saying, "It is not to be!" "What is not to be?" "You are not to go out. When General Thompson came to the Secretary this morning, with the President's reference to him, to assign him to your place, he was told before he could act he (the Secretary) must see the President. The result of the Secretary's interview with the President was, you were to be retained, and General Thompson is referred back to the President for explanation. Thompson is in a rage about it.

Another illustrative anecdote, which, though it may not be wholly true, is so like others that are known to be so, that I venture to think it is at least founded in fact. A member of Congress appointed to a foreign mission consulted the President as to the choice of a secretary of legation. The President declined all interference, and remarked to the minister that the United States government would hold him responsible for the manner in which he discharged his duties, and that he would, consequently, be at liberty to choose his own secretary. The minister returned his acknowledgment, but before taking leave sought his advice in regard to a young gentleman then in the State Department, and who was highly recommended by the Secretary. General Jackson promptly said: "I advise you, sir, not to take the man; he is not a good judge of preaching." The minister observed that the objection needed explanation. "I am able to give it," said the general, and he thus continued:

On last Sabbath morning I attended divine service in the Methodist Episcopal church in this city. There I listened to a soul-inspiring sermon by Professor Durbin, of Carlisle, one of the ablest pulpit orators in America. Seated in a pew near me I observed this identical young man, apparently an attentive listener. On the day following, he came into this chamber on business, when I had the curiosity to ask his opinion of the sermon and the preacher; and what think you, sir? The young upstart, with consummate assurance, pronounced that sermon all froth, and Professor Durbin a humbug. I took the liberty of saying to him: "My young man, you are a humbug yourself, and don't know it." "And now," continued the old man, "rest assured, my dear sir, that a man who is not a better judge of preaching than that is unfit to be your companion; and besides," he added, "if he were the prodigy the Secretary of State represents him to be, he would be less anxious to confer his services upon you; he would rather be anxious to retain them himself."

As a general rule the dismission of officers was sudden and unexplained. Occasionally, however, some reason was assigned. Major Eaton, for example, dismissed the chief clerk of the War Department in the terms following:

Major ——: The chief clerk of the department should, to his principal, stand in the relation of a confidential friend. Under this belief I have appointed Doctor Randolph, of Virginia. I take leave to say, that since I have been in this department nothing in relation to you has transpired to which I would take the slightest objection, nor have I any to suggest.

These facts will suffice to show that the old system of appointments and removals was changed upon the accession of General Jackson to the one in vogue ever since, which Governor Marcy completely and aptly described when he said that to the victors belong the spoils. Some of the consequences of this change are the following:

1. The government, formerly served by the *élite* of the nation, is now served to a very considerable extent by its refuse. That at least is the tendency of the new system, because men of intelligence, ability, and virtue universally desire to fix their affairs on a basis of permanence. It is the nature of such men to make each year do something for all the years to come. It is their nature to abhor the arts by which office is now obtained and retained. In the year of our Lord 1859, the fact of a man's holding office under the government is presumptive evidence that he is one of three characters, namely, an adventurer, an incompetent person, or a scoundrel. From this remark must be excepted those who hold offices that have never been subjected to the spoils system, or offices which have been "taken out of politics."

2. The new system places at the disposal of any government, however corrupt, a horde of creatures in every town and county, bound, body and soul, to its defence and continuance.

3. It places at the disposal of any candidate for the presidency, who has a slight prospect of success, another horde of creatures in every town and county bound to support his pretensions. I once knew an apple woman in Wall street who had a personal interest in the election of a President. If *her* candidate gained the day, her "old man" would get the place of porter in a public warehouse. The circle of corruption embraces hundreds of thousands.

4. The spoils system takes from the government employé those motives to fidelity which in private life are found universally necessary to secure it. As no degree of merit whatever can secure him in his place, he must be a man of heroic virtue who does not act upon the principle of getting the most out of it while he holds it. Whatever fidelity may be found in officeholders must be set down to the credit of unassisted human virtue. In a word, the spoils system renders pure, decent, orderly, and democratic government impossible. Nor has any government of modern times given such a wonderful proof of inherent strength as is afforded by the fact that this government, after 30 years of rotation, still exists.

At whose door is to be laid the blame of thus debauching the government of the United States? It may perhaps be justly divided into three parts: First, Andrew Jackson, impelled by his ruling passions, resentment, and gratitude, *did* the deed. No other man of his day had audacity enough. Secondly, the example and the politicians of New York furnished him with an excuse for doing it. Thirdly, the original imperfection of the govermental machinery seemed to necessitate it. As soon as King Caucus was overthrown the spoils system became almost inevitable, and perhaps General Jackson only precipitated a change which sooner or later must have come.

While the congressional caucus system lasted, confining the sphere of intrigue to the city of Washington, politicians did not much want the aid of the remote subordinate employés of the government. But when the area of President-making was extended so as to embrace the whole nation, every tidewaiter, constable, porter, and postmaster could lend a hand. Well, then, do not burst with virtuous rage until you have duly reflected upon the fact, too well known, that the average disinterested voter can only with difficulty be induced even to take the trouble to go to the polls and deposit his vote. Without the stimulus of interested expectation how is the work of a presidential campaign be got done? Who will paint the flags, and pay for the Roman candles, and print the documents, and supply the stump? The patriotic citizen, do you answer? Why does he not do it, then?

The spoils system, we may hope, however, has nearly run its course. It is already well understood that every service in which efficiency is indispensable must be *taken out of politics;* and this process, happily begun in some departments of municipal government, will assuredly continue. The first century of the existence of a nation, which is to last 30 centuries or more, should be merely regarded in the light of the " Great Republic's" experimental trip. A leak has developed itself. It will be stopped.

The course of the administration, with regard to removals, excited a clamor so loud and general as to inspire the opposition with new hopes. The old federalists who had aided to elect General Jackson were especially shocked. Occasionally, too, the officers removed did not submit to decapitation in silence. The most remarkable protest published at the time was from the wife of one of the removed, Mrs. Barney, a daughter of the celebrated Judge Chase. Her husband's case was one of peculiar hardship, and she narrated it with the eloquence of sorrow and indignation :

My husband, sir, never was your enemy. In the overflowing patriotism of his heart, he gave you the full measure of his love for your military services. He preferred Mr. Adams for the presidency, because he thought him qualified, and you unqualified, for the station. He would have been a traitor to his country, he would have had even my scorn, and have deserved yours, had he supported you under such circumstances. He used no means to oppose you. He did a patriot's duty in a patriot's way. For this he is proscribed—*punished!* Oh! how punished! My heart bleeds as I write! Cruel sir! Did he commit any offence worthy of punishment against God or against his country, or even against you? Blush while you read this question; speak not, but let the crimson negative mantle on your cheek! No, sir; on the contrary, it was one of the best acts of his life. When he bared his bosom to the hostile bayonets of his enemies he was not more in the *line of his duty* than when he voted against you; and had he fallen a martyr on the field of fight he would not more have deserved a monument than he now deserves for having been worse than martyred in support of the dearest privilege and chartered right of American freemen.

Careless as you are about the effects of your conduct, it would be idle to inform you of the depth and quality of that misery which you have worked in the bosom of my family, else would I tell a tale that would provoke sympathy in anything that had a heart, or gentle drops of pity from every eye not accustomed to look upon scenes of human cruelty with composure. Besides, you were apprised of our poverty; you knew the dependence of eight little children for food and raiment upon my husband's salary. You knew that, advanced in years as he was, without the means to prosecute any regular business, and without friends able to assist him, the world would be to him a barren heath, an inhospitable wild. You were able, therefore, to anticipate the heart-rending scene which you may now realize as the sole work of your hand.

The sickness and debility of my husband now calls upon me to vindicate his and his children's wrongs. The natural timidity of my sex vanishes before the necessity of my situation, and a spirit, sir, as proud as yours, although in a female bosom, demands justice. At your hands I ask it. Return to him what you have rudely torn from his possession; give back to his children their former means of securing their food and raiment. Show that you can relent, and that your rule has had at least one exception.

The severity practiced by you in this instance is heightened because accompanied by a breach of your faith, solemnly pledged to my husband. He called upon you, told you frankly that he had not voted for you. What was your reply? It was, in substance, this: "That every citizen of the United States had a right to express his political sentiments by his vote; that no charges had been made against Major Barney. If any should he made, he should have justice done; he should not be condemned unheard." Then, holding him by the hand, with apparent warmth, you concluded, "Be assured, sir, I shall be particularly cautious how I listen to assertions of applicants for office!"

With these assurances from you, sir, the President of the United States, my husband returned to the bosom of his family. With these rehearsed, he wiped away the tears of apprehension. The President was not the monster he had been represented. They would not be reduced to beggary—haggard want would not be permitted to enter the mansion where he had always been a stranger. The husband and the father had done nothing in violation of his duty as an officer. If any malicious slanderer should arise to pour his poisonous breath into the ears of the President, the accused would not be condemned unheard, and his innocence would be triumphant. They would still be happy.

It was presumable also, that, possessing the confidence of three successive administrations, (whose testimony in his favor I presented to you,) he was not unworthy the office he held. Besides, the signature of a hundred of our first mercantile houses established the fact of his having given perfect satisfaction in the manner he transacted the business of his office.

In this state of calm security, without a moment's warning—like a clap of thunder in a clear sky—your dismissal came; and, in a moment, the house of joy was converted into one of mourning. Sir, was not this the refinement of cruelty? But this was not all. The wife whom you thus agonized drew her being from the illustrious Chase, whose voice of thunder early broke the spell of British allegiance. When in the American Senate, he swore, by Heaven, that he owed no allegiance to the British Crown; one, too, whose signature was broadly before your eyes, affixed to the charter of our independence. The husband and the father whom you have thus wronged was the first-born son of a hero, whose naval and military renown brightens the pages of your country's history from 1776 to 1815, with whose achievements posterity will not condescend to compare yours, for he fought amidst greater dangers, and he fought for independence. By the side of that father, in the second British war, fought the son, and the glorious 12th of September bears testimony to his unshaken intrepidity. A wife, a husband, thus derived—a family of children drawing their existence from this double-revolutionary fountain—you have recklessly, causelessly, perfidiously, and therefore inhumanly, cast helpless and destitute upon the icy bosom of the world; and the children and the grandchildren of Judge Chase and Commodore Barney are poverty-stricken upon the soil which owes its freedom and fertility (in part) to their heroic patriotism.

The reader ought to be informed, I think, that his friend and benefactor, Major Lewis, opposed this fatal removal policy from the beginning to the end. "In relation to the principle of rotation," he once wrote to General Jackson,

I embrace this occasion to enter my solemn protest against it—not on account of my office, but because I hold it to be fraught with the greatest mischief to the country. If ever it should be carried out *in extenso*, the days of this republic will, in my opinion, have been numbered, for whenever the impression shall become general that the government is only valuable on account of its offices, the great and paramount interest of the country will be lost sight of, and the government itself ultimately destroyed. This, at least, is the honest conviction of my mind with regard to these novel doctrines of rotation in office.

APPENDIX B.

JOINT SELECT COMMITTEE ON RETRENCHMENT.

Concurrent resolution of the two houses, passed by the 39th Congress, in July, 1866.

Whereas the financial condition of the United States demands the exercise of a rigid economy in all departments of the government, in order to sustain the credit of the nation and to relieve the people at the earliest possible day from the burden of excessive taxation; and whereas there is reason to believe that in many departments of the service abuses have for a long time existed, and still exist, in the perpetuation of useless offices and sinecures, in extravagant salaries and allowances, and in other unnecessary and wasteful expenditures: Therefore,

Resolved by the Senate and House of Representatives, That a joint select committee be appointed, to consist of three members of the Senate and five members of the House, to be styled " the Joint Select Committee on Retrenchment;" that said committee be instructed to inquire into the expenditures in all the branches of the service of the United States, and to report whether any, and what, offices ought to be abolished; whether any, and what, salaries or allowances ought to be reduced; what are the methods of procuring accountability in public officers or agents in the care and disbursement of public moneys; whether moneys have been paid out illegally; whether any officers or agents or other persons have been or are employed in the service without authority of law, or unnecessarily; and generally how, and to what extent, the expenses of the service of the country may and ought to be curtailed. And also to consider the expediency of so amending the laws under which appointments to the public service are now made as to provide for the selection of subordinate officers after due examination by proper boards; their continuance in office during specified terms, unless dismissed upon charges preferred and sustained before tribunals designated for that purpose; and for withdrawing the public service from being used as an instrument of political or party patronage; and inquire into the accounts and statements in reference to the government debt, and the management thereof, and the mode of depositing and keeping of the public money, and all accounts relating thereto. That said committee be authorized to sit during the recess of Congress, to send for persons and papers, and to report by bill or otherwise; and that said committee may appoint a clerk for the term of six months and no more.

Concurrent resolution of the 40th *Congress, March,* 1867.

Resolved by the Senate and House of Representatives, That the joint select committee on retrenchment, raised by a concurrent resolution of the two houses at the first session of the 39th Congress, be, and the same is hereby, revived and continued for and during the 40th Congress, with all and the same powers and duties appertaining thereto in said 39th Congress, and with power to appoint a clerk, and with power in its members to administer oaths; and that any vacancies in said committee be filled by the presiding officer of each house, respectively.

By a resolution adopted July 19, 1867, one senator and two representatives were added to the committee, which consists of Senators Edmunds, Williams, Patterson of New Hampshire, Buckalew; and Representatives Van Wyck, Randall, Welker, Halsey, Jenckes, Benjamin, Benton.

At a meeting of the joint select committee on retrenchment, held in the city of Washington, July 20, 1867, it was, on motion,

Ordered, That so much of the inquiries referred to this committee as relates to the mode of appointments to the public service and the abolition of useless offices be committed to a sub-committee consisting of Senator Williams Representative Jenckes, and Senator Patterson.

To ―― ――.

SIR: You will please answer, in writing, the following questions, at your earliest convenience, and return your answers (with such comments on the condition of the civil service, and the best method of making it more effectual, as you may see fit to add) to the undersigned, one of the members of said committee on the part of the House of Representatives.

       Respectfully, yours,

T. A. JENCKES,
For Sub-Committee on the Civil Service.

QUESTIONS.

1. Are you in the civil service of the United States; and if so, in what official capacity?

2. When did you enter upon the duties of your office?

3. State whether you have served in any other office or offices, and what offices, and during what period or periods of time?

4. What was your employment before your appointment to your present office, and before entering the service of the United States?

5. Have you received a collegiate education? and if so, state where and when; and if not, state where and how you received your education.

6. Previous to entering the civil service, were you examined with regard to your qualifications for the place to which you were appointed? if so, state when, where, and by whom; relate the full particulars of such examination.

7. What evidence of your qualifications was submitted to the appointing power other than such examination?

8. By whom was your appointment made, and by whom were you recommended for the office you now hold?

9. State the annual income of your present office, and whether it is a larger or less sum than your income previous to your appointment.

10. Had you ever pursued any course of study with a view of fitting yourself for the duties of the office you now hold, or of any office you have held under the government of the United States? if so, state where, when, and with whom.

11. Is there any printed book or manual which sets forth the duties of your office? if so, name it, and refer to the portions of it relating to such duties.

12. To whom do you make report concerning the performance of the duties of your office, and at what times, and what is the nature of the reports? Describe particularly the character of such reports, and if the last which you have made is in print, annex a copy; and if not, state where it can be found.

13. How many hours in each day, on an average, are you actually employed in the service of the government, and what are your office hours?

14. What number of persons are under your official control; into how many classes are they divided, and what is the number of each class; and how many are employed permanently, and how many temporarily?

15. State the character of the employment of each class, and how many hours each day they are employed.

16. State the number of applications for employment in subordinate offices you have received since you have been in office, and what number of these have been successful, and how many have been rejected.

17. Have those who have received appointments under you given evidence of their fitness for such employment by any test examination? if so, state the number of those who have been examined, the offices to which they have been appointed, and state by whom such examination was conducted, what subjects it embraced, and what standard, if any, was adopted as the test of fitness for the employment to which the appointment was made.

18. State whether any persons have been appointed to the subordinate offices under you without examination; and if so, how many, and to what offices, and whether they are still in the service, and upon what recommendation or supposed qualification such appointments were made.

19. State the previous occupation of your subordinates, and whether any of them pursued any course of study before appointment with the special view of qualifying them for the service, or whether they were taken indiscriminately from the various employments of civil life.

20. How many among your subordinates have been appointed for merit and qualification alone, without political or personal influence, and without regard to political or personal considerations?

21. What is the usual mode of application, how supported, and how urged?

22. Are the recommendations of the personal and political friends of the applicant preserved and placed on file?

23. State how many of your subordinates have served in the Union armies; how many have been connected with the press in any capacity; and whether there are not different grades of efficiency among them in the same class.

24. State how many have been appointed within two years; how many more than two years and within four years; how many more than four years and within six years; how many more than six years and within ten years; how many more than ten years and within fifteen years; and how many above fifteen years.

25. State how many are under twenty-five years of age; how many over twenty-five and under thirty; how many over thirty and under forty; how many over forty and under fifty; how many over fifty and under sixty; how many over sixty.

26. State what number have been removed since you have been in office, and what portion of these removals have been for political considerations.

27. State whether there is any system of promotion among your subordinates; and if so, what it is based upon; what are its rules; how are they applied, and who has the final decision upon any question of promotion.

28. State whether there is among your subordinates, or in your department, any rule constantly acted upon by which merit shall be advanced, and which will insure a career in your particular branch of service to any deserving person who enters the lowest grade.

29. State whether you have not known meritorious persons to be discharged, and their places filled by others not before in the service, who have been backed by political influence.

30. Have you not known such new recruits to be placed over the heads of meritorious persons already in the service ?

31. Between what ages do you find your subordinates most diligent and efficient ?

32. What classes of appointees do you find the least diligent and efficient ?

- 33. Suppose all new appointments were to be made in the lowest grade only, and out of candidates who shall give evidence of their fitness for appointment by passing a rigid test examination conducted by competent persons, and that no promotions should be made to a higher grade unless the candidates for promotion should pass a similar test examination for such higher grade, would not the efficiency of the service be thereby increased ?

34. Could not an equal amount of work be accomplished under such a system by a less number of persons than are now employed ?

35. If the employment was assured and certain, and promotions granted only to seniority or merit, and no discharge permitted except for cause, could not a higher grade of talent and a better quality of persons be induced to enter the government service ?

36. Are there any females among your subordinates ? If so, state what proportion their compensation bears to that of males for the same service, whether they compare favorably or not with males for diligence, attention and efficiency, and whether the general efficiency of the class would not be improved by a system of appointment for competency alone, and promotion from merit or seniority, or retention in office during good behavior ?

37. State any matters which in your judgment would tend to make the civil service more efficient and economical ?

APPENDIX C.

EXTRACTS FROM REPLIES OF PUBLIC OFFICERS TO INTERROGATORIES BY THE COMMITTEE.

William Hunter, Second Assistant Secretary of State:

No. 3. As a clerk in State Department, May, 1829, at $800 per annum; and gradually, by promotion, to my present position.

No. 33. Have no doubt that the measures referred to in the above question would be wise for the public good.

No. 34. If officers of this department were appointed under the system referred to, I am of the opinion one-third less could perform the duties now required.

No. 37. The civil service would be more efficient if employés were not so often changed.

I have no doubt that the measure referred to would be wise for the public good. Examination, however, to be worth anything as a test of fitness, must be conducted by persons not responsible to the appointing power, and the examiner, to be impartial, *must be ignorant of the State from which a candidate may hail, of the persons who may recommend him, and perhaps even of his name.*

If officers of the State Department were to be appointed under the proposed system, at least one-third less would be required for the present work, although the business of the department in its diplomatic and consular branches has perhaps doubled within seven years.

He lays great stress upon experience, and expatiates upon the absurdity of appointing men to diplomatic and consulate missions without knowledge of the language of the country to which they are sent. He thinks it might be as well to appoint inmates of deaf and dumb asylums.

J. F. Hartley, Assistant Secretary of the Treasury:

No. 32. The uncertainty of position under the present system is inconsistent with hearty and entire devotion to public service.

No. 36. There are; with compensation less than one-third of average compensation of male clerks; principally employed in counting currency, notes and bonds, and are better adapted for that service than males, and in other employments compare favorably; efficiency would be increased by creation of grades, and merit rewarded by promotion.

All clerks in the Secretary's office receive their appointments upon a written report of the board of examiners established in accordance with the act of March 3, 1853. The object being simply to inform the minds of the board as to the general intelligence of the candidate and his capabilities for the performance of the duties to be intrusted to him, and the special positions to be filled being very diverse in their character, it is obvious that no uniform and arbitrary standard can be prescribed.

From August 1, 1865, to February 4, 1868, 9,092 applications for appointment in the Treasury Department have been filed, of which 1,512 have been successful.

Applications are considered and appointments made for the entire department in the Secretary's office. * * * The Secretary can of course have personal knowledge of the character and the qualifications of but few of the applicants. * * * The younger clerks are apt to regard their positions only as temporary, and to act accordingly. * * *

The Assistant Secretary contends that the proposed test examination is now actually in force in the department, but fails to adduce adequate testimony to that effect.

No. 37. In reply to this inquiry I have to remark that stability in the tenure of office and adequate compensation are indispensable to any healthful reform. The services of competent persons cannot he procured or retained as a general thing on any lower scale of compensation than is paid for similar services elsewhere. It can hardly be expected that the services of expert accountants or members of the legal or other professions will abandon the higher rates received in their respective pursuits to serve the government for $1,800 per annum, the highest grade of clerkships provided by law. Yet their qualifications are indispensable to the successful performance of official duty in some branches of the Treasury. Of late, special acts of Congress have granted additional compensation, which to some extent, and as a temporary relief, have mitigated the evil. What is needed, however, is a permanent system. If greater stability were imparted to the tenure of office and no removals made except for cause, as in the army and navy, the services of experts, with the needed special qualifications, could doubtless be procured at rates somewhat lower than those prevailing in other pursuits subject to vicissitudes both of employment and compensation; the fixedness of revenue being an ample equivalent.

In my judgment no preliminary examination will afford the requisite assurance of qualifications for the special duties to which clerks are to be assigned. It is doubtless true that general intelligence and scholarship may be satisfactorily ascertained in that way. The more important duties in this office are, however, in the main, so purely arbitrary and technical, depending so much on specific statutes, judicial decisions, and departmental regulations, that no previous training can materially aid in their performance. Nothing in my judgment but an actual trial will exhibit or develop the fitness of candidates for offices in this branch of the Treasury Department. Upon satisfactory evidence of character, capacity and general acquirements will be best ascertained by such trial under temporary appointment. This procedure is the more important if the tenure of office is to be permanent, and the incumbent displaced only on the establishment of charges of neglect of duty, or other misbehavior in office. Under such a system, not only could a "higher grade of talent and a better quality of persons be induced to enter the government service," as suggested in the 35th interrogatory now before me, but the suggestion made by the 34th question would also apply, viz: that "an equal amount of work could probably be accomplished by a less number of persons than are now employed."

As further expressive of my own views upon this subject, I respectfully refer to a communication of the 31st ultimo, addressed by the Secretary to the chairman of the Finance Committee of the Senate, in regard to a proposed reorganization of the department.

N. Sargent, Commissioner of Customs :

TREASURY DEPARTMENT,
Office of Commissioner of Customs, January 4, 1869.

SIR: I have the honor to acknowledge the receipt of your circular, with interrogatories propounded by the Sub-committee on Retrenchment, to which I reply as follows :

1. I am, as Commissioner of Customs.

2. On the 20th day of May, 1861.

3. I have served in other offices, viz: Sergeant-at-arms of the House of Representatives during the 30th Congress: Recorder of the Land Office part 1849–'50; Register of the Treasury from October, 1851, to April, 1853.

4. I am a lawyer by profession, but was for a number of years an editor and owner of a daily paper in Philadelphia; afterwards correspondent of the United States Gazette, under the *non de plume* of Oliver Oldschool. For a few years previous to entering my present office I prosecuted claims before Congress and the departments, and carried on a small farm, which I still carry on.

5. I have not. I received my education in Vermont, partly under a private tutor and partly at an academy in Brattleboro', and partly also by my own studies, "without a master."

6. I was not.

7. I was well known to General Taylor, Mr. Fillmore, and Mr. Lincoln, from whom I received my appointments, who were satisfied with my qualifications for the positions they respectively tendered me. General Taylor, through Mr. Clayton, Secretary of State, first tendered me the office of secretary of the Mexican commissioners, which I declined on the ground that I did not understand the Spanish language. General Taylor was pleased to say that I was the first man he ever knew who declined an office because he did not consider himself fit for it, and then offered me the office of Recorder of the Land Office, which I should have declined if I could without giving offence.

8. By Mr. Lincoln, recommended by many senators and members of the House of Representatives, though Mr. Lincoln did not ask for or look at any of these. I knew him and he knew me well.

9. The salary attached to my office is $3,000 per annum, but during the past year I have received 20 per cent. additional, under an act of Congress. I think it is larger than my income was previous to my entering the office, but is less in comparison with the cost of living now and then.

10. I had not; and had to learn the duties by study and application.

11. The duties are only to be learned by a study of the revenue laws, the treasury regulations, treasury circulars, and the recorded correspondence of the office from 1790 down to the present time, contained in some forty volumes of records.

12. I report annually to the Secretary of the Treasury, and enclose my last two annual reports. I have to occasionally make other reports upon cases referred to me by the Secretary, as they arise in the course of business—some quite elaborate, some less so.

13. I am usually in my office by half-past eight a. m., and remain till after four p. m. ; sometimes return to the office and labor the whole evening. Since I have held the office, I have never, for a single day, failed to sign all official papers, except when absent from the city.

14. I have under my control 35 persons, divided into 7 classes, viz: 1 chief clerk; 3 clerks of class 4; 8 of class 3; 10 of class 2; 9 of class 1; 1 assistant messenger; and 3 laborers; all permanently employed.

15. The employment of the different classes is as follows: 1 chief clerk; 1 clerk of class 4, bookkeeper; 1 accountant; 1 special agent; 1 of class 3, estimates; 1 law clerk; 6 accountants; 6 of class 2, accountants, 1 miscellaneous, 2 copyists, 1 record; 1 of class 1, copyist; 1 assistant bookkeeper; 6 accountants; 1 acting messenger; 1 assistant messenger; 1 laborer, acting as clerk; and 2 as laborers. All employed seven hours each day.

16. I am unable to answer this.

17. All who have been appointed under me have undergone test examinations. Those examinations were conducted by myself or some one appointed by me for that purpose, under my supervision. They were examined particularly in arithmetic and bookkeeping questions, being put to them of a character likely to arise in the performance of their duties; also in other branches, as history, grammar, geography, &c.

18. One or two clerks have been transferred to my office from others, of whose examinations I knew nothing. I think one, at least, is now in my office. As to the remainder of the interrogatory, I cannot answer.

19. The previous occupations of my clerks are exceedingly various. Some have been lawyers, some school teachers, some bookkeepers, some mechanics, and one has been in the office since he was a boy, now 64 years ago, nearly, and who is a good, efficient clerk yet, at the age of 78.

20. I do not know that any one has been appointed on political grounds since I have been at the head of the office. Four or five were appointed at my solicitation, because I knew their qualifications, and needed just such men. Three of these were lawyers. They have

proved to be all I expected—most valuable assistants. I never inquired about the politics of any one, except during the war, and then only to satisfy myself that he was loyal; and I allow no political, nor, indeed, any other discussions, among the clerks.

21. Appointments are made by the Secretary in all cases.

22. This should be answered by the Secretary.

23. Nine have been in the army; 8 have been connected with the press. There are different grades of efficiency among my subordinates in the same class.

24. Twenty have been appointed within 2 years; 7 have been appointed more than 2 years, and within 4 years; 2 have been appointed more than 4 years, and within 6 years; 3 have been appointed more than 6 years, and within 10 years; 1 has been appointed more than 10 years, and within 15 years; and 2 have been appointed more than 15 years.

25. Seven are under 25 years of age; 7 are over 25, and under 30; 6 are over 30, and under 40; 5 are over 40, and under 50; 6 are over 50, and under 60; and 4 are over 60.

26. Nine of my employés have been discharged; none for political causes.

27. There is no *system* of promotion, except that when a vacancy occurs I endeavor to have it filled by a lower-class clerk.

28. It is impossible to advance meritorious clerks in my office, for the reason that the number of each class is limited, and I have but few, and am allowed but few, of the higher grades, although mine is a *revising* bureau. (See my remarks on this subject at page 7 of my annual report.)

29. Nothing of the kind has happened in my bureau since I have had charge of it. I should protest most earnestly against it.

30. Answered in 29.

31. I find nearly all my clerks diligent and prompt in their attendance. The older ones, however, are more sedate, and apply themselves to business more steadily than younger men. When I say the older, I mean those from 30 to 60 years of age, and two over that age; they are as regular, steady, and diligent as the sun.

32. Answered above.

33. I answer most decidedly in the affirmative.

34. I do not doubt it.

35. I have not a doubt of it.

36. I have now no female employés. I have had some experience of them, and had some very good female clerks; but, as a general rule, they are less reliable and efficient than males, and more difficult to govern. I should be unwilling to trust such duties to them as my clerks have to perform: that is, the revising and settling long and intricate accounts, involving innumerable questions of law and practice, and not unfrequently the unraveling of confused and erroneous statements, and pursuing errors through a long series of returns. I have never yet seen the woman equal to such a task. Some of them make very good copyists.

37. Answered in interrogatory 47.

38. I find great and indeed insuperable difficulty in enforcing the revenue laws on the frontier and seaboard through the regular officers of customs; though I take pleasure in saying that I think, as a general thing, these officers were never more vigilant and faithful in the performance of their duties than they have been for the three years past, and are at the present time, especially on the northeastern, northern, and northwestern frontier. But there are among them incompetent, inefficient, unfaithful, and unreliable men. In some of the seaboard districts, the number of these is considerably greater in proportion to the number employed.

39. "What changes are necessary, in your judgment, in the present system to make the service more efficient and economical?"—In my judgment the present system should be discarded altogether. At present custom-houses are conducted in the interest of party politics, and have been so conducted for over 35 years. Since offices were proclaimed to be "the spoils of victors," they have been seized and used as such by both parties, appointments of customs officers being made, not with a single eye to the interests of the government, but with an eye, first, to the interests of the dominant party; and secondly or lastly, to the public interests. If both could be served by an appointment, very well; if not, the first must be served at all events, and of course the latter suffers. If all appointments were made upon competitive examinations, the appointees assured of permanent employment, (if not forfeited by demerit,) and of advancement in position and compensation when merited by length of service or by capacity, fidelity, and assiduity in the performance of duties, I do not doubt that a higher grade of men—higher as to education, character, integrity, and social standing—could be obtained for the same compensation.

40. What would be the gain in the revenue from customs by the change I have suggested I have no means of knowing; but that there would be a gain by reason of the more strict and prompt enforcement of the revenue laws, and the increased vigilance in preventing frauds by means of false invoices, smuggling, &c., I do not doubt. The expenses of collecting the revenue would be somewhat lessened, inasmuch as a less number of officers would be needed.

41. Answered as far as it can be above.

42. There is no rule or regulation under the present system by which delinquencies among subordinate officers are certain to be reported. I think such failures to report are not unfrequent; reason, because it is not the interest, nor is it felt to be the duty of any one to

report such delinquencies, even if known; but they may not be known to any officer other than the guilty one.

43. It undoubtedly would, for the reason that the duties would then be performed by men of integrity, and actuated by a high sense of moral responsibility to God and the community, who could bring into the service increased vigilance, honesty, and fidelity.

44. With customs officers of the character described in this interrogatory, I do not doubt that a great saving to the government might be secured in the single item of the prevention of frauds on the revenue; but I have no data from which to estimate the amount, even approximately. I am satisfied that our revenue is immensely defrauded, especially in some of the large cities—New York, for instance—and that much of this could be prevented by such a system of appointments as is hereinbefore indicated. Perhaps if I were to say that a million of dollars a year might be thus saved I should not speak extravagantly.

45. Very far from it.

46. As a suit of clothes made for the boy do not fit the man, for the same reason a revenue system framed with admirable skill and adaptation to the condition of the country in its infancy, is not fitted to its present vastly increased territory and commerce.

47. I answer this interrogatory in the negative; but I think that the fidelity of customs officers might be better secured, and their vigilance and assiduity increased, by concentrating the whole business relating to commerce and navigation in one bureau or department, the head of which should exercise a more direct and rigid supervision of these matters than is now possible, and especially in regard to the efficiency, integrity, and fidelity of the officers and their subordinates, and the economy, or want of it, in the various branches of the service. The commerce and navigation of this country are of sufficient magnitude and importance in my judgment to constitute a department, and require all the administrative abilities of its head. So long as they are appended to another department, the head of which is compelled to devote his time and energies to multifarious matters of great magnitude and urgency, aside from these, it is not in the nature of things that they can receive the attention and consideration which their importance demands, however anxious he may be to perform his whole duty, and look after all the interests committed to his care.

J. M. Brodhead, Second Comptroller of the Treasury:

No. 3. Clerk and chief clerk from 1830 to 1837, and from 1840 to 1853; from February, 1853, to October, 1857, Second Comptroller of Treasury.

The least diligent and efficient appointees are those who have strong political backers or influence in Congress especially, and who are thereby emboldened to neglect their duties. The efficiency of the service would be increased by the adoption of the system suggested in the 33d question, and an equal amount of work could be accomplished under such a system by a less number of persons than are now employed. A higher grade of talent, and a better quality of persons could be induced to enter the government service if promotion were granted only to seniority or merit, and no discharge permitted except for cause.

No. 33. Yes.

No. 34. Yes.

No. 35. Yes.

The same system would also promote the efficiency of the female clerks. They have 25 per cent. less than a first-class clerk. In diligence, attention, and propriety of conduct they are superior to clerks of the other sex, and in efficiency they compare favorably with them, considering the difference in pay. I have too much respect for women, however, to be in favor of employing them in public offices.

I have not time to go in the general subject of the civil service, but believe that my own office would be rendered more efficient by the transfer to it of competent clerks from the offices of the respective Auditors, whose work is subject to the revision of the Second Comptroller, so that no original appointment should be made to this office. As it now is an inexperienced clerk, just appointed from the mass of the people, may be set to revise the work of experts, and the freshly indentured apprentice is required to detect the errors and perfect the work of the master workman. The salaries should of course be larger, so that the transfer would be a promotion; but fewer clerks would be required, and the expense would be no greater.

Thomas L. Smith, First Auditor of the Treasury:

No. 3. Before present appointment was register of the United States Treasury for 16 years.

No. 17. Yes; by board of examiners, few have been rejected.

No. 33. The rules that govern the office is to test qualifications by examination before appointment to first class, and promotions to each class are made upon examination, in direct reference to qualifications for promotions.

John Wilson, Third Auditor of the Treasury:

No. 3. From 1831, with intervals, to the present time.

No. 17. Every clerk is subjected to a rigid examination: the questions are those that occur daily in the duties of the office, conducted by the chief clerk, subject to the examination of the Fifth Auditor and myself, constituting a board of examiners.

No. 32. Those who are backed by great political and congressional influence feel independent of the head of the office, and above the reach of salutary rules and regulations.

33. Precisely the course suggested in this question is pursued in this office, except that candidates for higher grades are selected because of their superior talents and general excellence in the discharge of their duties. This is a much safer basis of promotion than any test examination; and, in my opinion. all appointments should be made in the first class, and all promotions be made on merit alone, as the hope of reward is the best stimulus to exertion in a well-balanced mind. Such are our rules here, simply to secure the greatest efficiency in the official corps.

34 and 35. The answer to this question (34th) substantially is given in the answer to the 33d question, and to the 35th I reply there is no doubt that such a system would secure higher grades of talent and a better class of persons in the government service. It would establish and promote a proper *esprit de corps*, in which every member would be interested, and which each and all would be proud and anxious to sustain.

36. There are 15 female clerks in this office, who receive about 75 per cent. of the amount paid to male clerks for similar service, with whom they compare favorably for diligence, attention, and efficiency. As they are chiefly copyists, the only examination that should be required is of their penmanship and spelling. It is difficult to determine the best method of increasing the efficiency of these employés. In my opinion, they should receive precisely the same compensation as is paid to male clerks for similar duties; should be promoted to positions and duties suited to their sex and abilities, and receive the compensation ordinarily affixed to the duties they may be called upon to perform. Perhaps mere copyists should be paid by the hundred words a fair compensation, and then each would receive full equivalent for her service, the rate to be fixed so as to enable a good copyist to earn $1,200 per annum.

37. As far as lies within the jurisdiction of this office, I have endeavored to state in my annual report some matters which. in my judgment, would tend to make the civil service more efficient and economical. (See Doc. 3, herewith, pp. 15, 16, 17, and 18.) The suggestion of commutation of pensions, with consent of the pensioners, on the principle somewhat of life annuities, would take more money out of the treasury at once, but would finally materially reduce the expenses of all the agencies, and ultimately close up that branch of business. Legislation that would prevent the payment of fraudulent claims, perpetuate testimony in such cases, and limit the time in which all claims shall be presented, would relieve the government from erroneous expenditures on that basis. All claims of the same general character should be passed on by the same tribunal to insure uniformity of decision, and legislation to that effect should be had. The Treasury Department should by law be made the exclusive financial agent of the government. To this end all supplies for the several departments should be purchased under existing laws, or such as Congress may pass hereafter for that object, by suitable officers to be designated for that purpose. Those officers should then certify the accounts for such articles furnished, with the contract, to receiving officers, designated by law, who should certify that the articles so purchased are of the quality, quantity, and price specified in the contract. The accounts thus certified to be sent to the proper department for administrative examination, and if approved. to be forwarded to the accounting officers, who, by law, have charge of the matter. If the accounts are found correct, and so stated by the proper auditor, and admitted and certified by the Comptroller, the amount so found due to be paid by the Treasurer of the United States, by draft, sent direct to the person who furnished the supplies. In this way the government would have vouchers for every dollar paid out, so far as the purchase of supplies is concerned, and there will be no risk of defaulting disbursing officers. Those officers will then only have property accounts to be adjusted, and there will be little or no risk of loss in those cases. This mode cannot be adopted in paying officers, soldiers, and sailors, but a system might be adopted of dividing the country into districts, with a paymaster for each, &c., to whom the necessary funds could be transmitted by the middle of each quarter to settle up the liabilities of that quarter; said paymaster to be required to return his accounts and vouchers within ten days after the end of each quarter under severe penalties; no money to be sent to him for a succeeding quarter till such accounts had been rendered for the preceding quarter; and in no case should money be sent to *any* disbursing officer to a greater amount.than is covered by his bond, the bond to be increased as circumstances may require, at the discretion of the Secretary of the Treasury, and under such rules and regulations as he may prescribe. The same remarks to apply to pension agents; and the signing of such bond by principal and sureties to act as a lien on all their property at the time the bond was given. Clear and judicious laws that would carry out these ideas would, in my opinion, materially accelerate the settlement of accounts, reduce expenditures, and avoid risk of loss of government money.

Stephen J. W. Tabor, Fourth Auditor of the Treasury:

No. 3. For five years as county judge and two years as treasurer and recorder of Buchanan county, Iowa.

No. 17. Yes, *thoroughly*, by a board of examiners, consisting of the Hon. C. M. Walker, the Fifth Auditor, Darius Lyman of the Secretary's bureau, and myself. embracing reading, writing, arithmetic, grammar, geography, history, bookkeeping, spelling, and composition.

No. 32. Those who imagine they have outside or political influence to retain them in office.

No. 33. All new appointments are made in the lowest grade only. They are promoted because they have given evidence of their fitness. But must answer the inquiry (33) in the affirmative.

No. 34. Some additional regulations in accordance with the idea in No. 33, but more ample, would have this effect.

No. 35. Most assuredly, and this is beyond question the true principle. Faithful and competent clerks should at least have the same certainty of employment that professional men, tradesmen and mechanics do outside.

No. 36. There are, at $900 a year, and perform their duties satisfactorily. The other inquiries answered affirmatively.

I think an arbitrary examination of a technically scholastic character applied to other clerks and other employés of the government who have learned their duties at their posts, and who are competent for their performance, would be unjust and detrimental to the public service. The experience of a clerk is of great value. That, united to sound sense and good natural parts, makes a clerk excellent. Any rule, no matter how stringent, may be adopted for new applicants, but clerks who are actually performing their duties in the best manner should not be displaced because they are not versed in the learning of the schools.

Summary from reports from this office.

The annexed table, collected from the Fourth Auditor's reports, shows a falling off in business in seven divisions of his office of nearly one-third of the total amount of accounts settled in 1866 and 1867 ($76,576,675 65) as compared with preceding year, while there has only been an increase of business in one division, leaving a balance of falling off of business of $10,973,456 52.

While it appears that one additional clerk is required in the one division (naval agents' disbursements) in which there was an increase of business to the extent of $22,800,702 10, it does not appear that there was any reduction of force in the other seven divisions, in which the decrease amounted in the aggregate to $33,774,158 62.

In the face of this falling off it is, on the contrary, surprising that 11 new clerks should have been appointed in 1866 and 1867. The forces under his control at the present seem to be larger than they were at any time previous to his accession to office, (1863,) 59 persons having been appointed since that period, and only 18 dismissed.

Falling off in the business of the Fourth Auditor's office.

Letters received in 1865 and 1866	70,117
Letters received in 1866 and 1867	36,321
Decrease	33,796
Letters recorded in 1865 and 1866	97,088
Letters recorded in 1866 and 1867	68,152
Decrease	28,936
Allotments registered in 1865 and 1866	3,043
Allotments registered in 1866 and 1867	1,820
Decrease	1,223

$45,983,986 03	Cash requisitions, 1865 and 1866	$45,983,986 03	
	Cash requisitions, 1866 and 1867	34,518,733 85	
	Decrease		$11,465,252 18
8,948,593 03	Cash refunding req'tions, 1865 and 1866	8,948,593 03	
	Cash refunding req'tions, 1866 and 1867	2,208,006 13	
	Decrease		6,740,586 90
2,599,269 30	Prize money, 1865 and 1866	2,599,269 30	
	Prize money, 1866 and 1867	1,042,099 56	
	Decrease		1,557,169 74
4,100,276 24	Navy pensions, 1865 and 1866	4,100,276 24	
	Navy pensions, 1866 and 1867	1,228,242 25	
	Decrease		2,872,033 99
46,724,957 34	Paymaster divisions, 1865 and 1866	46,724,957 34	
	Paymaster divisions, 1866 and 1867	36,331,198 33	
	Decrease		10,393,759 01
797,752 49	General claims, 1865 and 1866	797,752 49	
	General claims, 1866 and 1867	598,347 45	
	Decrease		199,405 04
$109,154,834 43			$33,228,206 86

	572 clerks, navy agents, 1865 and 1866, account 441 vouchers, 113,554....	54,657,975 99
	672 clerks, navy agents, 1865 and 1867, account 52 vouchers, 184,900.....	77,458,678 09

	Deduct increase.........................		22,800,702 10
1,195,999 84	{ Allotments, 1865....................	1,195,999 84	
	{ Allotments, 1866....................	650,048 08	
	Decrease................................		545,951 76
$110,350,834 27	Decrease as against 1865 and 1866............		$10,973,456 52

SUMMARY.

Transactions in 1865 and 1866 in all divisions............................	$110,350,834 27
Decrease in 1866 and 1867 in seven divisions........................	33,774,158 62
Transactions in 1866 and 1867 in seven divisions	76,576,675 65
Business transacted in 1866 and 1867 in the eight divisions, (increase against 1865 and 1866 $22,800,702 10)...........................	77,458,678 09
Total business in 1866 and 1867.......................................	154,035,353 74
Decrease as against 1865 and 1866..................................	10,973,456 52
Total business in 1865 and 1866......................................	165,008,810 26

Total forces January 1, 1868, 92. Estimated salaries $150,000, for the transaction of business amounting in 1866 and 1867 to $154,035,353 74, but steadily decreasing.

C. M. Walker, Fifth Auditor of the Treasury:

No. 3. Law clerk, &c., in the office of the Secretary of the Treasury, for two years.

No. 17. Yes: examination conducted by myself and some person in the department designated by the Secretary, embracing different subjects, and tested pretty fairly the candidate's qualifications, his knowledge of accounts, orthography, composition, arithmetic. grammar, &c.

No. 32. Those who are too youthful, or those who have little capacity for business or knowledge of affairs, depend solely on political, personal, or other such considerations, for their retention in office.

No. 33. Yes.

No. 34. Unquestionably; if incompetent clerks could be weeded out and skilled and competent men retained at increased salaries.

No. 35. Most unquestionably.

No. 36. Seven; $900 per annum; lowest class of male clerks receive $1,200; compare favorably with males for diligence and efficiency, &c.

The "civil service" cannot be made a career so long as the principle of rotation in office obtains, nor while the maxim of to "the victors belong the spoils" is followed. It will, in my judgment, be a fortunate day for our government when both these principles are discarded, when merit, fidelity, and capacity shall govern in all appointments, and when the civil service shall be made to approximate what it is under other civilized governments, viz: a career. * * * New appointees are frequently placed over the heads of old ones by reason of superior talents, competency, or qualifications. Mere length of service is not conclusive as to a man's qualifications; for he may have been a mediocre man to begin with, and a new man may be far more deserving of promotion. There can be no question but that the efficiency of the public service would be increased by some reform substantially like that suggested in question No. 33.

If incompetent clerks could be weeded out and the appointment of any such in future prevented, the public business could be performed by a much less number of persons than it is at present. But to secure such superior qualifications higher salaries would have to be paid in these times. One of the greatest difficulties experienced is the frequent resigning of skilled and competent men, because they can do better elsewhere. I think it would be true economy to increase the compensation and decrease the number of government employés.

The lowest class of male clerks receive $1,200 per annum. The females receive each $900 per annum. They are employed solely as copyists, and answer very well for that. If they were not employed it would take about the same number of males to do the work done by them. The same principle of appointment, advancement, promotions, &c., should, in the main, apply to the female as to the male clerks.

Elevate the standard of employés, make appointments more difficult to obtain, exclude the paramount influence of political considerations, make merit and capacity the requisite in appointments and promotions, decrease the number of employés, increase to a fair rate the compensation of those retained, make the tenure of all offices as permanent as practicable, permit no discharges except for cause, and approximate the civil service, so far as possible, to a career or life pursuit.

H. J. Anderson, Sixth Auditor of the Treasury, for Post Office Department:

No. 3. In early life clerk of judicial courts for ten years, subsequently United States House of Representatives, from 1837 to 1841; governor of the State from 1843 to 1847; and United States Commissioner of Customs from 1853 to 1858.

No. 17. Yes; by a board of examiners, consisting of the Auditor, Hon. C. M. Walker, and Darius Lyman, of the Treasury Department; by written questions.

No. 33. Yes.

No. 34. Undoubtedly.

No. 35. Probably to some extent have that effect.

With the present rate of compensation to the lower class of clerks, I apprehend that it would be difficult to obtain a very high grade of talent for those places, unless the classification was so changed as to provide a larger number for classes three and four, being the two highest classes. Referring particularly to this office, the promise of promotion is so slow, that the lower classes of clerks get discouraged, and such of them as can find other employment resign their places. In this way we lose many of our most valuable clerks.

Hon. E. A. Rollins, Commissioner of Internal Revenue:

Almost all appointed with regard to political or personal considerations.

33. The efficiency of the service in this manner would be very much increased, though I doubt if all new appointments should be made to the lowest grade only until the service should be somewhat redeemed from its present condition.

34. It could.

35. Undoubtedly.

36. There are. The females are employed only as copyists, and females only are thus employed. In this service they compare, favorably, I think, with males for diligence, intelligence, and efficiency. Their efficiency, however, would be improved in the manner suggested.

38. There is very great difficulty. The service is full of officers appointed with too little regard to personal integrity or actual ability. I respectfully refer you, in this connection, to so much of my last report to the Secretary as relates to the civil service and which is herewith attached.

39. Appointments and promotions with less regard to political service and only upon competitive examination.

40. Immense gain to the revenue under existing laws.

41. Under the present system delinquencies in subordinate officers are not certain to be reported, because those whose duty it is to detect and report such delinquencies—the delinquencies, for instance, of assistant assessors—are oftentimes as inefficient as the delinquents themselves.

42. To a very great extent.

43. I annex herewith a statement showing the amount collected on distilled spirits in each collection district in the United States for the fiscal years ending June 30, 1865, 1866, and 1867.

44. The subject is very largely engrossing the attention of the Ways and Means Committee of the House of Representatives, but the receipts which the government should derive from this tax can only be derived through officers of integrity and ability. Legislation can do something, but more depends upon the character of the men who administer the law.

45. I cannot answer this definitely nor even approximately, but much more, I have no doubt, than the present receipts from distilled spirits.

The efficiency of the service, in this manner, would be very much increased, though I doubt if all new appointments should be made to the lowest grade only until the service should be somewhat redeemed from its present condition. * * * An equal amount of work could be accomplished under such a system by a less number of persons than are now employed. * * * If the employment was assured and certain, and promotions granted only to seniority or merit, and no discharge permitted except for cause, a higher grade of talent and a better quality of persons would, no doubt, be induced to enter the government service.

The following is the report relating to the reform of the civil service, contained in the Commissioner's annual report, lately presented to Congress:

There is no question of a higher personal interest to every faithful revenue officer, nor one of hardly greater importance to the public, than that which relates to the recovery of the revenue service from the reproach under which it has fallen. The failure to collect the tax upon distilled spirits, and the imperfect collections from several other objects of taxation, are attributable more to the frequent changes of officers, and to the inefficiency and corruption of many of them, than to any defect of the law. I write this in the advocacy and the defence of every worthy, honest officer, but I write it with shame. The legal evidence of its truth may never be found, but the moral evidence is patent to every thoughtful observer. The law can never be thoroughly enforced except in those districts where the officers, both principal and subordinate, in the revenue and judiciary departments alike, are earnestly determined that it shall be, nor except when the combined and active hostility of all those against whom it is enforced shall be insufficient for the removal of any officer opposed to their plunderings. The dishonesty of an assistant assessor, or an inspector, whose offences cannot be discovered, prejudices the efficiency and good standing of all his associate officers of every variety. and the community, ignorant of the exact nature and locality of the evil, ascribe to it undoubtedly a wider and more general existence than it really possesses. I honor more and more the officer who yields neither to temptation nor threats, and to him it is due, as it is due to the country, that the revenue service be rescued from the control of purely political favor, which has for many years too largely dictated the appointments in most departments of the government, and that it be more thoroughly interwoven with the highest interests of the treasury. Men should be appointed to place because they are needed, and because they are qualified, not because they are out of employment, and are the supporters of a political party or person. They are not thus employed in banks, counting-rooms, and factories. Every community has a right to expect and to require that the persons intrusted in it with important interests pertaining to the general government shall have earned its confidence in their integrity and ability.

The evil is inherent in the manner of appointments, and lies deeper than the present supremacy of any political party. Assessors and collectors are appointed by the President with the confirmation of the Senate. Their subordinates, except deputy collectors, are appointed by the Secretary of the Treasury, and under the long-continued practice of the department, upon the recommendations of the assessors and collectors of the districts where service is to be rendered. Political pressure, and combinations born of corrupt and corrupting purposes, too often remove and appoint assessors and collectors, and they in turn, while making recommendations for their inferior officers, are surrounded and overborne or deluded by politicians, or whiskey operators disguised as such. Their tenure of office, when secured, is uncertain and feeble, seeming to be strengthened rather by concessions to wrong than by exacting the rights of the government. This is not so in any other civilized and important nation on the earth. They have all passed through our present experience, and it will be fortunate for us if we shall profit by their example.

It is not within the purpose and scope of an annual report to consider at length the civil service of other countries, and indeed it was so fully detailed in the report of the Joint Committee on Retrenchment during the last Congress, and the necessities of this country in this behalf so fully portrayed, that little more need be done by me, perhaps, than to invite the attention of the Secretary of the Treasury to the report itself, with its accompanying papers, and to the remarks of Mr. Jenckes, of Rhode Island, upon its introduction to the House of Representatives. The subject, however, is of such vital importance to the interests with which I am charged, that I cannot forbear a brief reference to its controlling and principal features in several countries with whose institutions we are more familiar.

British statesmen had learned wisdom from the necessities of the distant colonial dependencies of the kingdom, and the character of its civil service had long been improving, but it was not until the famous order in council of May 21, 1855, that the patronage of the Crown and its officers at home was partially limited to those who should successfully pass the examination of the civil service commission then established.

The system is not so comprehensive as that of several countries on the continent, but its advantages are growing more and more apparent through all the departments of the government. There are in fact two examinations, one to determine whether a person has the minimum or standard qualification necessary to candidacy, and the other of a competitive character, in which all the candidates designated for a particular position participate. He who secures the greatest number of marks indicating degrees of proficiency, both in theoretical and practical acquirements, provided he has done well in all, receives the appointment. The commission, however, have a well established rule that "unless we are satisfied with the evidence produced of the moral character of candidates, we are bound to withhold our certificate. The number of persons rejected will suffice to prove that these precautions are by no means superfluous, even though the candidates are in most cases recommended by persons of some position in society."

The marks are published with the list of appointments, and the applicants and the public are made acquainted with the actual and relative standing of all who become connected with the service. A candidate must be free from debt before appointment, and must make solemn oath that neither he nor any person for him within his knowledge has, directly or indirectly, given or promised to give any gratuity or reward for obtaining, or endeavoring to obtain, him a position. Any officer arrested for debt is suspended, and, if not free from debt at the end of twenty-eight days, is superseded. The elective franchise is denied to all officers of the service. Promotions are made only after prescribed periods of employment, and only upon the application of the candidate himself. Should another make application for him, and he not be able to show that it was without his knowledge, he is punished for the offence by a reprimand; for the second of a like nature, by transfer; and for the third, by reduction. Promotions are earned, not given through favor, and are indicative of absolute merit. Officers are liable to be transferred to any place in the kingdom, and although periodical transfers are discontinued, the board reserves the right to transfer at pleasure without ascribing cause therefor. There is permanency in the service. Removals of those immediately connected with the inland revenue are never made for personal or political reasons.

I have examined a register of those now employed, and while I have not made an accu rate calculation of their average period of service, because of want of time necessary to do so, I am sure that it cannot be less than fourteen years. Many have served from 20 to 40 years, and a comfortable support is secured to all who shall be placed upon the superannuated list. Mr. Timm, after a long and honorable service as solicitor to the commission, has recently retired upon a pension of £1,800 per annum, and Mr. Trevor, from that of controller of legacy duties, upon an allowance of about £1,500, after a consecutive service of 41 years and five months. As many changes have been occasioned in the British service during the past year by death as by all other reasons combined.

The French revenue system is the result of nearly a hundred years' experience. Every officer in it below the minister of finance commenced his service in a clerkship or some more subordinate position, and the advancement which his fidelity and ability secured has never been hindered by political frowns or even by political revolutions. His appointment was without partiality, and public examination has awarded him his promotions.

For more than fifty years a semi-annual record has been kept of every man's official conduct as reported by different superior officers. This is a testimony and encouragement to faithful effort, and a security against malicious and unfounded charges. Under such a system it becomes almost impossible for an unworthy man to work his way to a position where his incompetency or his corruption can largely prejudice the reputation of the service or materially affect the revenue of the empire. Indeed, the corruption of an officer in France or England, or anywhere else where a proper system determines appointments, very rarely exists.

The civil service of Germany is superior to that of England or France. Throughout the entire confederation special education is added to the requirements elsewhere made of moral fitness, and a certain measure of attainments tested by competitive examinations. As with us there are normal schools for the preparation of teachers, and academies for those who are to officer our army and navy, so there are in Germany, at public charge, schools and universities for the special and appropriate education of those who are to become connected with the public administration of the laws. The higher the standard of requirements has been raised, the larger has been the number of aspirants for employment, because the elevation of the character of the service itself has persuaded men of the highest position and attainments to offer themselves as rivals for its honors and its emoluments The prominent and enviable position which Prussia has won among nations is due not more to the character of her people and the natural resources of the kingdom than to the careful preliminary training of those in the several departments of the government to whom her resources are intrusted, and whom she keeps in her service as long as they are worthy of her trust.

I am aware that the peculiarity of our institutions, and the fact that all political parties have learned to expect much actual service from their office-holders, may prejudice, and for a time prevent, in this country, the adoption of a system as universal and valuable as that of Germany, but the Constitution itself has elevated the national judiciary above the fluctuations of popular favor by appointment during good behavior, and there is equal need that revenue officers shall exercise their judgment and execute the law without fear of personal disadvantage. The rights of property adjudicated by all the courts of the country, State and national, in a single year are of small amount when compared with those which are passed upon in the various revenue offices during the same period.

H. R. Hulburd, Comptroller of the Currency:

No. 3. Clerk in office of Comptroller of Currency from January 24, 1864, to August 1, 1865. Deputy Comptroller from August 1, 1865, until appointment as Comptroller.

No. 17. Yes; all appointed under me, with reference to nature of work to be performed, and their intelligence, education, &c.

No. 32. The most inefficient are those whose applications are most strongly urged.

No. 33. Yes; provided the candidate should have reached a certain age, and received a good preliminary education.

No. 34. Yes.

No. 35. Yes; with the modification in regard to *seniority*, which alone would not be certain to advance the most meritorious.

No. 36. Thirty female clerks in my office as counters and copyists. They compare favorably in diligence, efficiency and attention to duty, with males. Classification of them by merit is just as desirable as of males.

The women are employed as counters of bank notes and as copyists. None of this kind of work is performed by men, and men could not do it better than it is now done by women.

The male clerks are all employed as bookkeepers or as correspondents, duties that could not be as well performed by women.

I think it would be well to have different grades for women. All are not equally meritorious, and some discrimination might, with great propriety, and I think with good effect, be made as to the grade allotted, or the compensation allowed. The stimulus furnished by the chance of promotion would operate with perhaps as much force upon the female mind as upon the masculine intellect.

No. 37. Better salaries should be attainable, by men of ability, in the civil service. During the last two years seven men, who by their ability and experience had become valuable to this office, have resigned, being offered higher salaries in active business. Banking institutions pay from $2,500 to $5,000 per annum to men for work which I am expected to have done, so as to defy criticism, at salaries of $1,600 to $1,800. This is a difficulty hard to be overcome.

F. E. Spinner, Treasurer of the United States:

No. 3. Auditor and deputy naval officer, port of New York, from 1845 to 1849. Member of Congress from 1855 to 1861.

23. Forty-seven of my subordinates have served in the Union armies; one in the United States navy; quite a large number, including females, in army hospitals. Nine have been associated with the press. There are different grades of efficiency among them in the same class. The pay of the several classes is now $1,200, $1,400, $1,600, and $1,800. Intermediate classes of $1,300, $1,500, and $1,700 would more equally distribute the pay according to service.

24. Of the employés in this office there were appointed—

During the years 1866 and 1867	100
During the years 1864 and 1865	119
During the years 1862 and 1863	48
Over six and less than ten years ago	10
Over ten and within fifteen years since	3
In the office over fifteen years	2
Total in office December 31, 1867	282

29. I am not aware that any of my subordinates pursued any course of study before appointment with the special view of qualifying them for the service; that they were taken indiscriminately from the various employments of civil life is evidenced by the following list of their previous occupations, viz: 7 accountants, 13 bankers, 18 bookkeepers, 27 clerks, 1 detective, 2 druggists, 1 editor, 5 farmers, 1 hackdriver, 1 housekeeper, 1 hotel steward, 16 laborers, 1 lawyer, 1 machinist, 8 mechanics, 14 merchants, 2 messengers, 1 minister, 1 page, 1 porter, 1 postman, 2 salesmen, 1 sculptor, 12 students, 1 surveyor, 24 teachers, 2 telegraphists, 1 county treasurer, 1 waiter, 1 washerwoman, 1 watchman, and of no particular occupation, 112; total number, 282.

32. The class of clerks that have the strongest political and other written recommendations are generally the "least diligent and efficient." Such are apt to place all hope of promotion on such recommendations, and seem not to think it necessary to be over attentive to the public business.

33. As a whole it is probable that "the efficiency of the service might be increased" by the course indicated in this question. But, in this office, the duties of the clerks are so diverse that it often happens that men fitted for a particular place can be had from the outside who better answer the requirements of the place than any one holding a lower grade in the office.

34. Am not prepared to say that "an equal amount of work could be done" by "a less number of persons" under such a system alone, but such a reorganization could be made as would certainly bring about such a result.

35. If "employment was assured and certain," and if promotions were made *only* on *merit*, the efficiency of the service would, no doubt, be greatly promoted thereby. But if such promotions were granted "to *seniority* only," the efficiency of the service would, in my opinion, be greatly damaged thereby. The power to withhold promotion or to dismiss for cause should not be impaired.

36. The compensation of the female clerks in this office bears about the proportion to that of male clerks for the same service as three to five. There is little difference between the two in regard to diligence, efficiency, and attention to the business of the office. The efficiency of the female clerks would be greatly promoted if they were classified according to merit only. Some female clerks are now equal to some males; yet, under present laws, some male clerks receive double the pay of any female clerk. Some female clerks do more than double the work of some others, yet all of them are paid the same salary.

37. With competent men at the heads of the various departments and bureaus of the government, the efficiency of all of them is assured. With incompetents in these positions, inefficiency must follow. Where a head is wrong, the whole body will be wrong; and no amount of legislative physique can give vigor and efficiency to a body that has a weak or an inefficient head.

N. L. Jeffries, Register of the United States Treasury:

No. 3. In military service from September, 1861, to October, 1866. From August, 1863, to August, 1864, was provost marshal general of States of Maryland and Delaware. From August, 1864, to September, 1866, on duty at the War Department as Assistant Provost Marshal General of the United States.

No. 17. There have been 81 appointments, 13 males and 68 females. All the male clerks have been examined as to their qualifications.

No. 18. The 68 female clerks were not examined.

No. 32. Those who rely on political influence.

No. 33. Yes.

No. 34. Yes.

No. 35. Yes.

No. 36. Yes. The compensation is much less. Those receiving $900 salary perform service equal to that of males receiving $1,600, in some cases. A system of promotion, depending on merit, adopted and *carried out*, would be of great advantage; but under present system of making appointments it would be impossible. Female clerks are as diligent and efficient as males.

S. M. Clark, Chief of Printing Division National Currency Bureau:

No. 3. Chief clerk of the office of construction in the Treasury Department nearly four years; subsequently engineer in charge of that office for about two years; and for the past five years have been the disbursing agent of the treasury extension.

No. 6. I was referred for examination in August, 1856, in this department, to a board of examiners appointed by the Secretary of the Treasury, consisting of Mr. Rodman, then chief clerk, and Major Barker, and Mr. McKean, two prominent fourth-class clerks. The "full particulars of such examination" were as follows: I was instructed by the then Secretary to appear before this board at a given time and place to be examined. I put in my appearance at the time and place stated in my instructions. Major Barker commenced the "examination" by saying: "You are from New York, I believe, Mr. Clark?" I replied that I was. He then commenced a detailed narrative of his first visit to New York, and gave me an interesting and graphic account of the disturbance created in his mind by the "noise and confusion" of the great city. The delivery of this narrative occupied, as nearly as I remember, about half an hour. I listened to it attentively, endeavoring to discover some point in his discourse which had reference to my (then present) "examination." I failed to discover any relevancy, and therefore made no reply. At the close of his narrative, without any further question, he said to his associate examiners, "Well, gentlemen, I presume there is no doubt but that Mr. Clark is qualified." Whereupon they all signed the certificate, and my "examination" closed.

No. 18. Yes; those pressed upon me by Congressmen; but few are now in the service, as I get rid of the undesirable whenever a reduction of force offers opportunity.

No. 19. The employments are specialties, requiring skilled experts who have been similarly employed in private life before; other branches of the work are new, and the hands require to be educated in it after being hired.

No. 32. Those recommended by members of Congress.

No. 33. Yes; the examination should be by the party who is responsible for proper execution of the work.

No. 34. Yes.

No. 35. Yes; if hired and promoted for merit, not seniority.

No. 36. There are; compensation half that of males, but they do not perform same class of service. But where service is same pay is equal. Appointments for competency alone, and promotions for merit, not seniority, improve general efficiency of the service.

No. 37. I infer that the committee intend that I shall here confine my reply to the efficiency and economy of conducting the division of which I have charge, though the question is framed sufficiently broad to cover the entire civil service of the government. I therefore, as a reply, reproduce the recommendation in reference to this division made in my report to the Secretayr, and through him to Congress, in November, 1864, as a reply to the question:

"RECOMMENDATIONS.

"The Secretary directs me to state what legislation, in my judgment, is necessary, if any, for the future operations of this division, and to make such recommendations for his consideration as my experience in the work may dictate.

"In my judgment, this division, which now only exists *ex necessitate rei*, should be organized by law as a distinct and separate bureau, to be entitled 'The Engraving and Printing Bureau of the Treasury Department.' The necessity for paper issues, in some form, is likely to be coexistent with the public debt, and the production of such issues in connection with the production of the currency for the national banks, and the large amount of printing and engraving required for the various drafts, checks, and certificates of the Treasurer, assistant treasurers, and disbursing agents, will give ample employment for such a bureau, if permanently organized and established by law. The internal revenue stamps, postage stamps, envelopes, postal money orders, and all similar work for other departments, could be more economically and safely produced by such a bureau than by the present method of contracting with individuals or private corporations. Much other incidental work would also naturally be done under such a bureau.

"The work should all be executed in a fire-proof building, to be erected and exclusively occupied for this purpose. A substantial but not costly structure should be built on the grounds adjacent to the Treasury building, and communication between it and the rooms occupied by the Treasurer of the United States should be made by a subterranean passage between the two buildings through which the printed values could be transmitted, thus avoiding such risk of transmission as attends the present method of carrying the finished money through the main halls and passages of the treasury, to which both the public and the treasury force have free access. The experience of the past two years in this division, in connection with the detailed descriptions which have been obtained of the construction of the buildings in which the Banks of England and of France prepare and issue their notes, will enable the interior accommodations to be economically and conveniently planned for the safe prosecution of the work, if such a structure should be authorized by Congress.

"The head of the bureau should be appointed by the Secretary of the Treasury, subject to confirmation by the Senate. Its affairs cannot, in my judgment, be successfully administered by a division of its responsibility under different heads. One chief, and one alone, should guide its details, under the general direction of the Secretary of the Treasury, to insure its economy, safety, and efficiency. Perfect integrity, with a familiar knowledge of all the details of the work to be done, should be combined in this head, and about him every possible guard should be thrown, to prevent all opportunity for fraud or malfeasance.

"A rigorous system of accountability—frequent, and where it is possible, *daily* adjustment of accounts—regular and systematic daily reports, to be carefully scrutinized and tested by competent officers not connected with the bureau, will be found essential safeguards; and these, if properly systemized and made of record, will, at all times, satisfy the department and the public of the daily condition of the trust. But no system, however ingeniously and skilfully devised, will compensate for lack of integrity; and *freedom from all desire of gain* should largely characterize the incumbent of such an office. Men of such character, amply qualified, are readily found, if sought for in the proper walks of life. They are to be sought for the office, as they are not seekers after office. The merchant and manufacturer find no difficulty in getting such men for private establishments, and government need not, if it seeks in the same quarter and offers like inducements for permanency upon proper discharge of the trust and performance of the duties. The salary should be sufficiently large to insure a maintenance with reasonable accumulation, and the tenure of the employment should not be subject to political changes. The employment should continue so long as the duties are well and faithfully performed.

"The employés upon the work should be hired and discharged, on their merits, by the head of the bureau alone, who should be held strictly accountable for the integrity and good conduct of all his subordinates, for the correctness of the accounts, and for the safe handling of all the products. To this end he should be empowered to make such rules and regulations for the guidance of these subordinates as he is willing, personally and officially, to abide the result of. Any method of business which places out of his control the complete power over his aids, or which lessens the belief and knowledge of that power among them all, will, I feel the strongest conviction, result in disaster. Experience proves that the adoption of such guides for the employment for these responsible mechanical operations, as usually guide appointments for clerical purposes, do not not result satisfactorily. The head of the bureau should select his aids solely for their fitness for the work and its responsibilities, irrespective of the locality of the applicant or of his professed claims for government patronage, or of any political or partisan influence which may be brought to guide such selection."

My experience in this division since this report was rendered confirms the entire propriety of these recommendations. The system of hiring or appointing parties simply because they have rendered partisan service is fraught with danger, tends to demoralize and degrade the service, and is an effective bar to the efficient, economical, and honest despatch of public business. Until this system is entirely done away with, the business will be, as now, badly, if not dishonestly conducted, at an unnecessary cost to the treasury.

A. B. Mullett, supervising architect, Treasury Department, Washington:

No. 33. I think appointments should be made, as a rule, in the lowest grade, and promotions made according to merit. I consider a practical test such as could be obtained by an appointment on trial, better than any test examinations. Many of the most worthless clerks in the department pass the best examinations, and probably could one still more rigid, while some of the most valuable could not. The duties of most of the clerks employed in the department require, beyond a good education, proficiency only in the special branch to which their duties are confined.

Nos. 34 and 35. Undoubtedly. At present the best talent cannot be retained in the higher grades of the public service for two reasons, viz: First, it is underpaid; and, second, no amount of capacity, honesty and fidelity, can secure the position.

No. 36. No.

No. 37. If civil officers were appointed for good conduct, at salaries sufficient to maintain them in a suitable manner, and provision made for retiring them on say half pay when superannuated, the civil service could and would retain the services of competent and efficient men in all of its branches, instead of being, as at present, considered by a large majority of its appointees as a mere temporary employment in which there is no inducement to perform any other duty than is absolutely required.

Benjamin Peirce, Superintendent Coast Survey:

No. 33. This is the practice now in the Coast Survey.

No. 34. Yes.

No. 35. Yes, undoubtedly.

No. 36. Yes; four. About the same as aids; they are quite intelligent.

No. 37. Appointments for merit alone.

The following suggestions are presented by instruction and under authority of Mr. Attorney General Stanbery:

(A.) In each bureau of the government an officer, with a tenure during good behavior, (who might be called a superintendent, director, or other name,) whose duty it should be to supervise the working of the system of business therein, under the command of the chief of the bureau. The present chief clerks occupy a position somewhat similar; but a precarious tenure is naturally opposed to regular, rigid, and complete system. Either the clerks would find their true level under such a supervision, or else the head of the office must bear a visible personal responsibility.

(B.) All clerks divided into two classes, viz: permanent and probationary. All permanent clerks to be of one grade, of a salary much higher than the present average. No appointment to be made in any case but from probationary clerks, after a certain period of probation.

(C) These to be appointed as all clerks are now appointed, and to receive a specific and equal compensation, say half as much as clerks. But their employment to cease at the pleasure of the appointor, and in all cases after one year's continuance. To be eligible for a second, probably a third, probation.

(D.) With some hesitation I add that the appointment of a person on probation, with his name and that of the persons on whose recommendation he was selected, might be published. The latter would work much good, but doubtless some evil. If a board could be useful in any event it might determine appointments to the probationary class.

I think it highly probable that more perfect system and a better *personnel* in the offices would make it practicable to conduct the public business *better* with much *fewer* clerks; I almost venture to believe, with one-half the present number. A very large proportion of the the labor is now, substantially, only to check a carelessness or dullness not provided for in private business establishments.

J. M. Binckley, Acting Attorney General:

No. 37. There is room for reform in method of business and standard of qualification, &c.

A. A. Harwood, Superintendent Lighthouse Board:

No. 33. Beyond a doubt.
No. 34. Yes.
No. 35. Certainly.
No. 37. Appointments for merit, and retention during good behavior; promotion by seniority.

Declares himself emphatically in favor of the proposed reform, by which the general efficiency of all classes in the civil service would be greatly improved.

He thinks that much of the inefficiency of an office is due to frequent changes in inferior positions, and declares it to be a lure to men who have failed in other avocations and a temptation to all who, not knowing how long they are to enjoy the fruit of their labors, proportion the amount and accuracy of work to the prospect of the harvest.

Assistant Secretary W. S. Otto, of the Interior Department:

A very large amount of money is, in my opinion, lost to the government by the frequent changes that are made in the appointments of persons to other offices who have no acquaintance whatever with the duties thereof. On becoming sufficiently familiar with them, they are too often discharged without an imputation upon their personal or official integrity.

The salary paid to clerks whose duties are merely those of copyists is very liberal, largely exceeding that paid for similar services in any other walk of life, or, as far as I am aware, by foreign governments. In the higher branches of clerical duty, demanding something beyond mechanical labor and routine, the clerks are not sufficiently paid.

The Assistant Secretary and the heads of bureaus in this department are not proportionately as well paid as the clerks. There is a singular irregularity in their compensation. The Commissioner of Patents receives $4,500 per annum, which is 50 per cent. more than is paid to either the Commissioner of Indian Affairs, the Commissioner of Pensions, or the Commissioner of the General Land Office. The duties of these last-named officers exact as much time and thought, and require as high an order of qualifications as do those of the Commissioner of Patents.

The disparity in the compensation of the heads of bureaus in this department and of officers holding corresponding positions in the War and Navy Departments, demands, in my opinion, the early attention of Congress. Every head of a bureau in the War Department receives, in pay and emoluments, more than a hundred per cent. greater salary than is paid to the head of a bureau in this department, except the Commissioner of Patents. It is idle to suppose that the duties of a Paymaster General or Quartermaster General are more arduous than those of the Commissioner of Pensions, or the Commissioner of the General Land Office. These officers in the War Department receive the "pay and emoluments" of brigadier generals. I presume that the attention of Congress has not been called to the subject, or such a distinction would not be made between officers whose position in the public service gives them an equal claim upon the country.

Was not examined and never pursued any special studies with a view of fitting myself for the office which I hold, nor did I produce any evidence of qualification. I have been circuit judge, and held other State offices in Indiana, but had no other evidence of qualification, excepting that I was known personally and by reputation to Ex-Secretary Usher, at whose suggestion I was appointed by President Lincoln.

There is no special printed book or manual setting forth the duties of my office.

Make no report to any one concerning the performance of the duties of my office ; confer habitually with the Secretary in regard to the business of the department, except that which relates to the appointment to office.

Under Secretary Usher possessed the appointing power ; the examination of each applicant should be thorough and efficient.

Do not know the previous occupation of subordinates, and whether any of them pursued any course of study with a view of qualifying themselves for the service.

Recommendations of the applicant are filed.

Unable to state how many of the persons employed in the department have served in the Union army and how many members of the press, and also unable to state the various periods of appointment and the various ages of the employés, and do not know how many have been removed since I have been in office.

Not positively know what the rules of office are, but have every reason to believe that promotion is governed exclusively by seniority, all other "things" being equal. Wield no longer the appointing power under Secretary Browning, and that this, as well as the final question of promotion, rests with the Secretary, and with him alone.

Very large amount of money is lost to the government by the frequent changes that are made in the appointment of persons to other officers who have no acquaintance whatever with the duties thereof. On becoming sufficiently familiar with them they are too often dismissed without an imputation upon their personal or official integrity.

Joseph H. Barrett, Commissioner of Pensions, with about 1,500 persons under his control, declares—

That an examination is made by his subordinate officers of new appointees, but fails to give detailed particulars of such examination. He admits that not one of the persons under his control pursued any special studies to fit himself for his duties. He is, on the whole, in favor of the proposed reform, and thinks that under the suggested system an equal amount of work could be accomplished by a less number of persons and a higher grade of talent and better quality of persons be induced to enter the government service.

Horatio Bridge, chief of Bureau of Provisions and Clothing, Navy Department, suggests :

To reduce the number of clerks 33⅓ per centum, dispensing with those of least capacity, industry and efficiency, and to add 25 per centum to the pay of those who remain or who should be afterwards appointed, would, as a general rule, in my opinion give more efficiency and economy to the civil service. But this result can only be secured by strict and impartial examinations, and by the assurance that faithful and efficient clerks will not be dismissed to make places for less valuable public servants.

A. B. Eaton, Commissary General of Subsistence :

No. 28. The rule of promoting the most meritorious and those of highest qualifications is sufficiently prominent, as a governing rule of action in this bureau, to insure promotion and a successful career to those clerks of the lowest grade who render themselves especially meritorious. This rule of promotion would have a much more successful effect if the number of clerks of the different classes were different in numbers, and consequently in salaries, from what they are now in this bureau. Now the clerks of this bureau (40 in number) are as follows: Of class one, (salary $1,200 per annum,) 24 clerks ; of class two, (salary $1,400 per annum,) 12 clerks ; of class three, (salary $1,600 per annum,) one clerk ; of class four, (salary $1,800 per annum,) one clerk.

I take this opportunity very strongly to recommend that a law may be enacted classifying and paying them as follows, viz : Class five, (salary $2,200,) one clerk ; class four, (salary $1,800,) six clerks ; class three, (salary $1,600,) 12 clerks ; class two, (salary $1,400,) 15 clerks ; class one, (salary $1,200,) six clerks ; messenger, (salary $1,200,) one messenger ; assistant messenger, (salary $900,) two assistant messengers ; laborers, (salary $720,) two laborers.

The present salaries paid the clerks of this bureau are too low to make their positions sufficiently desirable to hold them in the government service any longer than the time necessary to find other and better paying positions. Such salaries as are above proposed would insure to the government the services of those superior men who now, when better paying positions are offered them, vacate this office to be succeeded by others of less experience.

No. 29. Not in this bureau.

No. 30. I have not.

No. 31. I have not found that diligence and efficiency bear any special relation to age, except that very youthful or very aged persons are apt, from the almost certain accompaniments of those periods of life, to fail in accomplishing as much work as those of the intermediate period of life. In this bureau there is nothing to complain of either as to youth or age.

No. 32. Some of those who have been in the military service, and who on that account are encouraged to claim, and who do claim at the hands of the government and its responsible agents, special consideration, indulgence, and leniency, and who seem to have an idea that public sentiment will secure them their places even if they do not perform their duties very faithfully.

No. 33. The course stated in this question is that now substantially observed in this bureau and which works out good results. Such a general rule will, I think, usually be found to subserve the public interests. I suggest that all candidates should be examined to show that they possess the requisite qualifications. This bureau has often been saved from poor or worthless clerks by the Secretary of War having always required that, previous to appointment, they should be certified by a board to be qualified. None are promoted in this bureau who have not, in a lower grade, proved themselves competent for a higher. This proof, by an examination or from the personal knowledge of the senior officer in charge of the bureau or department, should be had.

No. 34. The more accomplished the clerks the more work will be done by them. Where the system of examination does not prevail, it would, I have no doubt, be an improvement to introduce it. It would lessen the number of clerks necessary to do a given amount of work, since its result would be an improvement of the *personnel* of the bureau or department in which they served. All such examinations should, however, be made by or under the supervision or orders of the head of the department in which the service is to be rendered, and not by a general board of examination for all government employés, as none but such head and his responsible assistants can know so well as they do the qualifications requisite for the special places to be filled.

No. 35. Undoubtedly, provided the salaries paid for "the government service" be placed upon a fair and just footing, so that such "better quality of persons" possessing "a higher grade of talent" would seek for, and, obtaining, would wish permanently to retain such government service. In this connection I respectfully, so far as this bureau is concerned, refer to my answer to question 28

No. 36. There are no females employed in this bureau.

No. 37. Not being in the "civil service," it may be that I am not the proper person to remark upon a matter that has no permissible place under the law or by custom in the military service. But, as I am directed authoritatively to state any matters which in my judgment would tend to make the civil service more efficient and economical, I give my opinion that nothing that I can state would conduce more to *efficiency and economy* in all departments of the service than to allow each person in the public service an exact, fixed, undeviating amount of pay for his services, to be established by law and beyond the possibility of misapprehension, and to make it a misdemeanor, with suitable punishment, for any person in any department of the public service, under any pretext whatever, to receive a single cent for his services except the precise amount allowed by law. It should be made a crime against the United States for any person holding any office whatever to receive a cent more than his law-allowed compensation. All fees, charges, percentages, commissions, perquisites, profits, gains, rentals, premiums, bonuses, discounts, abatements, reductions, drawbacks, rebates, set-offs, rents, preference-bribes, and the thousand other tricky words by which many office-holders cheat the government or the citizen who has dealings with it, or both, should be, by some means, swept away. Every citizen who is ever compelled or allowed to pay one cent that does not go directly to the United States treasury and is not known to be a legal charge, should be invited and required to make official report thereof. I but touch this broad field; it is a fruitful one for investigation with a view to "efficiency and economy."

St. John B. L. Skinner, First Assistant Postmaster General:

If the civil service should be placed on a permanent footing, with appointments only on examinations and entering at the lowest grade, with a discipline approximating to that of the naval and military service, on a plan somewhat similar to the one proposed by the Hon. Mr Jenckes at the last session of Congress, I doubt not the service would be greatly improved.

A. R. Spofford, Librarian of Congress:

33. Yes; but to do it here, the law must be changed.

34. I think, under such a system, followed three or four years, one, and perhaps, two assistants could be dispensed with.

35. Yes, everywhere.

36. No females as yet employed. Under competitive tests, I think half the number here employed might usefully be women, and that the resulting economy to the government would be great. For example, I know of educated and practically industrious women, who could do all that assistant librarians receiving $1,200 to $1,800 now do, and who would think themselves well paid at $1,000 per year.

Hon. Henry Barnard, Commissioner of Education:

37. My attention was first called to the mode and conditions of appointment to the civil service of the United States, in 1829–'31, by personal observation of the utter unfitness in previous preparation or in general knowledge and practical ability of several appointments, avowedly made on account of political activity; and of the detriment to the public interests, and to the respect of the people for personal integrity and official service, in the removal of incumbents acknowledged to be honest, efficient, and faithful to the Constitution, but not retained, because they had been silent, or had not been active for the successful party. Since then (1829–'31) I have been brought much into near observation of the constantly widening application of this vicious principle, that "to the victors belong the spoils," and of the dispensation of all official appointments between the executive and the legislative departments, mainly on the principle of personal and political influence. I have also improved the occasion of three visits to Europe, and of several consultations with officials in Belgium, France, and Prussia, as well as in England, (since the application of open competitive examinations to the East India service and to the civil service generally,) to inquire into the operation of other systems of appointment. As official visitor to the national schools of Annapolis and West Point, I have had opportunity to inquire into the operation of our mode of selecting candidates for the military and naval service. From these opportunities of observation and much reflection, I am compelled to say, that we have a more expensive and a less efficient public service than either of the countries named, and that, unless a new system can be speedily inaugurated, the people will lose all confidence in the integrity and patriotism of public men, and our civil administration will sink deeper and deeper in the "Serbonian bog" of political and selfish combinations and interests. The main features of such a system are, *first*, a rigid test examination, in which evidence of good moral character, thorough elementary instruction, and, as far as practicable, a developed aptitude for certain kinds of public service, should be required; and *second*, all persons who seek public office as the resort of proved incompetency for any private enterprise, or solely on the ground of personal and party affiliations, should be excluded from the start; and *third*, a scale of compensation and a system of promotion, which, while it leaves the heads of departments, divisions, and bureaus, in all new appointments, the selection of subordinates by proven aptitude for special work to be done, will give to men of experience, fidelity, and efficiency, constantly increasing pay and a feeling of security that they will not be removed except for proven incapacity.

A system of examination, appointment, and compensation, such as is sketched in your report and provided for in your act—such as has been tried and proved successful elsewhere—would make our naval and military schools less expensive and more useful, and at the same time reduce the number and increase the efficiency of the clerical force in every department of the government; it would diminish the opportunities of political corruption, reduce the dependence of public officers on political movements, increase the respect and attachment of the people to the government, and do more for common schools in every nook and corner of any State, than could be done by any amount of appropriation from the State or national treasury.

Let parents, teachers, and pupils know that the conduct and proficiency of pupils in school will pass into the scale of merit of a board of examination, open to all the youth of a locality or a State; that the recorded results of such an examination will, to some extent, evidence the fidelity of parents in securing the regular attendance of their children at school, as well as the ability of the teacher in the instruction of his pupils; that the favorable result of such examination will open to the successful candidates not only a public career, but be the best evidence that individual or incorporated employers could have of rudimentary training and practical ability of applicants for situations; and an interest will be awakened in public and private schools which does not at this time exist, and which no other government action can awaken.

Letter of A. T. Stewart, esq., of New York:

JANUARY 11, 1868.

In answer to your inquiry I have no hesitation in expressing the opinion that our government would be enabled to dispense with a vast number of its clerks and other employés, were those only selected who, upon examination by a competent board, were found qualified for the various duties required of them.

It would follow almost as a consequence that if fitness was to be the single test in public as it is in private employment, the experience of the incumbent would give him such an additional value to the public service that his retention would clearly be a matter of prudence and economy.

Respecting the method to be adopted in dismissal, I should think it advisable to have the power placed where it could be exercised promptly, but without reference to political or party purposes. If such a system can be created, the strife and bitterness of party feeling would be, in a great measure, obliterated, if not destroyed.

Finally, it would be material in adopting such a system to make public employment not only honorable but compensatory, by fixing the salaries with reference to the character and qualifications required for it.

To illustrate—I would not continue the anomalous practice now pursued with reference to the custom-house officials in the appraisers' and examiners' department, positions requiring men of great intelligence and probity, but with salaries attached entirely insufficient for respectable support.

Men competent to fill such positions of trust should be liberally remunerated if the government would be well served and have her interests protected.

Trusting that your committee will submit some plan by which our government can be served without making its agents mere instruments of political patronage,

Letter of W. A. Wellman, Boston, Massachusetts :

In compliance with the circular of the Joint Select Committee on Retrenchment, I beg leave to submit the following remarks and suggestions, which would in my judgment tend to make the civil service more efficient and economical. I am unable to answer such interrogatories separately, as some years have elapsed since I resigned my position in the custom-house at this port. The result of my experience and observations for more than a quarter of a century as clerk and deputy collector, I place at the disposal of the committee.

The date of my first commission was under the administration of President J. Q. Adams, when appointments were made without regard to political or party influences, and the number of officers was limited to the absolute needs of the service, and the most rigid expenditure of the public moneys. On the accession of President Jackson, I was in the midst of rotation in office, and witnessed the injuries often resulting from the appointment of inefficient and inexperienced persons, especially in subordinate positions, and much as the government suffered in consequence of their want of knowledge of the revenue laws and their application to the duties of their places and to the commerce of the country, I am sure the mercantile community were the greater losers by their frequent mistakes and delays in the despatch of business. On one occasion where a new collector, at a distant port, had removed all the old incumbents, and before the new appointees had learned their duties, I was deputed to act as temporary deputy, to prepare the required documents for vessels waiting clearance for foreign countries, and to expedite the general business of that office; and during the years 1829 and 1830, that operation was repeated at other places. Hence will be seen what delays and serious inconveniences arise under such a system of appointments. Fortunately for the mercantile public, the office clerks at this port, with few exceptions, remained undisturbed during the eight years of Collector Henshaw's administration, and the department at Washington had no occasion to question the faithful discharge of their duties.

As the deputy of the venerable Governor Lincoln, collector in 1841, I was authorized to assure his clerks that they would retain their places so long as they attended faithfully to their duties, and did not meddle in politics; and during his administration a better or more efficient set of officers never served the government and the public. But the political pressure was too great to carry this excellent rule into the other departments, and with all the vigilance and sound discretion exercised, mistakes occurred and the people were the sufferers.

With each succeeding administration rotation in office has been continued without regard, too often, to the qualifications or fitness of the appointees; the number of offices are greatly multiplied; the rules and regulations are more onerous and complicated, until at length merchants can no longer afford the time necessary to attend to their custom-house affairs, but are compelled to employ brokers for that purpose. That the cost of collecting the revenue has been augmented beyond all ratio of the amount collected, is too palpable for confirmation.

In my judgment it is in vain to attempt to reform these abuses short of an entire change in the laws regulating the civil service; and I am convinced that the people now demand such legislation as is proposed by your committee. With the enactment of a law providing for appointments from persons best qualified upon competitive examination; fixing the tenure of office during good behavior; grading the various branches of the service, and allowing promotions according to merit; and establishing a board of commissioners for framing uniform rules and regulations, the offices would be sought by worthy and competent persons, whom the people would respect, and with whom honest men would gladly co-operate in the detection of frauds and in the prompt execution of the laws of Congress. Under such a system the number employed might be much reduced, and the expenses of the service curtailed at least one-third of the present cost, and the public better served, and with more zeal and fidelity. The details for carrying into effect these reforms will be digested when the board of commissioners shall be established, and I shall be glad to offer some further suggestions at the proper time.

George F. Deming, superintendent United States assay office, New York city :

1. Yes; superintendent of the United States assay office at New York.
2. May 1, 1861.
3. Had previously held office as follows: from 1840 to 1846, director's clerk, United States mint; from 1850 to 1850, treasurer's clerk, United States mint; from 1854 to 1861, superintendent's clerk, United States assay office.
4. Employed six years in a merchant's counting-house in Philadelphia previous to entering the civil service of the government.
5. Educated in Maine. Received the usual school and academic training; was fitted for college, and spent one year as "university student" in a selected course at Bowdoin College.

6. I was examined with reference to my qualifications by Dr. R. M. Patterson, director of the mint, and the examination having been satisfactory, I was appointed director's clerk in January, 1840. This examination had reference exclusively to my qualifications for the duties of the office.

7. The testimony of mutual friends consulted by the director, and at whose suggestion and without solicitation on my part, the office was offered to me.

8. Appointed superintendent of the United States assay office by the Secretary of the Treasury, Hon. S. P. Chase, with the approval of President Lincoln, as required by law.

Recommended by my predecessor, S. F. Butterworth, esq., whose chief clerk I had been for more than six years; by the director and other officers of the United States mint; by the president and officers of the Bowdoin College, and by leading citizens of Brunswick, Maine, my native place; by officers of 11 banks and banking houses, the mayor and influential citizens of Rochester, N. Y.; by seventeen members of the New York State senate; by five bank officers and others at Albany, N. Y.; by the presidents of 16 banks and trust companies, and by nine of the leading private bankers in New York city; by Senator Fessenden, of Maine, and Governor Buckingham, of Connecticut. Other individual recommendations were presented, the list of which is not at hand.

9. Present salary of superintendent of United States assay office $4,500. It is larger than my previous salary.

10. I had, as stated in answers numbered 4 and 5, and in an experience of sixteen years in the actual performance of duties connected with the mint service, and studies incident thereto.

11. Only the pamphlet "Laws relating to the mint of the United States and its branches," and a pamphlet containing "Instructions relative to the transaction of business at the mint of the United States and its branches," copies of which are herewith submitted.

12. To the director of the mint at Philadelphia, quarterly and annually, and at other times when required. The quarterly reports embrace the details of the business of the assay office during the quarter, giving the amount of bullion deposited, and indicating its various kinds and the sources whence it is derived; also, the amount of bullion refined, and of fine bars manufactured. The annual reports embrace the same points more accurately stated for the year, and give also a statement of the condition of the office, and the manner in which the year's business has been performed.

In October of each year, the superintendent prepares and submits to the director a statement of the expenses of the assay office, with estimates of the amounts required to be appropriated by Congress for the support of the institution for the fiscal year next following.

Reports upon special subjects are also occasionally made by the superintendent to the Secretary of the Treasury.

The substance of the annual report of the superintendent is given in the annual report of the director of the mint to the Secretary of the Treasury. A copy of this report for the fiscal year ending June 30, 1867, is herewith submitted.

13. The office hours of the assay office are from 10 a. m. till 3 p. m., the customary business hours in New York city. I seldom leave my office before 5 o'clock p. m., and am frequently detained later in the evening.

14. Fifty-five persons are at present employed in the office under my superintendence, classified as follows: 1. Officers and clerks, 10 persons; 2. Assistants, 6 persons; 3. Doorkeepers, watchmen, &c., 13 persons; 4. Workmen, 26 persons; all employed permanently.

15. The superintendent has a general supervision of the business of the office; conducts the correspondence; makes reports of operations, and prepares estimates of annual appropriations needed; makes requisitions upon the Secretary of the Treasury for moneys needed to meet expenses; examines all bills against the office, and issues warrants upon the treasurer for their payment; supervises and checks the treasurer's calculations of the value of bullion deposits, and issues warrants for their payment, and generally looks after the economical administration of the office, and the fidelity of the persons employed therein.

The treasurer (who is also the assistant treasurer of the United States at New York) has the custody of all moneys and all bullion not in charge of the melter and refiner. He makes all calculations of value of bullion deposits upon reports of the assayer; makes payments upon warrants of the superintendent, and renders monthly and quarterly accounts to the department at Washington.

The assayer makes assays of all deposits of gold and silver bullion, and renders detailed reports thereof to the treasurer. He also makes assays of all bullion intended for fine bars, and determines, in conjunction with the melter and refiner, all doubtful questions relating to deposits of bullion.

The melter and refiner receive from the treasurer, and is charged in account with, all bullion deposited; conducts the necessary operations of melting, parting, and refining the same; guards against loss by wastage or otherwise; renders quarterly accounts to the treasurer of bullion received and returned, and once a year, as required by law, makes a thorough settlement of his account with the treasurer.

The clerks and assistants of these officers are engaged in the business of their respective departments, and the workmen who are mainly attached to the melter and refiner's department perform the various duties required by that officer.

The hours of public business are from 10 o'clock a. m. till 3 p. m. The workmen are on duty from 7 o'clock a. m. till 4 o'clock p. m., unless the state of business permits an earlier dismissal.

16. No record is kept of applications for employment. They are very frequent for the place of workmen, but are seldom successful for the reason that skilled workmen are required, and it is deemed the wisest policy to retain faithful employés and make as few changes as possible

17. As far as practicable and necessary, careful inquiry is made as to character and qualifications. As the duties of employés at a mint or assay office are special in their character, they have, for the most part, to be learned within the establishment. The only test of qualification which is practicable, therefore, is the consideration of general intelligence and capacity to learn. A brief trial in actual service has been resorted to in doubtful cases, and candidates thus proved unfit have been rejected.

18. No appointments have been made in this institution during my superintendence without careful examination or inquiry as to character and qualifications as above indicated.

19. Of the sixteen officers, clerks, and assistants in this office, three had received a previous training in the United States mint. These were men of scientific reputation. Six were taken from mercantile pursuits, and four were young men of good education and capacity, but without previous experience in regular business. Of the 39 workmen and others, 10 had been previously employed in the United States mint, and the rest were mostly mechanics of various kinds of the better sort.

20. Most of the persons now employed in this office have been appointed for merit alone. A few may have owed their appointments originally to political influences, but they are now retained solely on account of their qualifications. Political considerations have very little to do with my appointments. Good character, capacity, and, in the light of recent events, *loyalty*, are a *sine qua non.*

21. Most of the applications for places are made in person; but frequently by letter, supported by the recommendations of influential men.

22. All applications and recommendations made in writing are placed on file in the office of the superintendent.

23. The United States assay office at New York contributed 12 volunteers to the army and navy during the war of the rebellion. No person now employed in this office has, to my knowledge, ever been connected with the press. There are differences in skill and efficiency among employés of the same class.

24. Number of employés appointed—

Within 2 years	1
More than 2 and within 4 years	9
More than 4 and within 6 years	0
More than 6 and within 10 years	18
More than 10 and within 15 years	27

Office established in 1854.

25. Employés—

Under 25 years of age	3
Over 25 and under 30 years of age	2
Over 30 and under 40 years of age	10
Over 40 and under 50 years of age	19
Over 50 and under 60 years of age	14
Over 60 years of age	7

26. Since my appointment in May, 1861, only 10 persons have been removed, and of these removals not one was for political considerations. During the war two of our workmen were removed for carrying their partisanship to the point of practical disloyalty; but being excellent men in other respects, and never intentionally disloyal, they have been restored to their places.

27. No other basis of promotion than merit is recognized. We have no regular system of promotion, and no prescribed rules. The heads of the several departments recommend persons under them, from time to time, as worthy of promotion or increase of pay, and the superintendent, if he approve the recommendation, refers the matter to the Secretary of the Treasury, as required by law.

28. No specific rule of this kind exists; but practically appointments and promotions in this office are determined by the rule of merit.

29. I have known such cases; but none such have occurred under my superintendence. A bitter experience of political proscription during my first connection with the mint produced in my mind such an impression of its injustice as to make it forever impossible for me to become an agent for its execution.

30. I have known such cases; but they have been very rare in the mint service within my observation.

31. Difficult to answer. Other things being equal, I would give the preference to young men, say between the ages of 20 and 40.

32. Decidedly those that are made from political and personal considerations only.

33. I have no doubt that such a system of appointment and promotion would greatly increase the efficiency of the public service.

34. I think that if appointments to civil offices, and promotions in office, should be determined by the character, capacity, and meritorious conduct of the candidates, as is done in private business enterprises, the great army of office-holders might be reduced to half its present number, and that, too, with great improvement to the service.

35. Undoubtedly. One of the evils of the system of filling offices for political reasons only, is, that so many drones must be supported that the government cannot afford to pay for the highest grade of talent.

36. No females are employed in this office; but my observation at the mint in Philadelphia during my connection with that institution impressed me very favorably in regard to this class of employés. With such a system of appointment and promotion as is indicated in this question, I am confident that the government might profit greatly by the employment, in various ways, of respectable women.

37. Recapitulating, somewhat, the foregoing statements, I think the civil service would be more efficient and economical if the following principles should, as far as practicable, shape the policy of the government: 1. Candidates for appointment or promotion to be rigidly examined as to character and qualifications by competent examiners. 2. Permanence in office and promotion to vacancies in higher grades to be the assured reward of faithful service. 3. New appointments only in the lower grades; and no removals except for incompetency, inefficiency, unfaithfulness, or other causes which would constitute a bar to appointment. 4. No proscription for opinion's sake; but while entire freedom of political opinion and action is assured, conspicuous and noisy partisanship to be ground of removal. 5. Compensation to be sufficiently liberal to induce persons of the highest character and capacity to continue for life in the civil service. 6. A retired list, with reduced compensation, for such employés, broken down in the service, as should be found worthy by a competent board of examiners.

A. Loudon Snowden, chief coiner United States mint, Philadelphia:

To those who accomplish this great work will belong the honor of having inaugurated a new era in the history of our country. She will arise from the dust and cast off her old garments stained with the corruption of the times, and in a new and spotless robe march on to the accomplishment of her great destiny. The offices and officers of the land will not alone be benefited and elevated by this separation from the influences of partisanship, but our politics and politicians will feel the ennobling effect of this second great "Proclamation of Emancipation."

It is in view of all these important and vital considerations that I witness with profound satisfaction the efforts now being set forth by men of character and patriotism at Washington and elsewhere to reorganize the civil service of the United States upon a sound and enduring basis; and do I not speak but the words of soberness and truth in declaring that the man who most prominently identifies himself with this great reform, who labors most earnestly, and strikes the most fearlessly and effectively against the present defective and corrupt system, will insure for himself a place on the pages of our history and in the hearts of all true lovers of our country that can alone be occupied by him who does a great and enduring work in behalf of the highest and noble interests of our people and age.

The working of the contemplated system would afford in itself a premium for honesty and faithfulness in the discharge of duty.

Under its working a class of men would be induced to enter the public service who have hitherto declined to apply for office under the government. * * *

The offices of the country are comparatively few, and yet their corrupt and unnatural use is rapidly lowering the standard of public morals and making us a nation of office-seekers.

Make the tenure of office during good behavior, and even men of defective moral character will, from very selfishness itself, if from no higher motive, be directed into honest paths.

From the internal revenue department of the government alone there is this day a mighty river of corruption issuing forth, which, unless checked by some wise legislation, will not only deplete the treasury, but utterly demoralize our people.

As our institutions rest on the virtue as well as upon the intelligence of the people, these undermining and corrupt influences are most surely and fatally sapping the foundation of the republic.

Since the formation of our government, (always excepting the blighting cause of slavery,) no evil has so warred against its fair fame, or endangered its permanency, as the consequences that flow mediately or immediately from the corrupt use of the offices of the land for partisan or selfish purposes.

David Howe, collector internal revenue, Lincolnsville, Maine:

Is in favor of holding out inducements to the females to qualify themselves for clerkships in the civil service, and thinks that many branches of the civil service might be benefitted by so employing them.

George P. Sewall, assessor internal revenue, Oldtown, Maine, declares:

That the revenue service has no manual that is regarded as authority at the present day, the one published by Mr. Boutwell, under the act of 1862, having been rendered to a great extent useless by subsequent legislation, and it being now seldom consulted. He does not consider examination applicable to the revenue service, but declares that an equal amount of work could be performed under any system by a less number of persons than are now employed. He thinks that if employment was assured and certain, and promotions granted only to seniority or merit, and no discharge permitted except for cause, a higher grade of talent and a better quality of persons could be induced to enter the government service. In his judgment the pay of assessors and number of assistants should be reduced, and the labor of each increased; that so much of the revenue act as authorizes payment of a percentage on the collections of a district in excess of $100,000 should be repealed; that a minimum salary should be allowed assessors, to be increased on the basis of the number of special taxes they assess in excess of 2,500; that all assessment districts now existing should be abrogated on the first of May next, and collection districts again subdivided into assessment districts, containing at least 20,000 inhabitants, and an assistant assessor, now in service, resident therein, (if then living,) assigned to each, with power in the assessor to employ temporarily more than one assistant in a division, when authorized so to do by the Commissioner; that such proportion of the tax collected on spirits as the Commissioner deems expedient should annually be paid to the assessor and assistant, when the same is assessed, and that payment of a special tax as distiller, retail or wholesale dealer of spirits should legalize the business—the provisions of any State law to the contrary notwithstanding; that assessors should act as special agents of the treasury, when required, without other compensation than their regular salary and expenses, and that the officers in all collection districts should be, from time to time, examined and reported upon by such agents; that assessors and assistants should not be removed without cause, prescribed by law, and should be first heard by the judge of the district court of their State, at chambers, on specific charges filed, who should find and determine all matters of fact involved therein; that all officers of the revenue should annually return their pecuniary standing, and if their liabilities, except as trustees or administrators, exceed 10 per cent. of their property or means of payment, it should be regarded as cause of removal.

S. H. Devereux, collector of customs, Castine, Maine:

As matters now stand, a man *fights* his way into office; he spends long months of time, and generally all the money he has, and sometimes all that he can borrow. If he is successful he goes into his office, and if a man of strict integrity he will, of course, do as well as he can for the government, and do right. If he is not a man of integrity, he will think within himself that the office has cost him quite a large sum, and that he will probably be obliged to vacate the same in about four years, and now I intend to make the most of it. If he has other business he will hold on to it and carry it along with his official duties, and very likely he will pay more attention to his own business than he will to his office, and so the government receives but poor service oftentimes. If he is unsuccessful, he becomes soured against the government and against the party with which he has been associated, and perhaps he will never co-operate with the party again. The whole thing works against the welfare of the country. Every four years there is a bitter war about the offices. I think the present system is the source of more trouble in our nation than any one thing besides.

Let the officers of the United States be appointed during good behavior, and promoted according to their worth; let them have a salary sufficient for their support, and let it be fairly understood that if they do not conduct themselves uprightly and perform their whole duty they must leave and make room for better men; then, and not till then, there will be a much better state of things. Government officers would give their whole time and attention to the duties of their office, and they would, as a whole, be much more efficient. Let such a system be entered upon, and three-fourths of the bitter feelings and strife which we now have to endure every four years would disappear. Rebellion would not be so likely to show its head: and if it should, it could be put down in half the time. The army of office-holders which we *must* have in this country would be a steady stream, and would work well together for the true interests of the government.

I have been in this office about seven years. I have a large and extensive district, 75 miles of coast, with great facilities for smuggling and defrauding the revenue. I have devoted my whole time to the duties of my office, and think I now understand my duty well. I say that a new man *cannot* learn the business of this district in four years as he ought to know it. This being the case, of course the government will gain by appointing its officers during good behavior. Of course, I being already an officer, favor the new plan; but men who are in office ought to know best how things are working, and their judgment should be none the less valuable for holding office under the United States government.

E. S. J. Nealley, collector of customs, Bath, Maine:

Thinks that the system indicated would insure a more efficient and economical performance of the civil service. He adds as follows:

The simplification of the revenue laws, and the condensation of the different acts pertaining to navigation and collection of the revenue into one harmonious code together, (if practicable) A more stable and unchanging system of accounts and reports to the Treasury Department would also tend to insure accuracy and clearness in the understanding and execution of the laws, and require less labor in the custom-houses.

Isaac W. Smith, assessor of internal revenue, Manchester, New Hampshire, a graduate of Dartmouth college, a lawyer and former member of the State legislature, declares:

Female clerks are more attentive, diligent, and efficient than males, and make better clerks, and that he intends very soon to have none but female clerks in his office.

W. C. Kittredge, assessor internal revenue, (late attorney general of Vermont,) Fairhaven:

34. I say that, after the assessment of the annual taxes, which is usually completed in the months of March and April, I think a less number of assistants should be employed. If the present law should be modified, as proposed by the Committee of Ways and Means of the House of Representatives, I am quite sure that four assistants can faithfully work up this district—that is, one in each county. I should need two in each county for two months in the year. I think, further, that the same rule will apply to the three districts in this State.

W. L. Burt, postmaster, Boston:

I think the plan proposed in interrogatory 33 would be a good one, with limitations, for the Post Office Department, and an equal amount of work could be accomplished by a less number of selected employés. I do not think that any higher grade of talent or any better quality of persons would be induced to enter the government service than under present arrangements. We get a good deal better material than we pay for. My men are all overworked and underpaid. Other departments, like the custom-house, with a third less hours, with nothing like of mind and body this office requires, receive double the pay. My office runs day and night, week in and week out, without interruption, including Sundays and holidays, and no person in it is one-half paid. My own salary does not cover the risk of loss alone. My bonds are nearly $200,000, second only to the sub-treasurer's in this city. All my clerks handle money. My cashier receives and pays out between $2,000,000 and $3,000,000 yearly. My money-order clerks paid out upwards of $100,000 in the month of December alone, and in sums of $5, $10, and $20, and with odd dollars and cents, and so rapidly as to make it almost impossible to be accurate. The services required of the postmaster of the city of Boston, as performed by me, are not only a gratuity, but I actually pay for the privilege of rendering them. The salary received by the postmaster of Bangor, with two or three clerks, and with no such expense as an official in the city of Boston is subject to, is precisely the same as my own; and the city of Cambridge, with one-tenth the inhabitants of Boston, and no commercial business, and immediately adjoining the city of Boston, has four postmasters, two of them with salaries two-thirds as large as my own, and the united salaries of the four double the salary of the postmaster of Boston. The same inequality of compensation extends, I believe, throughout the department.

As to females, I have employed three, and their compensation is much lower than for males for the same service, and they are superior to the men in diligence, attention, and efficiency. If I had proper rooms in which to do my work, I would employ from one-third to one-half female clerks in this office, to the advantage of the department and the satisfaction of the public.

Our civil service needs a thorough reformation. It should not be possible for a man to hold any office that is a mere sinecure, like the surveyor of the port or naval officer in New York, Philadelphia, or Boston, and derive from it an income of $50,000 or $100,000 or more annually, and under offices of various kinds with similar results. Why should the United States marshal of any district like New York or Boston reckon his net receipts by hundreds of thousands of dollars annually, or even for his four years of service? And invariably men are selected for these offices without reference to capacity or fitness. Formerly the postmaster of Boston must have derived from the office an income of from $12,000 to $15,000 annually, but now there is no compensation directly or indirectly except the salary. The box rents alone in my office, which formerly belonged to the postmaster, amounts to between $25,000 and $30,000 annually. The compensation, in addition to a fixed salary, should always be graduated by a percentage upon the amount of pecuniary liability incurred and the amount of business performed in each individual office. This would at once remove the inequalities in my department, that is, the post office department; and if the money that is now paid was properly apportioned, every postmaster could be amply paid for his labors.

A. B. Underwood, surveyor, Boston:

29. I have known many meritorious persons to be discharged and their places filled by others who had not been in the civil service, though many of those appointed had deserved well of their country by meritorious services in the army or navy. I have always believed, I do not personally know, that meritorious officers were displaced for meritorious soldiers and sailors rather than have officers not so efficient because the political or personal influence brought to keep them was less strong than to keep the others.

30. The only classes of officers serving under me who are not comparatively independent of other officers, except myself or my deputies, are the weighers, gaugers, and measurers

and their foreman. There have been comparatively few changes in them. One young man, with very little business experience, about 22 years of age, I think, was appointed weigher at a salary of $2,000, to be the superior officer over a foreman 40 years of age, who had been a year or two in the service, whom I recommended very strongly to be appointed to the vacancy as qualified for and deserving the place. The young man was appointed against my earnest protest, the weigher being one of the officers placed under my direction by law. I think the deputies of the three principal officers at this port have always been taken outside of the service.

31. As in most branches of the public service or private business I f_d my subordinates in middle life to be most diligent and efficient, depending upon the kind of duty somewhat, say between 25 and 45 years of age.

32. The class generally the least diligent and efficient are those known as political appointments; those who are of the opinion they were appointed for some services done their political party or for some person having an influence on the appointing power; those who seem to believe that government places are not for performing any labor but eleemosynary institutions, where the faithful can be at rest.

33. I think the system proposed in question 33 for appointments and promotions, with a chance to vary in extraordinary cases under proper safeguards, would increase the efficiency of the service immeasurably.

34. An equal amount of work could undoubtedly be accomplished under such a system. I have already recommended to the collector the removal of six or eight inspectors provided I could be allowed to select the least efficient and retain the hard-working and the meritorious; and with the rest, on this condition, I believe the work could be done, not, however, if inefficient men were to be substitutes.

35. The great evil of the present system is, that there is no assurance in the least degree that if an officer does his duty efficiently and with fidelity to the government he will be retained. It is not for his interest always, as it should be, to be faithful to his employer's interests rather than that of others. At the larger ports the office of surveyor, I suppose, was created to divide the duties of the collector, and to have a responsible officer do what a collector could not, look after the outdoor officers and see that they discharge their duties faithfully and to the advantage of the government. The surveyor is the officer who, from the nature of his duties, should know, and does, the qualifications and abilities as well as the efficiency of these inspectors, weighers, &c. Yet there is no law or regulation that requires the surveyor to be consulted in the retention or removal of these men, and he is often the last officer who is ever asked on the subject. The officers learn by this that his opinion is of no account, and that fidelity and efficiency are not the requisites for retention in service.

If the system could be so changed that the really good and working officers could be retained it would be of an immense advantage to the service, and if promotion or deserts were added, better men, a higher grade of men, would be found in the service.

36. There is one female inspector under my direction nominated by the collector. She is employed only occasionally at the steamers.

37. Since answering question 27 I have received notice of some promotions made by the collector, which I doubt not will be detailed by him.

To make the customs revenue service efficient, (I am not familiar with any other branch of the civil service;) to enable the government to get a suitable return for the great amount of money paid by it to customs officers and employés; to have them work for the government's interests, and not somebody's else; to have them induced to be faithful and be reasonably saving of the public money, something must be done to change the present system of appointment and retention, (if it can be said that there is any system of retention now;) to do away with, or greatly modify, the principle of political or personal patronage in the employment of men, the influence of which now pervades every part of the service and overshadows everything else. This principle now maintains an almost irresponsible one-man power. One man now has the gift of livings, and can take them away at will. When, as at present, it is difficult for men to get steady employment in mercantile or other private pursuits, one man has it in his sole power nearly to give a comfortable livelihood or turn a man out to starve. There is no practical power which the government has to encourage its faithful servants and retain them and protect them, when it is for its own interest to have them protected and retained. The Constitution vests the appointment of subordinate officers, I believe, in the Secretary of the department, and he nominally appoints now; but the nominating power is so far from the appointing power now, and the Treasury Department has such an enormous amount of business on its hands, besides looking after the details of custom-houses, which have grown to be great institutions in themselves, that practically everything relating to the appointment and employment of men is left wholly to the will of the collector; and there is no check upon him whatever; nobody but he has a shadow of power, and if he abuses it, there is nobody who dares report it. I only speak of the system now and its tendencies—not of collectors personally, of whom there have been and are now many good and valuable men. Such is the overshadowing influence of the present principle in the service, that though there are at the larger ports two officers appointed by the President of a rank approximating that of collector, a naval officer and surveyor, yet neither of them has but a shadow of power in the looking after and the protection of the best interests of the government. I have the direction of the outdoor officers, but I would have no influence whatever to retain in the service the most valuable, experienced, and faithful inspector or weigher ever employed by this government; and at certain times in public affairs he would be as likely to be turned out as anybody else. I never know what officers I have to work with to-morrow. If the present system is to be retained in the main, I should certainly ask, for the public good, that surveyors might have by law some power to retain valuable officers, and to see that only those properly qualified are employed. The responsibility of nominating and the annoyances connected with it under the present system I should be glad to have left to others.

If a radical change were to be made, as I should certainly recommend, the nomination of proper officers of customs should be left not to one man, but a board or commission, after some thorough examination to be prescribed by law, the examiners to be named by law; they ought to be, of course, experts. A board of customs officers might be detailed, as often in the army. The commission might be made to consist of commissioners appointed for the whole revenue, or simply the customs service, who should be independent of any interest in the result, except the good of the service. An improvement over the present system would be, at least, to have appointees recommended by the collector, naval officer, and surveyor, as a board. *Three* would be more likely to be impartial than *one*.

Whatever the mode of nomination to the Secretary, the officers should hold office by some fixed tenure, either during good behavior, or if we cannot hope to obtain that perfection yet, then for some term of years, say four on one commission, with the certainty of promotion to vacancies, if any should occur, and the senior or other officer should be found qualified; the new commission to be for the same fixed period, say of four years.. Then an officer would have the certain assurance of holding office four years under each commission, if he did his duty, with a prospect of promotion for the same period, if a vacancy should occur. There should be authority given the superior or employing officer to suspend for misconduct, or manifest incompetency, or inefficiency, and if proven to the satisfaction of a board of officers, such officer to be dismissed. I think if the officer held a commission under the seal of the Treasury, and not a simple warrant issuing as now from the collector, it would have a good effect.

I should recommend more grades among customs officers, with a proportionate scale of compensation, with a difference of name, or have the difference simply that of length of service. There should be more places, to make promotion possible. For instance, there are 94 inspectors at this port, all paid alike: $4 per diem. There is a great difference in the capacity and merits of these men, as well as in the relative importance of their duties. There might well be *three* grades, paid say $3 50, $4, and $4 50 or $5 per day, respectively, with excellent results to the service.

I might continue making suggestions. Perhaps I have made sufficient to show what I consider the evils of the present system in the service.

Amasa Norcross, assessor of internal revenue, Fitchburg, Massachusetts, a lawyer, formerly a member of the State legislature, and officially connected with the revision of the statutes of the State of Massachusetts, declares:

The moral character of applicants for office should be fully established, and their fitness for the office should be ascertained by a competent board of examiners. This could be done but imperfectly at the inception of the excise law, as no persons had then been educated with a view to the service, but it is now desirable that some method for determining the qualification of revenue officers should be devised and adopted.

Charles G. Davis, assessor internal revenue, ex-representative, a graduate of Harvard college, and a lawyer of Plymouth, Massachusetts, show the necessity of adopting the proposed reform and also urges the independence of the revenue department under three commissioners, one of them to act as solicitor, and the doing away with the present conflicting interference of the Solicitor and officers of the Treasury Department.

Mr. Davis also declares that the only two revenue manuals in use, namely, Emerson's and Boutwell's, are very incomplete.

My experience is chiefly confined to the Department of Internal Revenue, with such general knowledge of the injury done to the civil service by frequent removals and political appointments as is common to most observing men.

I have no hesitation in saying that with regard to all the offices which require special knowledge, aptness, or experience, examinations and appointments and promotions for honesty and capacity merely would render immense service to the government, both directly and indirectly. Directly by procuring honest, efficient, and capable men, and by economizing the labor and time now wasted on and by inefficient and inexperienced men; indirectly by removing, next to the political power of slavery, the most corrupting power of political action now remaining, namely, the search for office, the temptation to the citizen to.

vote not as his unbiased judgment would and should under our institutions dictate. Our government rests on the intelligent will of the people, but it is not too much to say, perhaps, that a majority of the active men in an election are sometimes controlled or affected by iased motives. Remove, if you can, as far as possible, this corrupting element in our elections; teach men that ministerial office is not to be sought as a reward of party effort; that the officer is the servant of the people, and that he shall remain in office as long as he is worthy of it, and you will effect a revolution in the morals of politics, and we shall all breathe a purer atmosphere in public life. But as to many of the offices under the internal revenue law it must be understood that promotions cannot, from the nature of the case, be frequent, nor can some of them be well subjected to examination by a central board before appointment. This would be the case with assessors' clerks and with assistant assessors throughout the country, who might, however, be appointed only on the condition that they shall first have passed an examination by the assessor, such as may be provided for by the central authority, and shall not be removed except for cause.

But one of the leading defects in the present system of internal revenue arises from the organization of the department. Under the control of the Secretary of the Treasury, subject to decisions of the Solicitor of the Treasury, controlled, thwarted, and contradicted by the Auditors and Comptrollers of the Treasury, it is wanting in the independence which so important a branch of the government should have. Its officers never know when they are safe. A rule or decision is laid down by the Commissioner as to pay, or salary tax, or allowance of some kind, and months after he is overruled by the Auditor or Comptroller, who know less than he does of the workings of the internal revenue system. So with a Solicitor of the Treasury. What is wanted is a law officer of internal revenue, through whose hands every decision or letter involving the law appertaining to internal revenue should go. No Commissioner can have the executive ability to control all that goes out of his office and render his rulings consistent. A solicitor whose whole mind was devoted to the subject could control and regulate the decisions, and not involve officers of internal revenue in the inconsistencies in which we are now involved, and which have done much to disgust the taxpayers. It is not the fault of the Commissioner, but of the system. The solicitor should have all the power of the Commissioner, so far that he should not be over ruled in his views of the law. For all the above purposes I would have the internal revenue, and perhaps custom revenue, a separate department, in the hands of three commissioners, one of whom should act as the solicitor, and the department should have full control so far as it can constitutionally be done of the appointments, (subject to examinations, &c.,) of the paying, auditing and comptrolling of its own work. Mr. Welles suggests the appointment of naval officers, &c., to the assessor and collectorships. The objections to this course would be: first, they are not business men acquainted with the people, property, and habits of the several districts; second, there would be too much of the "martinet" in their dealings with the people. Under our government the people want civilians for civil business, and not men whose life and pursuits have led them away from the people. I should as soon think of making a manufacturer an officer in the navy as putting a retired naval officer into the assessor's office. The very cause of examinations, &c., suggested by you, is inconsistent with the idea of putting in men not trained to certain civil duties, who have been brought up in the army or on the sea.

John Nesmith, collector of the internal revenue, Lowell, Massachusetts:

Most certainly the efficiency of the service would be increased by the adoption of such a course. If official position was permanent, *a class of young men would fit themselves for holding office, while pursuing their studies,* and when appointed would do their utmost to discharge their duties well in the hope of advancement.

The present time seems a peculiarly favorable time to try the experiment, with the President and most of the heads of departments of one party and Congress of another. Any party having full control of the appointing power would with difficulty be induced to give it up for the purpose of trying an experiment. A good law regulating appointments, placing them outside of party influences, would, I fear, soon be evaded. The examiners would become the tools of the party in power. If the supreme court cannot be kept free from party influence, what hope have we that a board of examiners could?

Is it safe to conclude that because a system of this kind has to some extent been a success in Europe, where the heads of the government are hereditary, we can establish it here, and keep it in force long enough to test its utility. During a large part of the existence of our government we have given the dominant party the offices, and I fear a large part of our voters look upon the control of the offices as a right not to be given up for the purpose of forming a class of office-holders independent of the party in power; but to make the system a success it must be outside of party influence.

William H. McCartney, collector of internal revenue, Boston:

Sets forth the present evils of the revenue system, and particularly those wrought by government detectives, or secret treasury agents and department clerks, and declaring that the only remedy to neutralize, if not altogether to obliterate this evil, is to adopt the civil service bill.

I have the honor to submit that while a collector's subordinates are employed and governed, as I have before stated, namely, as personal clerks of the collector, appointed and paid by him, there are subordinate officers of the revenue in every district for whom he is not responsible, and who are appointed by the department, such as inspectors of spirits, tobacco, oil, and cigars, storekeepers of bonded warehouses, revenue and treasury inspectors, special agents, &c., but with whom he is daily brought in contact, who are appointed and hold their positions under other and entirely different circumstances. I don't think there is an inspector of spirits, oil, or tobacco, in this district, at present, who owes his position to political influence; but there have been such, I am convinced. And it is also true that there are to be found in every collection district certain revenue officers who act as detectives, being designated as revenue inspectors, or special agents, or something of that kind, and who must have been appointed, and who must be now retained in the service, through political influence alone; for they are, many of them, a shame and disgrace to the department, and they are so evidently unqualified and unfitted by nature to deal with public or private finances as to be the subject of daily complaint and comment. These persons do not study or seem to realize the material interests of the revenue. Gain is their controlling motive, and office their objective point. Their operations are in secret and in the dark, and no one is safe from their attacks; and the very nature of their employment, the covert and secret dealing, both with honest and dishonest men, begets fraud and corruption. It may be said that some of them have been of advantage to the revenue in the uprooting of frauds. So they have been, but this has been much more than counterbalanced through their nefarious raids on honest tax-payers; and it is a fact, according to my experience, that all the work they now perform, which it is desirable to have done, can be much better and more satisfactorily (to the tax-payers) performed by the proper and legitimate officers of each district.

Under the authority granted me in your 37th interrogatory permit me to say that a great deal of the odium which is now attached to the revenue service arises from the ignorance and mistakes of the department clerks; but, as I am convinced and do declare, *not* with the knowledge of the chief officer thereof, for it is a fact, according to my experience, that tax-payers, as a rule, are treated not as honest business men, but as thieves and marauders of the treasury, which is also true, to a very great extent, of their treatment of collectors and assessors. The great principle, that this nation is now laboring under the burdens of what is generally hoped will be temporary taxation, and that a great majority of tax-payers are ready and willing to meet all legitimate and reasonable taxation provided they can have the protection of the government in the transaction of their business, is lost sight of and abandoned, and it is much too apparent that the odious and offensive details of red tape and the spy and detective system have been substituted therefor. It may be urged that the departmental system is based on the experience of other countries where it has succeeded. To that I answer, that, as a principle, the American people don't believe in taxation at all, and that they only submit to this because it is *temporarily* necessary; and only then unless it is liberally and comprehensibly managed after American notions. For instance, it does not benefit the revenue to charge a respectable merchant five per centum on his monthly tax, if through inadvertence or by accident he does not pay his monthly tax on the last day of the month when it is due, but does pay it on the first day of the month following. And yet it is very frequently done, and a collector has no power in the premises. Nor does it benefit the revenue to practically stop the business of a large and respectable firm who have applied for permission to establish a bonded warehouse, because on the copy of the bond which is forwarded to the department the characters [L S] are not marked around with ink to show that the original bore a seal, and yet it has been done, and in face of the fact that the collector who took the bond certified that it was safe and good in all respects. I beg leave to add, in this connection, that I do not wish to incur the displeasure of any one in submitting this, and I have only determined to declare as I have because I think the interests of the people demand it. If it is asked how I would remedy this, I reply, that the remedy is to be found substantially in the civil service bill of last session, which cuts off the practice of appointing favorites and politicians.

Thomas Russell, collector of customs, Boston:

Is satisfied that the efficiency of the service would be increased by having a rigid test examination before each appointment and each promotion. Something might be accomplished in this direction by a circular from the department calling attention to the regulations and requiring that the examinations be less formal and more substantial than it has been heretofore.

I have nothing to add to the above except to repeat my firm belief that the civil service would be more efficient if every appointment and promotion were preceded by a rigid test examination, and that such appointments should depend wholly on the result thereof, provided that no persons should be admitted to examination without preliminary proof of good moral character satisfactory to the appointing or nominating power. Besides this good effect the appointing officer would be relieved from the almost incessant solicitations of applicants and their friends who now harass officers having the power of appointment, and which in my own case consumes much time which ought to be devoted to the legitimate business of the office.

E. R. Tinker, collector internal revenue, North Adams, Massachusetts:

Seventeen persons under his control are emphatically in favor of the proposed reform.

Francis A. Osborn, naval officer, Boston:

No. 34. From the nature of the work in this office, I think it questionable whether the force could be materially reduced, even under the system proposed in the preceding question.

No. 35. I think it very questionable. I have no doubt, from what I have seen at this port, that there are a plenty of applicants, of as high a grade of talent as the government service requires. Whether or not the most valuable applicants receive appointments belongs to another branch of the inquiry.

No. 36. I have no females among my subordinates.

No. 37. Without pretending to any original suggestions, I will say, briefly, that I believe it would greatly increase the efficiency, and therefore the economy, of the service to remove appointments entirely from the sphere of political influence, and to make original appointments and subsequent promotions dependent solely on ability and character. The investigation to discover the relative merits of the different candidates should be conducted by large-minded men, who would not consider simply the actual information of the candidate, or rely on a fixed routine of examination to achieve their purpose, but who would also look to the general ability, and capacity to learn, of the applicant, and would, with fitly-devised questions and conversation, adapted to each case, analyze him thoroughly to learn what amount of energy, of ambition, of conscientiousness, and of industry, might enter into his composition, to give a solid value to his mental acquirements, and who should make their classification dependent on the resultant of these qualities and acquirements.

Fixed tenure of office is also highly important. The appointee should receive a commission for an established time, which should be irrevocable during that time, saving for proved incompetency or inefficiency. Promotion should be made by seniority, excepting that a certain proportion of promotions for distinguished merit should be allowed. These latter promotions should be carefully removed from the influence of favoritism, and determined by a similar investigation to the one proposed above, with the additional element of the candidate's record while in office.

In establishing such a system care should be taken not to destroy the authority of the chief of a department over his subordinates by lessening their responsibility to him, as discipline must be the basis of any system of value. The chief should be empowered to suspend his subordinates for cause, or even dismiss them, his action in either case to be revised by the same tribunal that regulates appointments. Power might also be given him to inflict minor punishments for trifling offences, at his discretion.

John Sargent, collector of internal revenue, Boston:

Thinks that the appointment of none to office but those who gave evidence of fitness for the discharge of the duties to be required of them, and the undoubted evidence of unimpeachable integrity, would add greatly to the efficiency of the service, and lift from it that load of distrust and opprobrium which a large portion of the people believe it justly amenable to.

A great point in economy would be gained by dispensing with a large portion of the revenue inspectors, and providing that the duties which they were appointed to perform should be discharged by the assistant assessors, as they always should have been, it being, in his judgment, a legitimate part of the duty intended to have been discharged by them under the original revenue laws.

Alphonso C. Crosby, assessor internal revenue, first Connecticut district:

Instead of the appointment of inspectors, (responsible to nobody in particular,) who act as detectives, &c., the assessor should have the right to designate any one of his assistants whom he may select to special or general detective service. The expense of the present force of detectives may thus be nearly wiped out, with a gain (I believe) to the service and increased economy.

David F. Hollister, collector internal revenue, Bridgeport, Connecticut:

No. 33. I think the idea of a test examination a good one, provided the board of examiners would adopt such rules in the examination as would govern good business men in their own affairs. Many of our best practical business men would perhaps make but a poor show in an examination where a really much inferior man would appear very favorably. The one has a general knowledge of men and things, and would conduct the affairs of his office efficiently and with very little friction, while the latter, though appearing before the committee to much better advantage, in the practical discharge of his duties would make but an indifferent officer. It would seem to me that the examiners should be fully satisfied by competent *testimony* as to the business habits and the moral character of the applicant, and especially as to his habits for *sobriety*, and also his ability to discharge the duties of his office with efficiency, and at the same time not *offensively*—a most important consideration in the execution of any law. Law should be enforced, but not rendered odious, by those charged with its execution. A man may be possessed of a large amount of knowledge, of a superior education, and may answer satisfactorily all the questions of a committee, and yet be most obnoxious for reasons above suggested. It seems to me that a mere personal examination would, in many cases, fail to elicit all the required facts.

No. 34. In an office where there are grades, I should say, yes.

No. 35. Yes: without doubt. It is my firm conviction that the civil service of the United States, in all its branches, would be far more efficient, uniform, and economical, were the officers originally appointed with express reference to their qualifications for their respective positions, and not to be removed except for cause. I believe the custom which prevails so largely of removing officers simply on partisan grounds is a most baneful one, and tends to corrupt and demoralize the whole civil service. The country is great and has large resources, and may stand such a custom, but no private enterprise could. No sane man would conduct his own affairs, or those of a corporation in which he was interested, on any such principle. I further hold that the officer, be he who he may, and in whatever capacity he serves, is but the servant of the whole people, and that, in the discharge of his official duties, he should ignore politics, and to this end he should be independent of such considerations. As an individual and citizen, he should perform his duty in that capacity; but as an officer, in the discharge of his official duty, no man or party should own him.

No. 36. There are none.

No. 37. I have no further suggestions to make. Shall be glad if I have not been too prolix already.

John B. Wright, assessor 2d district, Connecticut:

No. 33. The efficiency of the civil service generally would undoubtedly be increased by the adoption of the course suggested by query No. 33, *provided* the examiners be thoroughly competent, and unbiassed by partisan, personal or other improper influence or consideration; but, in my judgment, neither our past history nor present aspects afford very strong grounds of confidence in the infallibility or incorruptibility of any board of examiners which may be appointed for the contemplated object.

No. 34. An equal amount of work could be accomplished under such a system by a less number of persons than are now employed, this answer being subject to the proviso contained in the preceding paragraph.

No. 35. If the employment was assured and certain, and promotions were granted only to seniority or merit, and no discharge permitted except for cause, a higher grade of talent and a better quality of persons could be induced to enter the government service.

No. 36. There are no females among my subordinates.

No. 37. I think of no matters, not already known to the committee, which would tend to make the civil service more efficient or economical. In this district both the collector and assessor (the principal officers) have been retained from their first appointment, when the internal revenue system was inaugurated, and, through their efforts, faithful subordinates have also been retained, while in one or two instances unfaithful and inefficient ones have been dismissed. In many districts, however, it has been otherwise. Faithful and efficient officers have been removed, and their places filled with men possessing neither ability nor integrity, and the consequent loss to the revenue has been immense. Threats of removal are often made by parties supposed to have great influence with the appointing power, for the purpose of influencing officers in their official action, and while I can say in all truth that no such threats have ever influenced my official action in the slightest degree, it is important for the interest of the government that officers be protected reasonably against such influences.

If your committee can devise means for the effectual protection of the civil service against the unscrupulous exactions of partisan politics, and against the malignant, revengeful spirit of wealthy and influential defrauders of the revenue, whose schemes of fraud have been or may be thwarted by official energy and vigilance, you will have rendered a service to government and to the country for which you will be entitled to their warmest thanks.

Henry A. Grant, collector of the internal revenue of first district, Hartford, Connecticut, after indorsing emphatically the proposed reform, makes the following suggestion:

My department of the civil service being collector of taxes only, I can speak only of that branch of the service and the two articles which have given me the most anxiety and trouble, viz: distilled spirits and tobacco. My opinion is a direct tax on the capacity of the still and on the leaf tobacco would more than quadruple the amount of taxes on each of these articles.

R. H. Avery, collector of internal revenue, 22d district, New York:

37. Have the laws enforced by the government against all officials in the revenue department that fail to expose frauds from fear of personal or political persecution, or from being in complicity with offenders for gain or profit; and for any neglect or failure to perform the labor requisite and necessary to detect any frauds that may be apparent upon information, or suspicion, such officers should be removed from office, or punished in some degree adequate to the offence or neglect. At the same time there should be a reasonable and fully remunerative compensation secured by law to all officers for services, so that as far

as possible all temptation for gain by bribery or corruption would be removed. I am fully satisfied that the enormous frauds which have been committed upon the revenue for some time past by the whiskey manufacturers and those connected with them in the "whiskey ring" could and would have been prevented, had the collectors, assessors, and other officers in their districts been faithful, prompt, and diligent in their efforts in detecting and exposing the fraud from the beginning. At the same time officers in each district should be united, and fully co-operate together; also with officers of other and adjoining districts. In my own and in adjoining districts, frauds were suspected by me as being committed, and I at once began a thorough and laborious investigation, which has resulted in the seizure of 14 whiskey concerns, a part of which have been tried by the courts successfully for the government; a part have been compromised by the Commissioner on favorable terms to the government, where fines and penalties have been paid to the government on compromise, amounting to over $10,000, within the year. About $100,000 of forfeitures, fines, and penalties now await judgment of court and now pending, besides several criminal suits for penalties and imprisonments, concerning which the revenue inspector of this district, J. J. Lamoree, esq., and the Hon. Wm. Dorsheimer, United States attorney, think I have ample proof to secure a verdict for the United States. I only make these statements as an illustration of the ideas I desire to convey, "to make the civil service more effectual." In other words, as in the divine code, "rewards for the faithful, and punishment for the unjust."

If my replies have not been pertinent in any respect, it has not been from any design; but I have been animated rather with the desire to aid you in your investigations. Anything within my knowledge I will cheerfully impart, if at any time requested.

M. B. Field, collector of internal revenue, New York:

33. I should say decidedly, yes; at least so far as clerical offices are concerned. The system suggested could be easily carried out in the great executive departments of the government. It might also be directly applied to an office of the magnitude of that of the collector of customs at this port. In these cases the employés are government officers. The persons employed in the office of a collector of internal revenue are his own clerks. He appoints them absolutely; they are paid by him. It appears to me that in order to carry out your idea so far as this class of office is concerned, two things would be necessary: first, to make these subordinates government officers, and next, to arrange for a system of promotions not only in the same office, but also from one office to another. For instance, an inferior clerk trained in my office might become competent to take the position of deputy in a smaller office. The plan of competitive examinations for the civil service is, however, to my mind, beset with difficulties. For superior positions I do not think that it would answer. Certainly, for all offices the possession of certain qualifications by the applicant should be a *sine qua non* with the appointing power. Assuredly there obtains in this country a deplorable practice upon this subject. In too many instances the candidate, upon Procrustean principles, is lengthened into a foreign minister or shortened into a local postmaster, upon the single consideration of his political claims. Fitness for the particular office is too seldom made a controlling consideration. I am at a loss to see exactly how this is to be effectually remedied, except by making the possession of a certain amount and kind of qualifications a legal prerequisite in every case. Still, superior places cannot be put up to competition through examinations. Preliminary examinations for admission into any service will, at least, exclude the grossly incompetent; but they furnish no positive measure of relative fitness for those who pass them. It has frequently happened that members of Congress have thrown open to public competition nominations to West Point and to the Naval Academy. The boy who would carry off such a prize from many contestants would naturally be expected to distinguish himself in his after studies. It has often been the case, however, that he has taken but low rank among associates appointed in the ordinary way without competition. Again, for the successful discharge of some duties, certain personal characteristics, apart from acquirements, are necessary; and these can hardly be made the subject of examination.

34. Speaking generally of the civil service, there is no doubt but that, with better trained assistants than we now have, more work could be accomplished with a smaller force.

35. I shall say most decidedly, yes.

36. I have no female subordinates.

37. I regret that I have not the time to enter more fully upon this subject. In reply to this last question I will only make a single particular reference. I have already spoken of the present system of compensating collectors of internal revenue as a vicious one. It is as follows: We receive first a salary of $1,500 per annum. Upon the first $100,000 which we collect we receive three per cent., or $3,000; upon the next $300,000 one per cent., or $3,000; upon the next $600,000 one-half per cent., or $3,000; upon all over $1,000,000 one-eighth per cent. Out of this we pay all our expenses, (deputies, clerks, rent, &c.,) except stationery and postage. Take the item of rent. It is an extremely variable one. In this city it differs enormously. Some collectors pay but a few hundred dollars a year; others are compelled to pay several thousands, according to locality. My rent is a very moderate one, so that I am not one of the sufferers by this difference. But why should the collector, say of the fourth, be compelled to pay for rent out of his own pocket three times as much as I am compelled to pay out of mine? Again: Under the existing sliding scale of commissions the collector who collects only a million is better off than he who collects a larger sum, for it has

been established experimentally that it costs more to collect the excess over a million than he one-eighth per cent. allowed for it. Hence many collectors have large amounts of taxes abated which might have been collected, and are lost to the government because they are unwilling to employ and pay for the additional assistance necessary for the collection. The tendency of the whole system is to induce collectors to employ *cheap* assistants, *insufficient in number.* That it *should not* be so I concede. But that it is so in many instances, I have reason to believe. My own collections have been so extraordinarily close upon the amounts assessed, that I do not see how, under any other system, I could collect more than I do. But this is not the universal case. Incidentally I may mention that I have long urged the establishment of a central bureau in this city for the collection of *arrears* of United States taxes. Not only do I believe that such a bureau would directly save large sums of taxes which would be otherwise lost to the government, by collecting them, but that it would also do so indirectly, by stimulating collectors to greater efforts to avoid the discredit of passing over to this bureau large sums which they might themselves collect by more exertion.

I will conclude by saying, in general terms, that I think that our civil service should be assimilated to those of Great Britain and some of the continental countries. Require the possession of certain qualifications as essential to appointment; reward merit and length of faithful service; make the tenure of office more dependent upon efficiency and integrity, and less so upon political caprice and favor. You will thereby secure more efficiency, and this efficiency will involve economy.

C. S. Franklin, acting naval officer, New York:

27. I have pursued a system of promotion, increasing the salaries of those deemed worthy, by permission of the Secretary of the Treasury.

28. I regret that I am not enabled to reply affirmatively to this question. There are, however, some few who have remained in the office many years, and who have been promoted from a low to a higher grade of clerkship.

29. I have.

30. I have.

31. Between the ages of 30 and 40.

32. Very young men, and the very aged. Professed politicians are not remarkable for their efficiency as clerks.

33. Most unquestionably.

34. Undoubtedly, if those employed possessed a greater degree of efficiency, and exerted greater industry, encouraged by the hope of advancement.

35. Beyond peradventure. If permanent employment and promotion were awarded to merit or seniority, and no removals permitted except for cause, the axe would thereby be applied to the very root of that "Upas tree" by which the efficiency of the revenue service is now poisoned into a torpor resembling death.

36. None.

37. My answer to question No. 35 covers the whole subject, and the only additional requisite would be the appointment of officers of executive ability and integrity of purpose.

John S. Walton, United States treasurer, New York:

33. I have always thought that no man ought to be appointed to office without being examined in reference to his personal character, and his qualification for the position he sought. Until this is done the government will never be properly served.

34. I believe that if such a system as that stated in question 33 were faithfully carried into effect, and the same principles applied to it as govern commercial houses, the work could be done by one-half of the present number of officers.

35. If the employment was assured and certain, and no discharge permitted except for cause, there would be strong inducements to seek public office, and the government would undoubtedly secure the services of first class men.

36. I have no females among my subordinates.

37. I think that nothing would tend more to make the civil service efficient than the adoption of a system by which a person once in the government employment, after a thorough examination as to character and fitness, would be assured that his position and advancement would depend upon his conduct. Unless there is security, few honest men will voluntarily seek public office. Only those whose misfortunes drive them to it, and those who expect to make more out of it than the salary belonging to it, will try to obtain it. If the salaries were liberal and the positions permanent, honest men, of moderate desires, would seek them, and devote their lives to the faithful performance of the duties belonging to them.

J. P. Murphy, assessor 29th district. New York:

29. There have been no meritorious persons discharged in this district, and their places filled by others not before in the service, on account of political influence.

30. In this district I do not place new recruits over the heads of meritorious persons already in the service. I have more respect for myself and the service than to do anything of that kind.

H. Rep. Com. 47——4

31. It is true that I do not find all of my subordinates equally diligent and efficient, yet it is impossible for me to say among which class of ages I find the greatest efficiency; I have some in each class, even among the oldest, who are equally efficient with the youngest and best.

32. I cannot make a class discrimination among my subordinates as to diligence and efficiency. I find them equally so as a class. The office of an assessor of internal revenue is a peculiar one, requiring certain qualities of mind and education, which can only be acquired by close personal application and practical experience in the duties of his office.

33. If it were possible or practicable to graduate the appointments in this branch of the civil service, and make promotions only to the higher grades from the lowest on passing a test examination, or on displaying peculiar fitness, by acts of efficiency, &c., I think effectiveness of the service would be greatly increased thereby, but I see no way that this can be done in the assessor's department. The only way that the assessor's department can be made respectable and efficient is, in the first place to secure the appointment of the right man to the office of assessor, give him the entire control of the assessments in his district, and also of the appointments of subordinates, hold him to a strict accountability for all his acts, and have him only removable for cause; require him to devote his whole time to the office, and pay him such salary that he could afford to devote his time, without resorting to outside business to obtain a living and support for himself and family; do this, and I think you will soon perceive a marked difference in the efficiency of this branch of the service.

34. The system of promotions and graduation of the offices of subordinates, as suggested by you, being to my mind wholly impracticable in this department, I cannot say what the effect or result of your proposed system would be; of one thing I am well convinced, that so long as the present subjects and objects of taxation are continued in the revenue law, this district, being about 125 miles long by from 20 to 40 wide, cannot be well taken care of and all the taxes assessed with a less force than is now employed.

35. I have no doubt if employment in the assessor's department was assured and certain on a display of merit, and no discharge permitted except for cause, and suitable inducement by way of compensation held out, a higher grade of talent and a better quality of persons could be induced to enter the service.

36. I have no females among my subordinate officers. I doubt whether any female could be found in this district, or any other, possessing the requisite qualifications to make a good assistant assessor; the duties of this place try most men as by fire, and if the nerves and firmness of a man can rarely be found to withstand the wily exactions of dishonest taxpayers, I doubt the experiment of filling their places with females.

37. The present internal revenue law, in my judgment, (and which has become confirmed by experience,) is defective, because of its making the assessor of a district in many things and particulars subordinate to the collector. An assessor cannot now make a seizure of premises or articles for cause, neither can he order or direct a prosecution of a delinquent. If he desires a seizure made, or a prosecution commenced by the district attorney, he must inform the collector, and if he deems proper, he makes an order therefor. Now, who should know best, the assessor who has had the whole matter in charge, and is presumed to know whether a violation has occurred or not, or the collector, who in fact knows nothing about the matter only as he is informed. My experience is that collectors very much like to cast all the blame and odium attached to the enforcement of the law on the assessor, and hence when complaints are made to them by assessors, interpose so many objections and quibbles to evade their responsibility, that assessors cease in disgust from making any further complaint, and so offenders go unpunished. To make a law respected, offenders should know that its penalties are sure of infliction. By giving to the assessor power and authority to act in all cases of infraction of law in all matters connected with the assessment of internal taxes, would make this branch of the service more efficient, and, therefore, more economical, because more taxes would be obtained.

Again, by strictly enforcing the rule, that assessors while holding such positions should not be engaged in any other business requiring any of their personal attention, much more efficiency would be obtained; my experience is, that an assessor will find plenty of business to engage his mind and attention, by looking after and supervising revenue matters in his district, without any other; this is an evil which must be remedied, in my opinion, before the service is made as efficient as it should be. It is not an unusual thing in many districts to find the assessor attending to his law office or store, and his assistants and clerks running the revenue; and when you find such a state of things, I will guarantee an inefficiently worked district. Besides inefficiency, there is a lack of uniformity among revenue officers, especially assessors; this grows out of ignorance or misconstruction of the law; this should be remedied if possible, but never will be, unless a different system is adopted. Now, assessors have no supervisory agent over them except the Commissioner of Internal Revenue. It is impossible for the Commissioner to personally visit but few of the districts; the great mass of them are, therefore, left without supervision or instruction, except such as they get by writing to him for, or such as are contained in circulars of a general character; this course will not produce uniformity, and, unless something is done, under the growing disposition to be liberal in the assessment of the revenue taxes, the government will be the loser to the tune of many thousand dollars. In my judgment it would be economy to divide the several States into one or more districts, containing several collection districts as now divided, according to the size, and appoint a qualified person to supervise the assessment and collection of taxes in the several collection districts under his charge. If a qualified person had several districts under his charge he would be enabled to establish a uniform system of assessments, and if a State was divided into one or more, by frequent meetings of these supervisors, a uniform system would soon pervade the whole State. You may think that my suggestion of multiplying officers is a strange way to economize; but I am well satisfied that by establishing a uniform system of assessments the revenue would be largely increased; besides, it would make each district and State bear its equal proportion of taxation.

Homer Franklin, assessor internal revenue, New York, thinks the proposed system would increase the efficiency of the service and an equal amount of work certainly be accomplished under such a system by a less number of persons, and that if employment was assured and certain, a higher grade of talent could be induced to enter the government service and *at less cost.* He adds:

I have long believed that the uncertain tenure of office is the most prolific source of corruption, both to officials and the public, and that no law can be framed that will be effective with corrupt ministers. Man is a creature of motive, and the strongest one is to get food and clothing. Assure him of these, and you withdraw any motive for him to look elsewhere. I am certain that my district could be better worked at one-half the present expense had I around me one-half the number whom I could select, if left alone to follow my judgment. It is a singular fact that some of my *worst—most worthless—*men are put upon me by recommendations from those so high in life that I sometimes blame our public leaders for the uses to which they lend their names. Armed with these certificates of every moral excellence, the veriest loafers are foisted into positions of trust, when perhaps the men who sign them would hardly trust the individuals to black their boots.

D. B. Owen, collector of customs, Cape Vincent, N. Y.:

The office I hold is now and always has been a political office, and is seldom retained by the same person for a longer period than four years. Every change in the administration at Washington almost invariably brings around the removal of the collectors of customs throughout the entire country. Being thus purely a political office, it is clearly evident that very often good and efficient men are removed to make way for others whose chief qualifications consist in great political influence. A new collector, controlled by those who aided him in his efforts to secure the appointment, is in turn compelled to discharge all or nearly all of the subordinates employed by his predecessor in order that he may satisfy the claims of his political friends. Dependent on them, as he was, for the office secured, he cannot act in the matter of subordinate appointments independent of them.

The practical result of such a system is that real merit and conceded ability are lost sight of in the scramble for positions by successful partisans. There is no standard to which men can conform and thereby retain positions for which they have become specially fitted by reason of long and faithful service. The operation of this political rotation in office is most injurious in its effects for the reason that no examination precedes a new appointment, and a man totally unfit to assume the responsibilities of a collector often secures a place which was acceptably filled by a valuable officer. Hence small inducements are offered to men possessed of proper qualifications, under the present system, to seek the collectorship, inasmuch as the salary paid such an officer is less—excepting in comparatively a few commercial centres—than what he could realize out of some stable business pursuit. As it is, confusion invariably follows the appointment of a new collector of customs.

The duties pertaining to the position are of such a peculiar and intricate character that men who have shown much ability in other pursuits frequently fail in this. Only those who have given the subject careful study can correctly estimate the importance of this consideration.

The import duties of the United States constitute no small portion of the revenues of the government, the collection of which involves a vast expenditure. Economy in its collection, as well as the firm and wise enforcement of the laws, is the object sought in framing laws amendatory to those under which the revenue is now collected. Few candid observers will deny but that the present enormous expense attending the collection of import duties and the prevention of illicit trade with foreign countries could be materially reduced by the inauguration of a new system in the appointment of collectors whereby the same would be placed beyond the reach of political parties and the term of office extended to ten or fifteen years or during a satisfactory administration of the duties of the office.

In briefly presenting these important considerations, I am painfully conscious of my inability to present any plan which will obviate the defects of the present system of selecting collectors of customs and their subordinates, as well as the length of time they should retain their offices; and yet, having considered this matter seriously, in the light of several years' experience, I will comply with your request and offer a few suggestions as the fruits of my reflections on this subject.

1st. Every candidate for the position of collector of customs should be carefully examined before a competent board with reference to his general qualifications for the office, and embracing particularly his knowledge of the duties of the office, the revenue laws, and the practical workings of the system.

2d. No dismissals of subordinates should take place except for incompetency or malfeasance.

3d. A grade should be established, so that faithful subordinates, after four years' service, should receive a small yearly increase in their salaries, thus encouraging them to remain in the government employ and more thoroughly discharge their duties.

4th. The term of office should either be ten or fifteen years or during the faithful and competent discharge of official duties.

That a law embodying similar views to those above suggested would prove to be a great national blessing I have no doubt. Grave defects exist in the present system. The manner of appointing important officers is open to the most shameful abuses and also to the severest criticisms. Under its operations, those who succeed in obtaining positions as collectors of customs, and prove themselves valuable government agents, are allowed to serve in a position they so creditably fill only for a brief period. Men of character and eminent abilities are loath to seek the position of collector of customs under the present *régime*, owing to the fact that at the end of four years he is almost certain to be superseded, thrown out of employment, and, in a great degree, unfitted for other pursuits. What is true as relates to the collectors of customs applies with equal and even greater force to his subordinates. Demoralization in the collection of the revenues breeds distrust in financial circles and tends to weaken public morals. Our financial system is of vital interest to the future welfare of the American Union. Prudence, as well as the lessons of history, teach us that wise and mature deliberations can alone work out needed and far-reaching reforms.

With a profound sense of the incompleteness of the ideas herein expressed, and also feeling that they will be of little service to your committee, they are, however, respectfully submitted.

John F. Cleveland, assessor internal revenue, sixth district, New York city, (appointed 1862,) after declaring himself emphatically in favor of the proposed reform, says that—

Such a reform should commence by subjecting any one, not elective, now in the civil service, to a rigid examination by a competent and impartial commission. Such as may be found competent and worthy should be retained, and such as are not should be dismissed, and no new appointment should be made without the requisite and satisfactory examination.

A. C. Churchill, collector internal revenue, Gloversville, New York:

Knows of no better way to reform the civil service than that proposed in the circular.

John M. Mason, collector of internal revenue, Yonkers, New York:

The great want of practical ability in the administration of our civil service is to be ascribed to the uncertainty of the tenure of office. The government service is looked upon as a sort of hospital or asylum for the relief of broken-down politicians, rather than as an honorable employment in which merit is to be rewarded, intelligence appreciated, and fidelity acknowledged.

Alonzo Alden, postmaster of Troy, New York:

I believe the civil service can be made more efficient and economical if established on the same basis with the military service with respect to appointments, tenure of office, and discipline, from the chief of department to his lowest subordinate, including all intermediate grades.

I am persuaded, also, from nearly two years' experience in a free-delivery post office, that the system of free delivery, established about four years ago, involves a great expense to the government without furnishing any corresponding equivalent.

I am now paying $11,000 per annum, and this is as cheaply as the system can be creditably maintained in this city of 50,000 inhabitants, and during the four years of the experiment the amount of postal business has not increased more than the natural increase resulting from the growth of the business of the city.

The system has, perhaps, rendered unnecessary two delivery clerks otherwise required. With an additional appropriation of $2,000 for clerk-hire, I can dispense with the 11 carriers, thereby making a net saving of $9,000 per annum and satisfying the patrons equally as well.

Forces in his office, 11 clerks and 11 letter-carriers.

He proposes to have additional clerks to the aggregate extent of $2,000 annual salary, and to dismiss the 11 carriers, who cost in the aggregate $11,000.

Abram Hyatt, assessor internal revenue, Sing Sing, New York:

Urges the enlargement of the districts, say, one collector and one assessor for each judicial district, (there being eight in the State,) to be examined by a board to consist of the Secretary of the Treasury, Commissioner of Internal Revenue, and the chairman of the Finance Committee of the House of Representatives. He would also have the office of assessor and collector in one and the same city or town, and hold them strictly responsible for the acts of their subordinates. He would issue no commission to any subordinate unless evidence of qualification accompanied their application. He would have no interference by officers from one district in another, save, perhaps, by a general agent or inspector, who, if he be a proper person, could be very useful. In other respects, he thinks the collector and assessors should be allowed to take entire charge of their own district and be held responsible accordingly. He would have each to give a sufficient bond for the faithful performance of his duty, both officers to be under salary.

Lewis Hall, assessor internal revenue, Jamestown, New York:

After fully indorsing the proposed reform, suggests that a department be created for each revenue agent or an officer of like powers who will be a connecting link between the district officers and the department at Washington, and who shall be made responsible for the economical and efficient operations of this department.

Joseph W. Gates, assessor internal revenue, Lyons, New York:

Urges that persons whose attention or any portion of it is occupied by any other business should not be eligible to an appointment in the revenue service; and that assistant assessors should have divisions so enlarged as to be constantly employed.

P. M. Neher, assessor of internal revenue, Troy, New York:

Hails reform with delight, but has misgivings in regard to its political practicability; yet he thinks there is much force and logic in subjecting candidates for responsible positions to tests of fitness and capacity, even though the machinery or powers were of partisan character, but is afraid that, by vesting the power now devolving upon heads of departments in a committee, must be productive of complications.

E. W. Puddington, collector internal revenue, Kingston, Ulster county, New York:

Advocates a system of stamps to be applied at the distillery upon payment of tax, which should be daily, so as to prevent fraud and deception.

Dwight Webb, esq., of the New York custom-house, makes the following statement:

It may be safely affirmed that there is no doubt of the prevalence of a wide-spread disposition to evade the revenue laws of the country. The distemper is indeed epidemic, and without a parallel in the history of the government. The change which has taken place in the national spirit, under our present tax and tariff laws, superinduced by other causes, is not only alarming, but must, unless checked, prove fatal to the collection of revenue. That it can long prevail without subverting the bulwarks of public credit is quite impossible. Not only individual avarice, but in many instances powerful combinations, able to direct and control the elements which constitute the social, political and financial forces of the country, are organized to this end, and without the restraints ordinarily dictated by prudence.

It is therefore evident the legislative and administrative departments of the government are compelled to choose between the means necessary to control the disease and the cause of revenue itself, either to withdraw the demands of the government or to enforce them. To insist on a withdrawal or to neglect to use means to enforce the laws would be, in fact, to abdicate authority altogether. It is with the American people, as elsewhere in matters of government, of the first importance to distinguish things of accident from those arising from permanent causes. The former may not demand immediate or vigorous measures, but the latter must be met. With us the difficulties which beset the collection of our high rates of imposts belong, most undoubtedly, to the latter category, and will, so long as such high rates prevail.

It must be apparent to all considerate men that the government has but one course to pursue, and that course is, to meet the issue with firmness commensurate with the magnitude of the interests involved. To do this successfully our legislators must here regard—

1. The inherent weakness of revenue laws as compared with other written laws.
2. The opportunities and inducements everywhere offered for their non-observance, and which will no doubt be found in exact ratio to the increase or diminution of the rate of duty imposed.
3. The duty of the government to protect legitimate commerce.
4. That salaries and gratuities to customs officials and others should be adapted to the nature and extent of the requirements of the revenue.
5. That not only all preventive means now employed, but even other measures more energetic, are requisite to their due enforcement, rather than those less so, and that they should be in proportion to the difficulties to be encountered.

1. Revenue laws are but positive rules enacted with a view to meet the financial wants of the government. They are not intended to inflict punishment on individuals, only in so far as to deter them from the violation of such laws, and do not, like laws against crime, appeal to the consciences of men for support and vindication. However necessary for revenue they may be, experience teaches that far the larger portion of the people have not in the past, and it may be reasonably inferred will not in the future, look on them in any other light than as so many threatened fines, penalties or forfeitures which they are at liberty to hazard or avoid ; that non-observance is not crime *per se*, like felonies or misdemeanors under State laws, and if successful in avoiding detection, may be regarded as a stroke of good luck, of which they may boast, and often do boast of, without, as they think, compromising their business reputation or personal integrity. If not successful they must pay the penalty, but in either case they stand acquitted of conscience ; or, in other words, they do not regard the fraudulent evasion of revenue laws as a wrong, *mala in se*, but rather a hazard to be run.

For these reasons it will be seen, and experience confirms it, revenue laws must ever depend for the most part, whatever be the system adopted, for their execution on external agencies and restraints, and not on the dictates of personal duty, patriotism or conscience. The well-known fact that revenue laws are regarded so, in so great a degree, is a weak point, and a primary one, in the whole system. The inducements to smuggle, and facilities everywhere offered or existing in one form or another by which detection may be avoided, only influence and direct those who are swayed by economy or avarice, bent on securing the inordinate gains of an illicit trade.

It should be observed, in this connection, that those who violate laws for the collection of the revenue are far more likely to escape detection than those who violate police or State laws, for the reason, in the former case, no personal right is invaded, no personal violence is suffered by any one, as is the case in assault and battery, theft, perjuries, murders, arsons, &c. Individuals, therefore, cannot be expected to take a particular personal interest, even if they know of violations, in seeing the revenue laws executed, such as will work a prevention of smuggling. No one cares to make himself obnoxious to those who are engaged in smuggling, without fee or reward to stand forth a party complainant, and without which, on the part of some one, the laws, although bristling with fines, penalties and forfeitures, and imprisonment, are but so many pieces of harmless composition, in phraseology elaborately dressed, but as respects public utility, weak and impotent.

Under State laws complainants, constables, justices of the peace, prosecuting attorneys, jurors, and judges of courts of record are all conservators of the public peace, all of which introductory and ultimate means are, in fact, all wanting in the administration of revenue laws, for presentments by grand jurors for smuggling seldom or never occur. So, too, such violations are never seen by the public at large, and there are reasons to believe that but comparatively few evasions are known even by those having the best opportunities of knowing ; nor are they immediately felt except by those who are engaged in the same line of trade, and not always then, though the effects are disastrous to honest and assiduous merchants, whether known or unknown.

The marked difference, therefore, between the two systems of laws is clearly seen and quite sufficient to show that the means for their execution must vary as their nature and the ends for which they were designed vary. In what may be called the motive or inherent power to secure their execution, there is no analogy between the two systems. So, too, as revenue laws are never intended for corporeal punishment, but for the collection of imposts, their terms or conditions, as well as their method of execution, are the mildest consistent with the ends which make their enactment necessary.

2. Another source of weakness is found in the fact that a large portion of our people disapprove of the whole system *ab initio*, on principles involving national polity, or they are opposed to the manner of levying imposts. Add to all the foregoing the uncertainty or difficulty of obtaining correct foreign valuations as a basis for *ad valorem* duties, (although the most equitable system,) the irregularity and frailty of the present system is made more and more apparent. To obtain the requisite evidence to overcome uncertainty, irregularity, and frauds, incipient and actual, notwithstanding all the guards thrown around it, requires a combination of efforts, a degree of skill, patience, and capacity on the part of customs officials as extraordinary as it is rare, and an amount of time, too, they are quite unable to bestow on this branch of the service. The number of invoices per day at the port of New York is on the average about 500, with corresponding entries, and when we take into the account that these are of every conceivable variety as to classification, quality, or value, it is not too much to say the greatest degree of fidelity, astuteness, and energy is insufficient to meet all the wants of the government and protect it against manifold frauds. So complicated is the present system that at every step in its execution it is beset with almost every species of opportunity and inducement for false invoices, false valuations, false classifications, false entries, irregular or false manifests ; and however vigilant other agencies of the government may be, it is but the language of experience and reason to say numerous and continued frauds may be expected in some form or other. And it is self-evident the higher the rates of duty the stronger the motive or inducement to evade the laws ; on the contrary, little or no efforts will be made to smuggle merchandise on which there is little or no duty imposed. For all these reasons, and others which might be given, it will not be considered

an exaggeration to affirm that the difficulties of an organic character inherent in the system itself, and which are common to all *ad valorem* systems everywhere, are well nigh insurmountable under high *ad valorem* rates.

Perfection of the means necessary to enforce laws now on the statute-books has become, therefore, the indispensable duty of Congress, rather than by direct or indirect legislation removing the frail barriers against frauds now existing. It is no unfounded assumption to declare that just in proportion as preventive measures are withdrawn, in an exact ratio will fraudulent appliances be multiplied and strengthened. Their abolition in whole or in part, which has been advocated during the last two years, originated and was set in motion by those who were engaged in defrauding the government, and should be measured and characterized by the nature of the motives which produced them, and should not be adopted and advocated by those who are bound by the most sacred obligations to give this great subject not a superficial but a most profound examination, and provide means for their effectiveness. The abolition in whole or in part of preventive means now at command of customs officials, would heretofore have been and is now popular with the perpetrators, designers, and abettors of fraud. They are no doubt now and will hereafter be unanimous in support of all sorts of legislation which will limit the powers vested in the officers of the revenue, and witholding inducements to activity on their part. But would the honest and assiduous merchant be better protected? Would the revenue be advantaged? Would the confidence in the ability of the government to meet its obligations be strengthened by legislation of this character? Would they not rather recommend more energy and certainty in the execution of our laws—the perfection or organization of revenue laws in such a way as to make them capable of diffusing themselves to a much greater extent, and by each successive step reproducing themselves? Though impersonal, they must be endowed with the same fruitful motives to action, be inspired with the same hopes and expectations and moving to the same ends as influence and impel the violators of the laws. This can only be accomplished by interesting in the cause of the revenue the love of gain, the fears, hopes, confidence, and moral sense of the people—even their appetites and passions; all of which, when taken together, are the only reliable directors of human action. The provisions of the laws must therefore be so framed that they may be the means by which individuals may accumulate money while they are vindicating them, as well as those who are designedly engaged in their violation. Legislation, however perfect on its face, without this inherent motive power to impel execution, will always be found in matters of revenue weak and impotent, shorn of all vigorous, practical utility. To overlook or deny these considerations, nay, indispensable requisites, would be to forego all the usual maxims of prudence and policy. It may doubtless be observed without seeming arrogance, if there be an American statesman who does not consider this a cardinal principle in laws of this character, he may safely be pronounced one who has yet to learn the rudiments of revenue laws.

It seems quite impossible that there can be two opinions on this subject. All good and considerate men will see the necessity of these requisites, and hence will be found on the side of an efficient administration thereof; and if in their judgment they are not vigorous enough to meet the exigencies of this period of high taxes and imposts, they will not fail to recommend others which will. They will not fail to see that statutes without an inherent motive power and without practicable sanctions are everywhere found, in practice, abortive, the *ignis fatuus* of weak and impracticable minds. They will all admit that matters of revenue are like all other affairs of civil government, to a very great extent under the arbitrary control of circumstances, and do not rest on logical analogies, however just or however perfect; that the great and essential questions are what measures will best secure the collection of imposts and afford the greatest protection to the mercantile interests of the country—not such as are carried on in a clandestine manner, but such as comply with the commercial regulations of the United States.

In this view, "money being the vital principle of the body politic," the vigor of the revenue laws is not only essential to the collection of the revenue but to the permanency of the government itself, and in the view of sound and well-informed minds can never be separated. Those who do not realize the importance of this as a condition precedent are certainly either misinformed or do not weigh the evidences of existing necessities at this time of unprecedented activity and license, directed in many respects by the most ungovernable passions.

3. Before adverting to the means necessary for the protection of the revenue and lawful commerce, it should be observed that, by section 91 of the act of March 2, 1799, of all sums received as fines, penalties, or forfeitures a moiety was credited to the United States, and one-quarter was given to the informers, if any, and the remaining one-fourth was equally divided between the collector, naval officer, and surveyor, or to the collector if no naval officer and surveyor; and if there were no informer, then a moiety was given to the collector, naval officer, and surveyor, as before stated. It was thought by the renowned statesmen of that period, fresh in their reading and practical application of first principles of legislation, directed, too, in a great measure, by the intuitive and unsurpassed powers, analytical and practical, of Alexander Hamilton, in this sphere without an equal, that the inherent motive power to impel the execution of revenue laws was a matter of transcendent importance. They saw and provided for the necessity of putting the complainant and violator of laws on the same level as

to monetary and other inducements. that the former as well as the latter should be made to contribute to individual advantage, and that the honest merchant who by paying imposts to the government should have a legal means within his reach to protect himself, by a vindication of the laws as against smugglers or the dealers in illicit merchandise, and thereby not only enable him to make an honest profit, but protect his capital in trade, which otherwise would be in jeopardy by the arts and devices of those who set laws at defiance. It will be seen that the act of 1799 does not provide, in any case, for the deduction of duties on merchandise that has been seized and condemned, nor from the proceeds thereof. The distributed shares, under the 91st section, were not lessened by the deduction, nor the force of the act impaired by it. A moiety was, from a wise design, given to those who should voluntarily put the government in possession of information requisite to bring delinquents to justice. This status of legislation has, in fact, been recognized or allowed to remain on the statute-books until the act of March 2, 1867, when, under pretence of economy, and, as has been alleged by some, to take from customs officials an inducement to mercantile oppression, duties are required to be deducted when there is a forfeiture of imported merchandise of the value of $500, or where such merchandise is released on the payment of the appraised value or of a fine or composition in money.

By sections 37 and 38 of a bill reported or prepared by a commission appointed by the Secretary of the Treasury, it was first proposed to deduct duties in all cases whatsoever, but subsequently modified so as to require the deduction of duties in all cases where the appraised value was $1,000; and by a subsequent bill, reported by a committee of the House of Representatives, it is proposed to reduce the compensation of collectors to an amount not exceeding that now paid to the assistant treasurers. How far or to what extent the latter bill is intended to affect the distribution of fines, penalties, and forfeitures is not known at this time, nor is it necessary here to consider.

The ruling object in these several proposed changes is the saving of money to the national treasury, and is, in itself considered, respectable; it wears the marks of honest legislation, whether wise or unwise, on a full and impartial examination of the whole subject.

But will such alterations in the law, if made, be found in practice economical? Will more money be received from imposts thereunder than would be under the provisions of the act of 1799? Those who favor and those who oppose such modifications of the act of 1799 are, no doubt, striving to reach the same end. However much prejudice there may have arisen and now exists in some localities, by reason of the different means to be used, candor, if allowed to speak, will, no doubt, convince all that the difference between them is a difference only of means, and not of ends. It is, therefore, not only proper but pre-eminently necessary to examine impartially, in the light of first principles, all the various primary considerations, such as are involved—the state of society; the financial and commercial spirit of the day; the varied and multiplied inducements everywhere prevalent.

By the provisions of sections 37 and 38 of the bill prepared by the commission appointed by the Secretary of the Treasury, it appears to be conceded to be inexpedient to deduct duties where the appraised value of the merchandise is less than $1,000, and this on the ground that no incentive will be given any order of men to give information, even if the merchandise be known to have been smuggled, nor inducement to customs officials, of any rank or order, to exercise extra official vigilance to prevent violations or evasions of the laws. The concession amounting to this, that there would not be any incentive, but that an inducement equal to one-fourth part is an affirmative requisite to the proper enforcement of laws throughout the length and breadth of the land, not in the large cities only, but everywhere, for these provisions are of universal and not of local application. Hence the motive power heretofore thought to be requisite for nine and seventy years, is still so recognized in part by the sections 37 and 38 of the proposed bill. It is difficult to see what good reasons can be assigned for limiting the incentive to amounts over $1,000. It will readily occur to every one, if really serviceable in cases where the amounts are less, it is equally so where the amounts are more than $1,000.

It must be apparent that the danger to the revenue in the maximum by reason of a deduction of duties, (thereby impairing the incentive,) is far greater where the appraised value is over $1,000 than when the amount is less than that sum. If it be inexpedient in the one case, why not vastly more so in the other? Is the sum of $1,000 the limit of the avarice or fraudulent propensities of men? Have importers, their aiders and abettors, been found to be trustworthy when their importations exceed that sum? Rather, does not experience, the least fallible of human guides, teach that in all our great commercial cities the greatest losses the revenue has sustained have been occasioned by reason of the infractions of the law in the introduction of large importations? Not small one, but large ones. Can a principle be applied with safety to foreign merchandise over that amount which prudence forbids to be applied to merchandise of a less amount? If there be a good and sufficient reason it is to be found elsewhere than in the instructive volume of revenue experience. Small importers are not the only victims of avarice or lovers of inordinate gain. So, too, an impartial investigation will not fail to show that the government needs most the inherent motive power of statutes touching importations of merchandise having the highest rates of duty, whether the amount of such importations fall short or exceed the sum of $1,000, and for the obvious reason that where rates are highest, there exists the greatest inducement to evade the requirements of the laws. With whatever motives or purposes these modifications of the act of 1799 are advocated, a full and clear analysis will exhibit the fact that it is not so much the value of any given package of merchandise as the rate of duty imposed which constitutes the incentive to smuggle it, and if any limitation to the principle be warrantable, it should be made on a very different principle than that of an arbitrary classification of amounts of value. If made at all, it should be by declaring that duties shall be deducted where the rate imposed does not exceed, say 15 per cent., leaving no deduction where it exceeds that percentage, and this for the reason there will be little or no inducement to violate the laws where the rate of imposts falls below that rate, but where it exceeds it duties are to be deducted, for the reason there will exist greater and stronger motives to evade the laws, and hence the encouragement to all who will aid the government in preventing evasions (if there be any limitation) should rest on this apparently self-evident proposition.

The results arising from the deduction of duties, when the appraised value is over $500, is seen in the following cases of condemnation by the courts, under the act of March 2, 1867: United States vs. 11 casks gin, net proceeds, $2,743 30; duties, $3,008 74; duties exceeding net proceeds, $265 24. There was an informer. It is hardly necessary to say he was disappointed, and charged bad faith on the part of officials. United States vs. merchandise, $12,546 20; duties, $8,010 90; balance, $3,382 70; collector's share, $281 82. In a case of the condemnation of cigars, net proceeds, $525; duties, $353; balance, $142 11: informer's share, $35 52; collector's share, $11 84. Condemnation of laces, net proceeds, $950; duties, $712 36; balance, 268 37; informer's share, $67 09; collector's share, $22 36. Another case of condemnation of merchandise, net proceeds, $1,024; duties, $711 06; balance, $227 80; informer's share, $56 95; collector's share, $18 98. In another case of the condemnation of 16 casks of gin, $950; net proceeds returned, $142 35; informer's share, $35 58. Net proceeds in another case of merchandise, $7,440; duties, $3,933 90; balance, $3,506 10; informer's share, $876 25; collector's share, $292 08.

Other cases might be given, showing the trivial amount distributable to customs official after duties are deducted, but tho above are quite sufficient. In all cases they are looked by persons who have given information as disproportioned to the hatred, trouble and time consequent on the giving of it. But this is not all. In many cases where information is given in good faith, after the lapse of many months, and sometimes years, and after repeated inquiries have been made, informers are told that the Secretary of the Treasury has exercised the power of remission, and that they get nothing. The reply is, "It is the last time I will give information to the government."

It may, therefore, be reasonably concluded, for the foregoing reasons, after looking at this subject in the light of personal interest, and in which the practical results under the statutes present it, little or no inherent motive power exists calculated to impel execution of the laws, but rather practical weakness and frailty. From whence the conclusion is inevitable that when the greatest restraints and most active agencies are practically requisite, just then all, or nearly all, are withdrawn, notwithstanding it is generally thought to be otherwise from what appears on the face of the act itself.

For nearly a century of high tariffs and low tariffs Congress uniformly invoked external agencies and restraints to check, as far as possible, illicit commerce by calling into requisition, amongst other means, the principle of selfishness—to check inducement by inducement—avarice by avarice—energy in disregard of law by energy in its execution. Such were the ceaseless and powerful agencies invoked, but which now an unwise spirit of economy or concealed fraudulent purposes would abrogate. This may not be from any evil design on the part of any one; it may have its parentage in fidelity to government, even; but its effects will be evil, as is too clearly seen by those having the best opportunity of judging. It is not done, it is true, by direct terms, but effectually done, nevertheless. Government ought at least to keep good faith with its subjects, particularly those whom it induces to serve it. Governments to be respected must first show themselves respectable. For it makes no difference, when the rates of duty are high, whether the government says it will give no gratuities or whether it says duties shall be deducted; the result is found, in practice, to paralyze all the sources of information by which evasion of revenue laws are mostly obtained.

Attention has been called to the prevalent disposition everywhere to evade the collection of revenue; that the whole current of society has set in that direction. Let it, therefore, be asked, do the authors of these propositions hope to purify the foul current by a withdrawal of restraints? to check it by passive concurrence? to overcome the monstrous evil by ministering to its gratification? On the contrary is it not "everywhere known that the habits and passions of men grow by what they feed on; that the love of gold grows faster than the heap of acquisition?" In this view the question at issue reaches further than the successful administration of revenue laws—indeed, to the stability of all republican institutions.

Again, the principal reason, and that which is most relied on, for insisting on the deduction of duties is that the government is entitled to duties in all cases. No one disputes this; all concede it to be true. But the merit or demerit of the question at issue is something other and different. So far as any one isolated case is concerned, were it all, all would concede that duties should be deducted. But it is not to one case only; it is to be applied to a class of cases; it is to be incorporated into a system of legislation made up of, and surrounded by, frauds, necessities, and facts the most formidable. It is, therefore, a question of practicability, to be followed by uniform practical results and their consequences; one of practical results, and not one of mere right. It is really not whether the government is entitled to duties, but how is it to get duties; not a question of right, but of ability to gain what is endangered or positively withheld, and the power of a preventive system at all times ministering to the advantage of the government; though silent none the less necessary and effective. It is not theory with which we have to do; we are brought down, as a people, to the cold atmosphere of arbitrary facts; to the selection or the securing of agencies to act in behalf of the government when it cannot act for itself. Hence, too, we are compelled to estimate, not what men ought to do but what they may be reasonably expected to do. Will any person who may have given information stand forth a party complainant a second time, after being the sole cause of the government getting high duties and one-half of the balance? he failing to get anything, or the merest trifle, if any, and but for whose agency the government would not have got anything. Will he a third time, a fourth time, even if he be in the possession of the most unquestionable evidence and the most valuable, after subjecting himself to the malice of the violators of the law, see the government get all, when without his aid it would have lost all? It may be said such is the duty of every citizen. Is it rational to suppose because it is the duty of every one that they will perform it? He who expects it may be set down as already the victim of an excessive credulity. To expect it is, in fact, to affirm that selfishness is no longer a characteristic of the human species, and that intelligent lawgivers are no longer to regard selfishness an element of society.

A rule, therefore, which will not admit of continuous and multiplied applications should not be insisted on. One which will not in practice bear frequent repetitions is a fallacious one, and will be found, without doubt, as injurious to the revenue as it is futile. In a wide extended country teeming with commercial enterprise, increasing in volume and power, and stretching out wider and wider, the civil power should be so organized that each successive application should increase its power and effectiveness and not weaken it. It should be able to diffuse itself by a permanent and judicious arrangement of subordinate principles and institutions. Without incurring the charge of empiricism, it can be stated that if legislation for so widely extended a territory, whether relating to revenue or other affairs of the government, be not organized in such a manner it will be divested of all of its inherent and corporate vitality, and will at no distant day be seen to be a most miserable failure.

Again, there is another branch of this subject of such transcendent importance both to individuals and the government that it demands a full examination. Reference is had to the protection which the government is bound to give to honest traders, those who pay imposts; having paid duties to the government, and thereby increased the cost of their purchases, they are entitled to protection from low prices instituted and caused by those who have set revenue laws at defiance. If the government fail in this, it sacrifices the honest supporter of the government in order to shield the smuggler. How to do it is a question of ways and means, but the obligation to do it will admit of no two opinions.

If this protection be not afforded, the government may be safely pronounced remiss; and if so remiss will the capital invested in legitimate commerce be better protected or none protected? Although the agencies heretofore relied on during periods of high and low imposts, and herein contended for as indispensably necessary, may not be sufficient to meet the exigencies occasioned by present rates, but such exigencies do furnish the best of evidence adverse to an abolition of such agencies. Their inefficiency cannot furnish grounds for less stringent laws, but evidence for provisions which will give the necessary protection.

It is now openly affirmed by men of large commercial experience, and against whose commercial reputation aught cannot be said to their disadvantage, that during the two years last past they have been compelled to make purchases of houses they have strong reasons to think do not pay duties on their importations, the rates of duty being high, or go out of the business altogether; that they have been forced to this by dealers in illicit commerce who not paying duties, undersold them if they purchased at regular importing prices.

This will be more clearly seen and felt by supposing two men (and it is not a hypothetical case) go into business, of the same kind, at the same time, and invest the same amount of capital; one pays duties on honest and correct invoices, the other makes entries of merchandise on false invoices, from 12 to 25 per cent. below the actual foreign value. The latter will make from 12 to 25 per cent. while the former makes nothing. If the undervaluation be no greater, the former will be compelled to close his business altogether or become bankrupt; but suppose the difference be still greater, then the effects of a want of protection becomes more disastrous. Hence it must clearly be seen that the honest merchants are *per force* compelled either to go out of business, become bankrupt, or cheat the government; and hence the government, by withholding such protection, actually makes smugglers of otherwise honest men, and negatively furnish the strongest incentive to smuggling. In this view undervaluation on the part of importers in the absence of protection should no longer be considered a heinous wrong, but is most evidently extenuated by the remissness of the government.

It is not too much to say on this point, already the confidence either in the ability or the disposition of the legislative and administrative departments of the government is most sadly shaken. And why should it not be? The laws of trade are quite as intelligible and quite as imperative as those which regulate other departments of human affairs. It is not, therefore, a question simply whether the government shall have duties on imported merchandise actually levied, but a much broader and far reaching one, whether the government agencies shall be found, in practice, acting for or against the interests of those who are disposed to be law-abiding men. The collection of the revenue and protection to the mercantile interests of the country are indeed convertible terms. The one necessarily implies the other. The failure of one is a failure of the other. The idea, which prevails to some extent in high places, (to a too great extent,) that undeserved toleration and leniency may be exercised in matters of imposts or monetary demands of the government; that open fraud remitted and incipient frauds winked at without the most serious and unjust consequences, and for the purpose of avoiding charges of harshness and oppression, is a fallacy. The natural product of a diseased political sensibility is as incompatible with commercial safety as it is adverse to every reliable element of national character. Nothwithstanding all this, and in striking contrast with this want of protection, are the flagrant and persistent efforts being made to defeat the authorities in the laudable work of protection, denying their right and heaping calumny without stint or limitation on the heads of those who are found on the side of the government, whether in private life or in official stations. Under the systematic and unremitting agencies of wealth and position directed to these ends, to a great extent, the whole course of society has undergone a most deplorable change; "words" even "have lost their signification;" public sentiment is so debauched that to aid the government has become a personal reproach; skilful fraud evidence only of creditable capacity; systematic perjuries "masterpieces of cunning;" honesty a want of enterprise; execution of the laws unjustifiable oppression; praiseworthy efforts to protect the revenue and honorable assiduous merchants hireling meanness, stigmatized as the work only of base spies, corrupt and venal officials, unworthy of public or private regard. So far indeed is this carried, believed, and openly countenanced by a strong but yet still growing public sentiment, that to be known as being an officer or agent of the government in the revenue service constitutes a social ban, excluding all such from social position in which they would otherwise move and in many instances adorn. In short the whole structure of society has undergone a most marked and alarming change. Avarice and license has gained an ascendency, setting the laws at defiance, calumniating their constituted guardians, and before which the ablest, the wisest, and the purest of the land may well stand amazed and confounded, and with energy turn their attention to guarding well the foundations of all law and order.

The strength of purpose, extent of commercial transaction, and financial influence and activity bearing on this subject may be estimated by the statistics, a portion of which is hereto annexed, marked ——, showing that of all the vast amount of European productions which find American markets, only about nine per cent are imported directly by Americans, a fact which speaks its own importance.

There is still another side to this matter, the full development of which lies in the womb of the future. Without any disposition to reflect or cast unjust reflections on any order of business men, it, however, should be stated, that certain leading branches of importing business is now almost exclusively in the hands of foreign houses, or foreigners not owing allegiance to this government nor purposing ever to become citizens. What few American houses are now connected with such branches of business pay a commission to foreign houses to purchase for them abroad, or order for them. What are all the reasons or incentives to this it may not be easy or necessary to state. The fact is, however, some of the leading features are, European producers or manufacturers send out or they adopt a foreign house already doing business in this country, which they style their agent; then adapting their productions to what they term "the American demand or trade," ship, under color of consignments, such products to their (so-called) agent, invoicing such imported merchandise at or about the cost of manufacturing, claiming that such articles have no value in the principal cities of the country where they are produced. This may be believed by some and appear plausible to others; but let an American go to Europe and apply as a purchaser for such identical manufactures, and he is unable to buy a dollar's worth at the prices set forth in the invoices presented by such agencies in this country for entry. The result is, as before stated, such branches of the importing business is nearly or quite all in the hands of foreign houses. And the tendency is growing stronger every year, all in this direction, touching all other branches of the importing business. By reason of the opportunities afforded by the system of ad valorem duties, Europeans by finesse and by fraud are controlling the spirit and substance of American commerce on its own soil, and driving Americans from their own markets. How much further this will be allowed to prevail is to be determined by our national legislation.

Protection, in each and every of these respects, is a requisite which should not be postponed. The demand for it is most natural. Success or adversity is necessarily its concomitant. It may hence be not out of place to observe that, justice and justice only is the centre of personal national safety. She can, in the commercial world, as well as elsewhere, if invoked, establish order and security to all alike.

Hence combined individual selfishness, social predilections and power have not hitherto, as we have seen, been silent nor inactive. And as the American people and interests are now situated, it is idle to suppose that they are sleeping now. However much selfish pretensions, petulant invectives, and virulent hate may have done, or fraudulent purposes may conspire to do hereafter under false names and false pretences, the prominent fact will not go unobserved, that the cause of revenue and protection to the mercantile interests of the country is the cause of national safety, without which public and private prosperity in this sphere may be hoped for, but cannot be rationally expected.

But again, the provision for deducting duties in the cases before designated will defeat the object for which its projectors design it. It will always be in the power of those having a knowledge of infractions to make such knowledge known of act upon it or not. They may, however, defer until they know that the merchandise shall have passed from the possession of the guilty parties, and beyond the reach of the government, in which the only remedy will be an action *in personam* for the value, and from the sum received no duties will be deducted.

If the imported merchandise seized amounts to $500, duties will be deducted. It will therefore always be for the interest of persons giving information to wait till the merchandise has disappeared before complaint be made or official action is had. This is easily done. All that is required to effect it is to defer action. A little delay on their part defeats the deduction of duties. But this is not all. If the parties smuggling are permanently located, have a place of business, and are pecuniarily responsible, while the government would not have security in the first instance, they would most likely in the end ; but if itinerant or irresponsible, the government would not have security, as would be the case if the *res* were seized, and would most likely fail to collect the amount of judgment recovered. A moment's reflection will show how much better and safer it will be so to frame the statute that not only the part going to informers and customs officials should not be subject to the deduction of duties, but by such non-deduction induce the most speedy action for the security of the government. This, too, shows the exceeding impolicy of the attempt recently promulgated of making punitory laws remunerative, as unwise as it would be humiliating to national character.

It having been shown, by reason the most plain and conclusive, that an inherent motive power is most indispensable, and which is confirmed by the large and numerous frauds which have been experienced, it is only the part of consistency and honest dealing on the part of those who advocate the deducting of duties to name a substitute for the incentive heretofore relied on for the execution or impelling power of revenue statutes ; for to do away with the motive power heretofore known to be of the greatest utility, without furnishing or proposing some other argues, nothing less than culpable ignorance or fraudulent complicity with those who evade or resist the laws. Either conclusion would be as disagreeable as the effect of a wrong course would be disastrous, for to conclude for any reason that our national legislators are indifferent to the welfare of the revenue or the wants of legitimate commerce ought to be considered entirely inadmissible.

It is charged that distribution under the act of 1799 is liable to great abuses, that merchandise liable to condemnation has been released to claimants on the payment of amounts less than the duties alone, and this by the collusion of customs officials, United States district attorneys, and counsel for claimants. If there have been instances of this kind, a remedy should be provided, but in such a way so as not to take from the revenue system the strength requisite—the vital principles of its power. The remedy should not be allowed to take away the keystone of the arch, without which it will be found falling about our heads, more fatal to the government than to smugglers—indeed, fatal only to the government. It would be quite easy to provide that in all proceedings *in rem*. it shall be unlawful for United States district attorneys, collectors, and other officers to stipulate or consent to release any goods, wares, or merchandise on condition that the party claimant confess judgment in a less sum than the appraised value thereof so subject to forfeiture, without the approval of the Secretary of the Treasury, in writing, which approval shall be placed on file, and be a part of the records of the courts where judgment by confession shall be entered ; and in case judgment by confession shall be entered without such approval, the goods, wares, and merchandise so released shall be liable to seizure and forfeiture the same as if no proceedings had been had in the premises. If this should not be quite sufficient, others might be easily devised.

Again, it is said that in the most populous revenue districts the compensation of collectors, naval officers, and surveyors far exceeds any just limit. In a few districts the amount received justifies this declaration ; but the number is less than a dozen. The amount, however, received in these instances is not so in consequence of considerations such as are involved in the fixing of salaries given to other classes of government officials. It will be admitted, if candor shall prevail, that such compensations arise from the necessities of the government over and above such as are connected with the discharge of duties appertaining to other official stations of a totally different nature. They are the results of the indispensable motive power necessary to impel the execution of the statutes in overcoming frauds, incipient and actual, and without which there would not, for the numerous reasons heretofore specified, be vigor to enforce them. It is the gist of the preventive principle which experience has taught to be wise, and which is, in fact, the most effective and important for the welfare of the people. If large sums are received, it arises from the extent and volume of commerce on the one hand, and the prevalent disposition to evade the laws on the other, and it cannot be said in any just sense that the government is a loser by it, but it can be truthfully said the government is a gainer by it, however virulent may be the charges against customs officials. The government cannot be said to be a loser in that it never had; and when, too, it gets one-half of what is recovered, and will otherwise be successfully smuggled in by far the greater number of instances.

The instances, be it said to the credit of American revenue officers, when customs officials have acted corruptly, when all the facts are known, are not frequent. They have seldom occurred—so unfrequent, indeed, that, in a legislative point of view, they are to be regarded only as particular defects rather than as radical defects in the system itself—from hitherto unforeseen defects rather than having their origin in permanent causes, and of constant and continuous operation. Nothing leads to greater mistakes or is more to be feared than errors of this kind. Admitting the instances of collusion and complicity to be as marked and flagrant as stated and insisted on in some quarters, they should not be grounds for wholesale and sweeping suspicions, nor should such suspicions become the sole basis of legislation. If so, it would not be reasonable nor even safe to stop with customs officials. It would be quite as rational to charge those who are earnestly at work to overthrow the present preventive system with complicity with smugglers, that they are in the pay of smugglers. Such an inference would not be far-fetched, but pertinent in view of all the facts. Intelligent lawgivers will, however, dismiss the whole system of expedients dictated only by suspicions as unwise and uncalled for, and which system in a broad and politic view of this whole subject demands a higher order of legislation. But there is another side to this branch of the subject—one, too, which no competent legislator will fail to regard. Reference is had, first, to the nature of the duties required in the collection of the revenue in the most populous districts; second, the order or measure of abilities requisite thereto; and third, what the reasonable returns of such abilities or attainments may be estimated at in other departments of business life.

But there is still another side to this subject, one which no competent legislator will be likely to disregard, for it is no part of American statesmanship to run delirious after an idea, but rather to measure its practical fitness; it has more regard for utility than theory.

The opinions entertained in some quarters that salaries of collectors, naval officers, and surveyors should be rated by considering only the time required and the price of labor in the market, or rather the willingness of men to serve the government without regard to attainments and personal fitness on the one hand, and the nature, extent, and consequences of duties to be performed or neglected on the other, it is thought will not bear an intelligent examination. If adopted and applied to the revenue service it will hardly fail of being in more respects than one the prolific parent of national profligacy or legislative misdirection, when the nature of the duties are pleasing rather than distasteful, ministerial rather than inquisitive, popular rather than odious, trivial rather than laborious, increasing the political and social status of incumbents rather than lessening it; in all such instances it is conceded salaries may be rated to a great extent with safety. But when the duties which are to be performed are the opposites of all these, it must follow other important considerations must enter into and should be allowed to provide for the necessities of the government.

The duties of customs officials are evidently the latter of those above enumerated in almost if not quite every respect. Hence men of sufficient qualifications to perform the duties with advantage to the government will be successful in other departments of life, which hold forth greater promises of reward than $4,000 or $6,000 per year. They will not assume laborious and odious duties for a like amount of compensation, connected as they are with personal malice and hostility, and oftentimes without cause, with the general impression of bad faith, peculation, and even oppression, however honest or trustworthy they may be. As a general proposition those who are best qualified for such offices enter upon the duties only from motives of self-interest or personal advantage, offered and secured by the terms of the law. They do not do so from the love of official position or patriotism, nor for a limited salary assume voluntarily labors of such a gigantic character as such duties impose in the largest revenue districts. In fact it may be safely stated nothing but a strong appeal to individual love of gain on the part of the government will for any length of time secure the government the advantages arising from the services of qualified appointees, endowed by nature with force of character requisite to such duties.

Even where the laws are most clearly evaded will collectors institute suits against a man or firm if commanding influence, who alone or with the aid of his friends shall be able to displace him as readily as against some person or persons without influence. Will he do so in a critical case, or where there is likely to be strong opposition, as readily without a personal interest as with? Will competent men everywhere be found of so little regard to their own interests or reputation, or of so self-sacrificing a turn of mind, as to disregard all personal considerations—care nothing about the effects of administrative acts where wealth and influence are brought against him? Or, rather, will not there be stronger reasons to expect that, without a personal interest, laws in many cases will be a dead letter, and where, too, there are strong reasons for their execution arising from the extent and flagrancy of the frauds perpetrated?

The results may be summed up as follows: competent men, if receiving but a limited salary without a personal interest in the seizures made and suits instituted, will either disregard the interests of the revenue by failing to make seizures and institute suits when the public interest dictates for fear of losing their position, or fail to do so because there is no motive to move them thereto; or they will neglect to look after the interests of the revenue, preferring to give their time to business outside the custom-houses which promises better. In either case the revenue is made to suffer from the very nature of such a system.

It has already passed to a political maxim, "that a power over a man's subsistence amounts to a power over his will." So, too, men take but "a slender interest in what is short-lived and is of but little advantage;" and it is so particularly where "there is little or no inducement for them to expose themselves on account of it to any considerable inconvenience or hazard," which always, sooner or later, when wealth, political and social, are opposed and have an opportunity to display themselves.

If no personal interest be given officials the greater will be the inducement to commit, directly or indirectly, corrupt practices and peculations, "for experience, the least fallible of human guides," shows how easy it is for even many otherwise good men to persuade themselves that, as they bear the burdens of office, they are entitled to a compensation commensurate with the labors performed and the hazards run, even beyond the stipulated amount given by law, and that if they have not the terms of the law on their side they have at least a moral right to more than it gives. In public life it should be borne in mind that personal interest has as much to do in keeping men honest as the restraints of the law.

To avoid the inducements of a corrupt character their legal rights and personal independency should be in proportion to their labors and risks and responsibilities from whatsoever source they may come; their opportunities to accumulate money in accordance with the law sufficiently strong to deter them from doing anything which would involve its withdrawal. They should not be placed for the good of the government in a position to have their fortitude weakened by interested parties "operating on their fears nor corrupting their integrity by appeals to their necessities or their avarice."

It is believed if a system of the kind proposed be adopted, it will furnish inherent causes which will not fail to defeat itself. It may safely be pronounced in advance to be the offspring of incompetency and ignorance. It is only necessary to add that, in balancing the subordinate agencies and institutions of great nations, the element of self-interest often is made to perform quite as important a part as economy or disinterestedness.

The uniform experience of political communities have taught, when they are unable to help themselves, it is always wise to call for the assistance of individuals, moneyed though they be, by personal interests.

. 5. The following reasons, supported by facts of no ordinary significancy, show the necessity for a modification of several provisions now on the statute-books, and the enactment of other provisions for the protection of the revenue, and the rights of parties, and also to prevent our revenue system from becoming the victim of *ex parte* investigation, irresponsible agencies, favoritism, and every evil influence, which must in time follow:

1. The act of March 3, 1863, section first, and other sections and acts bearing on the subject of undervaluation, is believed to be greatly deficient, inasmuch as under the ruling of the courts it requires stronger proofs, and such as are far more difficult to obtain, for the government to prove undervaluation in an action against a consignor than against an actual purchaser. It is extremely difficult for the government to show a guilty knowledge on the part of a consignee, who alleges he enters his goods as per invoice forwarded by his principle, and to make him liable who sells for a commission of five per centum, and remits the balance of the proceeds of sales.

In consequence of this distinction or the greater latitude to false and fraudulent appliances under the forms of consignment, and the success which has attended practices of this character, a very large proportion of European importations have been admitted to entry at a very low foreign valuation, and the amount is believed to be increasing in consequence.

The total amount of such consignments of woollen goods as compared with sales, shipped to America from the following consulates, to wit, Bremen, Cologne, Aix la Chapelle, Brünn, for the months of July, August and September, 1867, were as follows:

1867.	Consignment.	Sales, currency thalers, 69 cts. American money.
July	75,252,462	1,641,403
August	45,827,990	890,555
September	25,094,028	1,245,059

Currency thalers, 69 cents American money.

The above figures were taken from the records of the consulates above named by one of the most intelligent and trustworthy agents of the Treasury Department, and in which the most implicit confidence can be placed. The amount of sales as compared with the consignments of goods shipped to America is hardly worthy of notice, only as it reveals a practice and a motive. From evidence obtained by the same agent who has been in Europe over two years, he is of the opinion that the average undervaluation of woollen goods and wines and drugs combined will not fall below 35 per centum. He is also of the opinion that the ratio or difference between sales and consignments above set forth will hold good in all the principal consulates of Europe, and also the rate of undervaluation.

Silk ribbons shipped from Lyons, total amount, first six months of 1866, francs... 25, 695, 835

Consigned.. 19, 271, 876
Sold.. 6, 423, 959
                                                            ———————— 25, 695, 835

Undervaluation estimated at 15 per centum.

Silk ribbons shipped from Zurich, first six months of 1866.................... 10, 751, 005

Consigned.. 9, 138, 354
Sold.. 1, 612, 651
                                                            ———————— 10, 751, 005

Undervaluation 18 per centum.

Silk ribbons shipped from Basle, first six months of 1866, total in francs...... 7, 323, 582

Consigned.. 6, 884, 372
Sold..   439, 210
                                                            ———————— 7, 323, 582

Undervaluation 18 per centum.

It will be seen that the proportion, in this article of merchandise, between consignments and actual sales holds good.

It is only necessary to add that the wine and champagne trade, as well as the above kinds of merchandise, are entirely in the hands of the manufacturers, and the system of undervaluation on consigned goods runs through the entire line of trades, and there is no doubt extends to others in the same ratio. They are either invoiced at or a small percentage above the manufacturers' prices, instead of the wholesale price, and are kept in the hands of foreigners to the exclusion of the American merchants by such system of undervaluation, besides defrauding the government of a large portion of its revenue.

These figures need little comment. They speak their own importance, point out the evil and suggest the remedy. Purchaser and consignee should be placed on the same level by our laws. Our laws should be so clear and specific on this subject that no foreign consignor could by any appliances whatsoever make entry of his goods at a less foreign value than an American purchaser; that no indirection shall avail him, no means be at his command by which he, who has no permanent interest in the welfare of our institutions, shall be able to drive Americans from their own markets and at the expense of the revenue of millions annually, as is now unfortunately the case.

Of the 157,000 (or thereabouts) invoices, of which entry is annually made at the port of New York, there is good reason to believe from the above figures and information from other sources that four out of every five set forth a foreign value less than the actual wholesale price required by our laws, or in other words, 400 of every 500 daily entered at New York are fraudulent.

It will be said no doubt that they are for the most part passed by the appraiser nevertheless, from which it is true an inference may be justly drawn that the appraiser is derelict of duty. No design of this kind is however intended directly or indirectly, even by implication. The appraiser no doubt for the most part arrives at his conclusions by comparing the invoices of different importing houses. He knows little or nothing of foreign valuation from his own personal knowledge of European wholesale prices, and as the figures and investigation made in Europe show that there is in all, or nearly all, the principal consulates an almost uniform system of undervaluations, it is not at all to be wondered at that the foreign values arrived at at New York by the appraisers by comparison and other means should disagree, with wholesale prices obtained in Europe by personal observations and statistics, and particularly so when less than 15 per cent. of all the importations are by American purchasers and 85 per cent. under the form of consignments and by foreigners. Such being the case comparison of invoices of one importing house with another is only another way of establishing undervaluation as foreign values at the expense of the revenue.

3. For the foregoing reasons, commencing with the inherent weakness of revenue laws in themselves considered, the necessity for the giving of gratuities to the third persons as an inducement to give government officials information and customs officials for extra vigilance, the systematic frauds perpetrated under cover of consignments, the unreasonable delays in the courts of the trial of causes in many cases, it is not to be wondered at that the Secretary of the Treasury has found it necessary to employ a large corps of special treasury agents to report on cases at all stages of their investigation. Nor is it at all strange that

under the various statutes giving specific powers in certain cases taken in connection with the general and sweeping power "to superintend the collection of the revenue," he should assume to act through agencies appointed by himself, which sound policy dictates should be wholly left to the judicial tribunals of the country when the amount gives the courts jurisdiction.

The policy which obtained until quite recently of confining the duties of such agents (limited in number compared to those now employed) to ferreting out and detecting frauds, was unobjectionable and judicious, but the extension of their assumed jurisdiction of erecting all over the country where interest, caprice or malice may dictate self-constituted examinations, making *ex parte* reports based on the rumors or statements of interested parties not confronted by opposing interests, is a system fraught with such numerous and monstrous consequences that no enlightened statesman can approve. As before observed, under the circumstances this may be justifiable on the part of the Secretary, but as a system it cannot be too severely reprobated. The means at the command of customs officers, their own experience and competency, and the efficiency of the courts ought to remove at the earliest day possible a system antagonistical to the genius and laws of the country, and subject to every vice.

Again if the system were in itself admissible the experience had under it, the character of men employed as such for the most part, the means used to secure such appointments, the rapid changes which take place, preclude the idea of competency on the part of such agencies and safety to those whose interests are involved, assuming that in all cases the agents are honest and directed by a laudable purpose to serve the government without doing injury to any one.

But when it is known that most of these agencies are sought for political or purely personal ends, that many are appointed without the requisite education, without any experience in revenue matters, and without sound characters when best known, the system becomes too dark and repulsive for comment.

But waiving considerations of a personal character and looking at the system so inaugurated as a system in vogue, the most deplorable feature is that in far the larger number of cases of any magnitude reported to district attorneys for prosecution in the courts at some time during some stage of the proceedings, the same is subjected to the considerations and reports of treasury agents, and although the laws do not by any means place the Secretary above the courts, or independent of the courts, except to a limited extent, nor were they designed to do so, yet practically the course now pursued by the Treasury Department has reached that end. So serious is this matter that an instance has occurred that after the collector had reported large frauds to the district attorney and had made full report of his acts and doings to the Treasury Department, the party who was used in the commission of the fraud, the one who actually committed the acts, procured from the department the appointment of a treasury agent and received instructions to investigate such and other frauds. This might have happened or have been the result of a well practiced imposition. It would be charitable to look at it in this light, but the facts are after his history and agency in the frauds was made known to the department, he was not only not dismissed but employed in other districts by the department. In other cases evidence points to the conclusion that parties who have committed large frauds on the revenue, fearing detection, have made use of influences at their command to secure the appointment of one of their own number as an agent of the treasury through whose offices and manipulations when the same were discovered they were able to compromise by the payment of a small sum or escape altogether.

Enough however has been stated to show that the effect of the system as it now obtains would not, if we had a properly organized system, be superintending the collection of the revenue, but an interference with the collection of the revenue.

And perhaps the worst of all is that the labors and ends reached by such agencies paralyzes and interrupts that silent invisible power of the law, the substantial growth of time and precedent, which, while it protects the rights of all parties, never fails to give the strongest support which legislation can receive, a power able to defend all orders of men "from the law and even the lawgiver from himself," arising from the conviction that the law is a living entity and not a mere form, which interruption, though in behalf of claimants, by the force of such precedents will not fail of being even to them the fruitful cause of other irregularities and frauds. This spirit is inherent in the system itself.

If the course of judicial proceedings shall become subject to such informal *ex parte* action as appears to be coming into general practice, all protection by the courts will fail; and not only this, but it is difficult to see, on the one hand, the practical boundary of the power of remission, and on the other what degree of protection and stability under it legislation will be able to afford the revenue; for "the precedent of to-day becomes the law of to-morrow."

4. The practical effect of the act of March 2, 1867, has worked badly in many respects for the interests of the revenue. After the experience of 14 months it is believed that the act should be greatly modified; in fact that the interests of the government require the repeal of the act, with the exception of such provisions as gives to the officer making the seizure one-fourth of the fine, penalty, or forfeiture, in case there be no informer; and section 2, which provides for the application and issue of warrants by the United States district judge for the seizure of books and papers.

The amount of clerical duties imposed in consequence of providing for the distribution of fines, penalties, and forfeitures, by the Secretary of the Treasury, instead of by collectors, as previous to the passage of this act, both by the collectors and the department, appears to be wholly unnecessary, and is attended with every species of delay. Although the act was intended to benefit the subordinate officers making seizures, and also informers, it is not too much to say that the delay in the adjustment of such items has produced so much complaint that the cause of it is extremely prejudicial to the service, and embarrassing to collectors, naval officers, and surveyors, and that so much of the act should be repealed.

It has been already stated that proofs of no ordinary significance pointed to the conclusion that from 85 to 90 per cent of all importations from the continent of Europe were imported under the form of consignments—that their average undervaluation is about 35 per cent. It has also been stated, a fact of the greatest importance, that the appraisers at the several ports of entry do not arrive at the foreign values which becomes the basis for duties so much from a personal knowledge of the wholesale market value of such importations in the principal cities in the countries from which the same are imported as they do by comparing one invoice with another—the invoices of an importer not known to them with those known of acknowledged commercial reputation. This they are, no doubt, compelled to do for want of a more satisfactory and practical method; for it is not to be supposed that appraisers at the port of New York, or elsewhere, are to be found who are personally conversant with the wholesale market value of all importations they are called on to appraise, in the countries from whence they are imported.

As before stated, only about 9 per cent. are actually imported under the form of purchases, that 91 is under the form of consignments, and that the undervaluation is equal to about 35 per cent. it follows that the system, so general, of comparing one invoice of consigned goods with another, is, in fact, to a very great extent, but a method of fixing by appraisement a false foreign valuation as a basis for estimating duties. It has been frequently said by the Hon. Hugh McCulloch, Secretary of the Treasury, and confirmed by others, that the government did not collect more than 50 per cent. of the duties it was entitled to under the law. Many have been unwilling to give credit to this statement. If the figures before given and confirmed in different ways be taken as proof, it can easily be seen how the larger part of such failure to get legal duties occurs, independent of other causes.

This is not intended to cast any reflection on appraisers, but to show, while the law devolves on them an important duty and high official trust, it has not by any systematic method provided them with the means necessary to perform such duties intelligently or satisfactorily to themselves even. The true test of a statute on this subject is to furnish the requisite information to appraisers. Its aptitude to perform this function can only be seen by practical results. The defects of the present statutes is seen from the fact that as there are collected from $120,000,000 to $130,000,000 at the port of New York per annum, there is a loss to the revenue of from at least $30,000,000 to 40,000,000 every year. This state of things should be obviated. Demanding the attention of the law-making power it should be remedied. Instead of Congress giving so much attention to matters of minor details and the bestowal of patronage, as has been the case in some instances, this maelstrom of frauds, false and fraudulent practices and appliances, and persistent mercantile assumptions, should be rendered impossible by more perfect and practical legislation. Various methods might be adopted to this end. The following is suggested for consideration as a substitute for those provisions, or as additional to the provision relative to the powers and duties now devolving on general appraisers, appraisers, and assistant appraisers:

1. At the time of making oath as to the true value by the owner or consignee before a consul, full samples shall be lodged or filed with such consul showing the contents of each package duly labeled, with all the necessary particulars.

2. That there shall be established three commercial agencies, or three consuls to be named to perform this duty, one in Great Britain, one in France, and one in Germany, under the supervision of a capable man with commercial experience, with authority to employ a staff of experts in various branches of all kinds of merchandise.

3. That consuls shall transmit abstract weekly reports, accompanied by samples filed, to the designated agencies, and also transmit a weekly report of the market price of all articles of merchandise susceptible of being quoted in commercial price-current.

4. That such commercial agents shall systematize such consular reports, and classify the samples of the goods so received by them, and weekly transmit them to the collector of the port of New York, for his guidance and information, and that of the appraiser; and also a duplicate copy of such reports to the Secretary of the Treasury.

The adoption of a plan of this character would enable the several commercial agencies to report weekly the true value of all kinds of merchandise, and quote understandingly the goods appraised in this country. They would, too, be enabled, from having all the samples of goods shipped, to at once detect any undervaluation, and could report, at any time afterwards, the specific facts at once to the collector or Secretary of the Treasury, when required. In case of any question in regard to the value of any kind of merchandise in this country, by forwarding the same with samples, or otherwise, to the commercial agency of the country from which the goods were imported, the matter could, with such means at command of the agent, be determined at once, and thereby prevent many delays here, and no doubt be the means of avoiding much litigation in the federal courts.

It need only be added, that by the adoption of this plan the government officials will have full statistical information in regard to the value of all kinds of foreign goods, with little or no additional expense, and which, it is believed, would soon be found of indispensable importance in all matters of revenue. It is the system which would be adopted by an intelligent private firm were the same necessities to exist for acquiring the same information, which fact, once admitted, is an unanswerable argument in favor of its adoption by the government.

In conclusion, all who shall take the trouble to look over this whole subject, in all of its parts, will not fail to see how much must ever depend on the proper execution of the minute details of which it is composed; that however perfect the code may be made by the repeal of provisions now existing and the enactment of others, the final success of the revenue code must depend on the ability with which its several provisions are executed. The history of states and nations everywhere discloses the great fact that not more than one-half, nor even that much, is accomplished when a code or organic act is adopted. "The administration of a system of polity is the larger part of its establishment." Arrangement and perfection of details can only secure success, and this can only come of industry, exactness, order, time, and experience; and these again need not be looked for where personal inducements are wanting. Nor is there anything in the nature of the public service which can or should overcome a rational demand for permanent and well-paid labor. Whoever demands it or expects it, is unconsciously or inadvertently the advocate or indorser of the parent of irregularity, incompetency, and license, which everywhere are the ministers of political vice. No part of the public service is made up of such an infinite number of details, and each so intimately attended with losses, and on which so vast an amount in money is made to depend, as the collection of *ad valorem* duties for a great nation. Each successive step should be performed with accuracy and despatch, and without which, no matter how perfect the legislation, or who may be appointed collectors, the system will, to a greater or less extent, prove a failure. On the other hand, if each part in detail be duly attended to, the concurrence of parts properly executed strengthen each other, different divisions and departments furnish each their *quantum* in the organism, and thus perfection of the whole arises by degrees, like the several orders of a Palladian palace, crowned with success, giving a permanent revenue to the government, and protection to its law-abiding subjects.

To this end, therefore, the system of appointing proper men for the execution of our revenue laws is of the most primary and vital importance. So much so, that it is not out of the way to say, that unless reformation begin here, it is less than useless to hope for a better administration of our revenue laws, however many other changes may be proposed.

However enamoured the advocates of the present system of appointments and tenure of office may be, it is confidently asserted that both rest on a false and mistaken basis: that the highest considerations demand that ascertained competency should be made requisite to every appointment under our revenue code, and when appointees are once found to be qualified by education and habits, they should hold their positions during good behavior, and that promotion should be made from the number found to be competent and deserving. Rapid succession in appointments, even when qualified, is inconsistent with every idea of certainty, regularity, and a high order of ultimate success; nor is there on the part of appointees that stimulus to excel when appointed, or to exhibit by their conduct a high order of uprightness. While, on the other hand, feeling they hold their positions by a feeble tenure, and at best cannot hold it long, there is always an inducement to make the most out of it possible, so they escape the penalties of the law. The practical extent of these observations is difficult of measurement in matters of revenue. Those most familiar with the collection of the revenue, both customs and internal, attach the most importance to them; for it has been well said, "it is a general principle of human nature that a man will be interested in whatever he possesses in proportion to the firmness or precariousness of the tenure by which he holds it; will be less attached to what he holds by a momentary or uncertain title, than to that he enjoys by a title durable or certain, and of course will be willing to risk more for the sake of the one than of the other. The remark is not less applicable to a political privilege or honor or trust, than to any article of ordinary property." It is as applicable to subordinates as to those holding the most exalted stations. It is worthy of remark, if time and training be essential requisites in the army, the navy, and the judiciary, it is believed to be hardly less so in the revenue service. If money be the vital principle of the body politic, then, too, it is not too much to say, to some extent, the permanency and efficiency of the army, the navy, and the judiciary are dependent on the successful administration of the revenue system of the country. For when it shall be made to appear, if ever, by the architects of political indifference and fraud, that our system for the collection of the revenue is inadequate, followed as it soon would be by a want of confidence, then will commence the dark catalogue of national evils whose consequences no friend of the government can estimate, nor their end foresee.

Letter of Hon. J. W. Hunter, of Brooklyn, New York:

My past experience has been sufficient to convince me that almost any change would be for the better. It could hardly be worse than the present system of *political qualifications*.

I think the public service could be performed by *well trained, well educated* men, assured of permanence in office during good behavior, and when meriting promotion to receive it, for about one half the amount now expended.

Questions No. 33, 34 and 35 I can answer most decidedly in the affirmative.

F. S. McNeely, postmaster at Trenton, New Jersey, an emphatic reformer, suggests abolition of franking privilege, and the leasing out of stamp stands instead of appointing stamp clerks, by which an annual saving of $100,000 would be effected:

Allow me to say something in regard to the "franking privilege." For nearly 20 years I have seen it abused most shamefully; and it is my decided opinion, that to correct the abuse, you must abolish the privilege. The abolition of the frank would very largely increase the revenues of the Post Office Department. I have in the lobby of this office a news-stand, at which postage stamps and stamped envelopes are sold. The news dealer pays three hundred dollars ($300) a year rent for the privilege of having said stand. A stamp clerk would have to be employed if the stamps were sold by me. By this arrangement the government saves at this office thirteen hundred dollars ($1,300) annually. If this plan was generally adopted, the government would save at least $100,000 annually.

John B. Headley, collector, Morristown, New Jersey:

Urges the discharge of the vast army of revenue inspectors and agents, the selection of collectors and assessors with particular reference to ability, honesty, and integrity, and not on account of political influence; a fixed salary from $2,500 to $6,000, in accordance with amount of labor and size of district, &c., holding them to a strict account for all frauds committed in the district, and to be removed at once if found guilty by the district attorney.

C. E. Wright, collector of internal revenue, 12th district, Wilkesbarre, Pa.:

2. A plan for the schooling and training of the assistant assessors would result in much good. The assessor is generally distant from the most of his assistants, and their instructions generally derived by letter, in answer to inquiries from them. At stated times they should be assembled by the assessor and catechised. It would establish uniformity and correctness in their work; or, if an agent of the department should make the tour of each district once a year, at least, it would be to a good end. The whole efficacy of the system hangs on the action of the assessing power. No doubt great losses are occasioned by the laches and inability of the under-assessors.

3. Perhaps the greatest evil occasioned the system of internal revenue is the traffic, of an illicit character, in spirits. The ingenuity of man seems baffled in attempts to counteract these frauds. In all parts of the country the railroad trains are shifting immense quantities of spirits from State to State, the tax on which has not been paid. If it were possible to control these common carriers by any congressional legislation, they should be restrained from carrying any cask which has not marked on it the evidence of "tax paid." I have in my district but one revenue inspector, and it is out of the question for him to keep watch of the great number of railroad depots, I presume more than a hundred. I know that the officers of one of our roads direct their subordinates to keep watch of the markings of casks of spirits, but this case is the exception to the rule. The transportation of copper stills, worms, &c., is usually by the same means of conveyance.

4. The subject of taxing whiskey is a problem that seems destined to fail of solution. For my own part I have become satisfied that there is but one way to secure this tax. It should never leave the premises where it is made until it has paid its tax, and when the distiller has failed to pay on a certain amount he should stop operating. The loss, the amazing loss, on this commodity, is that it is permitted to pass from place to place without payment of its tax. The system of bonds, given for particular purposes, fails in its purpose.

5. Though it may not strictly fall within the scope of your circular, I will mention lastly that the receipts of revenue in this State have been essentially diminished by removal of the tax on coal and iron. In this district the sum of receipts has fallen from $1,000,000 to $400,000. This tax was paid (I mean the tax on coal) the most promptly and easily of all. Coal operations becoming chiefly confined to large and wealthy corporations, the stock of which being much of it owned by capitalists of the Atlantic cities, it was easily paid. And the same remark applies to iron companies. The imposition of those taxes again, as they were, would materially increase the sum of revenue.

If there is any other point on which, at any time, you desire information of me, I shall be happy to give it.

J. Lee Engelbert, assessor 7th district, Pennsylvania:

37. In my humble opinion the efficiency of the civil service could be promoted by the employment and retention in office of officers who have shown by their abilities and acts qualifications for honesty and faithful performance of the duties devolving upon them for

the interests of the service and satisfaction of tax-payers. Employment being assured at a fair remuneration for services rendered would certainly cause a higher grade of talent and a better class of persons to enter the government service and remain therein.

Should the tax on manufactures be removed and the revenue for the government be derived from income, spirits, tobacco, luxuries, succession and legacy tax. I would respectfully recommend the reduction of the number of assistant assessors, the most efficient being retained in the service: let their whole time be devoted for the public good at a fixed salary; this would insure proper and diligent attention to assessment of taxes, because at present in our rural districts considerable ground is travelled over, some of the assistants having eight townships, requiring conveyance, and the small amount of tax sometimes assessed will not warrant the approval by the assessor of a large bill in the assistant's favor for services rendered.

C. S. Phillips, assessor internal revenue second district, Pennsylvania :

In my opinion the head of every department should give undoubted evidence of his fitness for the position. I do not think that such fitness can only be acquired by rising gradually from the lowest to the highest grade. I do not think that such a system would work well. New men of the necessary qualifications, and of well-known character in the community in which they live, should be appointed to the head of each department. An efficient chief makes efficient subordinates.

In all public offices I believe an equal amount of work could be done, and better done, by a less number of persons than are employed.

It is impossible briefly to give a full opinion of the merits and demerits of the system embraced in this inquiry. Fresh men, taken from the walks of active life, infuse more energy into an official department than men who have always lived in it. The latter are apt to become listless and indolent. It is the nature of the man who lives for a long time upon a fixed salary to become so. Care should be taken in selecting the heads of the different civil departments in the State. Political influence ought not be the sole or chief recommendation. A board of well-known merchants or business men, in each congressional district, might be selected, who should examine and pass upon the merits and qualifications of the candidates. The heads of the departments should be held strictly accountable for their subordinates.

The proposed system appears to me contrary to the spirit of the age, deriving its origin from governments unlike our own. Fresh men taken from the walks of active life infuse more energy into an official department than men who have always lived in it. The latter are apt to become listless and indolent. It is the nature of the man who lives for a long time upon a fixed salary to become so.

T. Wilkins, collector of customs, Erie, Pennsylvania, declares as follows :

Since I have held the position of collector my experience has sustained me in the opinion that the duties of a revenue officer are so far professional that their proper administration depends as much upon the knowledge derived from study and continued experience as does a successful practice at the bar.

Josiah P. Hetrick, collector of internal revenue, Easton, Pennsylvania, in reply to a demand for further testimony than in his first report, sends a communication setting forth the fact that the revenue act of March, 1867, reduced the collection in his district from $1,300,000 to $700,000 by taking off the tax on pig iron and leather, which makes a moneyed aristocracy of the furnace men and tanners, to the detriment of the lumber men of the district. His full report is herewith annexed :

The new revenue act of March, 1867, reduced the collection in my district from $1,300,000 to about $700,000. This was caused by taking off the tax on pig iron and leather, which never should have been done, inasmuch as the furnace men and tanners were then and are now clearing 150 per cent., and are becoming a moneyed aristocracy in the midst of an industrious community of lumbermen, manufacturers, mechanics and merchants, who pay me the $700,000 revenue tax which I collect annually. To collect $700,000 in small assessments, spread over five counties, requires as much labor as it did to collect one or two millions in large assessments, yet I am "running the machine," (and I believe it is well run, and with the approbation of the department,) with two-thirds of the subordinates formerly employed. This is done by securing men of temperate habits, ability and industry.

I am of the opinion that the revenue service relating to assessments might be made more efficient and economical. In some divisions of a district there are too many assistant assessors. They are paid $5 per day, and in many cases have but little duty to perform.

It is of vast importance that assistant assessors shall be honest and competent men, and before they are appointed by the department should pass through a thorough, searching investigation by the assessor of the district.

William McSherry, assessor internal revenue, Littlestown, Adams county, Pennsylvania, an ex-member of Congress and ex-State legislator, fully indorses the proposed reform, and states as follows :

I do not think there is a branch of the public service in which it is so important that competent and faithful officers should be retained than that connected with the assessment of internal revenue taxes. I refer particularly to the assistant assessors. So long as the system remains such as it now is, it requires months for an assistant assessor to become familiar with the duties of his office, it matters not how well he may have been educated nor how successful he may have been in transacting other kinds of business. Whenever changes are made in a district it disarranges the business of the district for months and causes much trouble. I believe if the services of competent and faithful officers were more generally recognized by the government and the public it would be a great stimulus to encourage them in the discharge of a duty which is generally odious to the public, and in many instances not remunerative to the occupant of the office.

T. C. Gummert, acting assessor internal revenue, Brownsville, Pennsylvania, offers the following suggestion :

Only appoint those of good moral character and able to stand a close examination. Abolish assistant assessors attending daily to distillery; it is a humbug; get an honest man for store-keeper and make distillers pay him, thereby lessen expenses of assistant assessors; many are now paid $125 to $135 per month that could not earn $90; make assessor's pay $2,000 per year and no compensation but office rent and fuel; assistant assessor $1,000 per year and not allowed to do anything else. And, finally, amend section eight of internal revenue so that in place of assistant assessor being the acting assessor, make the clerk, when competent, the assessor, so that I and any others situated as I am shall be honorably rewarded for past services, and for merit alone. And to make my assertions good, I refer to all citizens of this place, and especially O. P. Baldwin, republican postmaster at this place, and to the assistant assessors of 1st, 2d, 3d, 4th, 10th, 12th, 13th, 14th, and 15th divisions, half of whom are republicans and the rest democrats. Hoping that you may carry out your good intentions in this respect by calling at the Commissioner's office, ask for reports of 21st district, and make a decision in my case.

T. J. Jordan, assessor internal revenue, Harrisburg, Pennsylvania :

Urges the abolition of all bonded warehouses, these being, in his opinion, the chief centres of fraud. He further recommends that all cases involving whiskey frauds should be adjudicated by the courts, and not in the departments.

William P. Lloyd, collector internal revenue, Mechanicsburg, Pennsylvania, strongly advocates the adoption of the proposed system, fully indorses and quotes the opinions of Commissioner Rollins bearing upon the subject of reform, and declares :

Under such a system an equal amount of work might be done at least in the assessors, and collectors' departments of internal revenue *by half the number of persons now employed.* Assistant assessors, as they are required to visit the distilleries in their divisions once a day, might then be intrusted with both their own duties and those of storekeepers at warehouses of as small capacity at least as those of my district, and the checks to fraud which are now endeavored to be imposed by multiplying officers would be much more surely and effectually accomplished by the ability, honesty, and responsibility such a system would secure in the appointees.

F. Z. Hoebner, assessor of 6th district, Allentown, Pennsylvania :

Urges the reduction of the assistant assessors and the exclusive devotion of all their time to the duties of the office of the assistant assessors.

Collector of customs at Philadelphia :

Desires that the tests of qualification should include experience, sobriety, and general good character for stability and industrious habits.

D. E. Nevin, assessor internal revenue, Allegheny, Pennsylvania :

The adoption of a stable civil service, similar, in some respects, to our military system, with, perhaps, a little more regard in it to merit than to seniority in the matter of promotion, would, undoubtedly, draw a superior grade of talent and a higher degree of integrity into the government service.

John B. Warfel, assessor internal revenue, Lancaster, Pennsylvania:

Has little faith in examinations, but is in favor of a probationary service, and of reform based thereupon.

R. L. Wright, assessor internal revenue, Frankford, Pennsylvania:

A plan for the schooling and training of assistant assessors, to whose want of knowledge most of the present evils of the revenue service arise, must do much good.

James B. Ruple, assessor of internal revenue, Washington, Pennsylvania:

Declares that his views have been fully and intelligently expressed by Commissioner Rollins in his report of February 29, in letters respectively dated June 17 and July 15, 1867, and January 15, 1868, addressed to the Secretary of the Treasury.

Abram B. Longaker, collector of internal revenue, Norristown, Pennsylvania:

Suggests monthly conferences between the collector and assessor and the assistant assessors with a view of securing a uniform assessment, of detecting fraud and evasions of the revenue laws.

He does not think the per diem allowance for assistant assessors should be reduced, but urges a reform in the license to tobacconists, who should be compelled to pay their taxes on all cigars manufactured during each month or else increase the bonds for each hand.

Henry H. Bingham, postmaster, Philadelphia:

Emphatically in favor of reform; thinks the peculiar character of the post office labor would not admit of the whole proposition of question 33. A rigid test examination, however, conducted by competent persons to test the fitness of candidates for appointment, would, without doubt, increase the efficiency of the service, and allow of an equal amount of work to be accomplished by a less number of persons than are now employed.

A uniforming of all the employés of the civil service would be a progressive step. Test the experiment by uniforming the carriers employed by the Post Office Department.

Enforce by legal enactment that all appointees for general work service in the public offices should enter said service at a certain salary, and the increase of said salary to depend upon the parties' merit; and said increase to be only permitted after a certain length of service, and the increase to be specific. Increase the salary of employés after every three years of service upon the same basis as the "forage" ration in the army.

Forbid by law the discharge of employés in the civil service for political reasons, so that when men enter the serve they may regard it as their life profession. Increase the salaries of employés in the civil service so that they may live honestly, and thus take the temptation to commit theft out of their thoughts.

He has under his control 327 persons not subject to test examination, but dismissed if, after month's probation, they are unfit.

Among the carriers the system of promotion is of emolument under specific law. They enter upon their service at $800 annual salary; if found meritorious after six months' service, it is raised $100, and after a year another $100, making it $1,000, which is the end of the carrier's promotion.

John W. Douglas, collector of internal revenue, Erie, Pennsylvania:

Removed one of his subordinates upon the ground that he was *a consistent thief and an inconsistent preacher*; declares himself emphatically in favor of the proposed reforms; animadverts upon the system of paying commissions or irregular compensation to revenue officers, and urges the adoption of fixed salaries for all government officers. He is satisfied that permanency of employment, a system of promotion and examination, and regularity of compensation will tend to make the civil service more efficient and economical.

F. E. Volz, collector of internal revenue, Pittsburg, Pennsylvania:

Thinks the collectors and assessors of internal revenue should be paid a salary in full for services, and the percentage, now allowed, cut off. Likewise that the salaries be established in proportion to the amount assessed and collected and the other labor necessarily required to be done in the offices.

The government should have the appointment of all subordinates in these two offices.

Wesley J. Rose, collector internal revenue, Johnstown, Pennsylvania:

States that the efficiency of the service would be greatly promoted by the adoption of the system indicated. Such a system would secure competent and faithful collectors and assessors. These officers should be left perfectly free and untrammelled in the selection of all their subordinates, and should be held to a strict account for the actions of the same. Whiskey inspectors and storekeepers should be appointed by the collector and should hold their offices during his pleasure.

Collectors and assessors should be directly under the control of the Commissioner, and all subordinates under the control of the collector and assessor, and each should be held responsible for a faithful discharge of official duty.

Charles H. Shriner, collector of internal revenue, Mifflinburg, Union county, Pennsylvania:

After declaring his opinion that the adoption of the proper system would increase the efficiency and integrity and diminish the cost of the service, *urges government "to dismiss all spies and informers who are sent out to harass the people and eat out their substance."*

B. F. Martin, collector of internal revenue, Columbus, Ohio:

Declares himself emphatically in favor of the proposed reform, and recommends an establishment somewhat similar to the English civil service, in which case the government would be better and more economically served; since no prudent man will abandon the business of his life and devote his whole time and mind to a mere temporary position, liable to removal, regardless of his fitness or faithfulness. * * * *

The government plan is at variance with the experience and course pursued by every successful business man. They do not employ inexperienced persons to manage difficult and intricate affairs. Yet the government intrusts her immense resources at random, without examination, to the management of unqualified persons, and even these are removed, perhaps, just as they begin to comprehend their duties, to give place to a fresh supply of novices.

Answer to the last question:

37. In so far as the civil service would relate to the assessment and collection of the internal revenue tax, I would respectfully suggest:

1. That the law for the assessment and collection of this tax be *short*, *concise*, and *explicit*, without ambiguity, so that the *intention* may be gathered correctly from the language used, thereby avoiding many discussions, rulings, &c., which are made necessary by the crude and imperfect law now in force.

2. I would lop off much of the machinery now in vogue in the office of Commissioner of Internal Revenue, and consequently made necessary and in operation in the local offices of assessors and collectors of the several districts, and would reduce as near as could be the system of accounts to a mere cash account of debtor and creditor, with collectors, charging collectors with amounts of lists, crediting them with cash paid to treasurer, and with insolvents.

3. I would establish a separate bureau for internal revenue entirely independent of the Secretary of Treasury. The Commissioner to have the entire control of all matters relating to internal revenue.

4. I would suggest for that office a man of undoubted integrity, a good lawyer, and possessing an extraordinary degree of firmness, so that when a decision is once made and communicated to local officers, they may not be taken by surprise in the frequent overruling of decisions upon questions involving substantially the same facts in each case.

5. I would take from the Commissioner, or "any other man," the power to compromise any crime or offence for a violation of law, and the power to compromise any debt or demand due the government, and would leave these matters with the courts, where they of right belong, and would insist on prosecution, through the courts, against all who evade or violate the law for gain nor would I, however, make the penalty for its violation disproportionate to the offence, but would in all cases protest against all "let ups" until the party convicted shall have paid the penalty.

6. I would dismiss from the service any and all officers of any grade whenever their work, unexplained, gives the least evidence of incompetence, inefficiency, or dishonesty.

7. All officers of the government, including inspectors of all kinds, storekeepers, of bonded warehouses, &c., should be paid by the government, and none paid by parties who are engaged in the business of distilling, as inspectors and storekeepers are now paid.

8. All should be well paid, of course having reference to the business capacity required, responsibility incurred, and labor performed by each, and with a due regard to the character and position of the office which he holds.

9. All officers in the several districts under the grade of collectors and assessors should be appointed by the assessors and collectors of the districts, to whom alone they should be responsible for the faithful and honest discharge of official duties.

10. I would decrease the number of articles upon which tax is levied; decrease the number of occupations which shall pay a special tax, and consequently decrease the number of assistant assessors, and would have a less number of persons employed in the civil service in all the various branches of the government, and would in that process, I think, make the

civil service more efficient and economical; I would by all means sustain the local officers in the discharge of official duties as against those whose pecuniary interest is antagonistic to the government, until it appear *prima facie* that the case is against the government, and that its officers are wrong-doers. Finally, with something like I have here indicated, it is my judgment that a tax of $2 per gallon on distilled spirits or a greater or less sum, may be collected, and the "civil service made more efficient and economical."

John S. Hogin, assessor of internal revenue, Xenia, Ohio, after declaring that he knew meritorious persons superseded by inferior ones and fully indorsing the proposed reform, states the multiplicity of authorities by which the revenue department is trammelled to be the bane of the service:

He urges the establishment of a separate bureau of internal revenue with a practical and accomplished head, who shall be held responsible for the faithful administration of his department. Let the law be so modified that the Commissioner can call to account and immediately remove any assessor, collector, inspector, or other person acting in a subordinate capacity in his department for failure to faithfully perform the duties of his office with an eye single to the best interests of the government. Let each assessor appoint his subordinates, and be held responsible by the Commissioner for their actions as officers. Inspectors and storekeepers of distilled spirits &c., &c., should be paid by the government and not by the proprietors of distilleries, as is now the case. Under the present law an inspector is paid by the distiller a fee of eight cents per barrel for inspecting spirits, which, upon an average, will not amount to the wages of an ordinary day laborer. The result of this low-wages system causes the inspector to be finally controlled by the distiller, (his paymaster,) with a view of making a fortune before the illicit collusion upon the part of the inspector is discovered.

The same is true of the storekeeper; although he is paid better wages, he is not paid by the right and proper party. It is a natural result that the laborer should be controlled to a greater or less extent by the party that pays him his wages, especially when that party holds out glittering inducements.

W. P. Richardson, collector internal revenue, Marietta, Ohio:

Employment and promotion on account of merit is the best method, but will never be adopted. Every office in our government depends directly or indirectly upon the will of the people, and will, I am satisfied, so remain. No "civil service corps" can be created which would be more efficient or economical than the present employment, unless it is given a permanence wholly incompatible with the spirit of our institutions and the opinion of our people in regard to the tenure of office.

It is possible that a body of men, selected as suggested, might perform the duties of their several positions better than they are now discharged, and, indeed, the same plan might be extended so as to embrace most of the offices within the gift of the people, State and national legislatures included, from which we might expect like favorable results; but what probability is there of the exercise of so much prudence and self-denial on the part of our people?

My acquaintance with the condition of the service and the character of the officers and subordinates is not such as to warrant recommendations for its improvement.

I would suppose that if the number of persons employed were reduced to the minimum, those retained possessing the highest degree of capacity and integrity, and paid as little as such services could be obtained for, the service would then be as economical and efficient as it would be possible to make it.

George B. Arnold, assessor internal revenue, Mount Vernon, Ohio:

Declares that the proposed system would operate with peculiar benefit to the revenue service. He urges the extension of the penitentiary provisions of September 5, revenue laws, to *five years*, and that they should be enforced. He is satisfied that millions of dollars of *just* and *legal* revenue tax lie dead and uncollected all over the United States, by reason of delinquency, want of energy, and comprehension of revenue officers, not alone in whiskey and spirits, but in tobacco and cigars, legacies and successions, licenses, and indeed all classes of internal revenue tax. He would like to take a contract (say for the State of Ohio) to assess and recover all *just* and *legal* revenue taxes that have legally accrued from liability during the last four years, and which have been lying uncollected, and even unlooked after, allowing him a commission of 25 per cent. on the amount that can legally be collected, without extortion or oppression, but legitimately. He has no doubt that the same applies also to other States. One good and faithful revenue inspector, appointed for and embracing two or three revenue districts, might make himself very useful at a salary of $1,000 to $1,200 a year, and *actual expenses paid out by them;* but the appointment of one revenue inspector to a single rural district does not afford them *half* constant, legitimate employment, and they generally manage somehow to get per diem pay for *full time*, and frequently charge up in their bills expenses, such as railroad fare, &c., when they are travelling on a free railroad pass. It seems to me people are getting very much demoralized in regard to their jurat or oath to official papers in the revenue service.

The office of assistant assessor is the very *initium* or starting point in the internal revenue system, and the action of assistant assessors depends a great deal upon the promptings and energy of the assessor.

It is very important, therefore, that assessors should be themselves vigilant, and constantly stir up and prompt their assistants. I have seen the need of this almost every day, and thousands and thousands of dollars of revenue tax has been added to our lists in this district, which probably would have slept in the pockets of tax-payers, had it not been for promptings to special scrutiny and vigilance and energy on the part of our assistants.

George J. Anderson, collector of internal revenue, Sandusky, Ohio:

Declares himself emphatically in favor of reform, and demands that *the penalties for defrauding the government, whether by tax-payers or government officials, be more stringently enforced.*

F. Van Derveer. collector internal revenue, Hamilton, Ohio, states

That all his 18 subordinates have served in the Union army, and declares that this is a prerequisite in all appointments made by him or upon his recommendation.

Carr B. White, assessor internal revenue, Georgetown, Ohio:

Evades the questions relating to reform upon the ground that there are no grades in his office, but suggests to make the tenure of office commensurate with a diligent and faithful discharge of duty. He urges to hold the Commissioner of Internal Revenue responsible for assessors and assessors for assistant assessors, giving each power to suspend or dismiss for neglect or inefficiency of duty, in which case he thinks the revenue would be increased one-fourth, with same or less expense to the government.

He declares that the great frauds on the revenue are in the collection of tax on whiskey and tobacco. Most of this could be prevented by holding the assessors and collectors responsible for it. But little fraud could be practiced if the officers did their duty. The storekeeper or inspector must be suborned, to succeed at the distillery or bonded warehouse, but, to make the matter easy, the assessor, assistant assessor, and collector must be in the ring. The ring being able to pay more to these officers than the government, the avaricious find it hard to resist and generally yield. They expect to hold the office but a short time, and want to make what they can while they do hold it; hence, many who yield, if they were sure of retaining office during good behavior would not.

George M. Woodbridge, assessor internal revenue, Marietta, Ohio:

Evades the questions touching reform upon the ground that they do not apply to his office, but declares that in the rural districts, such as his, it was not economy to put up the per diem of assistant assessors to $5, and the abandonment of the requirement that 10 hours' work should constitute a day, he characterizes as unfortunate.

James Lewis, assessor internal revenue, Bucyrus, Ohio:

I have no doubt if the employment was assured and certain, that more efficient and better qualified persons would enter the service.

I believe after the annual assessment is made the expenses of the service in this district may be materially reduced, by making each county an assessment division, and having one assistant only therein, except perhaps in the counties where distilleries are located.

If Congress should pass a bill relieving manufacturers generally from tax on their productions, one assistant assessor would be sufficient to each county. This would lessen the expense of assessing the internal revenue in this district about 33 per cent., and the work could be as efficiently done as at present. All of which is respectfully submitted.

J. M. Connell, assessor of internal revenue, Lancaster, Ohio:

I received on the 14th instant a circular dated January 20, 1868, issued by the Joint Select Committee on Retrenchment, and signed by you for sub-committee on the civil service, in which I am requested to answer in writing certain questions appended to the circular, concerning my connections with the civil service of the United States, and to furnish "such comments on the condition of the civil service and the best method of making it more effectual as I may see fit to add."

In response, I will answer the first 13 questions, touching particularly my own relations to the service and fitness for it, in one connected recital.

I am assessor of United States internal revenue for the 12th district of Ohio; was appointed by the President and confirmed by the Senate on the 18th day of June, 1866, and entered upon the duties of the office July 14, 1866.

I was in the civil service of the United States in the years 1857–'58 as chief clerk of the bureau of the First Comptroller of the Treasury, in which bureau I served 13 months, terminating my service by voluntary resignation to return to my professional pursuits. Before this I had served as district attorney, eighth judicial district of Indiana, for one year. I was in the military service of the United States during the rebellion, as colonel of the 17th regiment Ohio volunteers, for 30 months, resigning, when unfit for duty by reason of disease contracted in the service, to take my seat in the senate of Ohio, to which elected while in the field. I served two years in the senate of Ohio.

Prior to my appointment to the office of assessor I was engaged in the practice of law. I was admitted to the bar in 1850, when 20 years of age.

I had no collegiate education; was educated in private schools and academies, terminating my course of study at Greenfield Academy, a boarding-school in this county, at the age of 16, at which time I had pursued a course of six years' study of Latin, four of Greek, six months each of French and German, and two years of higher mathematics and natural sciences. I then entered upon the study of the law, and continued therein four years, until admitted to the bar.

I have ever since principally relied upon my profession for support when not in public service.

I have computed the income of my present office for the year 1867; it was in that year $2,700, not equal to the average of my annual earnings in my profession when steadily pursued.

It is needless to state that I was not subjected to any examination in regard to my qualifications for my present office.

I have understood that I was appointed by the President, with the advice and approval of the Commissioner of Internal Revenue and of the Secretary of the Treasury, my qualifications being certified to by those who recommended me for the position, and being further attested in the faithful and satisfactory discharge of public duties in the official positions of trust I had held. I was recommended for this office by leading business men of my district, by Senator Sherman, by the members of Congress from my State with whom I had personal acquaintance, by Governor Anderson, members of the legislature of Ohio, and by my military record, professional standing, and prior official experience.

I make such official reports to the Commissioner of Internal Revenue as are required by law and regulations, or become necessary in the performance of my duties. None are in print. But I would here suggest that if the committee wish to learn something of the history of whiskey frauds, and of the conduct and character of the revenue officers of this district, an examination of my report to the Commissioner of Internal Revenue of an investigation of alleged frauds by Emmitt Brothers, distillers, dated February 1, 1868, and on file in the office of the Commissioner, may prove both instructive and interesting.

My office hours and labors are as they were when practicing my profession; my office is open and public business transacted from 7 o'clock a. m. to 9 o'clock p. m. No arrearages or delays are allowed. All reports, entries, records, and correspondence are made and completed without delay, and as required by law and regulations.

To the questions from 14 to 33, having reference to subordinates employed in this district, I will also present one answer covering all of the inquiries.

The assessor of this district has the appointment of one clerk for his office, and on his recommendation the assistant assessors of the district are appointed by the Secretary of the Treasury. After I had entered upon my duties as assessor, I found, as I believed, too many assistants employed. I reduced the number, discharging six, and continuing in employment eleven; also one assistant in addition was appointed to be placed in charge of Emmitt Brothers' distillery, which has been running constantly for more than a year, producing an average yield of 2,500 gallons distilled spirits per day.

In country districts like this, assistants are constantly employed only in the large towns, of which there are three in this district. Eight assistants, therefore, assessing in country divisions are occupied only a few days in each month, except when making the annual assessments upon incomes.

I have had about 20 applications for appointment as assistant assessors, eight of whom have been appointed on my recommendation. By consolidating divisions I reduced their number six, thus discharging six assistants; of the remaining eleven two resigned and six were removed. Three who had served for several years were retained.

The removals were made for the following causes: absence from division and neglect of duty, one; inefficiency, three; to give place to men of superior capacity who had served in the union armies, two. Nine assistants (including one in charge of the distillery) have been appointed on my recommendation for merit and qualifications, political and personal considerations being subordinate thereto; the three retained in office were so retained without regard to political considerations, because of their fitness for their positions; two of them are republicans, one a democrat; of the nine new appointees, six are republicans and three democrats.

Of course none of these assistants were subjected to the test of examination by a committee. As I am in a great measure responsible for their acts, I satisfied myself of their fitness. They were selected, as your committee would select its clerk, or as a banking or business house would choose its employés, for their integrity, industry and qualifications.

1. Over 50 years of age, is an able lawyer of thirty years' practice, high character, qualified by education, experience, integrity, habits and ability, for any position under the government. Has had four years' experience in his present position, and knows more of his duties than any committee that could be selected to examine him in regard to them.

2. Over 50 years old, has been a merchant for many years, a correct business man of strict integrity, energetic, good business education, clear-headed and faithful in discharge of duty; he too has had four years' experience in his present position.

3. 50 years old, formerly proprietor of a printing establishment, competent and faithful, with good judgment, and four years' experience in his present position.

4. Over 50 years of age, a lawyer of good standing, well educated, able, faithful and zealous.

5. Over 50 years of age, of large business experience, formerly a canal superintendent, good education and abilities, active and faithful, and peculiarly well fitted for his position.

6. Over 30 years old, a merchant who left his business to go into the army, where he lost an arm; of correct habits, good education, faithful and well qualified.

7. Over 30 years old, farmer and schoolmaster, well educated, lieutenant and captain in the service for four years, well qualified for his position.

8. Over 50 years old, farmer, formerly county auditor, a superior man in every respect, fine education and large business experience.

9. Over 50 years old, a lawyer of good abilities, high character, great industry, and a first-class officer.

10. Over 30 years old, a good lawyer, well educated, of correct habits, faithful and fitted for any government office; was colonel of a regiment in the late rebellion, and was greatly distinguished in the service.

11. Over 60 years old, was clerk of court for many years, of high standing, large official experience, a first-class man, with no defect as an officer except age.

12. Over 40 years of age, a physician, highly educated in European schools, of great abilities and large experience; fit for any government office; was in the military service in the war of the rebellion.

These appointments have been made on my recommendation, which was given in nearly every instance because of my personal knowledge of the fitness of the appointees; and I may here say, by way of general answer to several of your inquiries, that in this district, since my accession to the office of assessor, the employés of the United States revenue service have been as carefully selected with reference to qualification and merit, and with as little regard to personal or political considerations, as the employés of any private business establishment in the district.

Promotions in the revenue service in the country districts cannot occur, as the law requires each assistant assessor to be a resident of his division; nor does long service, without zeal and high character, (which neither education, competitive tests, nor constant employment can give,) add to the efficiency of revenue officers.

Under the present system there can be no grades of office in the assessment districts. The same duties are to be performed by all assistants, and all should be equally well qualified. The frequent changes in the revenue laws prevent officers from acquiring permanent and useful knowledge of official duty by experience.

If it be desirable that those who execute the laws should be prepared for that service by a course of study and experimental labor required by law, it is also essential that those *who make the laws* should "pass rigid test examinations" to give evidence of their fitness for their duties before being allowed to discharge them. The imperfections of the internal revenue system, and errors in its workings, are mainly attributable to defects in the law, and the cumbrous and unwieldy machinery prescribed by law for its execution. I have no hesitation in saying that so far as I have knowledge or information in regard to the character, experience and ability of the officers of the internal revenue service, they not only compare favorably with the lawgivers of the nation, but have merit and ability above the average standard required for the making of a respectable congressman.

As you have called for my "comments on the condition of the civil service, and the best method of making it more effectual," I will very frankly state that, in my judgment, nothing could be more disastrous than an attempt to create a civil service system in analogy to military service in the regular army, and borrowed from the governments of Europe least popular and most antagonistic to republicanism.

The theory is totally opposed to our system of responsibility to the people, is exceedingly unpopular, and its adoption would be temporary. It would only tend to derange our executive system for a time, and could not last two years before it would be made a political test question, and it would be buried with the party which advocated it by a popular majority that would be overwhelming. A permanent army of civil-service men, nearly as large as our armed forces during the war, fastened upon our government, irresponsible to the people, and creating a distinct caste, segregated from and independent of the people, would become so offensive in this free government as not only to arouse a great political storm, but to cover with popular odium all connected with it.

The tendency of the popular will and judgment *is towards making all offices elective;* even the judiciary in perhaps all of the States has been made elective through this tendency; and so jealous are the people that it has long been difficult to maintain a small regular army, and a military establishment as large as the proposed civil establishment would never be permitted. Our people learned to appreciate the great efficiency of the volunteer service during the war, and were taught that from the farm, the office and the workshop could be furnished soldiers and officers superior often to the hotbed growths of a permanent military service establishment.

Even, therefore, if the proposed civil service system would be more efficient for the execution of our laws than the present, its unpopularity would be an insuperable objection to its adoption. It would be too ephemeral to be of any benefit, and the derangement of the public business by its brief use should prevent its adoption.

I cannot, however, believe that the system proposed would secure more competent officers or better and more prompt and faithful discharge of public duties. It is the people's business that is to be done, their interests to be cared for, and any removal of the people's agents from direct responsibility to their principals would be unwise and improper.

While in the Comptroller's office at Washington I had good opportunities for testing your proposed system, for up to that time it was acted upon in the departments. A majority of the clerical force of the Treasury Department were old clerks with assured positions, trained for years in the department, and rising in grade by promotion for seniority and merit. In the bureau of which I was at the head of the clerical force were some clerks who had been in the service for from 20 to 50 years. I found it true that few died, none resigned, and removals seldom occurred. The old clerks, the "civil-service men," were numerous enough to control and shape the business of the department. I saw daily the effects of such a system in the creation of a "circumlocution office," such as was satirized by Dickens; "red tape" circumscribed everything; dreary routine wore out all energy and life in performance of duty; the civil-service men walked the treadmill of daily duty as patiently and lifelessly as blind old horses, "assured of their positions." They put in so many hours of each day in feeble, slow efforts "how not to do it." Arrearages accumulated, ancient precedents clogged all rapid action, and served as pretexts for needless delays, unjust settlements, and unintelligent rulings. I can imagine no worse fate for a young, vigorous, energetic man of brains than the stifling life of a department clerk under this circumlocutory system of service, and no more inefficient way of doing the public business.

In the comptroller's office I had the assistance of three or four clerks newly appointed and fresh from active life, with hopes of return to the outer world of life and action, who looked upon rotation in office as safety to themselves, and as beneficial to the service in frequently infusing new blood and vigor into the executive offices. I can remember well one John Bedel, a young lawyer from New Hampshire, fresh, active, and hopeful, whose official duties were performed with zeal and intelligence, who was not satisfied merely to sit six hours a day at his desk, but who averaged 10 or 12 hours a day of hard, exciting, official labor, who almost terrified the dreary, sleepy old clerks by his energy, and who in a day would get through more actual work than any two of the old civil-service men could do in a week. I noticed many such cases, and all satisfied me that the civil service in the departments needed reform by adopting a system of frequent changes, and bringing the employés of the government more directly under the control of the people.

In all popular governments short, prescribed terms of service in civil office is an unvarying rule. Experience, justice, and sound judgment all justify it. Life tenures of office are odious in all republics; they are corrupting and paralyzing, and no State constitution now exists which recognizes them. In no constitutional convention in the last thirty years have there been found politicians or statesmen who had the hardihood to defend the life tenure-of-office theory. Experience, therefore, certainly shows that the innovation proposed in the civil service bill is unpopular, dangerous, and without precedent.

You will excuse the freedom and extent of my comments. I understood them to be invited, and I felt glad of the opportunity of stating freely and at length my views. I now give them without personal or political bias. Politically I am without party affiliation, and personally I cannot in any way suffer by the adoption or rejection of the proposed civil-service system.

I have only to add, in response to the 37th question and last, that my experience and observation have led me to believe that in the execution and administration of the internal revenue laws, it would be well to abolish the offices of district assessors and collectors, and substitute a deputy commissioner of internal revenue for each State, with his office at the capital of the State, and with the same powers within his jurisdiction that are conferred upon the chief commissioner at Washington, though subordinate to him. The clerical force of his office would not be more costly than the allowance for clerk-hire to the district assessors now is. There should be one inspector or police agent for each State, subordinate to the deputy commissioner, and one United States assistant treasurer under his control and orders. With this system adopted there would need to be but one collector in each county in the State paid by salary, (or the county treasurer might be authorized to receive United States taxes,) and but one assessor for each county where the total internal revenue taxes would not exceed $100,000 per year, (the number proportionally increased in counties where larger assessments would be made,) to be paid by commissions not to exceed $2,000 each per year.

I know that this system would be better, more efficient, and more economical than the present, and I could give many reasons for its adoption, and merely suggest that I believe the district system causes or encourages and furnishes facilities for the commission of nearly all of the great whiskey frauds.

I have not the slightest idea, however, that Congress will ever make a change such as I have suggested, for the reason that politicians, the men who get into Congress, generally *first* look to political results even regardless of the interests of the country, and district assessors and collectors, with their subordinates, furnish too often an active corps to manage conventions and secure nominations in the interests of congressmen to be dispensed with.

In fact, I fear that civil-service bills, civil-tenure laws, and projects for the reformation of the civil service, have had their origin or adoption in the fears and jealousies of politicians who think more of the success of "the party" than the good of the country, and who would cripple their adversaries by depriving them of political appliances that they would gladly use themselves, if they still had the manipulation of them.

O. L. Mann, collector of internal revenue, Chicago, Illinois:

37. I am of the opinion that the efficiency of the civil service can be greatly increased by the adoption of a carefully arranged system of examination of candidates for appointment to government offices, and a plan for promotion for meritorious services.

There are a large number of general and special agents connected with the revenue department whose services could be dispensed with if certain modifications of the law are made.

Duncan Furguson, assessor, Rickford, Illinois:

33. Certainly. Just what is wanted.

34. It could in populous districts, but in the rural districts the extent of territory that would be in a division, if they were made larger, would be inconvenient to the tax-payers.

35. Most unquestionably. Until this mode is adopted in the civil service of the country, I have no hesitancy in stating that the class of men who will be desirous of entering it will not be of a high grade of talent or likely to make efficient officers, nor generally would they be of a high standard of honesty or integrity.

36. None.

37. There is no doubt but that great frauds have been committed on the revenue, and I presume they will continue to be perpetrated until the present system is altered nearly to what is suggested in question 35. Men who enter the service now are generally of that class who have no particular business or profession, and who want some temporary employment until something better turns up; and I need not say that many of such a class will not hesitate to take bribes to look over frauds, when they think they can do so without detection. When officers can be turned out of office at any time without any charge being preferred against them and without any reference as to whether they have been good and efficient officers or not, it cannot be expected that a high state of attainment will be reached. I may be more in favor of the course suggested in question 35, from having been educated in Scotland, where very nearly this course is adopted, and although the tax on high wines is higher than with us, yet there is no difficulty in collecting the tax, and frauds either by the distiller or of officers conniving at the frauds are of rare occurrence.

Permit me to suggest, that, in my opinion, revenue officers who have been found guilty of, or in any way implicated in frauds, have not been punished in such a manner as to be a terror to others from following in the same course. When an officer is found to be concerned in any way in these frauds, he ought to be punished with the utmost rigor of the law. But how is it done? One of the officers in this district, a distillery inspector, (now discharged,) was implicated with the distiller in a fraud to a large amount. It was proved in an investigation before the United States commissioner by the district attorney that the fraud was committed by the distiller, and that it was impossible to have been done without the officer being cognizant of the fact. The distiller was allowed to settle by paying a fine of $2,500, and the inspector by paying a like fine. The back taxes assessed by me on the liquors fraudulently conveyed away amounted to over $26,000. Was that any punishment for a fraud of this amount?

I presume that in very few districts have there been fewer changes for political consideration than in this.

R. B. Noleman, collector of internal revenue, Centralia, Illinois:

The present system of collecting by one general deputy seems to work satisfactorily to this office, but tax-payers in some instances complain at not having local deputies. In districts situated as this is, where we have more frequently to inquire who will accept, rather than who is the most competent, it is a difficult matter to adopt any system based upon merit and competency. I have but four subordinates—three deputies and one clerk—and none of these have been appointed or hold their situations from any other consideration than that of

In the assessing department of this district there have been many changes, both of assessors and assistant assessors; and many of these changes have been made without reference to the qualifications of the incumbent or the applicant, but entirely from political considerations, which has necessarily caused a great falling off of the revenue in this district during the last year. You will find herewith annexed answers to some of your interrogatories, corresponding to the numbers in the same.

W. C. Flagg, collector internal revenue, Alton, Illinois, thinks—

The civil service could be improved by the three following steps, *taken together*:

1. Increasing salaries and making them fixed, not contingent at least on matters beyond the control of the officer.

2. Severe tests of ability and integrity applied to all applicants, and statedly to all incumbents.

3. A wider margin of discretion to officers so approved, that the spirit rather than the letter of the law might be executed.

Nathan M. Knapp, collector of internal revenue, Winchester, Illinois:

I will venture a suggestion; that is, in regard to the revenue agents or foot-loose inspectors. It seems to me that the amount of good they do the government is hardly equal to the expense. In every county there are two or more revenue officials, who from their knowledge of the people are better qualified to judge in cases of fraud or evasion than a stranger, and who will often secure to the government all its rights without expense and vexatious litigation, where an inspector moved by a desire to do something or to make something must involve the government and citizens in a controversy upon technical grounds, fruitless in the end and calculated to bring the government and the revenue system into odious disrepute. I think there are too many inspectors.

Jackson Grimshaw, collector of internal revenue, Quincy, Illinois:

No storekeepers, inspectors, or officers of any class should be paid fees or any other compensation by the tax-payer. Government should pay all compensation to officers and should not directly or indirectly compel tax-payers to pay storekeepers, inspectors, &c., fees. Moieties or shares should be abolished and government officers should rely on government for compensation and costs of seizures. All money made by seizures should go into the Treasury Department to be used as taxes, and no portion used up as moieties or shares.

Quincy D. Whitman, assessor internal revenue, Ottawa, Illinois:

Among other things I think it would be a great saving to the government if the services of the large number of special revenue agents, that are now swarming through this section of the country pretending to detect frauds on the government, could be dispensed with. There are, perhaps, some honest ones among them; but it is well known to all revenue officers, as far as my knowledge extends, that, as a class, these agents, (or, as they style themselves, "government detectives,") while they pretend to work for the interest of the government, work for themselves, and many of them have become wealthy in their operations. I believe, as a general thing, one general revenue inspector is all that is required in one district.

C. M. Hammond, collector internal revenue, Joliet, Illinois:

Dispense with special treasury agents in a great measure.

H. L. Bryant, assessor internal revenue, Lewistown, Illinois:

No. 34. In this particular branch of service, I believe an equal amount of work could be accomplished better under such a system, but not by a less number, because county lines are the boundaries of the different divisions in the district, and residents of the counties are better acquainted with the persons and business of a county than a stranger would be, although residing in a contiguous county.

No. 35. I think they could.

No. 36. There are not.

No. 37. I would respectfully suggest, in answer to interrogatory No. 37, that the very short period of time I have been in the service of the government of the United States, and from my limited experience, my opinions or suggestions would not perhaps be entitled to very much weight. Notwithstanding, I will give my idea of such matters as have come under my cognizance and seem to me to need reform.

In relation to the office of revenue inspector: this officer is employed by the government at an expense of five dollars per day, and his duty is that of ferreting out frauds upon the revenue. He is not always appointed from the district or districts in which he is to act, and consequently is a stranger to the localities through which he travels, and is not presumed to know of the secret places where illicit manufactures may be carried on, and where frauds may be perpetrated.

In my short experience I do not know of any beneficial result to the revenue arising from his efforts. By the law as it exists, it is the duty of the assessor of his district to report any frauds upon the revenue that may come to his knowledge to the collector, whose duty it is to make seizures, arrests, &c. Under the present system, by the time the assessor has notified the collector of a fraud that he has ferreted out, the guilty parties may, and frequently do, get wind of the matter, and make their escape.

In my judgment it would tend to make this branch of the service more efficient and economical to dispense altogether with revenue inspectors, and not only empower but require the assessor of his district to canvass the same; and when he detects frauds on the revenue, to make arrests and seizures as an executive officer. As I understand the law, the assessor, as far as frauds upon the revenue are concerned, acts merely as a spy or informer.

If the office of revenue inspector could be safely dispensed with and the duties of this office be performed by the assessor, as suggested, it strikes me that it would be an immense saving in the expense of conducting this branch of the service.

David T. Little, collector, eighth district, Illinois:

No. 34. An equal amount of work under such a system could be accomplished by a much less number of persons than are now employed.

No 35. If the employment was assured and certain, and promotion granted only to seniority or merit, and no discharge permitted except for cause, I am of the opinion a much higher grade of talent could be induced to enter the government service.

No. 36. There are no females among my subordinates.

No. 37. The action of Congress in the abolition of the bonded system, through which the major part of the enormous frauds upon the revenue have been committed, meets with my hearty approval. Under the operation of the new law, the chief source of fraud upon the revenue, in my judgment, has been closed up. The most satisfactory evidence of this fact is that there are but a very few distilleries in active operation in the northwest. The statistics in the Treasury Department show that, while the tax upon distilled spirits ranged from 20 to 50 cents per proof gallon, more revenue was paid into the treasury of the United States in any given time than has been collected and paid since the tax was increased to $2 per proof gallon in the same stated time. The only hypothesis upon which this state of facts can be explained is, that the inducements to fraud and collusion between officers and manufacturers are so great under the present system of taxation that a general demoralization of subordinate officers and distillers has been the result. I therefore respectfully recommend to your honorable committee the careful consideration of the question of the reduction of the tax upon distilled spirits as a means of increasing the revenue of the government. On account of the inadequate compensation paid to revenue inspectors, general inspectors of spirits, and United States storekeepers, I would respectfully recommend that the law be so changed as to reduce the number of these officers and an increase of the per diem of those who may be retained or hereafter appointed to these places. By this change in the law a higher class of business talent, and a higher standard of morals, could be induced to enter the civil service. I think in my district one efficient officer could discharge all the duties embraced in the office of storekeeper where the distilleries are located in close proximity to each other, as in cities and towns that now have three, four, six, and even more. I think that the law as it now is with reference to the compensation of collectors is imperfect in many parts. This class of officers receive more for their services than they should in many cases, while in many other cases the pay is inadequate to insure the services of good competent men. I think that collectors and deputy collectors should be paid a sufficient salary to insure the services of good men, and that the commissions now provided by law on the collections of a district should be discontinued. I deem it proper to state in this connection that, if the law was so changed, the collector of the eighth district of Illinois would receive a less compensation for his services than he now does. The law authorizing the appointment of an almost unlimited number of itinerant revenue agents, most of whom are appointed through political influences and without regard to their qualifications, should be entirely abolished; this change alone in the law would save the government an immense amount of money. The same duties now performed by them are also enjoined upon the revenue inspectors of districts, and by whom the duties could be as well and efficiently performed, particularly if the pay of revenue inspectors was increased.

Jonathan Biggs, assessor 11th district, Salem, Illinois:

In answer to the 37th and last question, I am constrained to believe that the interest of the civil government would be subserved if those, and only those, who are duly qualified and diligent in their duty be retained in the service of the government. From my short experience in this department, I have become fully satisfied that in many instances where changes have been urged on political grounds, the government is always the loser. And so long as this practice is pursued there will remain uncollected large amounts of revenue which is justly due.

W. S. Cunningham, collector of internal revenue, Danville, Illinois:

Retain men for merit and integrity; take the service out of politics as much as possible; punish unfaithfulness surely and severely, but investigate both sides of all cases when charges are preferred.   Tax whiskey $1 per gallon on capacity of still, and enforce the criminal law against delinquent distillers and whiskey thieves.

Hageman Tripp, assessor internal revenue, 3d district, Indiana:

No. 37. Select men for merit alone; have them realize that their retention in office depends upon the discharge of their whole duty, and that they must earn promotion by diligence and labor.   Throw *party* to the dogs and you would make the civil service quite respectable, as well as more efficient and economical.

G. N. Stevenson, collector of internal revenue, Aurora, Indiana, after expressing his approval of the proposed reform, and after stating that he is in favor of adopting the same system for the civil service as that governing the army, explains as follows:

I have no comments to make further than to explain my answer to question 33 in so far as it relates to the test by which qualifications for office should be determined.   I think the test should not be a strictly educational or theoretical one, and that a general knowledge of business, and particularly of such business as may be similar in its details to that of the office to which an applicant may aspire, should have fully as much weight as theoretical acquirements such as are obtained by a course in a collegiate or commercial institute.   In proof of this position, I would state that two of my subordinates best prepared to stand an examination like the one last alluded to have proved to be of the least account.

William Grose, collector internal revenue, New Castle, Indiana:

In the revenue service, in my judgment, a serious error exists in the great number of revenue agents, inspectors, and detectives, that have been appointed with their unlimited expenditures.   Their present duties should be performed by collectors, deputies, assessors, and assistants.

My observations satisfy me of the total incompetency of a great number of the assistant assessors.   In this district we have three efficient, industrious, and competent assistants, two totally incompetent, and one neglectful of the duties of his office, following the legal profession closely to the detriment of the revenue.

A. H. Brown, collector of internal revenue, Indianapolis, Indiana, after declaring himself emphatically in favor of the proposed reform, states:

We have noticed that the principal sometimes filled the subordinate places with relatives, or the relatives of politicians to whom he was indebted for favors.   Selections for examinations (candidates) should not be made from relatives of the principal or of his political friends, but from meritorious young men.

Advocates the priority principle only when accompanied by *merit*.   Frequent examinations might correct the evil of continuing in place an inferior officer simply because he held the oldest commission.   He advocates an annual salary for assistant assessors instead of the per diem compensation, and states that a chief clerk with $1,000 is allowed in his district, though the services of such an officer are required for only three months.

A. J. Pope, collector internal revenue, Sigourney, Iowa:

33. I believe it would be the best system that could be adopted.
34 and 35. In my opinion, yes.
36. There are no females among my subordinates.
37. The adoption of a system that would secure the appointment to office of competent persons without regard to personal or party considerations; that would make retention and advancement in office dependent upon faithful and meritorious conduct; that would not make removals upon the representations of "rings" or cliques, but only upon proven charges of incompetency or dishonesty.

I make these suggestions because of the fact that to learn the duties of the service is not the work of a day only, but should be the study of years.

D. B. Henderson, collector internal revenue, Dubuque, Iowa:

I am bitterly opposed to the present system of giving moieties to informers.   It is a great source of corruption; does more to make expense to the government than to lessen expense. It causes unwarranted seizures and persecutions; it taints the action of officers who seize or prosecute, and brings unprincipled and avaricious men into the service.   So baneful has been the influence of this system upon the public that they are predisposed to take the side of violators, believing that the hope of gaining a moiety has induced some government agent to take advantage of some accidental or inadvertent step made by the party who is prosecuted.   Every lawyer who defends violators of the laws of the United States, thunders the words "moiety" and "blood money" at the juries until the government agent appears a Shylock and the whiskey-thief an Antonio.   Let officers be carefully selected, well paid, and give them no compensation but their salaries and commissions.

Cole Noel, assessor internal revenue, Adel, Iowa:

So far as concerns the sub-revenue branch of the civil service, I would, upon further consideration, respectfully make the following suggestion:

If the time from which special taxes commence running (May 1st) were changed to January 1st, to correspond with income tax, and the annual assessment were ordered in January instead of March, I have strong reason to believe that the work of assessing and collecting would be more thoroughly, more easily and speedily done, and, of course, more economically, and that it would result in an increase of revenue to the government.

Jos. E. Lancaster, collector of internal revenue, Nebraska City:

Examinations alone could not decide in that part of the country; as in addition to business talent, the positions for the revenue require industry, pluck, and considerable knowledge frontier life.

F. Renner, assessor of internal revenue, Nebraska City:

Urges a heavy special or license tax as a substitute of the present tax upon distilled spirits; further, the more efficient administration of justice and the withdrawal of the power of compromise from the judicial officers. No procrastination in revenue cases, as quashing indictments, entering *nolle prosequi*, &c., should be permitted in the revenue cases, and all decisions be prompt and decisive.

District attorneys should never be permitted to have law partners actually acting as attorneys for the defendant while carrying on the prosecution for the government.

J. C. Geer, collector internal revenue, Boise City, Idaho Territory:

Suggests that the civil service be placed upon the same footing as the military service as far as the tenure of office is concerned. He knows from experience that it is simply impossible to defraud the government out of one dime without either gross negligence or complicity on the part of the officials. He urges upon Congress the necessity of doing away with the present army of useless agents and the adoption of some such system as proposed, and of using a fair proportion of the money saved by abolishing all useless appendages of the government in paying honest and efficient officers a fair salary, in which case the service would, in his opinion, be better performed, and at less aggregate cost to the government than in any other country in the world.

He states that there are two special Indian agents in Boise City, Idaho Territory, who are drawing $1,500 per annum each, and *literally doing nothing*. He does not suppose for a moment that they are the only agents paid by the government for doing nothing. Let economy reach those ornamental gentlemen as well as the hard-working revenue officer.

D. Mills, assessor internal revenue, Dakota Territory:

No. 1. Under the present system of appointment, which is but a system of party affiliation or favoritism, it often happens that those are selected whose only qualifications are that they are good political managers; and such a recommendation does not speak well in a moral point of view.

No. 2. It may happen that a person is appointed to some position who, at the time of receiving the appointment, was not conversant with the routine of business, but by study and perseverance has become master of the situation. In such a case it would be but poor reward for his diligence and labor to be cast to the winds simply because the political complexion of the times had changed.

No. 3. Let the appointee at the time of receiving the appointment understand that he will be continued in position so long as he is a faithful and competent officer and consults the interest of his government, and in so doing his own. I believe that under such a condition of things the government would be vastly the gainer; that officers engaged in the service of the government would discharge their duty far better I have not a doubt. But as it now is there are a thousand temptations to neglect some portion of their duty. Some influential person is to be conciliated, or he will use his influence to get me out of office; but were it known by the officer that he would be removed only for neglect of duty, he would at all times do his duty. I have not a doubt millions might be saved to the government by adopting such a line of policy. Politics should not enter into the consideration, for I know of none who would not make any sacrifice to save our country from wrong. We may differ as to the best means to arrive at the same end. We cannot take a difference of opinion as an evidence of disloyalty.

F. W. Swift, postmaster, Detroit, Michigan:

35. Emphatically; yes. This is the great curse of the service. The uncertainty of their positions debars many, whose services would be very valuable to the government, from accepting them. This is especially the evil in the postal service and should be remedied.

36. There are eight females among the clerks of this office. I consider them fully as competent as males; quiet, unobtrusive and diligent in the performance of their duties. For

this service I recommend their employment. I believe the service would be vastly benefited by a system of appointment and promotion for merit alone, and retention in office during good behavior.

N. G. Isbell, collector of customs, Detroit, Michigan:

I think the efficiency of the service would be increased by such a system of appointments as is indicated in this interrogatory, (33,) providing the rule of removing for cause is strictly enforced.

Under such a system I have no doubt an equal amount of work could be accomplished by a less number of persons than are now employed.

In this country, where there are so many fields of private enterprise inviting the energies of young men, I do not think a higher grade of talent would be attracted to subordinate public service by the conditions named in this interrogatory (35) than now seeks such service for temporary purposes and on account of business disappointment; but if the appointing and promoting power were protected from political influences, persons of less talent and qualities for usefulness would be excluded from the service.

Under the license given me to state any matters in my judgment that would tend to make the civil service more efficient and economical, I have to say briefly, in regard to that branch of the service in which I am engaged, that though great improvement has been manifest within the last few years, I am of the opinion that the customs service of the country at large is more loosely and extravagantly officered than any other branch of the civil service of long-established standing with which I am acquainted. This comes partly from the necessarily irregular character of most of the service, making it difficult for persons in charge to know when subordinate service is laboriously discharging its full duty or when "shirking" labor; but mainly from the fact that it has long been the practice of political parties and politicians in power to seek positions as "tide-waiters," where the duty is supposed to be nominal, for persons who are supposed to have rendered, and are expected yet to render, some service to their parties, but who are not qualified by energy and application to maintain themselves in private business dependent upon energy and integrity. Though I cannot complain of any such interference in my own case, I can conceive of cases where collectors and others in charge of subordinate service might overlook inefficiency on the part of employés, fearing that their own tenure of office might be affected by thus incurring the disapprobation of friends who have influence at court. The public at large have also arrived at a very low standard of morals on this subject of official responsibility in the customs service, doing great injury to persons engaged in its duties. It is generally supposed that the custom-house is full of fat sinecures, and when a man receives an appointment to the service, and, in answer to the inquiry of his friends or acquaintances as to the worth of his office, says his salary is "two," "three," or "four" dollars per day, the reply is, "Oh, yes, I know that is the *salary*, but what is the stealing?" Thus encouraging him to think that to obtain compensation beyond the provision of the law will be regarded as legitimate by his friends and the public. For this crying evil of which I have spoken, in the official organization and administration of the service, there can be no remedy but in subjecting *all* appointments of collectors to a rigid test of fitness, and prohibiting their removal, except for cause well supported. The same rule should be applied to the subordinate service, making the tolerance of inefficiency on the part of subordinate service one of the causes for which a collector may be removed.

F. W. Curtenius, collector of internal revenue, Kalamazoo, Michigan:

Does not think that the service of females could be made efficient in the collecting department, or brought within the range of propriety.

In regard to the collection of the revenue, he declares that men of large incomes have not always been deterred from rendering false and fraudulent returns from the fact that they have relied too much upon the interposition of senators and representatives to have their penalties and fines remitted by the department, and in some cases have measurably succeeded. They seem to overlook the fact that favors bestowed upon the guilty result in great injustice to the innocent and honest tax-payer.

George Q. Erskine, collector of internal revenue, Milwaukee; appointed 1867:

37. There are two or three points I will give you my opinion upon. The law as it now stands, requiring the tax on all high wines to be paid at the distillery, is right. This law will save millions to the treasury the coming year. I think that storekeepers of distillery bonded warehouses (class A) should be required to be at the distillery at all times when the distillery is running, and distillers not allowed to run unless they are there. The office of assistant assessor in charge of distilleries would, in that case, be unnecessary, as it is now, in my opinion, of no benefit to the government. I think the bill before Congress requiring the stamping of all packages of tobacco and all cigars is a step in the right direction. It appears to me that the law relating to the collection of taxes on tobacco and cigars is very inadequate to the detection of frauds, and should be thoroughly revised. The bill introduced, I think, by Senator Patterson, looking to the doing away with the appointment of special

treasury agents and others, and in their stead having 25 agents to be nominated by the President and confirmed by the Senate, will save the government a large sum of money. Besides, I think it will improve the efficiency of the revenue service. I state my views on these points with some hesitancy, in view of my limited experience.

J. H. Warren, collector of internal revenue, Albany, Wisconsin :

Fully agrees with the report of Commissioner Rollins, and with the remedies he proposes. The present evils of the revenue service are not as much due to the defectiveness of the law as to the indolence, inefficiency, and corruption of revenue officers.

To remedy this, the Commissioner should have the power to remove for cause any revenue officer and to appoint his successor.

To require a man to be responsible for the proper administration of a department so important as that of the revenue of the government, and at the same time deprive him of the authority to select and govern his subordinates, seems to me unjust, unwise, and highly prejudicial to the best interests of the government.

He is powerless to remedy the evil growing out of the practices of the corrupt and inefficient for the reason that he has no authority to remove them and appoint in their stead honest, capable, and diligent men.

Until this power is given to the Commissioner I am unable to understand or conceive how he can even retrieve the revenue service from the reproach under which it is rapidly falling.

Luke A. Taylor, assessor of internal revenue, Prescott, Wisconsin :

Suggests a law giving the entire amount of fines for fraud to the informant, who should be responsible for costs if the case failed. This would secure increased revenue by removing temptations to combine with offenders in the commission of frauds, and take from the transgresser the ability to compromise with officers or others who may have discovered the cause of complaint.

Jacob S. Bugh, assessor internal revenue, Wautoma, Wisconsin :

Twenty-four persons in favor of the proposed reform. Urges that the office of general inspector of spirits and the office of inspector of tobacco, snuff, and cigars should be abolished, and the duties now performed by such inspectors devolve upon assistant assessors.

He further urges the collection of taxes on distilled spirits at the still, and the abolishing of all bonded warehouses.

He attributes the present evils of the revenue system to the frequent removal of revenue officers, and to the failure of the courts to heartily co-operate with revenue officers in the enforcement of the law, particularly that relating to distilled spirits.

C. Shuter, collector of internal revenue, Sparta, Wisconsin :

Thinks the proposed reform will most undoubtedly be beneficial, as is satisfactorily known in the English system of examination for civil officers.

37. I would suggest that the pay of assessor and collector of internal revenue should be graduated according to the amount of labor and responsibility of their offices ; that all fees or commissions should be discontinued ; all subordinate officers of the revenue, as deputy collectors, inspectors, &c., should be paid by the department ; that the bonds of the several officers of the government should be graduated according to the amount of responsibility or amount of moneys passing through their hands, and not, as now, according to the office they hold. All inspectors are required to give bonds in $5,000. I have two inspectors of cigars in this district, the amount of whose compensation is less than $25 per annum, and they consent to act at all only to oblige me. My office as disbursing agent requires me to give bonds to the amount of $10,000 ; the amount disbursed by me to others than myself will not average $850 per month, and which disbursements are made monthly by me as soon as money is received for the purpose. I think it of the utmost importance that all civil officers should be qualified for the offices with which they are intrusted, and that politics should not be considered a necessary qualification. I am of the opinion that but too many holding responsible positions are totally unqualified, and that the whole of their duties are performed by their subordinates. I would respectfully call your attention to the great disparity between the compensation of collectors in thickly and sparsely-settled districts. The commissions of the former are very large in many instances, while in the latter both salary and commissions amount to the sum paid to not high-class clerks.

Thomas Moonlight, collector internal revenue, Kansas :

36. There are no females among my subordinates. Females could not be employed except as clerks in my department.

37. I have said so much in the 36 preceding that there is but little left to say. One of the greatest curses of the revenue department is that of secret special agents. They are rotten to the core, and may very justly be termed the leeches of the revenue department, for, having the confidential private ear of the department, their every word is believed, to the injury of both tax-payers and revenue officers. There is not a revenue officer to-day but who

is at the mercy of these secret agents, and must do their bidding, right or wrong. For instance: a collector makes a seizure; a special agent slips in, and having the private ear of the department, lays before the different officers a statement of facts which blinds the department; the collector is ordered to release at once, and is threatened with beheading, perhaps, while the agent has rolls of greenbacks in his pocket for the part he has played. The fraud continues, and so the thing goes on. Sweep away all political interference with the offices; make the civil service as near as possible to the military, and with a discriminating judgment in making the first selection of officers to fill all the offices of trust and profit, from the highest to the lowest; fraud will hide its head and secret detectives will have to look for some honest way of making a living. I only wish I were present to talk with you instead of writing, but I presume you have much better counsel.

Thomas L. Sternberg, assessor of internal revenue, Lawrence, Kansas:

Rather evasive on the subject of reform, but elaborately calling attention to the vast difference in the compensation of assessors compared with the amount of labor performed by each, which is lighter in eastern and populous than in remote western and scantier districts.

John S. McFarland, assessor of internal revenue, 2d district, Kentucky:

Is rather inclined to believe that if the employment was assured on account of merit alone and no removals permitted except for cause, that it might and would be the means in the course of time of redeeming the employés in the revenue department from the terrible suspicion that now rests upon them, in consequence of the frequency and magnitude of the frauds committed upon the revenue.

He thinks that a uniform salary of $2,000 should be allowed assessors and no commission allowed unless their assessments exceed $300,000 or $400,000. This change could be made without increasing the aggregate cost; I presume it would be reduced; as the law now stands they only get $1,500 salary, less five per cent. on $500 thereof, unless their assessments exceeds $100,000, and their commissions upon sums above that until their pay may reach $4,000. But in my district, and I presume in a great many others, under the $1,000 our assessments do not reach $100,000; consequently we have to live and support our family on $1,675 per annum; and I assure you, at the present rate of house-rent and provisions, I have precious little left of my salary to buy clothes with.

John R. Beckley, collector of internal revenue, Shelbyville, Kentucky, (52 persons under his control:)

37. It is my opinion that if the appointments in that grade of the service were made from candidates whose fitness for the appointment was evidenced by passing an examination conducted by competent persons, and the candidates should be required to produce testimonials of their integrity, honesty, moral and social worth, with assured and permanent employment, with promotions granted only for seniority, merit, or fitness, and no discharge permitted without good and sufficient cause, the efficiency of the service would be greatly increased.

F. C. James, collector of internal revenue, Mount Sterling, Kentucky, (9th district,) suggests:

That in frequent instances laws have been made and instructions issued that do not as well apply to widely extended, sparsely populated districts, situated in rural regions at great distances from the great commercial centres of the country, as to the more compact and densely populated districts. Frequently such regulations are of such a nature that the application of them is almost impossible. If the districts themselves were graded, and the regulations of the department made to suit the different grades, many difficulties under which we of the remote and weaker districts labor would be done away with, and the result would be advantageous perhaps to an economical and certainly to a more efficient execution of the revenue law.

W. J. Landram, collector of internal revenue, 8th district, Kentucky:

No. 37. I am of the opinion that assistant assessors ought to be paid only in proportion to the number of lists they take; and not $5 per diem for the days employed, and three cents per list, as under the present law. This objection to the law as it now stands is peculiarly applicable to the rural districts, where nearly all the assistants pursue some vocation in addition to that of assistant assessors; and when, no doubt, they often charge the $5.03 for every day they enter a list, even though the assessment against the tax-payer amounts to less than the compensation of the assistant assessor. There is no incentive to action other than his oath to do his duty, and a lazy assistant doubtless often waits for many a tax-payer to come to him who never comes, because he is satisfied the officer is too indolent to look him up. If the amount of his pay depended alone upon his vigilance, the revenue would be *materially* increased and the cost of the assessments doubtless diminished.

All will admit that it is more trouble to *collect* than to *assess* the tax. It is more laborious, more complicated, more perplexing, and more dangerous. And yet, if we examine the subject closely, it will be seen that the pay of the one who assesses is largely in advance of the one who collects. Take this district, for example.

The pay of the assessor, clerk, and assistant assessors for the nine months ending December 31, 1867, was as follows, after deducting tax :

April	$1,141 91
May	1,184 18
June	797 70
July	578 61
August	805 62
September	1,434 79
October	1,599 79
November	1,067 11
December	1,271 05
	9,880 76
Salary of collectors during that period, including tax	1,125 00
Commissions on amount collected, $63,296 67, at 3 per cent	1,898 96
	3,023 96

Thus it will be seen that while the cost of assessing during the nine months is near $10,000. The cost of collecting is not *one-third* that sum.

Out of the $3.023 96 cents aforesaid, the collector has to pay his deputies and the expenses of his office. It is true that all the taxes assessed during the period aforesaid have not yet been collected; but that will not *materially* affect the great disproportion between the relative cost of assessing and collecting. Whether this disparity exists in other districts I do not know, but think the probabilities are that in the rural districts particularly something of the kind will be found.

This is a mountainous district, composed of 18 counties, containing at least 150 miles square, embracing about one-fourth of the territory of the State; no railroads yet in operation, no telegraph, and no turnpikes except in three counties; the mails are carried chiefly on horse-back, except in some four counties. The population is sparse, and although the people are loyal to the government, it is difficult to obtain officers of the first order of qualifications, on account of the collections being small and the commissions correspondingly insignificant.

Rolfe S. Saunders, collector of internal revenue, Memphis, Tennessee:

Urges the preparation of a well-arranged digest of the revenue laws, rulings of the department, regulations, decisions of the courts, &c.

Samuel F. Cooper, collector of internal revenue, Van Buren, Arkansas:

No. 37. I would respectfully suggest that the present method of assessing and collecting revenue, with its scale of fees for subordinate officers, is both expensive and unjustly discriminating in its operations. My deputy collectors, as a class, are superior to the assistant assessors in talent and responsibility. Their labors often greater, yet their compensation bears no comparison to that of an assistant assessor. This district comprises 19 counties. It is cut up into 10 little divisions, with an assistant assessor in each; not one of them allows his revenue duties to interfere in the least with his regular business or profession, and all their charges are fearfully *constructive*. They charge not only for the days actually employed, but for the days upon which they are *ready and willing to be employed.*

I have carefully studied this matter, and am satisfied that the plan of dividing a district into petty divisions, with an assistant assessor to each, is a pernicious one, and opens a wide door to perjury and fraud. Four men, real live working men, could do the work of this district better than it is now done by ten, and at much less expense. The deputy collectors, as well as assistant assessors, should be appointed by, and responsible to, the Secretary of the Treasury; and above all, both should receive the same compensation, and no assessor or collector should henceforth be appointed till he shows a creditable record as a subordinate. And present incumbents, high or low, should by all means be required to give evidence before a proper board of examiners of their fitness, intellectually and *morally*.

States that he had 100 applications for employment since November 15, 1866, when he came into office. The oath prescribed by the act of July 2, 1862, render it almost impossible to procure suitable persons to fill the positions. Would probably have had 300 or 400 more applications had the parties been able to take the oath.

He advocates the payment of stated salaries to the employés in the collector's office, and to assistant assessors and their subordinates. This he thinks would secure competent men, which cannot be obtained under the present system, collectors being now compelled, from the small compensation received for their services, to employ deputies and clerks at rates for which honorable and competent men could hardly be expected to work.

Bernard Zwart, collector internal revenue, Ironton, Missouri, is emphatically in favor of reform, provided religious morality be also made a test.

He submits suggestions in paper A for the more efficient execution of the revenue laws, and in paper B about the tax on distilled spirits, &c., which are herewith annexed:

A.

The mode of collecting revenue and accounting therefor I consider deficient for the following reasons, to wit:

1st. It does not hold the collectors sufficiently responsible, and if they are so inclined it allows them the use of large amounts of money belonging to the government for a long period without the proper means to detect such use.

2d. It often operates harshly and unjustly on collectors, in large districts which are sparsely settled and where mail facilities and other means of communication are unsafe and unreliable, in holding them responsible for uncollectable taxes, which are too often assessed by assistant assessors on parties who are insolvent or are not liable to assessment.

First. To obtain an additional check on collectors I would suggest that all blank receipts issued by the department to collectors should be provided with or bear the impress of a stamp representing the money value for which it is to be a receipt, ranging from the smallest to the highest amount of tax assessed; that every collector should draw the receipts on quarterly requisitions based on the tax assessed on each quarterly list by him received from the assessor, the amount of which receipts should be charged to the collector, and against which he should be credited with the amount of money deposited each month. The daily collection book of the collector should contain an additional column showing the amount of receipts drawn by him from the department, as well as a column for total collections and total deposits, so that the difference between the aggregates of the first and last named columns will show the amount of stamped receipts and money he should have on hand at any time, and enable inspectors (to be appointed for that purpose) to verify the collector's accounts whenever desired. The collectors should also forward a monthly abstract from this book to the department and further be required to impress their own official seals on each receipt, and the collection of any taxes without issuing the proper receipt therefor, stamped and sealed as above stated, should make them or their deputies respectively, on conviction thereof, liable to punishment by fine and imprisonment, the fine to go to the informer, even if he induced the issuance of such receipt without the required seal and stamp.

This provision of law should be printed in large letters on stiff paper, and by the government furnished to all civil officers to be posted up in their offices in a conspicuous place, and a failure to do so should make the offender liable to punishment.

At the end of every quarter each collector should return to the department the stamped receipts remaining on hand at such time and belonging to the quarter for which he makes return; with the amount thereof he should be credited, provided he furnish within three months thereafter the proper vouchers to show that said taxes were not collectable and ought to be abated, as now provided for.

Second. For the protection of collectors and saving of considerable expense to the government, I would suggest that it should be provided by law that if any assessor return to the collector any assessment which is uncollectable at the time of the assessment by reason of the insolvency of the party assessed, his own liability to assessment, or other good cause, such assessment should be charged to the assessor (who should also be required to give bond) and credited to the collector on proof of the existence of such cause at the time of the assessment.

For the protection of the government and the assessor the latter should be furnished with blank applications for assessment of the different taxes and duties, at the head of which applications should be printed the provision of the law imposing such tax, and such application should contain a clause admitting that the applicant comes within such provisions, and be signed by the party applying, and any person liable to such tax and refusing to sign the proper application at the request of the assessor or assistant assessor should not be assessed but reported by the assessor to the United States attorney of the proper district for prosecution under section 73, act July 30, 1864, which section ought to be so amended as to make the offence punishable by imprisonment in all cases coming within the provision, as well as by fine, a moiety of which fine should go to the informer. This is necessary, as too often parties are assessed who are not liable under the law or who are really insolvent at the time, so as to make it impossible for the collector to collect the tax, thereby causing a vast amount of useless labor and consequent expense to the government, which might be saved by the exercise of reasonable diligence on the part of assessors and their assistants besides; as the law now stands parties who have no property liable to distraint too often carry on their business without paying their special taxes therefor, thereby defrauding the government and also doing an injustice to the well-disposed citizen without adequate means of redress.

In relation to all manufactured articles subject to duty it should be provided that the same shall be liable to assessment and seizure in the hands of any party after removal from the place of manufacture, unless the same be duly tax paid, which fact should be made to appear either by the proper stamp or collector's certificate, the expense of which certificate should be paid for by the party obtaining the same.

B

From observation in this district and elsewhere, I think that unless the tax on distilled spirits be reduced considerably, say to 50 cents per gallon, no spirits of any amount can be manufactured with the certainty that the tax thereon can be collected, because a high tax, as is now imposed, is too strong an inducement for fraudulent practices to be withstood by the generality of men engaged in that business; it is true that by strict surveillance and extraordinary exertions on the part of officials large frauds may be prevented for a while, especially when the market is glutted, but it is to be feared that such vigilance on the part of the officers will be but temporary, or at the utmost spasmodic, as their attention will be diverted by other official duties, or former exertions will be followed by corresponding inaction.

Most men engaged in the business of distilling seem to consider the existing law a violation of their rights, and look upon smuggling as merely a "*male prohibita*," not a "*male in se*;" and as the profits are enormous, if they succeed they are willing to pay the penalty, if detected, and in proportion as their means and ill-gotten gains give them influence, they will try to use that influence to the detriment of the government and public morality in the corruption of officials whenever possible, and whenever this fails, in denouncing and persecuting honest officers whom they find to be incorruptible; the result whereof is, that all officers connected with the revenue department fall into disrepute, and are looked upon with contempt by the honest masses, and that large amounts of revenue, which would be paid cheerfully if the tax were not prohibitory, are lost to the government.

Besides, the imposition of prohibitory taxation on any manufactured article has a tendency to drive men of moderate means (who are often the most conscientious, and satisfied with a reasonable profit) out of the business, to the detriment of the national industry, because such men cannot compete with their more wealthy neighbors, by investing their means which they need to carry on their business in the tax imposed, especially when, as it seems to be mostly the case with distilled spirits, their manufacture will not sell in the market for enough to pay the tax itself; hence the capital invested by such men in the erection of buildings, and the necessary stills, vessels, &c., becomes a dead capital for all practical purposes, which not seldom works the ruin of worthy citizens.

To establish a system of taxation which must under all circumstances prevent fraud is wellnigh an impossibility, yet it would seem that a system of moderate taxation of distilled spirits might be devised under which the manufacturer would fulfil all his obligations to the government rather than to run the danger of interference with his business by a non-compliance with the requisitions of the law, and which at the same time might stimulate him to devise and invent improvements in the mode and instruments of manufacture so as to produce the greater amount of the article taxed, from the same materials.

But to do this, the tax should be imposed upon the raw material instead of on the product, and as it has been ascertained to within a fraction what amount of spirits of a certain strength can, under existing circumstances, be obtained from a given amount of grain, it would only be necessary to impose such restrictions and safeguards on the manner of using the necessary materials for distilling purposes, that it would be impossible under any circumstances to perpetrate frauds therein, without almost certain detection.

If such a plan was adopted, by prohibiting distillers from grinding their own grain, or having it ground elsewhere, without a permit from the collector, describing the quantity and weight of the grain, place where to be ground, time allowed therefor, and for its conveyance to the distillery, and also the time within which it is to be placed in the fermenting tubs and worked off, it would seem that but little difficulty could exist to prevent a full assessment of the tax; or the fermenting tubs in every distillery might be numbered in regular order, which number, together with the capacity of the tubs (which latter should be proportionate to the distilling power of the still) and be branded thereon, and a record thereof should be kept in the collector's office; ten days before the first of the month the distiller should hand in to the assessor a statement in triplicate, designating by their numbers and capacity the fermenting tubs which he desires to fill for fermenting purposes, on each day in the month, also those from which he desires to draw for distilling purposes, (allowing only sufficient time for the purpose of fermentation,) and those which shall be empty at any given time in the month. From this statement the assessor should ascertain the tax, and forward the duplicate of such statement to the collector, and return the triplicate, with his certificate, to the distiller, to enable the inspector to ascertain at any time whether the proper fermenting tubs are filled, in use, or emptied as designated.

Or, if it be not considered desirable to assess the tax on the raw material, the tax might be assessed and collected by means of stamps of the value of the tax, to be procured by the distiller from the collector, and by the inspector to be attached to the barrel or keg containing the spirits and by him cancelled in a proper manner; the distiller should, however, obtain a credit of, say, three months, on all such stamps by him purchased, provided he gives therefor sufficient security to the collector to prevent loss to the government. This is necessary to enable the distiller to dispose of his distilled spirits by the time that he should pay the tax; and such distillers as should pay for the stamps in cash at the time of purchase should be allowed a sufficient discount thereon. Each inspector and distiller should make his returns as now required.

Tax on tobacco and cigars.—This tax I think should be collected by the use of stamps in the manner as last above suggested in relation to distilled spirits.

John H Fox, assessor internal revenue, De Soto, Missouri, makes the following suggestions:

As the tax has been taken off from cotton, and probably will be from a great majority of all industrial pursuits, that the revenue laws be so amended that assessors make returns of their monthly assessments to their respective collectors on or before the 10th of each succeeding month, in place of making same by the 20th of each succeeding month; and if the collector's time for making the collections be also shortened ten days, it will give him ample time, and I think have a tendency to lessen the delinquent list by one-half.

The collector should also make it the imperative duty of his deputies to visit all parts of their respective divisions to make the collections, and not make it the duty of the tax-payer to hunt him up to pay his tax. This I find to be a very general complaint among the parties that have been assessed with an annual or monthly tax. They seldom ever get a notice from the deputy collectors unless the penalty is attached, and then they are required to ride from 1 to 25 miles to settle the tax. My assistant assessors have from six to eight places, in each county, where they make regular appointments to meet the tax-payer. Each assistant sends out his notices a month ahead, besides giving each known tax-payer an individual notice to meet him on the appointed days. This gives general satisfaction; but the deputy collector sends out circulars, calling on the tax-payer to meet him at the county seat and settle their taxes, and never sends individual notices unless the penalty is attached.

I do not name this as applying to my district alone. It appears to be a general complaint, and ought to be remedied.

I have no other suggestions to make at present, and hope that the answers and suggestions may meet with your approval.

John Van Lear, assessor internal revenue, Hagerstown, Maryland:

Thinks the introduction of a civil service, with some such mode of appointment as is pursued in the army; some such means adopted as are combined under the heads of questions 33, 34, and 35, to regulate the appointment, advancement, and continuance in office, would greatly advance the personnel of the service; some such regulations as would allow transfer from one sphere of duty to another within it—from the customs to the internal revenue, and *vice versa*.

If all supervising officers of the internal revenue were required to give bond for their faithful performance of duty, I can see no reason why, in this department, the collectors and assessors might not be transferred; the assessor performing the duty of the collector, and *vice versa*. Not only should this transfer take place as the appointments to these offices now stand, but a civil service instituted, which would have no bounds by States or congressional districts, that they might be ordered for duty over the United States, would add greatly to the efficiency of the department. Then, too, in the districts where the assessment is small, power should be given the department to consolidate with the larger.

If honesty were made the basis of all the other requirements, then intelligence, then determination, the expense of collection of the revenue would be lessened and the amount collected increased. It is impossible to collect the revenue without, at some one point, for the time, trusting to the integrity of the subordinates; hence the vital necessity of having all honest.

The pay of the offices is sufficient to secure good and competent men, and if a system of examination were introduced which was known to be thorough, the applicants would be less, and the service benefited by those who were successful.

This may be all brought about by such a system as was proposed to Congress at its last regular session.

I think that phrase, older than Shakespeare, "to the victor belong the spoils," has about as much sin on its head as any theory advanced by mortal man.

The only objection I have ever seen against the adoption of a civil service as is herein alluded to, which had in it a semblance of plausibility, is that same effete prejudice, which the war of the rebellion exploded, against the regular army, that it foisted a horde of idle, useless cormorants upon the people, whose industry was taxed for their maintenance. Good and true men had begun to believe in the cry against them until the war for the Union showed the latent value of McClellan, Grant, and Sherman.

I hope that I have not uselessly consumed the time of the committee in making these general remarks; it certainly is not my intention; and I close them by saying, that I know of nothing suggested for efficiency and the general good of the civil service which will bring about a more happy result to a tax-ridden people—who have endured the heat and burden of a war unparalleled in its magnitude and its concomitant taxation with such uncomplaining firmness—as the adoption of a civil service, the groundwork of which is suggested by questions 33, 34 and 35 of the circular from the Committee on Retrenchment.

E. H. Webster, collector of customs, Baltimore:

33. The efficiency of the service would be greatly increased if the course indicated by this (33d) interrogatory was generally followed in cases of appointments and promotions, but in some cases it might be beneficial to make new appointments in grades above the "lowest grade only." The lowest grade in this office, for instance, is that of watchmen, boatmen, messengers and porters. who receive $2 50 per diem. It would not be possible to secure the services of officers in these humble positions, who, as a general rule, could afterwards be safely advanced to much more important and responsible positions; especially would this be so if promotions were infrequent, as they necessarily would be were removals only made for want of efficiency; but I repeat that strict examinations of all applicants for appointment and promotion would be very beneficial to the public service.

34. If public officers were more efficient they would of course perform more labor than under the present system, and fewer officers would be required.

35. If employment was assured and certain, and promotions granted only to meritorious officers, and removals only made for want of efficiency in the discharge of official duty, I believe "a higher grade of talent and a better quality of persons" would be "induced to enter the government service," and that the public interests would be greatly subserved thereby.

Wm. H. Smith, collector of internal revenue, Easton, Maryland:

Is satisfied that the only sure way to enforce the revenue law is to create a civil service such as recommended by the Commissioner in his report.

William Welling, assessor internal revenue, Ellicott's Mills, Maryland:

37. I am of opinion that if the policy indicated by your questions is adopted, efficiency and economy in the administration of the civil service will be promoted.

George C. Tyler, collector of internal revenue, Onancock, Virginia:

Thinks the plan suggested by question 33, together with a fair remunerative salary to officials, would be a great improvement on the present system. It would perhaps be better to give to collectors and assessors a salary each, ranging from $3,000 to $5,000, according to the amount of duty devolving on them, without additional commission or percentage, except reimbursement for expenses incurred in extraordinary work, (to be judged of by the department,) and taking from the collectors the burden of paying for services of deputies, clerks, and office expenses, the government paying all subordinates of collectors as now it does for assistant assessors. With such an arrangement, in a little while, there would arise a mutual respect and confidence in the whole official corps, which it more than now obtains, and which would inspire the officers with a commendable vigor, and desire to be faithful and to please. It would be well to clothe officials with power to summon, and compel assistance, in certain cases where it is necessary to seize and distrain on account of infractions of the law, or in collecting the revenue.

John B. Ailworth, assessor of internal revenue, Drummondtown, Virginia:

Thinks that some plan should be adopted for the purpose of reducing the expense of assessing the income tax, which, in a purely agricultural district, yields but little income to the government. The deduction of the $1,000 exemption allowed the farmer exempts almost the entire community from the payment of any income tax. It is a fact that the very best tax-payers to the State do not pay a cent into the federal treasury, and this causes great complaint on the part of those who pay special taxes. I think the exemption should be reduced, or that such a modification of the law be made as will authorize the Commissioner of Internal Revenue or the assessor in certain localities to dispense with such a general visitation on the part of assistant assessors as the law now seems to make obligatory.

John H. Hudson, assessor, Richmond, Virginia:

Declares that the internal revenue service could be made more economical, efficient, and profitable to the government if the laws now under contemplation by Congress were made plain and explicit, the duties and responsibilities of each officer clearly set forth, and he held strictly accountable for the proper administration of his office.

John M. Donn, assessor of internal revenue, Norfolk city, Virginia:

The adoption of the proposed system has his fullest sanction, based upon convictions derived from many years of observation of the present system.

John H. Oley, collector of internal revenue, Kanawha Court House, West Virginia:

Urges the abolishment of all systems of fees and commissions, and the appointment of a fixed salary for each officer, with allowance for proper and necessary expenses.

A. G. Leonard, assessor of internal revenue, Parkersburg, West Virginia:

37. I think if more care was taken in securing proper persons to fill the various and firmness of character, with a due regard for the experience, educational and social acquirements of the applicants, the service would be vastly improved. I am firmly of the opinion that, if such men could be selected and induced to enter the service, there would be no necessity for resorting to the very questionable policy of reducing the tax on spirits and tobacco, thereby seeming to acknowledge that there is not virtue and integrity enough left in the land to execute the laws.

In addition, would suggest that all officers of government should give bonds with suitabl security conditioned for the faithful performance of the duties of their office.

Again, would say that suitable checks should be so arranged that no government money could possibly come into the hands of one officer without a fair charge on the books of another. There is at this time no check on the collectors in the return of unassessed penalties. They are required now to return monthly, on form 58, all unassessed penalty. This form is received by the assessor and charged up to the collector, without *any mode whatever of verifying its correctness* in this particular. And now, to secure the proper officers, I suggest, instead of revenue inspectors—who, so far as my experience goes, are very expensive without much efficiency—for each district, as now exists, that there be one revenue agent, who should be appointed to have the supervision of three districts, with suitable compensation; that he be appointed from the most experienced and efficient officers now in the service in the various districts; that three of these agents should form a board for the examination of all applicants for office in the various districts and divisions, and without their recommendation no appointment or promotion should be made in the several districts or divisions over which they have for the time being the supervision.

Average pay per month, for the year 1867, of assistant assessors.

First division	$105 93	
Second division	121 53	
Third division	127 09	
Fourth division	51 30	
Fifth division	83 40	
Sixth division	30 52	
Seventh division	47 38	
Eighth division	92 31	
Ninth division	22 78	} Average per month each division.
Tenth division	18 88	
Eleventh division	68 22	
Twelfth division	35 49	
Thirteenth division	117 74	
Fourteenth division	120 58	
Total	1,042 58	

General average of each division per month, $74 42.

W. Grant, collector of internal revenue, Greensboro', North Carolina:

In favor of reform; submits that owing to the scarcity of railroads, telegraphs, and mail facilities in his district, and in the south generally, frauds on a small scale are more easily perpetrated than in the more densely settled districts of the north, small distillers and manufacturers "running the blockade" with wagons into adjoining districts.

He suggests as a remedy the prosecution and arrest of such parties, and the seizure of property removed in violation of law wherever found. Under the present law, violators of the law escape with impunity.

He urges that manufacturers before shipping tobacco should be required to procure permits from the collectors of the district to ship the same, the manufacturer at the same time giving his note, with at least three good securities, to be regarded as additional security for the payment of the tax.

He advocates the appointment of those who have served in the Union army as collectors of internal revenue throughout the south, upon the ground of its securing a more co-operative system between collectors, and of contributing materially to the suppression of fraud and increase of revenue.

He boasts of having collected in nine months about $571,000, while his predecessor collected only in 12 months about $336,000, though under his administration the distilling of grain was entirely prohibited by General Sickles, and more than a hundred distilleries had been at work under the 12 months of his predecessor.

William E. Bond, collector internal revenue, Edenton, North Carolina:

I think some system should be adopted which would enable a collector in districts like mine, entirely rural, covering a large area of territory, where the collection is attended with a great deal of expense, trouble, exposure, and some danger withal, to pay his subordinates better compensation (without working for nothing himself) than I can afford to do. As I have before remarked, it appears to me that the best system in public service is to pay good men a good price, and render them directly responsible to the department. Would it not be best, therefore, to place the deputy collectors on a fair salary, and hold them bonded and directly responsible to the department, and, at the same time give such compensation to the collector as will be fair and right, and allow him to secure the services of a No. 1 man as clerk.

Suggestion in respect to the collection of taxes from delinquents scattered over a wide expanse of territory:

In my replies to the questions propounded by you, I neglected one suggestion which I designed to make, and which I regard as highly important everywhere, and absolutely indispensable in districts like this, covering a large extent of country with few modes of communications, and even scanty mail facilities. It is simply impossible for a collector in a district like this, with a weak force at his command, to collect from a large number of delinquents, scattered everywhere through the country, by actual personal distraint. Under the present revenue law suits cannot be instituted in the United States courts against delinquent tax-payers unless authorized by the honorable Commissioner of Internal Revenue, and he is of opinion, as the law seems to indicate, that it requires a separate authorization for each suit. There are some 800 or 1,000 delinquents scattered through the 15 counties of this district, and it would take me and my deputies at least six months or more to collect from them by actual distraint, to the entire neglect of the other duties of my office, and at least 12 months if we gave necessary attention to other imperative duties. But I am satisfied that if the power were given me to institute suit in the United States court, much the larger portion could be collected very soon, for in ninety cases out of a hundred, the service of a writ would be the end of the proceedings, the parties would raise the money "by hook or by crook," and pay. The cost of the proceedings would not be so great to the delinquent as by distraint. The suggestion I would make, therefore, is to invest collectors with the power to institute suits in the United States courts for the recovery of tax claims. The law could be framed so as to protect the government from imposition in the way of costs incurred on account of useless and unnecessary suits, by providing that in all cases in which the collector could not vindicate the justice of the claim by getting judgment, he should pay the costs himself. This would have another good effect; it would enable the collector to silence just complaint on the part of those who have paid, that "others are not made to do so too." The law provides for distraint I know, but, as before remarked, it, in districts like this, is a slow and expensive process, not quick enough to silence complaint, and cannot be done, in any great number of cases, without the neglect of other important duties.

I do hope this suggestion may receive your favorable consideration and be incorporated in the law. The collectors being heavily bonded officers, it appears to me that every possible advantage should be accorded to them.

Jesse Wheeler, assessor internal revenue, Greensboro', North Carolina:

In favor of the proposed reform; urges legal provisions and regulations with a view of checking the system of blockade runners.

About three-fourths of the revenue of his district (5th district of North Carolina) is derived from the tax on tobacco. A very considerable portion of it, that is assessed for tax, is removed from the district in wagons by pedlars. Under present regulations fraud cannot be prevented. He suggests to accompany each removal (not in bond) by a permit from the collector of the district, properly identifying the parcels or packages covered by the permit, and said permit to be indorsed by every revenue official to whom it is shown so as to prevent it from being used twice.

He recommends the same provisions in regard to tobacco, which may be offered for less than the tax, that there is in regard to distilled spirits, except in cases of tobacco accompanied by official certificates attesting to it having been damaged after it had been manufactured.

H. H. Helper, assessor internal revenue, Salisbury, North Carolina, believes:

From his knowledge of the duties of public officers at Washington and other large cities, that *at least one-third more work* should be done by each and every employé than is.

C. W. Dudley, assessor of internal revenue, Bennetsville, S. C.:

Prefers his subordinates to be in all cases of the Caucasian race, and thinks that the officers of this government should all be "*white people*," if white people are to be ruled by them. He is emphatically in favor of the proposed reform, and says the great thing was to put the right man in the right place, without regard to the complexion of their politics. Give authority to good men and they will not abuse it. Find them wherever you can, among all political parties, and the government will be administered in the only spirit any wise man ever supposed a republic could exist.

He inveighs strongly against officers addicted to drink, and if he had the power would select officers only from persons abstaining from the use of wine or strong drink. He advocates modification of test oath, so as to make citizens eligible for office who are at present debarred from the civil service under the operation of that oath.

Assistant assessors are now paid $6 50 per diem, or $2,034 50 annually. Total cost in his district $22,387 50; while citizens with proper qualifications could be employed at $1,200 per annum, making an annual saving of $9,179 50.

F. A. Sawyer, collector of internal revenue, Charleston, South Carolina, (graduate of Harvard College, and a teacher all his life :)

Has no doubt that the plan proposed would be of advantage; but the fact that many a man makes a first-class subordinate, but will be quite unfitted for a principal and controlling position, should never be ignored.

W. H. Watson, assessor 4th district, Georgia :

I am satisfied that the interest of the civil service of the United States and the general welfare of the government requires that a board of examination should be established to judge of the qualifications and examine each and every applicant for a position in any department before entering upon the duties of his office; political influence alone should hardly be taken into consideration, except, perhaps, merely to introduce the applicant to the notice of the board. In the majority of cases parties should apply in person and be required to furnish some record of their antecedents. In a great many instances the compensation of government officials and subordinate officers is too great, while in others it is insufficient; but that is a subject that belongs to the heads of the departments, and is a difficult one to legislate upon, and no general rule could be made to apply to every case.

W. P. Kellogg, collector of customs, New Orleans :

33. Should the course proposed in this interrogatory be pursued, I have no hesitation in saying that it would unquestionably add to the efficiency of the service. Until this or a similar system is adopted, I think we can look for no great improvement, where so much necessity for improvement exists.

34. Unquestionably it could.

35. Undoubtedly such would be the case.

36. There are no females employed in this custom-house.

37. I believe that the course proposed by the tenor of the interrogatories numbered 33, 34, and 35 would very much tend to make the civil service more efficient and economical.

E. G. Cook, collector of internal revenue, 1st district, Mississippi :

In my district half the counties are not assessed more than will pay the cost of assessing and collecting. Several of them are assessed from $1,000 to $2,000, of which not one-half can be collected.

The labor to assess the tax and to collect in a county of 1,000 square miles is as great for $500 as for $10,000. The assessor must travel over the whole territory, and it will take as long to see and examine a citizen who will make no return of tax whatever, as it will to enter the items and tax of $10 or $100 : so an assessor may and they do work and properly charge for services when there is no apparent return of revenue to be collected.

Then the collector will perform nearly the same service by going over the same extent of country to see all whose names are returned, and very often must go a second or third time. There can be no legal notice through the post office, as there is no mail service in any county in this district except, probably, to supply the county seats; all other small post offices are not supplied, and the sending of notices is a mere waste of time. The deputy collector, for this travelling over a county of 1,000 square miles two or three times, can only get at most three per cent.; this on $1,000 would be only $30—this for horse hire and two or three months' hard labor and one month in making out the returns required on 102, 47, 46 and 53.

No one can be had for the compensation provided by law, and something must be done or the poor divisions omitted in the annual assessments.

I think it would save to the treasury if some plan can be devised by which no division shall be taxed if the whole tax will not pay the expense of assessing and collecting the tax therein.

To illustrate: the county of Green has been assessed not as much as $50 for two years. and yet the assistant assessor may have been required to " proceed through every part of this county," &c., (see act of Congress,) but finding all too poor to be charged anything, made no report on 23, but charged for the labor actually performed per diem.

Expecting some assessment, a deputy collector was engaged to collect all assessed in that county, make all returns, and detect all violations of revenue laws, at a salary of $100. Now,. he has collected only $10 special tax on one physician, and this all that was assessed and collectable. The assistant assessor is compensated by per diem. He will continue though nothing be assessed; but no deputy collector can be had, because the amount, $100, is too small to require annual attention, though but little be done, and then the supposition will be that he makes no adequate return of revenue for his pay.

I know as well as I can know anything future that at least ten counties in the first district of Mississippi will not be assessed enough to pay the assessors and collectors reasonable compensation for the labor actually required in assessing and collecting; and then I am equally certain that not one-half will be collected of what may be assessed.

I am certain that I could not have secured the services of competent men by examination. No one is prepared to discharge the duties of assessor and collector at first, and it is hard to learn.

I requested (by letter to Commissioner Rollins) an officer to be sent to me when I was first appointed who would be recommended by deputy commissioners of internal revenue, but have failed to secure such a one. I expected a Mr. Payne, who declined coming; then Mr. Lawton came last; he knew little more than one whom I had in the office.

I have been under the control of treasury agents both general and special, and am still no expert in the office, and my deputies less so. Several have declined, and I think all will.

The cotton tax repealed leaves this district a charge upon the revenue department, unless no assessment or collection be attempted in many divisions.

Whether a county or division of a district should be omitted for any one year may be left to the discretion of the assessor of the district or the joint determination of the assessor and collector, or to the honorable Commissioner of Internal Revenue, if the facts and suggestions made by me on the 6th and 7th pages be considered at all in reference to such action.

The following officers of the customs answered the principal questions relating to the proposed reform affirmatively:

O. Utley, collector, Middletown, Connecticut.
John Brooks, collector, Bridgeport, Connecticut.
R. R. Bolling, surveyor of customs, Louisville, Kentucky.
William P. Kellogg, collector of customs, New Orleans, Louisiana.
Washington Long, collector, Passamaquoddy, Maine.
Stephen Longfellow, collector, Machias, Maine.
E. S. J. Malley, collector, Bath, Maine.
Thomas Russell, collector, Boston, Massachusetts.
John M. Fiske, deputy collector, Boston, Massachusetts.
A. B. Underwood, surveyor, Boston, Massachusetts.
Francis A. Osborn, naval officer, Boston, Massachusetts.
John Vinson, collector, Edgartown, Massachusetts.
William Silvey, collector, Newark, New Jersey.
James Brady, collector, Fall River, Massachusetts.
William A. Pew, collector, Gloucester, Massachusetts.
William Standly, collector, Marblehead, Massachusetts.
John H. Folger, collector, Nantucket, Massachusetts.
Lawrence Grinnell, collector, New Bedford, Massachusetts.
Enoch G. Currier, collector, Newburyport, Massachusetts.
N. G. Isbell, collector, Detroit, Michigan.
T. Harmon, collector, Belfast, Maine.
S. K. Devereux, collector, Castine, Maine.
E. H. Webster, collector, Baltimore, Maryland.
H. A. Smythe, collector, New York, New York.
C. P. Clinch, assistant collector, New York, New York.
J. H. Stedwell, deputy collector, New York, New York.
Abram Wakeman, surveyor, New York, New York.
James S. Benedict, special deputy surveyor, New York, New York.
C. S. Franklin, acting naval officer, New York, New York.
John C. Grannis, collector, Cleveland, Ohio.
John Young, collector, Sandusky, Ohio.
J. W. Cake, collector, Philadelphia, Pennsylvania.
D. N. C. Baxter, naval officer, Philadelphia, Pennsylvania.
William Harbeson, surveyor, Philadelphia, Pennsylvania.
Thomas Wilkins, collector, Erie, Pennsylvania.
W. R. Taylor, collector, Bristol, Rhode Island.

George W. Neff, surveyor, Cincinnati, Ohio.
T. P. Chandler, assistant treasurer, Boston, Massachusetts.
A. Loudon Snowden, chief coiner, mint, Philadelphia, Pennsylvania.
Seth W. Macy, collector, Newport, Rhode Island.
Charles Anthony Colector, Providence, Rhode Island.

The following officers, in other branches of the service, answered the main questions affirmatively:

W. D. Mann, assessor of internal revenue, Mobile, Alabama.
John M. Oliver, assessor of internal revenue, Little Rock, Arkansas.
John Edwards, assessor of internal revenue, Fort Smith, Arkansas.
Alphonso C. Crosby, assessor of internal revenue, Rockville, Connecticut.
John B. Wright, assessor of internal revenue, Clinton, Connecticut.
Samuel Wilson, assessor of internal revenue, Fernandina, Florida.
John Bowles, assessor of internal revenue, Augusta, Florida.
W. H. Watson, assessor of internal revenue, Atlanta, Georgia.
Duncan Ferguson, assessor of internal revenue, Rockford, Illinois.
Quincy D. Whitman, assessor of internal revenue, Ottawa, Ohio.
Henry L. Bryant, assessor of internal revenue, Lewistown, Illinois.
Jonathan Biggs, assessor of internal revenue, Salem, Illinois.
William C. Kueffner, assessor of internal revenue, Belleville Illinois.
Samuel H. Halmon, assessor of internal revenue, Tamaroa, Illinois.
Joseph G. Bowman, assessor of internal revenue, Vincennes, Indiana.
J. G. Harrison, assessor of internal revenue, New Albany, Indiana.
Hageman Tripp, assessor of internal revenue, North Vernon, Indiana.
Richard H. Swift, assessor of internal revenue, Brookville, Indiana.
H. W. Shuman, assessor of internal revenue, Milton, Indiana.
David Braden, assessor of internal revenue, Indianapolis, Indiana.
David Turner, assessor of internal revenue, Crown Point, Indiana.
George D. Copeland, assessor of internal revenue, Goshen, Indiana.
George Meason, assessor of internal revenue, Muscatine, Iowa.
Lucius L. Huntley, assessor of internal revenue, Dubuque, Iowa.
John Connell, assessor of internal revenue, Toledo, Iowa.
William T. Ousley, assessor of internal revenue, Paducah, Kentucky.
John S. McFarland, assessor of internal revenue, Owensboro', Kentucky.
William M. Spencer, assessor of internal revenue, Lebanon, Kentucky.
J. Crockett Sayers, assessor of internal revenue, Covington, Kentucky.
James H. Veazie, assessor of internal revenue, Baton Rouge, Louisiana.
Nathaniel J. Marshall, assessor of internal revenue, Portland, Maine.
George P. Sewall, assessor of internal revenue, Oldtown, Maine.
Thomas K. Carroll, assessor of internal revenue, Church Creek, Maryland.
William E. W. Ross, assessor of internal revenue, Baltimore, Maryland.
John Van Lear, assessor of internal revenue, Hagerstown, Maryland,
William Willing, assessor of internal revenue, Ellicott's City, Maryland.
Charles G. Davis, assessor of internal revenue, Plymouth, Massachusetts.
Otis Clapp, assessor of internal revenue, Boston, Massachusetts.
Phineas J. Stone, assessor of internal revenue, Charlestown, Massachusetts.
Alexander H. Morrison, assessor of internal revenue, St. Joseph, Michigan.
G. Thompson Gridley, assessor of internal revenue, Jackson, Michigan.
Westbrook Divine, assessor of internal revenue, Ionia, Michigan.
Levi Bacon, jr., assessor of internal revenue, Pontiac, Michigan.
Henry Raymond, assessor of internal revenue, Bay City Michigan.
William McMicken, assessor of internal revenue, Mantonville, Minnesota.
John H. Fox, assessor of internal revenue, DeSoto, Missouri.
Joseph A. Hoy, assessor of internal revenue, LaGrange, Missouri.
Mack J. Leaming, assessor of internal revenue, Pleasant Hill, Missouri.

Frederick Renner, assessor of internal revenue, Nebraska City, Nebraska.
George M. Henning, assessor of internal revenue, Farmington, New Hampshire.
Isaac W. Smith, assessor of internal revenue, Manchester, New Hampshire.
Bolivar Lovell, assessor of internal revenue, Alstead, New Hampshire.
Benjamin Acton, assessor of internal revenue, Salem, New Jersey.
Robert Rusling, assessor of internal revenue, Hackettstown New Jersey.
Benjamin F. Robinson, assessor of internal revenue, Ridgewood, New Jersey.
Robert B. Hathorn, assessor of internal revenue, Newark, New Jersey.
William R. Cummings, acting assessor of internal revenue, Long Island City, New York.
John Williams, assessor of internal revenue, Brooklyn, New York.
Pierre C. VanWyck, assessor of internal revenue, New York city, New York.
David Miller, assessor of internal revenue, New York city, New York.
John F. Cleveland, assessor of internal revenue, New York city, New York.
Abraham Hyatt, assessor of internal revenue, Sing Sing, New York.
James C. Curtis, assessor of internal revenue, Coshocton, New York.
Benjamin Platt Carpenter, assessor of internal revenue, Poughkeepsie, New York.
Frederick Cooke, assessor of internal revenue, Catskill, New York.
John G. Treadwell, assessor of internal revenue, Albany, New York.
Philip N. Neber, assessor of internal revenue, Troy, New York.
Uriah D. Meeker, assessor of internal revenue, Malone, New York.
Alexander H. Palmer, assessor of internal revenue, Schenectady, New York.
Nelson J. Beach, assessor of internal revenue, Watson, New York.
Charles M. Dennison, assessor of internal revenue, Rome, New York.
William H. Wheeler, assessor of internal revenue, Oswego, New York.
William Candee, assessor of internal revenue, Syracuse, New York.
Joseph W. Gates, assessor of internal revenue, Lyons, New York.
Lewis Peak, assessor of internal revenue, Phelps, New York.
Curtis C. Gardiner, assessor of internal revenue, Elmira, New York.
James P. Murphy, assessor of internal revenue, Lockport, New York.
James C. Strong, assessor of internal revenue, Buffalo, New York.
Lewis Hall, assessor of internal revenue, Jamestown, New York.
Robinson Piemont, assessor of internal revenue, Elizabeth City, New York.
Jennings Piggott, assessor of internal revenue, Wilson, North Carolina.
William H. Worth, assessor of internal revenue, Fayetteville, North Carolina
Solomon Pool, assessor of internal revenue, Chapel Hill, North Carolina.
Jesse Wheeler, assessor of internal revenue, Greensboro, North Carolina.
H. H. Helper, assessor of internal revenue, Salisbury, North Carolina.
Joseph Hamilton, assessor of internal revenue, Hendersonville, North Carolina.
Obadiah. C. Maxwell, assessor of internal revenue, Dayton, Ohio.
John T. Hogue, assessor of internal revenue, Xenia, Ohio.
Milton W. Worden, assessor of internal revenue, Mansfield, Ohio.
James Lewis, assessor of internal revenue, Bucyrus, Ohio.
Melancthon W. Hubbell, assessor of internal revenue, Toledo, Ohio.
Elias Nigh, assessor of internal revenue, Ironton, Ohio.
George B. Arnold, assessor of internal revenue, Mount. Vernon, Ohio.
John Sargent, assessor of internal revenue, New Philadelphia, Ohio.
Anson G. McCook, assessor of internal revenue, Steubenville, Ohio.
Charles A. Harrington, assessor of internal revenue, Warren, Ohio.
John W. Frazier, assessor of internal revenue, Philadelphia, Pennsylvania.
Clifford S. Phillips, assessor of internal revenue, Philadelphia, Pennsylvania.
William B. Elliot, assessor of internal revenue, Philadelphia, Pennsylvania.
Thomas H. Forsyth, assessor of internal revenue, Philadelphia, Pennsylvania.
Francis Z. Heebner, assessor of internal revenue, Allentown, Pennsylvania.

J. Lee Englebert, assessor of internal revenue, West Chester, Pennsylvania.

John B. Warfel, assessor of internal revenue, Lancaster, Pennsylvania.

William Mutchler, assessor of internal revenue, Easton, Pennsylvania.

William M Post, assessor of internal revenue, Susquehanna Depot, Pennsylvania.

William McSherry, assessor of internal revenue, Littlestown, Pennsylvania.

Robert H. Foster, assessor of internal revenue, Bellefonte, Pennsylvania.

John B. Hays, assessor of internal revenue, Meadville, Pennsylvania.

A. G. Booth, assessor of internal revenue, Brownsville, Pennsylvania.

Daniel E. Nevin, assessor of internal revenue, Allegheny City, Pennsylvania.

James B. Ruple, assessor of internal revenue, Washington, Pennsylvania.

Christopher W. Dudley, assessor of internal revenue, Bennettsville, South Carolina.

John P. Holtsinger, assessor of internal revenue, Greenville, Tennessee.

William T. Tune, assessor of internal revenue, Shelbyville, Tennessee.

Joseph H. Travis, assessor of internal revenue, Paris, Tennessee.

Halsey T. Cooper, assessor of internal revenue, Memphis, Tennessee.

William C. Kittredge, assessor of internal revenue, Fairhaven, Vermont.

Thomas E. Powers, assessor of internal revenue, Woodstock, Vermont.

Henry C. Adams, assessor of internal revenue, St. Albans, Vermont.

John H. Hudson, assessor of internal revenue, Richmond, Virginia.

John M. Donn, assessor of internal revenue, Norfolk city, Virginia.

Jacquelin M. Wood, assessor of internal revenue, Lynchburg, Virginia.

John H. Freeman, assessor of internal revenue, Lexington, Virginia.

William M. Fitzhugh, assessor of internal revenue, Fairfax Court-house, Virginia.

George S. Smith, assessor of internal revenue, Marion, Virginia.

Albert G. Leonard, assessor of internal revenue, Parkersburg, West Virginia.

George B. Bingham, assessor of internal revenue, Milwaukee, Wisconsin.

Henry Harnden, assessor of internal revenue, Madison, Wisconsin.

Smith S. Wilkinson, assessor of internal revenue, Prairie du Lac, Wisconsin.

Jacob S. Bugh, assessor of internal revenue, Wautoma, Wisconsin.

Lute A. Taylor, assessor of internal revenue, Prescott, Wisconsin.

Henry A. Bigelow, assessor of internal revenue, Prescott, Arizona Territory.

David M. Mills, assessor of internal revenue, Elk Point, Dakota Territory.

Austin Savage, assessor of internal revenue, Boise City, Idaho Territory.

Charles B. Andrews, assessor of internal revenue, Mobile, Alabama.

William J. Patton, assessor of internal revenue, Little Rock, Arkansas.

Henry A. Grant, assessor of internal revenue, Hartford, Connecticut.

John Woodruff, assessor of internal revenue, New Haven, Connecticut.

David F. Hollister, assessor of internal revenue, Bridgeport, Connecticut.

W. A. Wilhaner, assessor of internal revenue, Fernandina, Florida.

Alex. N. Wilson, assessor of internal revenue, Savannah, Georgia.

Will. D. Bard, assessor of internal revenue, Augusta, Georgia.

James Atkins, assessor of internal revenue, Atlanta, Georgia.

Jackson Grinshaw, assessor of internal revenue, Quincy, Illinois.

Charles M. Hammond, assessor of internal revenue, Joliet, Illinois.

W. T. Cunningham, assessor of internal revenue, Danville, Illinois.

David T. Little, assessor of internal revenue, Lincoln, Illinois.

Leonard F. Ross, assessor of internal revenue, Avon, Illinois.

Nathan M. Knapp, assessor of internal revenue, Winchester, Illinois.

Willard C. Flagg, assessor of internal revenue, Alton, Illinois.

Benjamin F. Scribner, assessor of internal revenue, New Albany, Indiana.

Smith Jones, assessor of internal revenue, Columbus, Indiana.

Gillett V. Stevenson, assessor of internal revenue, Aurora, Indiana.

William Grose, assessor of internal revenue, New Castle, Indiana.

Austin H. Brown, assessor of internal revenue, Indianapolis, Indiana.
Norman Eddy, assessor of internal revenue, South Bend, Indiana.
William W. Belknap, assessor of internal revenue, Keokuk, Iowa.
David B. Henderson, assessor of internal revenue, Dubuque, Iowa.
Alonzo J. Pope, assessor of internal revenue, Sigourney, Iowa.
Thomas Moonlight, assessor of internal revenue, Leavenworth, Kansas.
John R. Beckley, assessor of internal revenue, Shelbyville, Kentucky.
Philip Speed, assessor of internal revenue, Louisville, Kentucky.
James W. Hudnall, assessor of internal revenue, Covington, Kentucky.
Robert M. Kelly, assessor of internal revenue, Lexington, Kentucky.
William J. Landram, assessor of internal revenue, Lancaster, Kentucky.
Fielder C. Barnes, assessor of internal revenue, Mt. Sterling, Kentucky.
Nathaniel J. Miller, assessor of internal revenue, Portland, Maine.
Peter F. Sanborn, assessor of internal revenue, Augusta, Maine.
Jeremiah Fenno, assessor of internal revenue, Bangor, Maine.
David Howe, assessor of internal revenue, Lincolnville, Maine.
William H. Smith, assessor of internal revenue, Easton, Maryland.
James L Ridgely, assessor of internal revenue, Baltimore, Maryland.
George W. Harrison, assessor of internal revenue, Cumberland, Maryland.
James Buffington, assessor of internal revenue, Fall River, Massachusetts.
William H. McCartney, assessor of internal revenue, Boston, Massachusetts.
John Sargent, assessor of internal revenue, Boston, Massachusetts.
Nathaniel S. Howe, assessor of internal revenue, Haverhill, Massachusetts.
John Nesmith, assessor of internal revenue, Lowell, Massachusetts.
Augustus B. R. Sprague, assessor of internal revenue, Worcester, Massachusetts.
Daniel W. Alvord, assessor of internal revenue, Greenfield, Massachusetts.
E. R. Tinker, assessor of internal revenue, North Adams, Massachusetts.
Frederick W. Curtenius, assessor of internal revenue, Kalamazoo, Michigan.
Chauncey H. Millen, assessor of internal revenue, Ann Arbor, Michigan.
Sluman S. Bailey, assessor of internal revenue, Grand Rapids, Michigan.
Edwin G. Cook, assessor of internal revenue, Hazelhurst, Mississippi.
Bernard Zwart, assessor of internal revenue, Ironton, Missouri.
W. J. Chandler, assessor of internal revenue, Pleasant Hill, Missouri.
Joseph E. Lanaster, assessor of internal revenue, Nebraska City, Nebraska.
James M. Lovering, assessor of internal revenue, Exeter, New Hampshire.
John Kimball, assessor of internal revenue, Concord, New Hampshire.
Chester Pike, assessor of internal revenue, Cornish, New Hampshire.
Elston Marsh, assessor of internal revenue, Plainfield, New Jersey.
George F. Carman, assessor of internal revenue, Long Island City, New York.
Alfred M. Wood, assessor of internal revenue, Brooklyn, New York.
Maunsell B. Field, assessor of internal revenue, New York city, New York.
Marshall B. Blake, assessor of internal revenue, New York city, New York.
Thomas E. Smith, assessor of internal revenue, New York city, New York.
John M. Mason, assessor of internal revenue, Yonkers, New York.
Edward W. Budington, assessor of internal revenue, Kingston, New York.
Theodore Townsend, assessor of internal revenue, Albany, New York.
Asahel C. Geer, assessor of internal revenue, Troy, New York.
Erasmus D. Brooks, assessor of internal revenue, Potsdam, New York.
Allen C. Churchill, assessor of internal revenue, Gloversville, New York.
George W. Ernest, assessor of internal revenue, Cooperstown, New York.
Laurence L. Merry, assessor of internal revenue, Ilion, New York.
Ralph H. Avery, assessor of internal revenue, Canastota, New York.
Silas F. Smith, assessor of internal revenue, Syracuse, New York.
Adrian R. Root, assessor of internal revenue, Buffalo, New York.
Charles W. Root, assessor of internal revenue, Fayetteville, North Carolina.

John Crane, assessor of internal revenue, Greensboro, North Carolina.

Samuel H. Wiley, assessor of internal revenue, Salisbury, North Carolina

Ferdinand Van Deweer, assessor of internal revenue, Hamilton, Ohio.

William W. Wilson, assessor of internal revenue, Urbana, Ohio.

B. Franklin Martin, assessor of internal revenue, Columbus, Ohio.

Eugene Powell, assessor of internal revenue, Delaware, Ohio.

George J. Anderson, assessor of internal revenue, Sandusky, Ohio.

Harry Chase, assessor of internal revenue, Toledo, Ohio.

John A. Hunter, assessor of internal revenue, Lancaster, Ohio.

Albert A. Guthrie, assessor of internal revenue, Zanesville, Ohio.

William P. Richardson, assessor of internal revenue, Marietta, Ohio.

Kent Jarvis, assessor of internal revenue, Massillon, Ohio.

Abraham B. Longaker, assessor of internal revenue, Norristown, Pennsylvania.

William M. Swayne, assessor of internal revenue, West Chester, Pennsylvania.

James A. Inness, assessor of internal revenue, Pottsville, Pennsylvania.

Joseph P. Hetrick, assessor of internal revenue, Easton, Pennsylvania.

Caleb E. Wright, assessor of internal revenue, Wilkesbarre, Pennsylvania.

Charles H. Shriner, assessor of internal revenue, Mifflinburg, Pennsylvania.

William Penn Lloyd, assessor of internal revenue, Mechanicsburg, Pennsylvania.

John W. Douglass, assessor of internal revenue, Erie, Pennsylvania.

Peter M. Gough, assessor of internal revenue, Franklin, Pennsylvania.

Fred E. Voltz, assessor of internal revenue, Pittsburg, Pennsylvania.

John M. Sulivan, assessor of internal revenue, Allegheny, Pennsylvania.

W. D. Brayton, assessor of internal revenue, Warwick, Rhode Island.

Fred. A. Sawyer, assessor of internal revenue, Charleston, South Carolina.

Elijah Simerley, collector of internal revenue, Elizabethtown, Tennessee.

James T. Abernathy, collector of internal revenue, Knoxville, Tennessee.

Joseph Ramsey, collector of internal revenue, Shelbyville, Tennessee.

Rolfe S. Saunders, collector of internal revenue, Memphis, Tennessee.

George C. Tyler, assessor of internal revenue, Onancock, Virginia.

Thomas L. Sanborn, assessor of internal revenue, Alexandria, Virginia.

Geo. W. Brown, collector of internal revenue, Kingwood, West Virginia.

John H. Oley, collector of internal revenue, Kanawha Court-house, West Virginia.

G. Q. Erskine, collector of internal revenue, Milwaukee, Wisconsin.

H. M. Lewis, collector of internal revenue, Madison, Wisconsin.

J. H. Warren, collector of internal revenue, Albany, Wisconsin.

J. C. Geer, collector of internal revenue, Boise City, Idaho.

W T Otto, Assistant Secretary Department of Interior, Washington.

Joseph H. Barrett, Commissioner of Pensions, Washington.

John Potts, chief clerk War Department, Washington.

A. B. Eaton, Commissary General of Subsistence of United States army, Washington.

A. A. Humphreys, brigadier general engineers United States army, Washington.

J. K. Barnes, Surgeon General of United States army, Washington.

Jos. Smith, rear admiral United States navy, Washington.

H. Bridge, Chief of Bureau of Provisions and Clothing in Navy Department, Washington.

P. J. Horwitz, Chief of Bureau of Medicine and Surgery, Washington.

John Lenthall, Chief of Bureau of Construction and Repair, Washington.

B. F. Isherwood, Chief of Bureau of Steam Engineering, Washington.

John B. L. Skinner, First Assistant Postmaster General United States, Washington, D. C.

George W. McLellan, Second Assistant Postmaster General United States, Washington, D. C.

A. N. Zevely, Third Assistant Postmaster General United States, Washington, D. C.

S. J. Bowen, postmaster, Washington, D. C.

T. P. Robb, postmaster, Savannah, Georgia.

Edward C. David, postmaster, Dubuque, Iowa.

Jno. J. Speed, postmaster, Louisville, Kentucky.

Geo. Fuller, postmaster, Bangor, Maine.

E. Schriver, postmaster, Baltimore, Maryland.

W. L. Burt, postmaster, Boston, Massachusetts.

Jno. R. Yarney, postmaster, Dover, New Hampshire.

F. S. McNeely, postmaster, Trenton, New Jersey.

Joseph Davis, postmaster, Albany, New York.

A. Allen, postmaster, Troy, New York.

A. Miller, postmaster, Raleigh, North Carolina.

H. H. Bingham, postmaster, Philadelphia, Pennsylvania.

J. J. Horn, postmaster, Easton, Pennsylvania.

J. H. McClelland, postmaster, Pittsburg, Pennsylvania.

Wm. Briner, postmaster, Reading, Pennsylvania.

Robert C. Gist, postmaster, Memphis, Tennessee.

C. J. Rawling, postmaster, Wheeling, West Virginia.

H. A. Starr, postmaster, Milwaukee, Wisconsin.

The following officers answer questions 33, 34, and 35, negatively :

Jesse S. Ely, assessor of internal revenue, Norwich, Connecticut.

Dudley Wickersham, assessor of internal revenue, Springfield, Illinois.

Robert M. Tindall, assessor of internal revenue, Okolona, Mississippi.

Benjamin C. Gunn, assessor of internal revenue, Utica, Michigan.

George W. Fish, assessor of internal revenue, Flint, Michigan.

William P. Tatem, assessor of internal revenue, Camden, New Jersey.

William A. Halsey, assessor of internal revenue, Port Byron, New York.

John Reed, assessor of internal revenue, Warrenton, North Carolina.

John H. Diehl, assessor of internal revenue, Philadelphia, Pennsylvania.

C. H. Hopkins, postmaster, Utica, New York.

C. W. Thomas, postmaster, Cincinnati, Ohio.

B. Embry, postmaster, Nashville, Tennessee.

J. S. Putman, collector, York, Maine.

The following revenue officers omit to answer the questions relating to the proposed reform :

N. K. Sargent, collector, Kennebunk, Maine.

A. G. Edwards, assistant treasurer, St. Louis, Missouri.

C. McKibbin, assistant treasurer, United States mint, Philadelphia.

George W. Lane, superintendent branch mint, Denver, Colorado Territory.

George B. Dickson, assessor of internal revenue, Wilmington, Delaware.

R. H. Carnahan, assessor of internal revenue, Danville, Illinois.

Cole Noel, assessor of internal revenue, Adel, Iowa.

Thomas J. Sternbergh, assessor of internal revenue, Lawrence, Kansas.

Thomas L. Morrow, assessor of internal revenue, Somerset, Kentucky.

Eben. F. Stone, assessor of internal revenue, Newburyport, Massachusetts.

Ivers Phillips, assessor of internal revenue, Worcester, Massachusetts.

Amasa Norcross, assessor of internal revenue, Fitchburg, Massachusetts.

Anthony J. Bleeker, assessor of internal revenue, New York city.

George M. Woodbridge, assessor of internal revenue, Marietta, Ohio.

Thomas G. Turner, assessor of internal revenue, Providence, Rhode Island.

Charles J. Hascall, assessor of internal revenue, Charleston, South Carolina

Peter M. Pearson, assessor of internal revenue, Washington, D. C.

C. H. B. Day, assessor of internal revenue, Dover, Delaware.
Robert D. Noleman, assessor of internal revenue, Centralia, Illinois.
Warren H. Withers, assessor of internal revenue, Fort Wayne, Indiana.
Jacob Weart, assessor of internal revenue, Jersey City, New Jersey.
Levi Blakeslee, assessor of internal revenue, Utica, New York.
Oscar J. Averell, assessor of internal revenue, Elmira, New York.
Samuel P. Allen, assessor of internal revenue, Rochester, New York.
William E. Bond, assessor of internal revenue, Edenton, North Carolina.
Henry Fassett, assessor of internal revenue, Ashtabula, Ohio.
Joseph Barnsley, assessor of internal revenue, Doylestown, Pennsylvania.
Chas. S. Dana, assessor of internal revenue, St. Johnsbury, Vermont.
Sam. R. Sterling, assessor of internal revenue, Harrisonburg, Virginia.
W. Johnson, assessor of internal revenue, Appleton, Wisconsin.
Chas. Shuter, assessor of internal revenue, Sparta, Wisconsin.
W. Davis, postmaster, Portland, Maine.
M. T. Willard, postmaster, Concord, New Hampshire.

The following revenue officers think the proposed reform inapplicable to their districts :

Edward Prentiss, collector of customs, New London, Connecticut.
H. N. Trumbull, collector of customs, Stonington, Connecticut.
Joseph F. Babcock, collector of customs, New Haven, Connecticut.
S. B. Upham, collector of customs, Portsmouth, New Hampshire.
Thomas Loring, collector, Plymouth, Massachusetts
Robert S. Rantoul, collector, Salem, Massachusetts.
Reuben Rockwell, assessor of internal revenue, Colebrook, Connnecticut.
Andrew J. Warner, assessor of internal revenue, Prophetstown, Missouri.
George I. Bergen, assessor of internal revenue, Galesburg, Illinois.
James B. Weaver, assessor of internal revenue, Bloomfield, Iowa.
Benjamin Gratz, assessor of internal revenue, Lexington, Kentucky.
Samuel L. Blaine, assessor of internal revenue, Maysville, Kentucky.
D. C. Palmer, assessor of internal revenue, Gardiner, Maine.
Nathaniel A. Joy, assessor of internal revenue, Ellsworth, Maine.
Nathaniel Wales, assessor of internal revenue, Stoughton, Massachusetts.
William S. King, assessor of internal revenue, Boston, Massachusetts.
Charles C. Esty, assessor of internal revenue, Framingham, Massachusetts.
Joseph P. Douglass, assessor of internal revenue, Columbia, Missouri.
Carr B. White, assessor of internal revenue, Georgetown, Ohio.
Willard Slocum, assessor of internal revenue, Ashland, Ohio.
Thomas J. Jordan, assessor of internal revenue, Harrisburg, Pennsylvania.
Daniel G. Hay, assessor of internal revenue, Cairo, Illinois.
John Boyd Headley, assessor of internal revenue, Morristown, New Jersey.
John B Weaver, assessor of internal revenue, Ashville, North Carolina.
L. B. Frieze, assessor of internal revenue, Providence, Rhode Island.

APPENDIX D.

OPINIONS OF THE EARLIER PRESIDENTS AND OTHERS.

PRESIDENT WASHINGTON ON APPOINTMENTS TO THE CIVIL SERVICE.

Letter to a naturalized citizen applying for an office :

Three things ought, in my opinion, principally to be regarded, namely, the fitness of character to fill office, the comparative claims from the former merits and sufferings in service of the different candidates, and the distribution of appointments in as equal a proportion as might be to persons belonging to the different States in the Union.

Letter to Mary Wooster, widow of General Wooster. He begs to be relieved from the personal attendance of candidates for office, and adds :

All that I require is (of candidates) the name and such testimonies with respect to abilities, integrity, and fitness as it may be in the power of the several applicants to produce. Beyond this nothing, with me, is necessary or will be of any avail to them in my decision.

Letter to David Stuart, New York, July 26, 1789 :

Nothing would give me greater pleasure than to serve any of the descendants of General Nelson, of whose merits when living no man could entertain a higher opinion than I did. At the same time I must confess there are few persons of whom I have no personal knowledge or good information that I would take into my family, when many qualifications are necessary to fit them for the duty of it. * * * Most clerkships will, I presume, either by law or custom, be left to the appointment of their principals in office. Little expectation, therefore, could Mr. Nelson, a stranger, have from this source. This latter consideration, added to the desire I feel of serving the son of my old friend and acquaintance, has induced me at all hazards to offer Mr. Thomas Nelson, his son, a place in my family.

Letter to Bushrod Washington, New York, July 27, 1789 :

You cannot doubt my wishes to see you appointed to any office of honor or emolument in the new government to the duties of which you are competent ; but however deserving you may be of the one you have suggested, your standing at the bar will not justify my nomination of you as attorney to the federal district court in preference to some of the oldest and most esteemed general court lawyers in your own State who are desirous of this appointment.

Letter to Joseph Jones, New York, November 30, 1789 :

In every nomination to office I have endeavored, as far as my own knowledge extends, to make fitness of character my primary object. If with this the peculiar necessities of the applicant could be combined, it has been with me an additional inducement to the appointment. By these principles, in a proper degree, have I been influenced in the case of Mr. Griffin, who is not only out of office and in want of the emolument of one, but has been deprived of the former by my means, owing to an opinion which prevailed here at the time among our countrymen that his accepting the temporary appointment of commissioner to treat with the southern Indians would not bring him under the disqualifying act of Virginia ; by which, however, it seems he has lost his station in the council of that State, and is now entirely out of employment. This circumstance, added to the knowledge of his having been a regular student of law, having filled an important office in the Union in the line of it, and being besides a man of competent abilities and of pure character, weighed with me in the choice.

Letter to William Fitzhugh, New York, December 24, 1789 :

Mr. Johnson has, as you supposed, declined the appointment of judge to the district of Maryland, and I have lately appointed Mr. Vaca to fill that office. Mr. Thomas, whom you recommend for that place, undoubtedly possesses all those qualifications which you have ascribed to him, and so far as my own knowledge of that gentleman extends he is justly entitled to the reputation which he sustains. But in appointing persons to office, and more especially in the judicial department, my views have been much guided to those characters who have been conspicuous in their country, not only from an impression of their services, but upon a consideration that they have been tried, and that a wider confidence would be placed in them by the public than in others, perhaps of equal merit, who had never been proved.

Letter to John Armstrong, Philadelphia, February 6, 1791 :

In a word, to a man who has no ends to serve and no friends to provide for, nomination to office is the most irksome part of the executive trust.

Letter to Monroe in reply to his letter opposing Hamilton's nomination as minister to England, Philadelphia, April 9, 1796 :

In reply to your letter of yesterday, I can assure you with the utmost truth that I have no other object in nominating men to offices than to fill them with such characters as, in my judgment, or, when they are unknown to me, from such information as I can obtain from others, are best qualified to answer the purposes of their appointment. * * * But as much will depend, among other things, upon the abilities of the person sent and his knowledge of the affairs of this country, &c., &c., &c.

To Timothy Pickering, Secretary of War, (private,) Mount Vernon, September 27, 1795 :

I shall not, while I have the honor to administer the government, bring a man into any office of consequence knowingly whose political tenets are adverse to the measures which the general government are pursuing ; for this, in my opinion, would be a sort of political suicide. That it would embarrass its movements is most certain. But of two men equally well affected to the true interests of their country, of equal abilities, and equally disposed to lend their support, it is the part of prudence to give the preference to him against whom the least clamor can be excited.

Letter to Edward Carrington, (private and confidential,) Mount Vernon, October 9, 1795 :

In the appointments to the general offices of the government, my aim has been to combine geographical situation, and sometimes other considerations, with abilities and fitness of known characters.

ADEQUATE PAY TO SECURE COMPETENT OFFICERS.

Washington's speech to both houses of Congress, December 7, 1796 :

The compensation to the officers of the United States in various instances, and in none more than in respect to the most important stations, appears to call for legislative revision. The consequences of a defective provision are of serious import to the government. If private wealth is to supply the defect of public contribution, it will greatly contract the sphere within which the selection of characters for office is to be made, and will proportionately diminish the probability of a choice of men able as well as upright. Besides that, it would be repugnant to the vital principles of our government, virtually to exclude from public trusts talents and virtue, unless accompanied by wealth.

If public servants, in the exercise of their official duties, are found incompetent or pursuing wrong courses, discontinue them. If they are guilty of malpractices in office, let them be more exemplarily punished.

PRESIDENT JEFFERSON.

Jefferson refused all offices to relatives. See Jefferson's letter to J. Garland Jefferson, January 25, 1810, and other letters.

Letter to Madison, November 29, 1820 :

This is the sample of the effects we may expect from the late mischievous law vacating every four years nearly all the executive officers of the government. It saps the constitutional and salutary functions of the President, and introduces a principle of intrigue and corruption which will soon leaven the mass, not only of senators, but of citizens. It is more baneful than the attempt which failed in the beginning of the government to make all officers irremovable but with the consent of the Senate. This places every four years all appointments under their power, and obliges them to act on every one nomination. It will keep in constant excitement all the hungry cormorants for office, render them, as well as those in place, sycophants to their senators, engage them in eternal intrigue to put out one and put in another, in cabals to scrap work; and make of them what all executive directories become, mere sinks of corruption and faction. This must have been one of the midnight signatures of the President, when he had not time to consider or even to read the law, and the more fatal as being irrepealable, but with the consent of the Senate, which will never be obtained.

Letter to Monroe, March 7, 1801 :

Deprivations of office, if made on ground of political principles alone, would revolt our new converts and give a body to leaders who now stand alone. Some, I know, must be made. They must be as far as possible done gradually, and bottomed on some malversation or inherent disqualification.

Letter to William B. Giles, March 23, 1801 :

Good men to whom there is no objection but a difference of political principle, practiced on only as far as the right of a private citizen will justify, are not proper subjects of removal, except in the case of attorneys and marshals.

Letter to Elbridge Gerry, March 29, 1801 :

The instances [of his removals] will be few and governed by strict rule, and not party passion. The right of opinion shall suffer no invasion from me. Those who have acted well have nothing to fear; *   *   *   those who have done ill, however, have nothing to hope.

Letter to Levy Lincoln, October 25, 1802 :

I still think our original idea as to office is best ; that is, for obtaining a just participation on deaths, resignations, and delinquencies.

Letter to Dr. Rush, March 24, 1801 :

Of the thousands of officers, therefore, in the United States, a very few individuals only, probably not twenty, will be removed, and these only for doing what they ought not to have done. I know that in thus stopping in the career of removal [the means on paritzan grounds] I shall give great offence to many of my friends. That torrent has been pressing me heavily, and will require all my force to bear up against; but my maxim is, "*fiat justitia, ruat cœlum.*"

In a letter to General Knox, March 27, 1801, he expresses himself to the same effect.

HENRY CLAY UPON THE SCRAMBLE FOR OFFICE.

Henry Clay said in his speech in the Senate, January 26, 1832, in opposition to Mr. Van Buren's nomination as minister to England :

I have another objection to this nomination. I believe, upon circumstances which satisfy my mind, that to this gentleman is principally to be ascribed the introduction of the odious system of proscription, for the exercise of the elective franchise, in the government of the United States. I understand that it is the system on which the party in his own State, of which he is the reputed head, constantly acts. He was among the first of the secretaries to apply that system to the dismission of clerks in his department, known to me to be highly meritorious, and among them one who is now a representative in the other house. It is a detestable system, drawn from the worst periods of the Roman republic, and if it were to be perpetuated—if the offices, honors, and dignities of the people were to be put up to a scramble, and to be decided by the results of every presidential election—our government and institutions, becoming intolerable, would finally end in a despotism as inexorable as that of Constantinople.

Josiah Quincy thus describes the office-seeking members of Congress, in a speech made in the House of Representatives on the 30th day of January, 1811 :

But as to that other class of persons who are open, notorious solicitors of office, they give occasion to reflections of a very different nature. This class of persons, in all times past, have appeared, and (for I say nothing of times present) in all future will appear on this and on the other floor of Congress, creatures who, under the pretense of serving the people, are, in fact, serving themselves; creatures who, while their distant constituents, good, easy men, industrious, frugal and unsuspicious, dream in visions that they are laboring for their country's welfare, are in truth spending their time mousing at the doors of the palace or the crannies of the departments, and laying low snares to catch, for themselves and their relatives, every stray office that flits by them. For such men, chosen in their high and responsible trust, to whom have been confided the precious destinies of the people, and who thus openly abandon their duties, and set their places and their consciences to sale, in defiance of the multiplied, strong, and tender ties, by which they are bound to their country, I have no language to express my contempt. I have never seen, and I never shall see, any of these notorious solicitors of office, for themselves or their relatives, standing on this or the other floor, bawling or bullying, or coming down with dead votes in support of executive measures, but I think I see a hackney laboring for hire, in a most degrading service ; a poor earth-spirited animal, trudging in his traces, with much attrition of the sides and induration of the membranes, encouraged by the special certainty that, at the end of his journey, he shall have measured out to him his proportion of provender.

But I have heard that the bare suggestion of such corruption was a libel upon this House and upon this people. I have heard that we were, in this country, so virtuous that we were above the influence of these allurements ; that beyond the Atlantic, in old governments, such things might be suspected, but that here we were too pure for such guilt, too innocent for such suspicions.

Mr. Chairman, I shall not hesitate, in spite of such popular declamation, to believe and follow the evidence of my senses, and the concurrent testimonies of contemporaneous beholders. I shall not, in my estimation of character, degrade this people below, nor exalt them far above, the ordinary condition of cultivated humanity. And of this be assured, that every system of conduct, or course of policy, which has for its basis an excess of virtue in this country, beyond what human nature exhibits in its improved state elsewhere, will be found, on trial, fallacious. Is there on this earth any collection of men in which exists a more intrinsic, hearty, and desperate love of office or place, particularly fat places? Is there any in which place and official emolument more certainly follow distinguished servility at elections, or base scurrility in the press? And as to eagerness for the reward, what is the fact? Let, now, one of your great office-holders, a collector of the customs, a marshal, a commissioner of loans, a postmaster in one of your cities, or any officer, agent or factor for one of your Territories or public lands, a person holding a place of minor distinction but of considerable profit, be called on to pay the last debt of nature, the poor man shall hardly be dead, he shall not be cold long, before the corpse is in the coffin, the mail shall be crowded to repletion with letters, and certificates, and recommendations, and representations. and every species of standing sychophantic solicitation, by which obtrusive mendicity seeks charity or invites compassion. Why, sir, we hear the clamors of the craving animals at the treasury trough here in this capitol. Such running, such jostling, such wriggling, such clambering over one another's backs, such squealing because the tub is so narrow and the company is so crowded. No, sir, let us not talk of stoical apathy towards the things of the national treasury, either in this people or their representatives or senators.

APPENDIX E.

TESTIMONY OF THE PRESS, REVIEWS, &c.

From the Chicago Tribune:

THE CIVIL SERVICE OF THE UNITED STATES.

Taking for a text the bill introduced in the last Congress by Mr. Jenckes, a writer in the current number of the North American Review commences an instructive article on the civil service in the United States with the words: "The condition of our civil service is deplorable." The statement is true. The picture the reviewer draws of the character and qualifications of our red-tape gentry is calculated to excite the just indignation of the people and to engage the considerate attention of every politician who is a statesman. For a generation before the war the essential qualification for the public service was an unconditional devotion to slavery. The atmosphere of Washington was pestilential. The intellectual inactivity and moral debasement could only be withstood by the most vigorous natures. And the writer claims that this state of things, than which nothing could be worse, has been but little improved. The departments are still "mental dormitories;" prison and school-boy discipline take the place of intellectual vitality, while self-respect and ambition are generally wanting. The writer would have us believe that the officers of our civil service, with few exceptions, constitute a class of privileged imbeciles, and that the civil service is a bureau of favored ignorance and preferred incompetency.

Such charges as these the writer sustains by incontrovertible facts. Our civil service system, or non-system, is radically vicious. While the requirements for the United States military and naval service are such as to attract the highest talent, and to stimulate the noblest ambition, our diplomatic and civil service, in connection with which are the most important positions in the government, are left to the favoritism of partisans. Merit and ability are supplanted by false notions of political gratitude. Men of the most diverse abilities, or of various grades of incompetency, at different times hold the same office. Public officers engaged in the same work are frequently unknown to each other. There is no *esprit de corps*, no harmony of action, no common end, save the too frequent unity of selfish interest. Whatever party is in power there is the same scrambling for spoils, the same seeking for the offices in the "gift" of a successful candidate.

The remedy proposed is the plan of competitive examination proposed by Mr. Jenckes. Of all civilized nations, the United States alone has not adopted such a system. Even Turkey, whose government the world is so unanimous to condemn to decadence and dissolution, appoints officers to its civil service according to a scale of merit. In Russia there are fourteen grades in the organization of the civil service. England, later to adopt this system, accomplishes its work with few officials and no fraud. France, since the First Napoleon, has maintained the system the Emperor advocated, "that all public offices should be filled by the most competent persons," and in all the vicissitudes in that most changeful fabric—the French government—the judicial and civil service form the only historic links which connect the present with the past. But it is in Germany, we are told, that the benefits of this system are most clearly manifest, and where it has reached its most perfect development. The rigid economy and system in this branch of the Prussian government contributed not a little to the recent wonderful development of strength, and enabled Prussia successfully to carry on a war without extra taxation. In Prussia every candidate for civil and diplomatic office must present his university diploma and pass a rigid examination. Once entered on this career the conditions of promotion are well-directed ambition and studious labor, with the prospect, in case of disability or old age, of an honorable retirement with a pension. From this class consuls, ambassadors, and diplomatists are recruited. In this department of the government some of the best talent of the nation is engaged, and to the cultivated minds of the European civil service, enriched by practical experience, the world is indebted for many of those works on social science which form the unconscious basis of so much of modern government. Stealing is rendered as unprofitable as it is dishonorable, and fraud is almost unknown. There are special courses of study for officers in this service. Political science, taxation, finance, and political economy are subjects of thorough investigation. The excise man must know something of chemistry, the treasurer of finance, the custom-house officer of commerce and tariffs. The civil and diplomatic service are as much a profession and convey as much distinction and honor as the naval and military profession. It is the introduction of a similar system that is advocated in the article above mentioned, and which we deem worthy of careful attention. It is neither "independent" nor "American," nor anything of the sort, wilfully to remain in ignorance, nor is it a signal proof of patriotism to reject the lessons offered us by the experience of older nations.

To the adoption of a system of competitive examination founded on the experience of other nations, only two possible objections can be made: one, that a bureaucracy would be thus created; a second, and one which presents more difficulties, is, that politicians would have fewer offices to dispose of.

The fear of an American bureaucracy as a result of a competitive system is absurd. Whatever may be the tendency in some countries of continental Europe, we certainly need not fear a civil army feeding at the manger of the state. The humblest clerk would be as much a candidate for the presidency then as now, and, in the majority of cases, with vastly superior qualifications. Indeed, the writer above referred to insists that there would not be a worse bureaucracy than the present system, which, in fact, has all dangers of a bureaucracy in that the officers are "incompetent and practically irresponsible." The names of the occupants of office change, but their characters do not, and rotation in office does not materially alter the condition of things. There remains the same unambitious oligarchy of incompetents. The political or partisan reasons for opposition to such a change are more apparent than real. If congressmen have fewer places at their disposal they will have more peace of their lives, fewer bores at their heels, and fewer soreheads threatening vengeance on them at their next election. Four-fifths of the labor, worry, and anxiety of a congressman's career under the present system comes from importunities of office beggars. Time which should be devoted to public business is wasted in racing from one department to another to satisfy the demands of this numerous and increasing tribe, or in listening to their stories or answering their letters. We believe that any member of the majority party in Congress would gladly consent to lose one-half of his salary if he could thereby free himself of the perpetual teasing of applicants for office.

It has been intimated that Mr. Wells, the Commissioner of the Revenue, will make some important recommendations on this subject in his forthcoming report, having special reference to the efficiency of the revenue service. We trust that Congress will take the matter into earnest consideration, and will not be satisfied with reforming a single department of the government, but carry the principle through every grade of the public service, that intelligence, honesty, and capacity are the first requisites for civil appointment, and that when a man shows himself faithful and competent he shall not be liable to removal for political reasons.

From the North American Review:

The United States have gone through a formidable convulsion, the outbreak of which was fomented to a great extent by wrong men in wrong places; by faithless and reckless public officers at home and abroad; by a demoralization of the public service, which was at the same time the cause and the effect of treasonable practices and debasement of appointments to public offices to the vilest uses. The moral atmosphere of the land is now gradually clearing up. The destructive era is drawing to a close, and the constructive era is beginning to dawn. We have purged our civilization from the degrading system of slavery. We are now impelled by all the considerations which are sacred to the lover of his country's fame to complete this task by reforming those evils in the public service of the country that grew up to a great extent under the fatal influence of sham democratic and slave-state supremacy. In a recent debate in the House of Lords on the subject of the English Reform bill, Earl Spencer referred very pointedly to the unwillingness of able and noble men to accept public service under democratic institutions. The fallacy of this proposition remains to be demonstrated by this republic, and it can and will be demonstrated.

Under a new system, offering adequate pay to the competent, and based upon the principle of open, competitive examination, young men of talent and ambition would seek public offices; and the same amount of intelligence that distinguishes all other avenues of American activity would appear in the civil service. As the service gained in efficiency its cost would diminish, inasmuch as ten competent persons, fairly compensated, might easily do the work of a hundred incompetent persons at low salaries. Indeed, it is estimated by a high authority that a saving of millions of dollars might in this manner be effected annually.

It may, on the whole, be said of England and other countries, that the civil service suffers as much from the incompetency of the highest officers as from that of the subordinate employés.

In the foreign service of England much improvement has taken place in the subordinate branches, the secretaries of legation being subjected to a severe examination. But the heads of the legations themselves, having been secretaries at a period when such stringent tests had not yet been introduced, are in many instances comparatively inferior men, often of elegant manners and social accomplishments, but not proficient in the higher branches of statesmanship and cosmopolitan culture, and thus incapable of grappling with the manifold relations of foreign countries, and unable to give to their own government comprehensive views of the respective countries to which they are accredited.

In France, the great political and social revolution of 1789 led to a revolution in the French civil service. The first Napoleon confirmed and established the principle that all public offices should be filled by the most competent persons. The system of examination has since been improved by Victor Cousin, the eminent philosopher and minister of public instruction in 1840, under whose auspices Mr. E. Laboulaye, since so well known in this country by his sympathy with American institutions, made a thorough examination of the systems of civil service in the various states of Germany. Mr Laboulaye's report, (appended to that of the congressional committee,) embodying the result of his careful investigations, has given a new impetus to the further improvement of the French civil service.

As far, however, as the highest officers of the state are concerned, they are liable to be changed by the caprice of the Emperor. But these arbitrary changes do not affect the civil service of France. This moves on with the regularity of clockwork and the inflexibility of fate. In a country liable as France was and is to be tossed about by political storms, the civil service may be said to be, next to the courts of law, the only organization which survives all changes, and furnishes an historic link between the past, present, and future generations.

The German states, particularly Würtemburg and Prussia, are more advanced than any other country in their system of examination.

In Russia all the government officers have grades. There are fourteen grades, all of them implying the rights of nobility, the fourteenth grade being the lowest in the scale. No one can be appointed to a public office in Russia without furnishing certificate of college education, and the offices are assigned according to the educational qualifications. Persons without such qualification are not entitled to any grade, but they may fill lower offices, as those of copyists, &c. They may be promoted, however, and there are not a few instances of copyists rising to the highest offices. Russia, however, is far from being purged of the abuses of favoritism, and the public offices swarm with mere parasites. But the principle of the civil service is, at any rate, established upon a sound theory, and the efforts of the present Russian government are strenuously directed to the enforcement of its practice.

In Greece, no person is admitted to the public service unless he has graduated at a university. In Italy, Portugal, Spain, Belgium, Holland, Switzerland, as in the German states, qualification tests prevail, together with the system of promotion. As an instance of this it may be mentioned that three of the foreign ministers residing at present at Washington, namely, those of France, Spain, and Portugal, had all held the post of director of their respective foreign departments previous to their nomination as ministers to the United States, and served in all the subordinate capacities of the foreign bureau before they attained to their present ambassadorial position. Lord Lyons, formerly English minister at Washington, has recently attained to the most exalted position in his profession by being appointed ambassador to the Tuileries, after having served from his earliest life in the various subordinate offices of the diplomatic service.

In the remote east—in China and Japan—the persons employed in the government offices are the most learned men of the empires; and the perpetuity of the ancient civilization of these remarkable countries may be in part accounted for by the character of their civil service organization.

Even in the mongrel empire of the Sultan of Turkey a test of qualification is insisted upon. To be sure, a pachaship may be wasted upon a favorite of the Sultana, and the governorship of a large province upon a hanger-on of the Porte or a partisan of the Grand Vizier; but smaller offices in Turkey and Egypt are generally bestowed only upon qualified candidates, accomplished Greeks, Armenians, or Levantines, who are as remarkable for their proficiency in languages and their general attainments as the Turkish or Egyptian "head" of the department is generally notorious for his ignorance. In fact, there is hardly a civilized country without a system of examination and promotion in the dispensation of its public offices.

Ours is probably the only country in the world where it does not exist in the civil service, though it exists in our military and naval service, the stringent discipline and efficiency of which are well known to all Americans. No doubt, the so-called localization of offices and political influences have heretofore impeded reform, nor do we desire to disregard this influence. Illinois, for instance, or Wisconsin, would be justified in complaining if their citizens were studiously kept out of all public offices, so that they might be filled exclusively by citizens of Massachusetts or of New Hampshire. The proper theory of the matter is, that all States should have the same right to competition, and that rejection should not take place upon any other ground excepting that of disqualification.

Another argument against the reform of the present chaos is the fear of a permanent bureaucracy, and of the anti-republican tendencies of such permanent institutions. We entertain no such apprehensions. A permanent bureaucracy is only dangerous when it is incompetent and practically irresponsible. We have already shown to what a great degree our service is now practically irresponsible, and we will proceed to show that it is a permanent institution, that we actually now have a permanent bureaucracy.

In the absence of a qualification test, it matters very little whether the incumbents of public offices represent the outgoing or the ingoing administration. If Jones, appointed in 1857, is of the same calibre as Smith, nominated in 1861, and Brown, in 1865, the fact of permanency is not in the least impaired by Jones being superseded by Smith, or by Brown supplanting Smith. Jones, Smith, and Brown, though three different persons, are, in point of fact, one and the same individuality as far as their unqualified office-holding and their unfitness are concerned. This, indeed, is the worst of all bureaucracies, when the hydra-headed brood of office-holders has positively one head, as far as qualification is concerned, and that head a dead-head. Unfitness is consequently perpetuated to such an extent that, although Jones is removed, and Smith dies, and Brown resigns, and White is promoted, the permanency of stupidity is more and more consolidated as time passes on and generation succeeds generation. The spectre "red tape," which we all imagined to have been buried amidst the rubbish of antediluvian monarchies, is thus actually haunting the public offices of the republic. The American citizen, buoyant with capacity, impatient of pedantry, finds himself, on crossing the threshold of government offices, suddenly transferred from the nine teenth century of steam and telegraphs to "the good old times of King George the Fourth."

From the National Quarterly Review:

The change in the condition of our national finances requires a proportionate change in our civil service; in our good old times, happily gone now, never to return, public officers were little more than clerks, and the employés of a large commercial house would not have exchanged places with them. Strangers to the public, the public neither knew nor cared to know them. To be an officer in the civil service of the United States was to live "the world forgetting, by the world forgot." Offices were really hereditary, and the traditional families lived on elegant incompetencies, preserving their names from popular praise or reproach by doing as little as their offices allowed; that little was less than enough to keep them from rusting, but nobody expected more. Now the scene is changed; they are no longer mere subordinates, supernumeraries in the drama of public affairs; they are become actors of the first importance; they administer the law; *inserviunt, non serviunt.* Their duties and their number have grown into equal importance. The army of officers of the internal revenue are, to a great extent, judges to themselves and the public, who have to deal with them, and nobody escapes; they decide on matters and on amounts of prodigious variety and extent; their office is, in many respects, more delicate than that of judges in the courts, for in the cases which they decide the government is at once judge and prosecutor; its officers must have impartiality and ability enough not to fail either as judges or as officers, not to injure either the government or the individual, not to forget what is due the treasury and what the citizen.

It is, therefore, just, right, and necessary to exact of those who are appointed to these offices knowledge and experience, as well as to require a thorough preliminary test of their fitness for appointment. It will no longer do to dismiss a tried and capable officer, like a house servant, with his month's wages. The higher the office, the less should change be allowed to please political adherents or to gain them. The civil service to be good, must be permanent; slow it may be in promotion, and severe in its requirements, but fixed, certain, safe, and dependent only on merit, capacity and good behavior.

The recent legislation on this subject by Congress was the first step in the right direction; Mr. Jencks's bill is the second; but the one without the other is incomplete and unsafe. One of the least pleasing facts of our present condition is the enormous number of candidates for public places; whatever may be the cause, the first result should be to require of every candidate, as conditions precedent to considering his claims for office, some test of his capacity; then from among those who have stood this examination, and that of antecedents and qualifications, to select the fittest, and finally to insure to men thus chosen the position they have earned, permanently, with the prospect of promotion according to merit and seniority.

As matters now stand, the amount of capacity required for any or all of the thousands of places that are in the appointment of the national government seems to be measured inversely in proportion to the duties to be fulfilled. The very phrase that has grown into fashion of "offices in the gift" of the appointing power, negatives the real truth of office as an employment in which the labor and the reward are fairly balanced. What merchant or manufacturer talks of the clerkships "in his gift?" He looks for the best man for the work to be done, pays a fair price, and builds up between them a tie of interest that grows with every succeeding year. A lawyer may not practice without a license, nor a doctor without a diploma, lest private and individual interests suffer, but the welfare of the whole public is staked on the chances of getting men good enough for the civil service.

* * * * * *

The example once set in the civil service of the United States will be followed in that of each State, and of the municipal and other local subdivisions; cities and counties will join States and the general government in a wholesome rivalry to make civil-service employment all that it should be, and in turn civil service will provide public officers as they should be. Political instruction and education for the civil service will become necessary; schools and colleges will add them to their course of study; special schools will be begun and supported; the public generally will be benefited by the opportunity and the occasion for learning anew its political duties; those who complete their studies will be rewarded by appointments, and having secured them by examination will continue their studies, making a practical application of them to the duties of their office, and doing those duties all the better for the prospect of a future secured to them by making promotion the reward of further tests of advanced studies.

From the Tobacco Leaf, New York :

HOW TO PREVENT OFFICIAL CORRUPTION.

In a recent article we took occasion to point out and regret the universal corruption which prevails in this country among our public men and officials. While it is true that, so far as the administration of the internal revenue system is concerned, much of this venalness may be properly laid at the door of that system itself, holding out, as it does at every turn, inducements and temptations to fraud, there is a more remote cause of the evil which no modification or improvement of that system would altogether remove. The real fault lies in the improper selection of men to fill places of public trust, and the cause of this improper selection is political favoritism. Here we get the kernel of this reeking mass of corruption. The party axiom, "To the victors belong the spoils," has wrought greater injury to the republic, by forcing weak, dishonest, and incapable men into places of trust and power, than all the material evils which have befallen her since the memorable Fourth of July, 1776. Indeed, it has now come to such a pass that no man can be chosen to public office among us unless he is willing to bind himself to fill the lucrative positions under him by the appointment of certain party followers—the jackals of the political camp—who are chosen without the slightest regard to their capacity for discharging the duties of the office, and whose only recommendation is that they have stooped lower and plunged deeper into the dirty tides of a popular campaign than any of their competitors. Of course no man of principle will bind himself to such a line of action, and the consequence is that he is thrust aside for some more available candidate. That this is repeated at the recurrence of every general election every one at all acquainted with the subject must know. What wonder, then, that our public officials, from the President downwards, are smitten with this moral disease? Party is elevated above principle, and, although we rejoice that we have had a few Chief Magistrates who have been comparatively free from such influences, the majority have succumbed more or less to this evil genius of our public affairs. It may seem quixotic to imagine that there will ever come a time when our public men will adopt for their motto the noble sentiment of Henry Clay—a sentiment which ought to be engraved in every public office in the land—"I had rather be right than President;" but we have not yet given up all hope of seeing our polluted officials rising from the slough in which they are at present involved and placing themselves on the high ground of an honest, faithful discharge of their duties, untrammelled by party affiliations.

If it is asked what remedy we propose for the present deplorable state of things, we answer, the taking the appointment to public positions, as far as possible, out of the hands of the politicians, who get themselves chosen to the most responsible and remunerative positions under government, and lodging it in a board of commissioners, who shall be known as the board of civil service commissioners, and who shall be composed of men above the reach of political corruption, if such are to be found. This civil service—resembling that of Great Britain—shall include all our foreign and diplomatic appointments and the organization of the different bureaus at Washington. To take away even so much power of appointment from the present incompetent and corrupt hands would be to inaugurate a reform among our officials the good results of which would be incalculable. The appointments of the civil service commissioners should be made solely on the ground of merit, and should only be made after a proper examination as to the general attainments and particular qualifications of the applicant for the position desired. Should such an examination but be generally established, what might we not hope for the future? Take, for example, the appointees to positions as inspectors under the internal revenue law. The earnest inquirer will hardly find a district throughout the country in which there are not many officials who know scarcely anything of the duties they have undertaken to discharge; and not a month passes in which letters are not received by the heads of the department containing the most childish and illogical inquiries with reference to the provisions and construction of the law, which a school-boy of twelve would be ashamed to propound.

But not only should the applicant for a situation in the civil service of the government be properly examined, he should be properly paid and provision made for him when, from age or disease, he has become unable to properly discharge his duties. As we have frequently remarked, the crying evil in the internal revenue department, and in other branches of official trust, is the inefficient remuneration of the employés. No man of proper business qualifications can afford to give up his regular calling for the small returns and insecure position of a government employé, and thus these positions fall into the hands of men whose services would be dear at any price. Civil service positions should be well paid, and an honest and intelligent discharge of duty should be required in return. A man should feel that he has a sure situation for his working days, and that he and his will be properly cared for when he can work no longer. This is the arrangement adopted by the British government, and both salaries and pensions are carefully and equitably adjusted, and based on the amount and quality of the service rendered.

We are glad to see that this important subject has already attracted the attention of our legislators, a bill—of which, however, we have net been able to procure a copy—having been introduced into Congress during its last-winter session providing for the establishment of a civil service bureau such as we have here indicated. With such machinery organized, we should not, when travelling abroad, be constantly put to the blush by meeting American diplomatic representatives utterly ignorant of the language of the court to which they are accredited and of the country to which they are sent. Such appointments are, unfortunately, very common, but they are none the less disgraceful and a stain upon the national escutcheon. With the organization of such a service the holding of public offices would be, in a measure, taken out of the hands of incompetent men, and a dignity be given to the public service unknown before. As at present managed, we should regret to see any friend of ours accept a situation under government, unless he possessed an independent income of his own, as we are certain that his integrity would be assailed by the most powerful temptations, and that even should these be successfully resisted, the vicious principle of "rotation in office" would oust him from his position at the next turn of the political wheel. These facts have caused office-seeking to be generally regarded as no better than a genteel kind of begging, and applicants as a set of worthless beings unable to procure any more permanent or remunerative means of livlihood. Thus true it is that public service has fallen low down in the public estimation, and the republic is suffering daily incalculable injury from a continuance of such a state of things. We might, were it necessary, go back to the days of the Pilgrims, and even later, when only the best men—best both in point of intellect and morality—were chosen to fill the places of public trust, and trace the gradual departure from that high standard until we reach the low level of the present day. But suffice it to say that this point has been reached, and that there is no hope for the future unless the people take hold of this monster corruption by the throat and insist that he shall be ousted from the high official places of the land. Well may Pope's lines be applied him:

> Vice is a monster of such hideous mien
> That to be hated needs but to be seen;
> But, seen too oft, familiar with its face,
> We first endure, then pity, then embrace.

We have embraced too long already; now let us have a loek at virtue's beautiful and benign countenance.

From the Newark Daily Advertiser:

THE CIVIL SERVICE BILL.

Mr. Jenckes, of Rhode Island, has a bill now pending in the House of Representatives, providing for an entire change in the present system of appointments to public offices. Everybody knows what the present system is. It hardly raises a question as to the capacity or integrity of an applicant, and makes official position exclusively the reward of partisan service. Ever since the time of Jackson, and the assertion of Governor Marcy that "to the victors belong the spoils," the inauguration of a President has been the signal for a general removal of those who hold, and a general scramble for the successorship of those who want, an office. During the present administration, it has been loudly and offensively proclaimed that those who eat the President's bread and butter must fight his battles, and so sweeping were the changes, and so little did they regard any qualification other than devotion to "my policy," that it is no exaggeration to say that the national treasury has suffered losses to the amount of hundreds of millions from the substitution of dishonest and incompetent men for experienced and honorable officers.

The army and navy, except to a very limited extent, during the great rush for shoulder straps incident to the war, have been almost entirely free from this evil. It is fair to say that as now organized and managed, the regular army is made up as exclusively as possible of men of capacity and integrity. It is very rarely indeed that its honor has been clouded by dishonest acts on the part of its officers, and the same statement may be truthfully extended to the navy. Yet these officers are not extravagantly paid, nor are they without those temptations to which so many men yield in the civil service. The fact that they are so generally honest is due to their training, to the method of their appointment, and above all to the fact that, so trained and appointed, they have naturally acquired a high sense of professional honor. Their social position depends almost entirely upon their rank and reputation in the service, and not upon the style in which they live.

Mr. Jenckes's so-called civil service bill proposes to apply to the civil officers the same rules of appointment that now obtain in the army and navy. Candidates for positions in the Treasury, the Interior Department, or the Post Office are to be required to pass a stringent examination, in competition with other applicants; and measures are also proposed to ascertain the general fitness and integrity of the candidate. There is nothing impossible about this; nothing even that can be considered inconvenient. It would require no great skill to devise a system of examination in accounts, in fiscal science, and in the history of treasury operations which would fairly test the ability of a young man to enter upon the duties of a clerkship under Mr. McCulloch. In the diplomatic service, so often disgraced by the uncouth ignorance of men who "must be provided for," the same rule should apply. They should be able to speak either French or the language of the country to which they are destined; they should be familiar with the customs observed in national negotiations, and, especially in consulates, they should be proficient in knowledge of the commerce of the port to which they seek to be assigned. We are glad to know that Senator Patterson, of New Hampshire, is preparing a bill to do for the foreign service just what Mr. Jenckes is trying to do for the civil service at home.

Under such a plan of competitive examination, with the added condition that appointees shall hold office during good behavior, a commission would be a certificate of character as a gentleman, entitling the holder to social position and recognition. The different bureaus would naturally draw to themselves men of purity and refinement. An *esprit de corps* similar to that existing in the army and navy would soon arise, and promotions would be looked upon as the regular reward of a faithful discharge of duty, so that there would be little disposition to change or retire. But the greatest benefit would be found in the removal of a terribly corrupting influence from our popular elections. Many people now vote for a candidate because, in event of his election, they will have a claim upon him for some subordinate position. The taint of self-aggrandizement runs through our whole political system. A bad man in power has a controlling influence over all his inferiors. Their food and shelter and the comfort of their families depend upon his favor. There is nothing more melancholy or more degrading, in our conceptions of human nature, than the timid subservience of the office-holder who changes his political opinions with every election, and thinks, acts, and votes with an eye single to his livelihood. There are other arguments that will suggest themselves, and we hope that they are sufficiently obvious to induce the passage, in Congress, of the civil service bill of Mr. Jenckes, and the foreign service bill which Senator Patterson is about to introduce. We shall have a purer political atmosphere when they become laws.

From the Iron Age, New York:

NECESSITY OF CHANGE IN THE MANNER OF APPOINTMENT AND CONTROL OF REVENUE OFFICIALS.

We append a memorial adopted at the Cleveland convention, praying Congress for a thorough change in the manner of appointing officers for the collection of internal revenue, and pointing out the evils attending the present system of collection. We suggest to our exchanges that they copy this memorial, and urge upon their readers the importance of having it extensively signed and sent forward without delay to Congress. The subject is one of the deepest and most pressing importance, as the incapacity and venality of the persons charged with the duty of collecting our excise taxes are so great as not only to have become a great national disgrace, but to threaten even the demoralization of the government itself. If a system cannot be devised by which men may be compelled to deal honestly with the public moneys intrusted to their charge, we may fear for the permanence of our institutions and the safety of the country, and no subject requires prompter or more judicious treatment than this at the hands of Congress. The following memorial (prepared by Mr. E. B. Ward, of Detroit) is just in time, and we hope it will receive a million signatures from all sections of the country. We trust the suggestion we make will be attended to.

MEMORIAL.

To the honorable Senate and House of Representatives of the United States in Congress assembled:

Your memorialists beg leave most respectfully to represent that the belief has become universal throughout the United States, that the interests of this country demand a great and decided change in the mode of appointments and removals, and in the qualifications of all others who are selected to execute the laws for the disbursement of the moneys belonging to the United States. The evils of the present system are so patent and so gross that the Secretary of the Treasury and the Commissioner of Internal Revenue both admit the impossibility of conducting the revenues and treasury of the country creditably or satisfactorily with officers appointed under the present plan.

All the ablest and most sagacious statesmen of the country, including Jefferson, Calhoun,

Clay, Morehead, Benton, Webster, and hosts of others, have during the time of their greatest political power lent the whole force of their influence and eloquence to change a system that, in the language of a most able and searching report to Congress on this subject, says: "That the present system of appointments is fettered by conditions destructive of the independence, reproachful to the patriotism, humiliating to the pride, degrading to the character of an American citizen," and it is patent to every one conversant with this subject that the time has already arrived when (as predicted by those far-seeing men) the finances of the nation can no longer be successfully managed by the men who seek and obtain appointment under the present crude mode of selection of public officials. It is true that some worthy men obtain office, but it is notorious that worth and fitness are the exceptions. The Secretary of the Treasury reports that large percentages of taxes on several of the leading articles subject to taxation are totally lost through the collusions and incapacity of the officials charged with their collection.

It is time that a thorough system of examination into the moral and educational fitness of all candidates for office should be put in operation in this country, as it has been in all European governments, and as is suggested in the able and practical report of the Commissioner of Internal Revenue, under the head of "civil service."

Believing that no subject will be presented to the consideration of Congress during its present session of more imperative importance to the well-being of this government than the one we now press upon your attention, we most respectfully solicit your earnest and early efforts for the removal of one of the greatest and most dangerous evils that now afflicts the overtaxed energies of this great nation, and threatens, if continued, the total demoralization of our whole collection system.

The humiliating confession of the Secretary that this government cannot collect its revenues owing to the corruption of its officers, is a flagrant disgrace, and no time should be lost in making such a change as will wipe this shame from the records of the government.

And your memorialists will ever pray.

From the Boston Advertiser, February 6, 1868:

THE CIVIL SERVICE.

To the Editors of the Boston Daily Advertiser:

It is a matter of encouragement to every true friend of our institutions that the attention of our legislators and business men is at last becoming interested in the subject of that branch of our government known as the "civil service." A committee of Congress has the matter under advisement. They have prepared a bill well adapted to produce one of the greatest reforms of the age. In these times when men are feeling for the solid foundations whereon to rebuild, it is well that this important department should be remodelled and brought into harmony with the spirit of our institutions and the intelligence of the age. It is a work in which the United States ought to have been the pioneer, but unwittingly it has been delayed till even the conservative governments of Europe are far in advance of us.

Time was when our government could afford—if a government ever could afford to tolerate an evil—to let its financial matters be managed in any way that would best suit the lax notions and convenience of those having them in charge. Its revenues were not only amply sufficient to meet all its demands, but were such that, after feeding all the parasites and vampires that naturally infested the system, it actually distributed among the people an accumulated surplus lying unused in its vaults.

But times have changed. The nation is now deeply in debt. Taxes are levied to meet our necessities. The people give a willing assent. The debt is theirs; the government is theirs; the officers of the government are their servants. Into the hands of these servants they give a free offering to be applied to the speedy cancellation of this debt. In doing this they demand faithful effort and honest service in every department of the government, that no part of the revenue be diverted from its legitimate purpose; that no post of responsibility be encumbered by an inefficient servant; that no funds be squandered to support an inefficient system of service that has outlived the era it served, or that has been perverted from its legitimate purposes to subserve the interests of mere partisans, if not to feed broken down politicians at the government expense.

We have before us a prolific source of evil in the matter of appointments to office. Look for a moment at the results following the appointment of a collector of customs at any of our larger ports of entry. While the new incumbent is yet without experience and with little knowledge possibly of the very first steps to be taken in the discharge of his new duties, to say nothing of the pressure of the daily routine of business devolving upon him, and the endless variety of perplexing questions involved in appeals from his decisions, and from other sources, to be considered and reported upon to the department, he finds himself surrounded with a clamorous horde of place-hunters who, like Æsop's hungry swarm of flies, give him no peace till they gain a foothold where they hope to engorge themselves at the expense of the government. They haunt him not only at his office during the hours of business, but at the street corner, at his fireside, and in short at any place and at any hour of day or night when he may be reached.

Once in the coveted positions they find not only something to do but much to learn before they can begin to do. And here to the government at least is the beginning of trouble. All the world knows that in such circumstances accounts were repeatedly returned from the departments for correction, to the frequent mortification of the chief officer and the great hindrance of the public business.

The business community are also included in the list of sufferers from this cause. Not a few can bear testimony to the vexations delays, the grievous annoyances, and sometimes the added expenses resulting from errors of construction or misinterpretations of the laws regulating the details of business by the inexperienced, if not incompetent, appointees that succeed nearly every new administration. I do not intend to imply that every new appointment is undesirable, but I do wish to be understood as being in favor of a system that shall make needed changes in such a manner that the public service shall not suffer thereby. The business of the government is not of a nature so simple and obvious that a man can know by intuition just how it is to be performed. Our business establishments, with a capital of a few thousand dollars, intrust their books and papers to no bookkeeper unless he is qualified for the position by a previous thorough course of training. But here is our government, an immense business establishment with the care if not with a capital of millions of dollars, appointing men to the care of its moneys and keeping of its accounts in a manner that, if followed by ordinary business concerns, would ruin 999 out of every 1,000.

The renowned Swartwout years ago demonstrated the imperfections of the system in one direction, and his imitators follow in so rapid succession at the present day it would seem to need no argument to convince the most incredulous of the imperative necessity of a radical change in the entire system.

From the Republican, Bellefontaine, Ohio:

THE CIVIL SERVICE BILL.

We are glad to know that this bill is gaining in favor with members of Congress, and that it is now likely to be adopted. This measure provides for the examination of applicants for office, and makes their appointment dependent upon qualification and moral fitness and not on the favor of politicians or the political services of the applicant. If adopted the measure will do away with the greater part of the corruption in the government and bring about a purity in the administration of government affairs that has not existed since the day when Jackson inaugurated the present corrupt system of appointing men to office for party services without any regard to qualifications or fitness for positions.

We know of no measure that would work a greater reform, or which we would more gladly see adopted.

From the Round Table, New York, October 26, 1867:

OUR CIVIL SERVICE.

The most anomalous of all our public officers is the Vice-President of the United States. The Paul Prys of the press give faithful accounts of the cabinet meetings, but with all their acuteness they have not yet been able to detect the Vice-President among the personages who constitute that solemn conclave. But how can the Vice-President be expected to discharge the duties which the Constitution assigns to him in the event of the absence, sickness, removal, or death of the President if opportunities for familiarizing himself with the functions of the Executive are altogether denied to him? When President Washington made a journey, even of the shortest duration, he never left the White House without first installing in it Mr. Vice-President Adams as acting President during his absence. President Johnson, on the other hand, has absented himself on several occasions from his post of duty without calling upon Mr. Vice-President Wade to officiate as President during his absence. The Vice-President having consequently nothing to do excepting during the session of Congress, when he officiates as President of the Senate, we suggest that he may profitably be placed at the head of the civil service commissioners to be appointed whenever Mr. Jenckes's civil service bill shall have become the law of the land. This will give the Vice-President something to do, and this functionary will cease to be a mere walking gentleman on the stage of affairs, and become a fully-employed public officer. The President might thus be relieved from attending personally to the selection of postmasters and other petty officials, and the time now wasted by the Executive in adjusting appointments and in granting interviews to supplicants for office might certainly be more worthily bestowed. The question who shall be postmaster at Kankakee or collector at Cohasset is no doubt one of transcendent magnitude, but we believe that the power of deciding upon it may safely be delegated to the Vice-President, while the President may employ himself in deciding upon questions of possibly somewhat greater importance.

Public opinion is in this, as in most other respects, far in advance of politicians. The people are disgusted with the present condition of the civil service, and it is due to the intelligence of American citizens that the public service of this republic should be organized upon the same principle of fitness and qualification which determines the appointment of persons to be employed in private establishments. Yet it may fairly be asserted that more care is bestowed by a New York lady upon collecting evidences of the qualifications of her maid than by the politicians upon those of public officers. With a test of qualification once established by law, the whole official atmosphere of the republic will be delivered from the taint of incapacity and turpitude which now weighs upon it like a nightmare. We shall then have men for Presidents and Vice-Presidents and other public offices who come from the highest intellectual and moral spheres of society, instead of from the very gutters and sink-holes of the land. This republic was founded by the gentlemen of America, by men of the noblest culture of heart and mind. Society in the early days of the republic was controlled by gentlewomen and gentlemen whose influence kept vulgarity at a distance, and blended republican simplicity of manners and living with the most delightful social virtues and accomplishments. A thorough reform in the civil service, such as proposed in the civil service bill, with the Vice-President as chief commissioner, will do much to restore official service and society to something of its original purity and respectability.

Thousands of educated young Americans, of gentlemanly nature and high attainments, who now are doomed to vegetate as briefless lawyers, idle divines, or unsuccessful merchants, would enter the lists as candidates for the civil service from the moment the latter shall be based upon a principle of qualification that holds out a fair chance to their talents and aspirations. Dunces, imbeciles, and rogues would be excluded by proper tests of qualification which they must necessarily be unable to meet. Washington, the national capital, now the seat of all the riff-raff and the incapacities of the continent, would soon become a city distinguished for its culture, if public officers, from the President and Vice-President down to the most obscure head of bureau and clerk, were selected from the most intellectual and refined, instead of from the most obtuse and coarse classes of citizens. Any one who doubts the propriety, not to say the absolute necessity, of a change has only to visit Washington on the eve of the meeting or during the session of Congress, or during some political excitement, and he will soon become less incredulous. He will see the hotels and principal streets, the lobbies of Congress, the departments, and the White House thronged with multitudes of men and women who look as if they had escaped from some bagnio. The men will look dirty and sordid, and the women haggard and forbidding, to say no worse. These people are office-seekers or office-brokers. A foreigner, unfamiliar with the chaotic condition of our civil service, might fancy that Botany Bay and the Dry Tortugas had poured out their inmates upon the capital. These wild, uncouth men and miserable women crowd the parlors of the White House, clamoring for bread, as if the government of the United States were a poor-house, and offices meted out to the needy like alms.

Evils of this kind can only be remedied by introducing tests of qualification and open competition. The thousands of individuals who now besiege the Executive and Congress and the departments in search of employment, without a shadow of qualification, should be left to the tender mercies of the charitable, if they cannot earn a living by honorable labor. The present system should be altogether abrogated. The power of appointment should be vested in the hands of a commission, who, as is proposed, shall decide as to the qualifications of the candidates for the public service. The President, the heads of departments, and the members of Congress need all their time for the proper discharge of their official duties. In relieving them from the present pressure for appointments to office, the public service will gain as much in efficiency, as far as the public men are concerned, as all other branches of the service will be purified and improved by limiting the tenure of office to successful competitors in open examination. By effecting this reform, the way may be paved for a nobler era in American public life, and in American society. We may then possibly show the nations of the world that, unlike the democracies of antiquity, which were destroyed by bad and incompetent men, who, unhappily, monopolized office and power, the American republic has the wisdom to perpetuate its life by pressing into its service the best and most high-toned, and not the worst and most ill-bred of its citizens.

From the New York Round Table, November 9, 1867:

The country has been lately shocked by the discovery of frauds in the Treasury Printing Bureau, and a congressional committee is now in Washington for the purpose of investigating these charges. Frauds will, unfortunately, occur in the best regulated services, and it would be hazardous to assert that the contemplated reform of the civil service will render them altogether impossible. But this reform bids fair, at all events, to diminish the difficulties which exist in the present chaotic condition of the civil service, by substituting for an army of irresponsible office-holders persons who have gone through the ordeal of a public competitive examination and of such other tests as the civil service commissioners may deem proper to apply regarding the integrity and trustworthiness of the respective candidates. The Treasury Printing Bureau is an immense establishment in which hundreds of men and women are employed who are not responsible to the state. They are responsible only to an officer as irresponsible as they are, who cannot be removed or suspended excepting with the consent of the Secretary of the Treasury, who, in his turn, wields also an altogether irresponsible authority, he or his predecessor having appointed the so-called Superintendent of

H. Rep. Com. 47——8

the Printing Bureau (who in the hierarchy of the treasury is only a clerk, though he actually exercises the authority of a superintendent) without either the knowledge or the consent of either house of Congress, or of any other responsible body or authority.

Now, this is a dangerous state of things. In the midst of our free institutions we find official bureaus, the operations of which are wrapped in mystery and darkness because they are carried on by irresponsible employés, appointed by the arbitrary power of one man, and that one man in most cases ignorant in regard to their moral and mental status, and hardly knowing their names. And how is it possible that one man, howsoever watchful and able, can vouch for the competency and integrity of thousands of clerks, directors, and superintendents?

In the eastern, western, and middle States, there are thousands of brave women who earn an honorable livelihood as teachers, and they hold a distinguished position among the most civilizing agencies of the country. The profession of teaching is sympathetic to womanhood, and gives a worthy occupation to the mind. But the task of the female copyists in the departments, and the quasi-factory duties of the girls in the printing bureau, are of a far less elevating character, and produce rather a bad than a good influence. However, if women are overtaken by poverty in Washington, there is little choice between keeping a boarding-house or going to the Treasury or poor-house. Five out of six Washington women keep boarding-houses, and rents and living being high, while on the other hand the tendency of congressmen to keep house is increasing, this business is already overdone and precarious under the best circumstances. At the same time Washington contains a larger number of poor, genteel families, than any other city of the Union north of Richmond, from the fact that the salaries in government offices are not adequate for the support of a large family, and also from the accession of many helpless and reduced women of the southern States. The number of those ladies has increased a thousand-fold during and since the war, and they are ladies, too, who have not been brought up like those of the east and west, in such a manner as to fit them for teachers even if their intellectual and moral sympathies gravitated in that direction. Hence the immense rush to the government offices of women of all ages and all conditions, good, bad, and indifferent, and the cry is still they come. Yet there is no reason why, if there be no legalized system of competitive examination for the men who apply for offices, there should be a discrimination made among the women. Nor should women be excluded from the benefit of public employment because they are women, or receive less pay when they give the same quantity and quality of work as men because they are women. Yet we have said enough for the present to explain the peculiar circumstances which increase the number of female applicants for office in Washington in addition to that of legions of men.

But what is a Secretary to do in the face of such a state of things? If he were a man of comprehensive statesmanship he would be the first to petition Congress for the abrogation of a power which he is physically and mentally unable to wield over such a mass of untested subordinates, and even if he happens to be only a second or third rate man, he must, at least, have enough common sense to exclaim, like Metternich, "After me the deluge!" But "deluges" are not things to be trifled with when they threaten to fill the land with the stenches of imbecility and corruption. To-day there is something wrong in the printing bureau, to-morrow in some other bureau. Congressional committees may sit until doomsday, and even unravel the meshes of some particular fraud or irregularity, yet no permanent remedy will be found until Congress strikes at the root of the evil by substituting competitive examination, and consequent law, order, and responsibility, for the present chaos and irresponsibility. Competent men and women should also be compensated in such a manner that they may not be obliged, as at present, to convert the federal capital into a nest of paupers. However, as long as the irresponsible system now in force prevails, the country has no means of ascertaining whether even the smallest pay is not too large, and the incumbents of office themselves must fret under this imputation of being overpaid, when, as far as the competent number of them is concerned, they are actually underpaid, at least in comparing their salary to that earned by merely muscular labor. The worthy, active, able, faithful government employé is actually wronged, while the public is still more grievously wronged, as far as the maintenance of the frauds of those employés is concerned who are unworthy to hold office. At present all is chaos and confusion, attended by injustice to the good, by immunity to the bad public servant, and by disasters to the public credit, to the honor and the dignity of the country. The proposed system of competitive public examination, and of the introduction of the principle of responsibility to the state in all public offices, high and low, may not afford a remedy for all the evils of which we complain, but few unbiased thinkers will deny that a considerable improvement may thus be effected in the civil service.

From the Round Table, November 23, 1867 :

*　　*　　*　　This is, however, only one case out of a thousand. Indeed, it would not be hazarding too much to assert that worth and aptitude are the very last things thought of in appointments. This is the cancer which gnaws at the vitals of the republic. If culture and character continue to be ignored, the democracy will become a pigocracy; and already there is not a ruffianly tavern-keeper in the land, or otherwise illiterate or venal clod, who does not think himself entitled to any office, simply because he meets congressmen in bar-rooms and knows how to buttonhole them in the nick of time. Corruption may not be always guarded against, whether the delinquent official be a gentleman of culture or an unlettered boer, and it is only by exacting bonds from officials, high or low, that the people can be efficiently protected against robbery and fraud. The commission charged with the competitive examination of candidates might also exact proper tests as to their moral character and integrity, so that culture and honesty may in future go hand in hand in the public service of the United States. Congress is about to reassemble, and, with the recent political events, office-hunters will soon throng the lobbies of the White House, of the departments, and the Capitol. The maxim that "to the victors the spoils belong" has wrought more evil in this country than any saying that ever fell from a politician's lips. Spoils refer to the property found upon the persons or in the camps of vanquished enemies. Now, to represent the offices of the public service as "spoils" which the victorious political party is justified in clutching as prize-money would virtually degrade this government to a freebooters' organization, with the additional infamy that a professional pirate is guilty only of destroying certain cargoes and ships, while a political pirate captures whole government organizations, inflicts damages that cannot be repaired, by contaminating the entire service and undermining the honor, dignity, and prosperity of the nation.

A plausible, often-quoted maxim thus becomes an execrable hydra-headed conspiracy, and while demagogues flatter the baser strata of the people by laying the spoils at their feet as a bait or bribe for their votes, the people are robbed, swindled, disgraced, and become the laughing-stock of mankind. During the turmoil of the last generation, while the republic was sowing its wild oats, with slavery at the south and incursions of hordes of immigrants north, it would have made wily old politicians smile to hear any one urge morality and efficiency in the public service and to advocate its purification by the introduction of a system of competitive examination and of rigid tests of qualification. But the republic is gradually emerging from this chaos. It is also becoming rapidly weaned from the fallacy that common schools and churches and facilities for the rapid acquisition of wealth are all that is required to make a government respectable and a people happy. It is only by welding culture together with integrity that the civil service can be purged from its present evils, and, at the same time, set an example to all other branches of American activity. This is not alone the indispensable condition for the improvement of the civil service, but that of the stability of democracy itself. Surely with cultivated, patriotic, and upright men in public places, the republic need not again present the mortifying spectacle to the world of fellow-citizens cutting each other's throats because they lacked the moral and intellectual power to settle their difficulties in a peaceable manner, as becomes Christian legislators and peoples of the nineteenth century. Since we had no tests of qualification for public functions, legislative action became pugilistic, official action arbitrary, and the public service inefficient, corrupt, chaotic. A better era is dawning, and the adoption of the Jenckes bill of competitive examinations will be among its most auspicious heralds, to be followed by many other measures in the same direction.

From the New York Round Table, November 30, 1867:

The Land Office is presided over by a functionary of great comprehensiveness of mind and indefatigable industry and energy, but as far as the subordinate officers are concerned, greater talent would certainly be infused in the service by the adoption of the competitive principle. This department is also under the official control of Mr Browning, who is thus the lord of all the lands which he surveys. Low down in the building, in the subterranean halls, where, as upon the altars of the ancient Greeks, light is always burning, is concealed the Census bureau. Having been without a head for many years past, it is to be supposed that Mr. Browning himself counts the population, male and female, their goods and chattels, their churches and schools, their penitentiaries and their asylums. Mr. Browning has altogether too many bureaus under his control, and good cannot be expected to come out of this comet with many tails.

The agricultural, land, and census departments hold, in some respects, cognate relations as far as many agricultural facts are concerned. Then there is the State Department, which receives agricultural reports from ministers and consuls. Again, there is perched at the top of Mr. McCulloch's caravansary a strange hybrid concern called the Statistical Bureau of the Treasury Department, which prints the commercial statistics received at the State Department and at the custom-houses, and which dabbles in what may be called "statistics at large," with an eye to the revenue. All these departments meddle more or less in agriculture, and some nibbling is done here and some there. Finally, there is the new Agricultural Department proper, which is supposed to be the great pastoral ocean which absorbs all the minor affluents of agricultural incidents and statistics, and from whence they irrigate the whole country in seeds, samples, cuttings, pamphlets, reports, model farms, experimental farms, and agricultural periodicals and publications. Many millions of dollars are annually paid for the support of these multitudinous organizations. Apart from the fact that the appointments made in them are irresponsible and unsatisfactory as long as they are not based upon stringent tests of qualification and integrity, we do not find any preconcerted device presiding over these establishments, so as to combine and simplify their labors and make them all concur in a well-defined aim of really national utility and progress.

Leaving out of question the statistical department of the treasury, as a thing to be altogether done away with, and considering the importance of the land, census, and agricultural departments, we believe the time has fully come for separating them from Mr. Browning's *olla podrida* and uniting them in one and the same, but independent, department   It will not be enough in future to present ponderous reports to Congress and make a meretricious display of activity.   The essential thing is that certain central facts of vital importance should be thoroughly ascertained, and then presented to Congress in as simple and lucid a manner as possible.   The distribution of property in lands as well as in real estate and railways should be ascertained in the most careful manner, it being of primary importance to know whether this tends towards monopolies in the hands of a few, as under feudal and semi-feudal institutions, or whether the effect of democracy actually is, as it is generally assumed to be, to diffuse the good things of this world in a more equal manner among the masses of the people.

Many of the facts presented in the reports of these offices do not seem to grapple with these and other central points, and are rather encumbered with a formidable array of dates and figures, which should be only dealt with as aims to the end of deducing facts and principles concerning the present status and future prospects of all the various classes of the population. But they are too much considered without regard to any ultimate result or principle, and the consequence is that, though we have so many gigantic bureaus and departments, we have very little positive information about matters in regard to which it is most needed. Another consequence is, that though we have so many departments, there is a constant call for the establishment of new ones, simply because with the present lack of intellectual power in official life there is hard-working industry without comprehensiveness of mind, and overflowing prolixity without unity of thought or aim.   Mr. Orestes Browning does not pretend to possess either the organizing genius of Carnot or the creative power of Bonaparte ; yet he is the Tycoon of 50 different bureaus, under the responsibility of which even those two master minds would have fairly staggered.   Mr. Browning has also official charge of the mining department; but Mr. McCulloch, too, coquets with mineralogy, and deputes a gentleman noted as an author of several funny books of travel to explore the mining resources of our new Eldorados!   This and other reports will be no doubt drawn up to the best of the ability of those who write them.   But who tested this ability ?   Where are the official vouchers to satisfy the country that they can depend upon the information contained in these reports? They are, indeed, even less trustworthy than newspaper disquisitions, because journalists select their writers according to their fitness, while in official life the framers of reports and employés are taken at random, with little or no regard to such qualification.

In advocating thus strenuously the infusion of more brains, the adoption of competition, examination, and the promotion of culture and merit, combined with integrity, to the highest places, we are satisfied that we are rendering the best service that can be rendered to the country.   Without greater unity of aim and comprehensiveness of ideas and culture in the prominent offices, and without the adoption of the competitive principle in the various branches of the service, the present intolerable confusion will become so much worse confounded that, in the end, the republic may come to grief for want of brains and want of conscience ; it is certainly becoming daily more seriously embarrassed for want of system and unity of thought and purpose in the various spheres of the government.

From the New York Round Table, December 28, 1867 :

The Treasury Department would work more efficiently by abolishing half of its bureaus. The same applies to the Interior Department.   The multiplicity of bureaus seems only to have been created for the purpose of constituting an outlet for office-seekers, and for the supporters of politicians.   If we need political Botany bays, they ought at all events to be as self-supporting as many penitentiaries are, and should not entail both extravagant expenditure and extravagant imbecility upon the country.   Another cause of our cumbrous and multitudinous bureaus is to be traced to the scarcity of master minds in our official spheres, and consequently to the necessity of letting things go by chance instead of devising methods for simplifying the organization of the public service, and for testing and sifting, and at the same time reducing in number, the persons employed in it.

The competition for public service being, under this bill, open to all classes of the population, each congressional district will contribute its ratio of candidates, so that the proteges of congressmen will all have the same chance of employment as heretofore, with this difference, that only those will be eligible who possess the requisite qualifications, as prescribed by the new bill.   Those politicians of the old school who hold to the doctrine that well-ascertained aptitude and integrity, as tests of public service, are incompatible with the chaotic nature of a rough-and-tumble democracy, form only a small section of what may be called the diabolical party.   Their objections may have considerable weight in bar-rooms, but begin to be scouted with scorn by the enlightened masses of the community.   Certain customhouse directors and heads of departments and hack politicians may regret the good old times, when they could with impunity disgrace the service of the country by cramming public offices with their satellites, but their lamentations will awake few sympathetic echoes except in the hearts of those who are hostile to the republic, and who chuckle with delight over this insidious method of bringing it into disrepute and tearing it to pieces.

The scramble for office which follows in the train of every presidential election, and which is the source of so much demoralization, will, in virtue of the adoption of the principle of qualification, lose, at all events, some of its most objectionable features. Intelligent and accomplished citizens of the republic, who have heretofore shunned contact with public life as long as it held out premiums only to incapacity and corruption, and no inducements to merit and probity, may in future be encouraged to devote their services to the state. Unless American democracy secures the co-operation of the most intelligent, of the best qualified, of the most highly cultured men, it will inevitably share in the end the fate of all previous democracies; attempts which were regularly shipwrecked in consequence of the fatal mistake that democracy means the exclusive rule of the lowest and most uneducated people of the nation. Mr. Jenckes's bill takes the first step toward better things, to be followed, we trust, by more comprehensive reforms, until we have secured the highest talent and most exemplary moral culture of the country for the service of the state.

The principal revenue commissioners take strong ground in their reports to Congress in favor of the principle of mental and moral qualification as a means of protecting the revenue of the country against the frauds and imbecilities that now beset it. These and all other unbiased functionaries are in favor of such a reform. They may have pet schemes of their own, and the Jenckes bill may not meet all expectations, but a gigantic reform like this cannot be expected to be carried out all at once. The best that can be done is to merge all minor differences for the purpose of adopting the Jenckes bill as an incipient measure, remedying some of the most crying evils, and paving the way for ulterior reforms. The republic is at present in a condition which requires on the one hand the utmost retrenchment of expenditure, and on the other, a complete reorganization of the public service. In the face of the southern reconstruction difficulty the republic is called upon to organize the new Territory of Alaska, and perhaps also that of St. Thomas. The lust for more land is not to stop at the Arctic or in the Antilles. The result of all this will be the creation of more public offices. Under the old system it might be as well to draw for these offices, so that the winner may clutch the prize and become a territorial officer or clerk. The chance would be as much in favor of the qualifications of these tricky wights as of those appointed under the old system.

With two immense sea-coasts—the Atlantic and the Pacific—to guard, the custom-house service alone will require armies of employés. The revenue service and the various departments will also increase their business to a vast extent. It will not be too much to assert that within a short period there will be more persons employed in the public service of the Atlantic and Pacific dominions of the republic than in all the European states together. Think of a hundred thousand employés selected at random, according to the caprice of a custom-house director or a secretary, or a hack politician, without guarantee of their qualification either intellectual or moral! The imagination shrinks from fathoming the consequences of such a revolting chaos. Indeed, it would seem as if the republic cared only for clutching empire, without the least thought or care of administering and preserving it, and making it conducive to the welfare of the people. Any savage chief may acquire empire by purchase or by conquest, but the preservation and the use of it depend altogether upon the intellectual and moral forces employed in its administration.

If we go on with our old system we shall present to mankind the spectacle of a nation which spreads from ocean to ocean and grasps one territory after another, without mental forces to administrate such a vast empire, and without moral force to have a public service distinguished for its integrity. We have already shown on previous occasions that, in spite of our costly legations and hundreds of consulates, England and France take the lion's share of the world's commerce, while our foreign ministers make desperate efforts to be admitted to court circles, and to be invited to the soirés of people of title and fashion. We have further shown that our multitudinous bureaus and troops of clerks obstruct rather than advance the public interests, and need to be curtailed as well as to be sifted. In view of all this, and of the additional territorial acquisitions to the republic, the people demand that Congress should procrastinate no longer in regard to the adoption of the bills which we trust to see introduced soon after the reassembling of this body for the greater retrenchment and better efficiency of the home and foreign service.

From the New York Round Table, February 8, 1868:

The task which the civil service reformers have before them seems to be this: To allot to each public office a certain number of employés, selected from the candidates for competitive examination, and, consequently, to reduce the number of the present civil force to a considerable extent; to do away with the present scale of increase of salary, (namely, from $1,200 to $1,400, $1,600, $1,800, &c.,) which is not sufficiently discriminative, and so fails to insure the best capacity; and to adopt in its stead a higher scale, discriminating between the merely mechanical clerks and copyists, who should not have a higher salary than from $800 to $1,200, and the employés whose occupations involve intellectual culture and knowledge of special studies, and whose salary ought not to be less than $1,800, and should gradually rise, in the scale of promotion, to $3,000 and $4,000. The heads of departments themselves should he subjected to a rigorous test of examination as well as their subordinate employés. The collector of the port of New York; for instance, offers no other qualification excepting that of being one of the hundred thousand merchants of the country. There is no doubt a fair number of merchants who have devoted special studies to all those intricate laws, regulations, and sciences a mastery of which is indispensable to the proper discharge of one of the most important administrative functions of the government. But, as a general rule, our merchants lack time for such studies, though many of them have enjoyed at least the advantages of collegiate education. Now, taking for granted that there are men whose whole life has been devoted to the accumulation of wealth in the importing or in the banking line, and who have yet found time to qualify themselves for the duties to which we have referred, how is the country to discriminate between the merchants and bankers who are qualified and those who are not, excepting by a legalized system of examination? Hence, the fact that a man has been a successful merchant or president of a bank does not carry sufficient weight to substantiate his qualification for an important public office. Not that we wish to underrate the experience of a laborious commercial or financial occupation; they are, no doubt, useful accessories in the administration of custom-houses, revenue and treasury departments. But they are only accessories, which, without special and additional qualifications, may rather prove obnoxious than otherwise, inasmuch as a collector or treasury man, of commercial and financial antecedents and experience only, must be but too apt to rush through his duties in a conventional and apparently smart style, and to scout all improvements, reforms, and comprehensive studies as useless or unpractical, simply because he confounds a governmental with an importer's office, and because anything that transcends his ordinary mercantile routine naturally appears to him visionary. Moreover, if a collector as important as that of New York, or a prominent treasury official, happens to be a person of only ordinary education and without special qualifications and accomplishments for his post, how can the public be expected to respect his administration, and how can he expect to be respected by his subordinates?

If he do not court a stringent examination, if he cannot produce the evidence of having pursued special studies for the fulfilment of his functions, how can we expect that he will exact a test of examination and qualification from his inferiors; and, if untested and conscious of his defective training himself, how can he be expected to pass a judgment upon the qualifications of other men? That such untested men can hold public offices at all is deplorable enough, but that the appointing power should be vested in their hands is positively silly. Think of the collector of New York, for instance, having the power of appointing 1,000 men in his office alone, without taking into account those he may recommend to other offices and those he may "swap." Such a state of things is not to be tolerated any longer, and our advice to the congressional committee is to begin by cleansing the Augean stable of the New York custom-house by taking the appointing power away from its present director and examining him and his employés in regard to their special studies and qualifications. It is only by overhauling one department after another that reform can be effected. The overhauling of the Treasury Department at Washington will also afford rich sport for the reformers. We have no doubt that several bureaus, particularly the statistical bureau, will be abolished altogether, as inflicting a large annual expenditure upon the country without compensating advantages. We have already stated on a former occasion that the custom-house reports, the commercial reports of consuls in the State Department, the census, land, and agricultural departments give all the statistics that are required. Any additional statistical laboratory is a luxury which the country can ill afford, and certainly not at the present time. Moreover, too many cooks spoil the broth, and we are satisfied that with the nibbling done in statistics here and there and everywhere, more money is spent in this country for the collection of loose statistics and statistics "at large," and for their fragmentary and chaotic publication, than for all the ministers of commerce and navigation in European countries together.

The time may come, and we trust soon, when this country will have a minister for commerce and navigation, who shall relieve the Secretary of the Treasury from the custom-house and surveyors' and naval office business, and the State Department from the commercial and maritime part of the consular business. If Congress were to decree to-morrow the abolition of the statistical and other similarly unnecessary bureaus, every tax-paying citizen would be relieved to the extent of the saving of the amounts now wasted upon these bureaus; while their disappearance would inflict no public injury or individual pang save in the hearts of those dismissed from office, and of the critics who might mourn over those delectable opportunities which formerly enabled them to expose gross blunders. We therefore again enjoin upon Congress the necessity of abolishing all useless offices, and the speedy enactment of the proposed reforms in the public service of the country, so that in future our civil and foreign establishments may attain the same efficiency as our military and naval service. As regards the prevention of frauds, and the securing of integrity in the revenue and other public departments, we have already suggested the adoption of a system of bonds; so that, whatever may be the other measures taken for testing the character of the person appointed, the people would be, at all events, guaranteed against loss consequent upon frauds, by requiring every person, particularly in revenue and financial departments, to deposit a certain amount of money as security for his integrity, to be refunded only within one year after his resignation or removal from the office. Unless such a system be adopted, we cannot see how the people can be protected against the defalcation of public officers; and the protection of an over-burdened people calls for the utmost solicitude on the part of the legislators of the country.

From the New York Round Table, February 22, 1868 :

The system of appointing deputies and assistants as accessories to every public office should be altogether abolished. That system exists only for the purpose of enabing the chiefs of the respective offices to neglect their duties. With the exception of the State Department no assistant or deputies should be allowed. Whatever assistance the head of a department, bureau, or any other office may require, ought to be afforded him by the clerical force; and not the least advantage of the adoption of the Jenckes bill will be that of making these forces so competent as to relieve the government from the necessity of spending large amounts for deputies and assistants. In not a few instances men of shattered health, unable to perform their duties, cling tenaciously to office and luxuriate in its prestige, while the assistants or deputies perform all the work. Obsequious papers publish, on such occasions, pathetic accounts of the declining health of the head of the department, which are very touching from a humanitarian, and suggestive from a pathological point of view. But why does a man who is avowedly unable to perform his duties not resign his office? If there were no assistant or deputy he would be obliged to do so; and as for exceptional cases of temporary illness, the chief clerk might be authorized to officiate in the absence of his principal, with the provision that, whenever the absence shall exceed one month the chief should retire and make room for a more healthy successor. In other instances there are heads of departments who figure only at cabinet meetings and at receptions; who have their names and that of the female accessories of their households printed in the local papers to satiety, but who perform very little work, their duties being actually done by the assistants. Nothing would test the mettle of these great men more efficiently than to give them an opportunity of ceasing any longer to hide the light of their genius under bushels of assistants; and as good things never come alone, nothing would contribute so much to the retrenchment and efficiency of the service. In regard to postmasters it is a notorious fact that many of them are mere holders of sinecures, being absent from their posts all the time, or most of the time, and the work being fulfilled by a deputy or clerk, so that the people are cheated to an extent which, if the double amount of salary thus required and the immense numbers of postmasters be taken into consideration, would take the community by surprise. Nothing can remedy this state of things excepting the enactment of a law providing for the dismissal of any postmaster who has been absent from his duty, (excepting on account of ill health,) and the dismissal of any postmaster who has been proven to have absented himself from his duty during a period of two months and longer, at any time within the two years preceding the enactment of such law. Postmasterships are in great demand for the very reason that, in many localities, they are practically sinecures. The same observation applies to some extent to custom-house, internal revenue collectorships and assessors. In some of these offices assistants may be indispensable, but we have every reason to believe that the revenue and custom-house would be rendered infinitely more profitable and efficient by abolishing a great number of the assistant collectors and assistant assessors. In consulates the system of appointing deputies and assistants is the curse of the foreign service. In some of the principal consulates the consul only makes his appearance for one or two hours during the day. With the exception of Liverpool, where an assistant consulate or vice-consulate seems to be indispensable, all other deputy or vice-consulates or assistant consulates, which now exist in the same places where there are consulates-general or consulates, should be permanently abolished. Cases of ill health are, or ought to be, very few and far between; and should they occur it would not be difficult to appoint a temporary acting consul. If the health of the consul cannot be restored after one or two months, he should yield his office to a person of a stronger constitution. At this time of reform of the civil service it is important that the principle of allowing deputies or assistants, excepting in a few stated or extraordinary cases, should be definitely abandoned.

From The Nation, May 28, 1868 :

With such facts plainly and tersely put, as they are in this speech of Mr. Jenckes, it is easier to find forcible arguments in support of the measure than to educe them from our general and theoretical belief in its efficiency. What are the substantial rewards which Mr. Jenckes promises for the fruits of his bill if it be made law? Double the amount of the present service at two-thirds of the present cost; a saving in the expense of the collection of the revenues of one-half the $15,000,000 which it now takes; and finally an addition of revenue from the subjects of taxation proposed to be retained by the Committee of Ways and Means of $50,000,000 in the internal revenue and $25,000,000 in the customs. In short the country will be richer by a $100,000,000 every year, if it adopt a law which will do more to elevate the politics of the country from the great Serbonian bog in which it is now bedraggled and bemired, more to make statesmen of our politicians, financiers and economists of our revenue officials, more to save the people from corruption, more to preserve the government from mischief, more to renew and restore and sustain the virtues of the republic than all the legislation of the last decade.

With a Constitution purified from slavery, with a government under it that has undergone the throes of civil war, of dissentions between its co-ordinate branches, and with a people honestly and heartily in earnest to maintain both the government and the Constitution, there is still a vice in the administration of the laws which almost palsies them. This mischief lies in the shifting, changing, uncertain, and gradually decaying condition of our civil service. Up to the breaking out of the rebellion it mattered little how the officers of the United States exercised their functions, for the government was seen rather than felt, it was an idea rather than a fact. All this changed with the rebellion, with the enormous efforts of the government to maintain itself, with the burdens put on the people by the success of these efforts, and with the taxes and the vast addition of revenue and outlay that were then voluntarily assumed. The task of adjusting these burdens to our capacity, to make sources of national income without destroying national wealth, has tested the fitness of our political system to do this work. In any other country than our own, with its youth, its wealth, its vigor, its unlimited expanse of territory, its growing tide of emigration, the government would have broken down. That it will not do so now may well call forth all our gratitude. That it may be strengthened and fitted for the work that it has yet to do, in developing the power and capacity of the country in industrial and in other directions, there must be a reform in that one thing which has hitherto been the pitfall of every political party, and the blighting curse of the young men who belonged to one or other of the great armies of our government by parties. This reform is, as we believe, effected by Mr. Jenckes's bill, at least it is aimed at; and as tentative legislation has been the best thing that we could get in other matters, so it may be the best, or in the end it may secure us that which is best, in our civil service.

From the Boston Post, May 29, 1868:

THE CIVIL SERVICE BILL.

If men of all parties would lay aside their differences on other questions for the moment, and in concert establish a general civil service system on which they are already substantially agreed, one important step would have been taken toward the permanent improvement of the administration of public affairs, whose necessity requires no further argument. The bill of Mr. Jenckes, of Rhode Island, is substantially one which will command the favor of the country. It provides simply that the power of appointment to civil offices below a certain grade shall be taken from the hands in which it is at present lodged, and given to a board of examiners, with the Vice-President at its head, to which all applications for place or promotion shall be duly preferred. This board the bill proposes to cloth with final authority in the case. Offices of all kinds are to be open to the competition of seekers, both male and female; but instead of appointments being distributed any longer for personal and party reasons, they are to rest on qualifications as they shall be made to appear, and on merit for services already faithfully performed.

Could a measure of this sort be fairly adopted and consistently maintained as the rule of our government, we assume nothing in saying that influential men of all parties would hail its immediate operation as a sensible relief from the pressure which is regularly brought to bear on larger and more comprehensive questions, too frequently to their injudicious or improper settlement. Interest in party matters will always be found powerful enough without adding anything to its incentives. It is only a detraction from the dignity of our politics, and a detriment to public affairs as therein involved, that considerations of office and personal reward should be suffered to crowd themselves in until they actually take control. The European governments provide for this much better. And if it be so necessary to separate the department of civil service promotions and appointments from general affairs under foreign governments, in a popular government like ours the necessity is very much more apparent. We have thus far consented to let matters run into a state of general confusion so far as this business is concerned; with the rapid growth of the country and multiplication of the needs of the public service, it becomes absolutely imperative that something like order and system should at length be established. Besides creating needless excitement and confusion on the organization of every new administration, this general scramble for party rewards sensibly diminishes the dignity of government operations, and tends to bring the serious discussion of momentous public questions into comparative contempt.

Such a plan as suggested, to be efficient and enduring, should be as simple as possible in its outline, and keep carefully clear of all partisan complications. A well-regulated civil service bureau would reasonably answer to these requirements, provided party hands were kept off of it and out of it by a solemn mutual agreement. Then service under government in this country, instead of being an object of greed and envy, from which every man's neighbor would be glad to see him ejected for the advantage of himself, would be elevated to the level of a separate calling or profession, in which a capable and faithful appointee might expect to spend the active term of his natural life. Such an acceptation of the matter by men of one side and another side, would instantly purge our politics of a great share of its bitterness and venality, and change the old temptations into the desirable forms of a worthy ambition. The public service itself would be benefited, and so would the recipients of public appointments, and at last parties themselves. There could not be any more conclusive reasons urged for the passage of any measure proposed.

It is not necessary to argue for the positive advantage of a trained body of men to whom is to be committed the routine work of a government yearly enlarging its interests as ours is. The only obstacle which will be presented to this plan with anything like seriousness, happens to be the very one which the plan itself aims to remove; that is the patronage with which members of Congress are now invested, and which has come to be regarded as a sort of essential perquisite to their position. It cannot be that high-minded men of any party would cling to an old, cumbersome, and corrupting custom, for reasons of such a character; on the contrary, they would see in such reasons only the more urgent inducement to be rid of the custom altogether. And we can add nothing to what we have already expressed on behalf of so sensible a proposition, except a desire to see Congress take up Mr. Jenckes's bill just as soon as it can bring its mind to practical business again, and establish a system of appointments in conformity to its general principle. Let our government machinery be made lighter rather than heavier as the nation advances with its development.

From the New York Evening Post:

THE CIVIL SERVICE REFORM.

The question of reforming the system of appointment to office under the United States is a contest between a horde of political managers on one side and the nation on the other. All the true interests of the people are in favor of ending at once and forever the use of official places and salaries as rewards for partisan zeal and efficiency; and of bestowing them only upon those who can really do the work. There is no difficulty in the theory of our institutions to be overcome; the only serious opposition to the reform is from those who profit by the abuses now practiced. The "managers" of parties, the "men of influence," whom the appointing power must not offend, the great powers of the lobby and the closet, whose importance depends on the patronage they are supposed to control; these are the obstacles to this most necessary reform.

The bill as now proposed aims at no sweeping change in the methods of government. Its provisions are as modest and gentle as a measure can be which aims to initiate a radical improvement in a great system. While it is simple in its plan, its adoption will afford a fair opportunity to test the principle of competitive examinations for office under a popular government, and it admits readily of being modified and extended, as experience may suggest.

By this bill the Vice-President or President of the Senate is made the head of a new "Department of the civil service," and president of the "civil service examination board," which is to consist of himself and four commissioners, who are to prescribe the qualifications for each branch and grade of the civil service of the Union, and to hold examinations of all persons claiming to be eligible under their regulations, and asking for appointments. The preference in appointment, in each branch and grade, shall belong to the applicants in the order of merit; but promotions may be made in the order of seniority from among those who have passed an examination, unless the department choose to order another. Special examinations may be demanded by any department of the government, or ordered by the board itself, to determine precedence and seniority in any grade.

A small fee may be required of applicants, to be paid to the United States. The board may prescribe general rules for the suspension or removal of civil officers for misconduct or inefficiency. They may employ "men of learning and high character" to assist in their examinations. The head of any department may send officers before the board for examination, to be dismissed if found incompetent. All citizens of the United States are eligible to examination and appointment under the act; the heads of departments to designate the branches of the service; which may be filled with females as well as males, and for these females shall be equally eligible.

All of the above provisions are limited to those officers, not postmasters, who are by law appointed by the President, the heads of departments and the courts, and do not require confirmation by the Senate. But section twelve permits the President or the Senate to send before the board any person whose appointment to an office requiring confirmation is proposed, to be examined as to his qualifications, either before or after being commissioned, the result to be reported to the President and to the Senate.

It is expected that this bill will be reported to the House within a few days. As it retains the essential features of the system which has produced such satisfactory results in Great Britain, and yet is far more simple, leaving all the details to grow up as circumstances require, it can scarcely fail to commend itself to the country. Any such measure may doubtless somewhat limit the patronage of the members of Congress, and thus a little diminish their importance, but no such consideration ought to weigh against the necessity of bringing greater intelligence and efficiency into the service of the government.

The contest is likely to be most severe on the twelfth section, which permits the application of a test of intelligence. not to clerks alone, but to secretaries, commissioners, auditors, collectors, assessors, foreign ministers, and consuls. It is of little moment whether this section be retained or not. Although it is by far the most important provision of the bill, and that from which the best results are to be expected in the end, yet it will be a great boon to the country if even the appointment of clerks and subordinates can be connected in some way with merit; and a fair trial of this experiment will inevitably lead to an universal application of the principle.

Give us the department of civil service and a board of worthy examiners, and however limited their power at first, the office holders of the future will, on the whole, be useful and honorable men. The passage of this bill will be a notice to quit to all the incompetency and idleness long pensioned on the treasury; ambassadors and consuls abroad, who know no tongue but their own, and speak that with vulgarity; collectors in great cities, who gather millions a year for the treasury and cannot tell on which side of their books to enter their payments, and chief clerks of departments who cannot spell three lines of a plain English document correctly, all these must go. The first vote for a civil-service bill is the knell of their official lives; and the proposed board of commissioners, once appointed, under whatever restrictions, is sure to become their guillotine.

From the New York Tribune:

REFORM IN THE CIVIL SERVICE.

One of the important subjects now before Congress is the movement of Mr. Jenckes, of Rhode Island, for complete reform in the appointment of public officers, clerks, &c., the object being mainly to secure for public station men who are properly qualified for the places to be filled. The principal points of the bill are these: It creates a department of civil service, the head of which shall be the Vice-President or the President of the.Senate, and there shall be associated with him four gentlemen, to be known as "the civil service examination board." This board is to prescribe qualifications of applicants for appointment in all grades of public service, with respect to age, health, character, knowledge and ability; to provide for thorough examinations in all cases, and for periods of trial or probation; to establish rules governing applications, and examining personally, or through others specially authorized, all who propose to take places under the government. There is also provision for graduated promotion, based upon merit and length of service, in testimony of which certificates are to be granted. Provision is also made for general rules governing the investigation of charges against any officer, suspension, removal, or other punishment. The commissioners may require an examination of any officer in service when the act goes into effect. The President and Senate may also require any person applying to them for appointment to undergo examination by this board, the result to be reported to the appointing power. It does not appear, however, that such report will be more than advisory.

The general objects of the bill are excellent. Men at all familiar with public business know that there are hundreds of officers in places of great responsibility who are in no degree qualified for the duties demanded of them. The doctrine of General Jackson, "To the victors belong the spoils," opened the door to an irruption of barbarians as little fitted for real public service as were the hordes of Attila to appreciate the grandeur and beauty of Roman civilization. In the distribution of these fitly-called spoils the most zealous, unscrupulous, and ignorant caucus managers or shoulder hitters have been put into places of vast responsibility upon no better qualification than that on some occasion they carried a primary election, and secured a nomination for their patron by the sheer strength of their fists, or, perhaps, by judicious bribery. Party service is, of course, everywhere a claim for preference when patronage is bestowed; but any triumphant party owes to its adversary as well as itself the recognition of fitness and merit in its appointments.

Another evil in our system is the uncertainty of tenure, even in the smallest places. No man, from Secretary of the Treasury to night-watchman in the public stores, knows how long his head may remain on his shoulders. Hence, among honest and zealous office holders there is a feeling of uneasiness that amounts to neglect of public interests. "Why should I work too hard, when a breath may throw me overboard?" they reason. Among the dishonest and unscrupulous the same uncertainty of tenure prompts to "make hay while the sun shines," and they do it with a will. Now, if the public service could be placed upon more assured foundation, if men filling say even the lesser places could feel certain that they would not be displaced except for cause after due trial, the character of the service would be at once elevated, the weight of responsibility would be felt, and all the influences of advancement for zeal and fidelity would begin to operate. Instead of a strife as to who should do the least, it would be who should do the best; instead of who should steal the most, it would be who should save the most. There are now in civil service more than 12,000 officers—an immense army for good or evil as the policy of the government may determine. It strikes us that Mr. Jenckes's bill aims at good results, and in so far we heartily commend it to the careful consideration of Congress.

From the New York Herald:

MR. JENCKES'S CIVIL SERVICE BILL.

The bill which Mr. Jenckes has introduced in Congress to regulate and improve the civil service of the government is a good one, though we doubt if it can become law or be made operative. He proposes to have all candidates for office pass a thorough examination by a board appointed for that purpose, the same as military and naval cadets are examined, and their qualifications tested and approved before they enter upon duty. This undoubtedly would give efficiency to every branch of the civil service. So far the bill should meet with no opposition; for though parties controlling the government may change, and removals be made for party purposes, there ought to be a test of competency in all cases. And we think the other feature of the bill—to make officers permanent during good behavior—is an excellent one; still, it is doubtful if this could be carried out, as the party in power could always find some pretext to remove obnoxious partisans. The principle is good all through, and we recommend Mr. Jenckes to urge the measure upon Congress and to try the effect of it.

From the New York Tribune:

A CIVIL SERVICE BUREAU.

We strongly hope that some such bill as that prepared by Mr. Jenckes may become law during the present session. It would relieve politics of three-fourths of its venality and corruption, and would purge our public offices of nine-tenths of their scoundrels and incompetents. It would greatly lessen the burden of appointments and removals which now presses heavily on the President and all the departments, and would furnish the Vice-President, who is now a sort of fifth wheel to the government coach, with something to do. Let us have a civil service department of some kind. No better plan has yet been devised than that of Mr. Jenckes.

From the Chicago Republican:

REFORM IN THE CIVIL SERVICE.

Taken in all its broad and deep consequences, no measure before the House has greater claims upon the votes of members than that of Mr. Jenckes, of Rhode Island, on reform in the civil service. Recently we gave editorially a brief and meagre outline of its provisions, but the importance of the subject, as well as the interest it is attracting among the masses of the people, lead us to print the bill in full.

The plan of distributing the offices of the government is full of present evil and future danger. With every change of administration, more than 50,000 of the appointees are expected to walk the plank. The same number of others take the vacated positions, generally unacquainted with the duties to be performed, and who are paid out of the public purse to learn what they are supposed, in theory at least, to know already. If they are disposed to become expert and efficient in the official routine of the grade and branch to which they are assigned, they have no assurance that the mysterious pressure of inside circumstances and outside intrigues, or the whims of their chief, will not at some unexpected moment turn them adrift. At best they can scarcely look for more than four years' lease of office. A new President, even if he entertain the same political views as his predecessor, brings more or less change, and no place holder can feel certain that he is not one who is to seek new quarters.

Thus the distribution of official stations under the government has grown into a vast hotbed of corruption. Promises of office are used by candidates to gather around them a body of adherents, who give their best energies to secure his triumph, not because he is the fittest man for the place he seeks, nor because his political principles are most conducive to the public welfare, but because his success is the stepping-stone to positions of honor and profit. In this way some one, plausible in address, and adroit in manipulating the machinery of nominations, finds his way into a clerkship for which he has no atom of qualification. Or it may be that some stump speaker, full of persuasive talk, but empty of real industry, obtains a fat place in reward for his unremitted use of his tongue, and fulfils its duties in such a slipshod way that he does not one quarter earn his salary. Of course the public interests suffer from such heavy inflictions of incompetency and laziness. No man in his private business would endure them for a moment. It is as if an extensive farmer should employ a haberdasher's clerk to oversee the cultivation of his crops, or a steamship company should select a captain for one of their boats because he possessed a voice whose stentorian tones could be heard above the raging of a storm. Individuals who acted on such principles would soon come to grief. If they cannot safely, neither can a nation. But the case is even more foolish and dangerous when to incapacity in office holders is added rascality. It is no proper recommendation to an application for an assessorship or a tax collectorship that he has exhibited remarkable aptitude in getting illegal voters through the naturalization mill, or has displayed wonderful ingenuity in manufacturing roorbacks on the eve of an election. It is no reason why a man should obtain the handling of the people's money that he knows every doubtful elector in his county, and the lowest sum that will purchase the support of those who are for sale.

Yet, under the present system of distributing the public patronage as rewards to be paid for partizan faithfulness and political services, instead of guerdons to be won by the capable and worthy, the national capital has become, to those who are behind the scenes and witness the daily hucksting of principle and place, as corrupt as the carcass of an old horse hauled out of sight and smell, but festering in the sun, bloated with putrified gases, swarming with maggots, and assailing with the most sickening stench the nostrils of any person who ventures into the neighborhood. This corruption does not characterize merely the administration of Andrew Johnson, but has appertained, in one degree or another, to all the preceding presidential terms for some decades. It is a natural and unavoidable consequence of the existing methods of filling the offices under the government. Its constant tendency, too, is from bad to worse. Every year introduces some new element of nefariousness not before practiced. In its present aspects it affords serious alarm to all thinking men, who see in its demoralizing influences a body of sappers and miners digging away the foundations of free institutions. The process is slow, but sure.

Here are some of the consequences that all can understand. The people have been amazed at the extent, audacity, and continued success of the whiskey frauds, in face of all the stringent laws that have been enacted to compel the collection of the dues. It is now officially known that these evasions could not take place without collusion or delinquency on the part of the revenue officials. From $60,000,000 to $180,000,000, according to various estimates, are thus lost annually to the treasury of the nation. But there are immense frauds committed in other departments of the revenue, all arising, in the main, from the negligence or the connivance of those whose oaths bind them to a conscientious discharge of their official duties. According to the lowest estimate, the aggregate of the losses from these evasions of internal taxation and customs will reach yearly the startling figure of $80,000,000, or enough to pay the principal of the national debt in 25 years, by drawing the means to pay the interest from other sources. This is an absolute loss to the people, and goes into the pockets of those who are continually lowering the standard of public morality.

When it is considered that this condition of affairs must grow worse and worse, it will be seen that Congress has before it a question of no ordinary magnitude and no little pressing urgency. It deserves to be considered in all its bearings; but whether the verbiage of Mr. Jenckes's bill is adopted or not, its principle is one that the people will demand shall be placed upon the statute book. If necessary, they will even go so far as to make it a point to elect men who will make it law.

APPENDIX F.

CIVIL SERVICE OF CHINA.

Literary attainments are the sole channel to the acquirement of office and of political advancement in China. All offices in China, from the highest to the lowest, are thus thrown open to all those classes of the people who have the requisite mental qualifications. Favoritism exists, of course, to some extent, particularly as regards Tartars connected by blood with the imperial family and noblemen; and the pressing necessities of the government have made, of late years, offices accessible to men of wealth, who can make up for the extent of their purchase-money and bribes for what they lack in intellectual accomplishments. But the rich, incompetent office-holder is laughed at by his subordinates and despised by his superiors. His position is altogether anomalous, and, in most cases, untenable. As far as the extent of the bribes are concerned, they vary according to the rank of the officer and according to the extent of his unfitness; so that culture and learning are duly appreciated even in such bargains, and the purchase-money decreases in amount in the same proportion that the office-seeker is more educated.

It is well known that one of the most remarkable features of Chinese polity is the very general diffusion of education, and the encouragement that, from a very early period, has been given to the cultivation of letters. Education is inculcated by positive precept, as well as encouraged by open competition for the highest reward. Among the 360,000,000 of Chinamen at least 200,000,000 are literati. Almost every man in this vast empire can read and write sufficiently well for the ordinary purposes of life. Nor is the education of females neglected, though it is not so well cared for as that of men. Books, on all imaginable subjects, from stories, tales, and comedies, romances, ballads, and fables, to religion, medical, meteorological, historical, philosophical, and legal works, issue daily from the press in Pekin and other great cities of the empire, the press being virtually free; though the publication of books is amenable to certain regulations, established by law, whilst treasonable or unpalatable political publications are punished with death. The more bulky and expensive works, as those on history, philology, and jurisprudence, are sometimes published by subscription; but are supplied to the libraries of the functionaries by the government. Libraries are seldom formed, to any great extent, by individuals. The grand collections of history, philosophy, and other standard national works, published by the direction of the sovereign, under the superintendence of the Han-lin, are distributed to the princes of the blood, the viceroys of provinces, presidents of departments, and to the learned of the empire; but, though they are rarely met with in the libraries of private individuals, it must be borne in mind that books are multiplied at a cheap rate, and to almost an indefinite extent; and the very peasant and pedlar have the common depositories of knowledge within their reach. Indeed, it would not be hazarding too much to say that, next to the United States, there are more books in China, and more people to read them, than in any other country in the world.

The great encouragement to this extraordinary and all-pervading cultivation of letters is that they open the door to official employment, and thus, while the state secures the most competent men for its service, it diffuses, at the same time, the blessings of culture. Indeed, it may be safely asserted that if this prospect of government employment were not held out to accomplished men, and to them exclusively, letters would not be cultivated to the same extent. With equal truth it may be stated that, if the effect of excessive absolutism in the form of government, of excessive superstition in the form of religion, and of excessive dislike of innovation, had not thus been neutralized by culture and talent and the highest capacity in the civil and military service of the empire, Chinese civilization would have long ago perished beneath the walls that shut it off from the outer world, and the land of Confucius would have fallen a prey to barbarism. The civil service of China is recruited from persons who have successfully passed through the competitive literary examinations; and, though corruption, and venality, and the influence of rank and wealth will exert their fatal influence in China, as everywhere else, the principle that public officers should only be selected from the successful competitors in the literary examinations is fully recognized, and is, in fact, the law of the land, while corruption and other sinister influences are, virtually, transgressions of the law.

The degrees of literary merit are four, viz: Sew-tsee, "men of cultivated talent;" Ken-jin, "elevated persons;" Tzin-sze, "advanced scholars;" and Han-lin, "the forest of pencils," or national institute. The examination for the first takes place in the country towns; for the second, in the provincial capital; for the third, in the imperial capital; and for the fourth, in the imperial palace. The examinations are very strict, and only a few out of numerous candidates receive titles. After undergoing certain preliminary examinations by the superintendent of the district, the scholar is recommended as a candidate for the first degree, the examinations for which take place twice every three years. The trial takes place in the county hall, which is divided into compartments just sufficient for the accommodation of each student. They receive themes, on which to write both in prose and verse, and are strictly guarded by soldiers to prevent their receiving any assistance. Those who have passed the first examination may become competitors at the second, which takes place once every three years. The examiners on this occasion are the imperial chancellor and the chief officers of the province; and the aspirants usually number 10,000, who are confined in cells, and guarded as already mentioned. The number that receive this degree are only about 72 in each province. The third degree is the result of a still more rigorous examination at the capital. Here, also, about 10,000 candidates enter the list, and, after being examined in the way described, about 300 of them are dignified with the title of Tsin-sze. The fourth degree follows, a very close examination of those who have already obtained the third, and takes place *in presence of the Emperor.* The successful candidates on this occasion obtain liberal salaries from the Emperor, and are employed to deliberate on all questions regarding politics and literature, to prepare public documents, &c. The three highest candidates are forthwith mounted on horseback, and paraded for three days round Pekin, signifying that "thus it shall be done to the man whom the king delighteth to honor." The chief of the three occupies the most enviable post in the nation, and yet a post to which all are eligible, to which all may aspire.

To succeed at any of these examinations, it is necessary to put forth extraordinary exertions. Each candidate is expected to know by heart the whole of the " *Five Classics*" and the " *Four Books*," (most of which were compiled by Confucius and his disciples,) as well as the authorized commentaries upon them, and to be well acquainted with the most celebrated authors of antiquity. The chief excellency of their essays consists in introducing as many quotations as possible from ancient authors; but they are deprived of all books and writings, being expected, as they say, "to carry their books in their stomachs." All this can only be attained by great application and perseverance. The first five or six years at school are spent in committing the canonical books to memory; another six years are required to acquire a good style; and an additional number of years, spent in incessant toil, are needed to insure success.

The most celebrated compositions in the Chinese language are the aforesaid Five Classics and the Four Books. The Five Classics are the Yike-King, "Book of Diagrams;" the She-King, "Collection of Odes;" the Le-Ke, "Record of Ceremonies;" the Shoo-King, containing the history of the three first dynasties; and the Chun-tsew, an account of the life and times of Confucius. Of the Four Books, the first two—Chung-yung, "the Happy Medium," and Taheo, "the Great Doctrine"—were written by Tsze-tsze, the grandson and disciple of Confucius; the third, called the Lunyu, "Book of Discourses," is the production of the different disciples of the sage, who recollected and recorded his words and deeds; while the last of the Four Books was written by Mencius, the disciple of Tsze-tsze, and bears the name of its author. The text of these nine books is equal in bulk to that of the New Testament, and it is not too much to say that, were every copy annihilated to-day, there are a million of people who could restore the whole of it to-morrow from memory.

Among the specimens of ancient poetry from the Shoo-King, the following is an address of the Emperor Chun to his ministers:

Koo, koong Khĕe tsai. When the chief ministers delight in their duty.
Yuen shyen Khĕe tsai. The sovereign rises to successful exertion.
Puh koong hee tsai. A multitude of inferior officers ardently co-operating.

To which the ministers responded:

Yuen shyen ming tsai. When the sovereign is wise.
Koŏ koong lyang tsai. The ministers are faithful to their trust.
Shyu tsĕ khang tsai. And all things happily succeed.

The four social classes of China were, in former times, the *Tsé,* or learned, who govern and instruct the rest; the *Nung,* the agriculturists who furnish food and material for clothing; the *Kung,* artisan or manufacturer, who clothed, built and furnished houses; and the *Shang,* who distributed and exchanged the productions of the other two among all other classes of society. But nothing like a division in *caste* ever appeared in China. On the contrary, every encouragement is held out to the children of the three inferior classes to aspire to the first.

The numbers of the first class or *Tsé*, or officers of the government and literary men, consisting of the members of the several boards, governors of provinces and cities, judges, treasurers, collectors, commissaries, inspectors and the like, with an enormous list of subaltern officers and literati, is estimated at about 500,000.

The salaries of the provincial officers are not high, as will be seen from the following list:

Governor general.....................	20,000 taels, at $1 50 =	$30,000
Lieutenant governor...................	16,000 ......do......	24,000
Treasurer...........................	9,000 ......do......	13,500
Provincial judge....................	6,000 ..... do......	9,000
Prefect.............................	3,000 ......do......	4,500
District magistrates, (according to size of district,) from..................800 to 2,000 ......do.1,200 to 3,000		
Literary chancellor..................	3,000 ......do......	4,500
Commander-in-chief..................	4,000 ......do......	6,000
General.............................	2,400 ......do......	3,600
Colonel.............................	1,300 ......do......	1,950
And other officers down to...........	130 ......do......	195

The civilians of different ranks are distinguished from each other by their costumes and ornaments.

There are 13 principal departments of government, viz:

1. The *Nuih Koh*, or cabinet, consisting of four principal and two joint assistant chancellors.

2. The *Kuin-Ki Chu*, or general council, probably the most influential body of the government, corresponding to the *ministry* of western nations and composed of princes of the blood, chancellors of the cabinet, president and vice-presidents of the six boards, and chief officers of all the other courts in the capital. The principal executive bodies in the capital under these two councils are the Luh Pu, or *six boards*. At the head of each board are two presidents, (shang-shu,) and four vice-presidents, (shilaug,) alternately a Tartar and a Chinese; and over three of them, those of revenue, war, and punishment, are placed superintendents, who are frequently members of the cabinet; sometimes the president of one board is superintendent of another. There are three subordinate grades of officers in each board who may be called directors, under-secretaries, and comptrollers, with a great number of subordinate clerks and their appropriate departments for conducting the details of the general and particular business coming under the cognizance of the board, the whole being arranged and subordinated in the most practical, business-like manner. The detail of all the departments in the general and provincial governments is regulated to the minutest matter in the same style: for instance, each board has a different style of envelope in which to send its despatches, and the papers in the offices are filed away in them.

3. The *Li Pu*, or board of civil office, has the government and direction of all the various officers in the civil service of the empire, and thereby it assists the Emperor to rule all people, and these duties are further defined as including "whatever appertains to the plans of selecting rank and gradation, to the rules presiding over the verdicts of degradation and promotion, to the ordinances of granting investitures and rewards, and the laws for fixing schedules and furloughs, that the civil service may be supplied." Civilians are presented to the Emperor, and all civil and literary officers distributed throughout the empire by this board.

There are four bureaus in this board. The first attends to the distinctions, precedence, promotion, exchanging, &c., of officers. The second investigates their merits and worthiness to be recorded and advanced, or, *vice versa*, ascertains the character each officer bears, and the manner in which he fulfils his duties and presents his furloughs. The third regulates retirement from office on account of mourning or filial duties to sick parents, and supervises the registration of official names ; it is through this bureau that Hwang Ngäntung, the governor of Kwangtung, has been degraded for not resigning his office on the death of his mother. The fourth regulates the distribution of titles, patents and posthumous honors.

4 The *Hu Pu*, or board of revenue directs the territorial government of the empire, and keeps the lists of population in order to aid the Emperor in nourishing all people ; whatever appertains to the regulations for levying and collecting duties and taxes, to the plans for distributing salaries and allowances, to the rates for receipts and disbursements at the granaries and treasuries, and to the rights for transporting by land and by water, are reported to this board, that sufficient supplies for the country may be provided. Beside these duties it obtains the admeasurement of all lands in the empire, and proportions taxes and conscriptions, regulates the expenditure and ascertains the latitude and longitude of places. One minor office prepares lists of all the Manchoo girls fit to be introduced into the palace for selection as inmates of the imperial harem—a somewhat incongruous duty, unless these girls be regarded as revenue from Manchooria. There are 14 subordinate departments under this board to attend to the receipt of the revenue from each of the 18 provinces, each of which corresponds with the treasury department in its respective province.

The revenue being paid in various ways and articles, as money, grain. manufactures, &c., the receipts and distribution of the various articles require a large number of assistants. This board is moreover a court of appeal on disputes respecting property, and superintends the mint in each province ; one bureau is called the " great ministers of the three treasuries," viz., of metals, silks, dyestuffs and stationery.

5. The *Li-Pu*, or board of rites, which has also under its control the regulation of the literary examinations, the number of the graduates, the distinction of their classes, the forms of their selection, and the privileges of successful candidates, with the establishment of government schools and academies. A "board of music" is also attached to this department, to cultivate a talent for music among the officials. The Chinese not being endowed with much innate musical genius, take this method of developing it by dint of study and application.

6. The *Ping Pu*, or board of war, which also regulates the navy department. The regulation of the entire army is committed to several departments, and the forces under each are kept distinct.

7. The *Hing Pu*, or board of punishments, partakes in part of the nature of a commercial and civil court of law; its officers usually meet with those of the censorate and Tali Sz', the three forming the San Fah Sz' or three law chambers, which decide on capital cases brought before them.

8. The *Kung Pu*, or board of works. The first bureau attends to city walls, palaces, temples, altars, and other public structures. A second bureau to military stores and utensils for the army, sorts the pearls from the fisheries, regulates weights and measures, furnishes death warrants to governors and generals, and takes charge of arsenals, stores, &c. A third bureau has charge of all water-ways and dikes, repairs and digs canals, erects bridges, oversees the banks of rivers by means of deputies stationed at posts along their course, builds vessels of war, collects tolls, mends roads, digs sewers in Pekin and cleans its gutters, preserves ice, makes book-cases for public records, and examine silks sent as taxes. The fourth bureau attends to imperial mausolea,

sepulchres, and tablets of meritorious officers buried at the public expense, the adornment of temples and palaces, and superintending of all workmen employed by the board.

The *mint* is under the direction of two vice-presidents, and the manufacture of gunpowder is specially intrusted to two great ministers.

9. The *Li Fan Yuen*, or court for the government of foreigners, *i. e.*, colonial office, all external foreigners, including the nomadic and settled tribes in Mongolia, Cobdo, Iti, and Koko-nov, as well as all internal and external barbarians, meaning all not Chinese, as well as the unsubdued mountaineers of Kweichau. The officers of the colonial office are all Mantchoos and Mongols, having over them one president and two vice-presidents, Mantchoos, and one Mongolian vice-president, appointed for life. Beside the usual secretaries there are six departments, whose combined powers include every detail of authority necessary for the management of all the various clans and tributary tribes; the Lama hierarchy in Mongolia, and in Thibet; the tributary visits of the Mohammedan beys in the southern circuit of Iti, the regulation of the salaries of Mongolian princes and nobles being all under the control of this department, which endeavors to disfeudalise the internal organization of these tribes by reducing the influence and revenue of the khans and beys, so as to elevate the people to the position of independent owners and cultivators of the soil.

10. The *Tu-chah-yuen*, or censorate, *i. e.*, all-examining court, is intrusted with the care of manners and customs, with the investigation of all public offices within and without the capital, the discrimination between the good and the bad performance of their business, and between the worthlessness and excellence of the officers employed in them, &c., &c.

The censorate when joined with the board of punishment and court of appeal forms a high court for the revision of criminal cases and hearing appeals from the provinces, and in connection with the six boards and the court of representatives and appeal makes one of the *Kiu King* or nine courts, which deliberate on important affairs of government.

11. The *Tung-Ching Sz'*, or court of representation, consists of six officers, and receives memorials from the provincial authorities, and appeals from their judgment by the people, and presents them to the cabinet.

12. The *Ta-li Szé*, or court of judicature, adjusts all the criminal courts in the empire, and forms the nearest approach to a supreme court, though the cases brought before it are mostly criminal.

13. The *Hanlien Yuen*, or imperial academy, is intrusted with the duty of drawing up governmental documents, historical, and other works. Its chief officers take the lead of the various classes, and excite their exertion in advance of learning, *in order to prepare them for employment*, and fit them for attending upon the sovereign. The body may be likened to the selection of learned men to whom the king of Babylon intrusted the education of promising young men, for although the members of the Hanlien Yuen do not to any great degree educate persons, they are constantly referred to, as the Chaldeans were by Belshazzar. Sir John Davis likens it to the *Sorbonne* (of Paris,) inasmuch as it expounds the sacred books of the Chinese. Its chief officers are two presidents, or senior members, who are usually appointed for life, after a long course of study. They attend upon the Emperor in the palace, superintend the studies of graduates, and furnish semi-annual lists of persons to be speakers at the "classical feasts," where the literary essays of his Majesty are translated from and into Mantchoo, and read before him.

Subordinate to the two senior members are four grades of officers, five in each grade, together with an unlimited number of senior graduates, each forming a sort of college, whose duties are to prepare all works published under governmental sanction. These persons are subject from time to time to fresh examination, and are liable to lose their degree or be altogether dismissed from office, if found faulty or deficient. Subordinate to the Hanlieu Yuen is an office, consisting of 22 selected members, who, in rotation, attend on the Emperor and make a record of his words and actions. There is also an additional office for the preparation of national histories.

The situation of a member of the Haulien is one of considerable honor and literary ease, and scholars look forward to a station in it as one which confers dignity in a government where all officers are appointed according to their literary merit, but much more from its being the body from which the Emperor selects his most responsible officers. A graduate of this rank is most likely to be nominated to a vacant office, though the possession of the title does not of itself entitle him to a place.

The *Kwohtsz Kien*, or national college, is a different institution from the Hanlien Yueu, and intended for teaching graduates of the lower degrees; the departments of study are the Chinese language, the classics and mathematics, &c., &c.

The *Kin Tien Kin*, or imperial astronomical college, seems, from the account given of its duties, to be as much astrological as astronomical.

The highest officers in the provinces are the governor general, (often called viceroy,) who always rules over two provinces or else fills two high offices in one province, and the lieutenant governor. The 18 provinces of China are incorporated into 11 governments, over which are placed eight governors-general and 15 lieutenant governors, besides which there are 19 treasurers, 18 judges, 17 literary chancellors, 15 commanders of the forces, including two admirals, and about 1,700 prefects and district magistrates.

The departments of the provincial civil government are five, viz: administrative, literary, gabel, commissariat, and excise; the first being also divided into the territorial, financial, and the judicial branches. At the head of the first branch is the treasurer; over the second presides the judge of criminal affairs; the literary department is placed under the direction of an officer selected from among the members of the Hanlien academy, called director of learning or literary chancellor. The officers of the excise are appointed whenever necessary, either in the interior or on the coast, and are usually selected from among the members of the imperial household, and are subject merely to the control of the governor general.

The appointment of officers in China being theoretically founded on literary merit, the officers to whom is committed the supervision of students and conferment of degrees are naturally of a high grade. The literary chancellor of the province therefore ranks next to the governor general, more because he is specially appointed by his Majesty, however, and oversees this branch of the government, than from any remarkable degree of power committed to his hands. Under him are head teachers of different degrees of authority, residing in the chief towns of departments and districts, the whole forming a similar series of functionaries to which exists in the civil department. These subordinates have merely a greater or less degree of supervision over the labor of students and the colleges established for the promotion of learning in the chief towns of departments. The business of conferring the lower degrees appertains exclusively to the chancellor, who makes an annual circuit through the province for that purpose, and holds examinations in the chief town of each department of all the students residing within its limits.

The number and rank of the officers connected with the salt monopoly (the gabel or salt department) show the importance attached by the supreme government to this trade.

The commissariat department is unusually large in China, as compared with other countries, for the plan of collecting any part of the revenue in kind necessarily requires numerous vehicles for transporting, and buildings for storing it, which still further multiplies the number of clerks and hands employed.

That feature of the Chinese civil-service system which makes officers mutually responsible seems to lead the superior officers to confer such various duties upon one functionary, in order that he may thus have a general knowledge of what is going about or under him, and report irregularities.

This system seems in no little degree to accomplish the designs of the present rulers to bind the main and lesser wheels of the huge machine to themselves and to one another in a very strong manner.

In order to enable the superior officers to exercise greater vigilance over their inferiors, they have the privilege of sending special messengers, invested with full power, to every part of their jurisdiction. The Emperor himself never visits the provinces judicially, but he constantly sends commissioners or legates to all parts of the empire, ostensibly intrusted with the management of a particular business, but required also to take a general surveillance of what is going on. The ancient Persians had a similar system of commissioners, who were called the eyes and ears of the prince, and made the circuit of the empire to oversee all that was done. There are many points of resemblance between the structure of these two ancient monarchies; but the Persians had not the elements of perpetuity which the system of common schools and official examination give to the Chinese government. G .vernors, in like manner, send their deputies and agents over the province; and even the prefects and intendants despatch their messengers. All these functionaries, during the time of their mission, take rank with the highest officers according to the quality of their employers; but the imperial commissioners, who for one object or another are constantly passing and repassing through the empire in every direction, exercise great influence in the government, and are powerful agents in the hands of the Emperor for keeping his pro-consuls at their duty.

In addition to the division of power, and the checks upon Chinese officers already mentioned, there are other means adopted to prevent combination and resistance against the head of the state. One of them is the law forbidding a man to hold office in his native province, which, beside stopping all intrigue where it would best succeed, has the further effect of congregating all aspirants for office at Pekin, where they come in hope of obtaining some post or succeeding in the examination of literary degrees. The central government could not contrive a better plan for bringing all the ambitious and talented men in the country under its observation before appointing them to clerkships in the capital or scattering them over the provinces.

Moreover, no officer is allowed to marry in the jurisdiction under his control, nor own land in it, nor have a son, or brother, or near relative holding office under him; and he is seldom continued in the same station or province for more than three or four years.

Beside a system of assiduous espionage, there is a triennial catalogue made out of the merits and demerits of all the officers in the empire, which is submitted to imperial inspection by the board of civil office. In order to collect the details for this catalogue, it is incumbent upon every provincial officer to report upon the character and qualifications of all under him, and the list, when made out, is forwarded by the governor to the capital. The points of character are arranged under six different heads, viz : the undiligent, the inefficient, the superficial, the untalented, the superannuated and the diseased. According to the opinion given in this report, officers are elevated or degraded so many steps in the scale of merit, and whenever they issue an edict are required to state how many times they have been advanced or degraded, and how many times recorded. Officers are required to accuse themselves, when guilty of crime, either in their own conduct or that of their subordinates, and request punishment. Punishment for high crimes fully proven to have been committed by officers is death, either inflicted by the executioner or inflicted by the delinquent upon himself, this latter mode of compulsory suicide being deemed less degrading, rope being generally delicately furnished for that purpose to the culprit, with the intimation that he may hang himself, failing to do which he is decapitated.

The names and standing of all officers are published quarterly, by permission of government, in the Red Book. In this book the native province of each person is mentioned as well as his nationality, and further describes the title of the office, its salary and considerable other general information.

The following is a tabular view of the offices, boards, tribunals, courts and departments, arranged according to the Chinese statistics:

1. Six titular guardians of the monarch, ditto of the heir apparent. They do not constitute a court, but are great ministers, premiers, and governors general.

2. Board of the imperial family: 1 president, 2 vice-presidents, 2 assessors, 2 assistants, 4 managers, 2 directors of affairs, 2 secretaries, 2 directors of the halls, 2 ditto Chinese directors, 24 clerks.

3. The cabinet: 4 premiers, 2 deputies, 10 assistants, 8 recorders, 16 assistants, 4 registrars, 124 notaries, 46 ditto assistants, 6 ditto of the herald's office, 10 clerks.

4. Privy council: number of ministers not determined.

Chamber for abridging memorials: 4 arrangers, 4 receivers, and 9 preparers of the extracts.

Translator's office: 2 arrangers, 4 receivers, 4 recorders, 40 translators.

Executive chamber: 2 directors, 6 superintendents, 12 clerks.

Herald's office: 2 examiners of heraldry, (assistant ministers of the cabinet,) 5 secretaries and notaries.

5. Board of officers: 2 presidents, 4 vice-presidents, 13 ditto deputies, 16 ditto assisants, 11 directors, 5 ditto of the hall or office, 2 controllers, 71 clerks.

6. Board of revenues: 2 presidents, 4 vice-presidents, 13 ditto deputies, 53 ditto assistants, 29 directors, 6 ditto of the office, 119 clerks, 2 superintendents of the granaries of the capital, 2 ditto of the mint, 5 chief servants.

Officers of the three treasuries: 3 deputy presidents, 6 ditto assistants, 1 director of the office, 5 comptrollers, 4 chief servants, 15 clerks.

Officers of the Peking granaries: 2 grand inspectors, 28 superintendents, 2 ditto of the thoroughfares or passages, 4 clerks.

7. Board of rites: 2 presidents, 4 vice-presidents, 11 deputies, 13 assistants, 9 directors, 4 ditto of the office, 2 comptrollers, 38 clerks.

Office for casting money: 1 assistant president, 1 chief servant, 1 clerk.

Translator's office: Deputy president, 1 shaon king, 1 chief servant, 12 Corean translators, 2 superintendents of horses belonging to this board.

Officers of the board of music, forming a subordinate department of the preceding: 2 masters of the band, 2 ditto deputies, 30 musicians.

8. Board of war: 2 presidents, 4 vice-presidents, 18 deputies, 16 assistants, 11 directors, 5 ditto of the office, 2 comptrollers, 78 clerks, 1 superintendent of horses.

9. Board of punishments: 1 superintendent, 2 presidents, 4 vice-presidents, 46 ditto deputies, 44 ditto assistants, 26 directors, 6 ditto of the office, 2 comptrollers, 114 clerks, 1 treasurer of the fines, 2 prison keepers, 8 jailers.

10. Board of public works: 1 superintendent, 2 presidents, 4 vice-presidents, 22 deputies, 24 assistants, 21 directors, 4 ditto of the office, 2 comptrollers, 86 clerks, 1 assistant president of the reserve treasury, 2 treasurers, 2 clerks, 11 chief servants of the treasury.

Treasury of workmanship: 3 deputy presidents, 2 treasurers, 2 overseers, 7 clerks, 22 servants of the treasury, 2 superintendents of the mint, 2 superintendents of the glass manufactures, 2 ditto of the wards, 2 ditto of coal miners.

11. Foreign office: 1 president, 2 vice-presidents, 11 ditto deputies, 36 ditto assistants, 9 directors, 6 ditto of the office, 2 comptrollers, 97 clerks, 2 treasurers,

1 comptroller of the treasure, 2 clerks, 1 assistant president of the chamber of translation, 1 director, 2 Mongol teachers, 4 clerks, 2 superintendents of the buildings, 16 assistant presidents over the affairs of the nomades, 6 officers of miscellaneous nature.

12. Censorate : 2 censors, 4 deputies, 15 provincial censors, 2 secretaries, 2 general managers, 42 clerks.

Auditors of six-board : 2 chiefs, 2 ditto second, 8 clerks, 2 inspectors of the five cities, 5 reporters of the five cities, 5 attendants.

13. Imperial household establishment : 1 steward general, 1 deputy president, 59 assistant presidents, 12 directors, 5 overseers, 30 stewards of the interior palace, 30 ditto deputies, 12 treasurers, 20 overseers, 17 masters of. ceremony, 298 clerks.

Officers of the arsenal : 2 kings, 1 deputy president, 8 ditto assistants, 2 directors, 28 clerks, 8 treasurers, 3 superintendents of the storehouses, 3 ditto of bows, 3 ditto of arrows, 3 ditto of tents, 3 ditto of workmen.

Officers of the imperial stud : 2 kings, 1 deputy president, 6 assistants, 2 directors, 2 ditto of the office, 25 clerks, 17 grooms, 11 herdsmen overseers, 30 ditto of the Ling-ho district.

Officers of the imperial parks : 2 kings, 6 deputy presidents, 8 assistants, 3 directors, 32 park-keepers, 39 deputies, 2 treasurers, 59 clerks.

14. Court of requests : 1 master of requests, 1 ditto deputy, 2 counsellors, 2 secretaries, 10 clerks.

15. Court of justice : 2 kings, 2 shaon kings, 3 assessors, 2 pleaders, 1 ditto of the court, 2 comptrollers, 6 clerks.

16. National college : 2 presidents, 6 ditto deputies, 6 ditto assistants, 2 recorders, 2 candidates, 44 clerks, &c., &c.

Historiographical offices : 20 historians, 5 directors, 16 clerks.

Courts of memorials : 1 president, 2 deputies, 2 registrars, 6 clerks, 9 officers of various denominations.

17. Sacrificial establishment : 2 kings, 2 shaon kings, 3 assessors, 2 recorders, 2 scholars, 1 treasurer, 1 superintendent of the sacrificial cattle.

18. Banqueting establishment : 29 persons employed.

19. Board of the imperial studs : 29 persons employed.

20. Court of etiquette : 32 persons employed.

21. National institute : 56 persons employed, (including 27 teachers, 2 eminent scholars, 2 teachers of the Russian school, and 1 mathematical teacher.)

22. Astronomical board : 98 persons employed, (including 5 astrologers, 32 eminent scholars, and 48 students of astronomy.)

23. Medical board : 1 principal, 2 deputies, 15 imperial physicians, 30 attendants.

24. Travelling establishment : 1 director, 1 secretary, 10 clerks.

25. Board of the praetorian band : 40 persons employed.

26. Office of the principal king : 15 persons employed ; office of the secondary king, 13 persons employed.

27. Clergymen of the establishment : 24 priests of the altars of Heaven, earth, and the imperial tombs and the temple of the manes, 3 officiating priests at the sacrifices, and 3 assistants, &c., &c., &c. Priests of the tombs of departed sages are officers who are either lineal descendants of Confucius or eminent scholars. In the temple of Confucius there officiate 2 mandarins of 1st class, 4 of 4th class, 6 of 5th class, 1 of 6th class, 8 of 7th class, 10 of 8th class.

The whole number of clergymen who read mass, recite prayers, and burn tapers is 132, exclusive of the officers of the board of rites and of the household establishment. The priests themselves are regularly graduated mandarins, and eligible to any civil office which happens to become vacant. They are, in fact, civilians, only serving for a time in the temple, but for the time being real clergymen of the national ritual.

The supreme government allows to the grandees of the provinces and in the frontier towns a certain number of clerks and private secretaries, who may be considered as "confidential spies." They amount to about 100. The whole number of civilians is about 13,000, 4,000 of whom belong to the supreme tribunals.

Though merit is the theoretical test of qualification, the students of the national institute, the members of collateral imperial descendant, and noblemen generally are, to some extent, privileged and precede the literati, who have no patronage. The sons of Mantchoo officers, the privates of the praetorian band, have a right to be promoted to civil offices, and the attendants, clerks, and translators of the court are equally advanced to official positions. The eminent minister Sung was a mere translator, and many other foremost men have thus risen from the ranks, frequently from the privates of the praetorian band or body-guard of the Emperor.

But even in all these cases, where favoritism is the first prompter of the appointment, examination among the candidates is indispensable, so that the principle of intellectual qualification preponderates, on the whole, over all other considerations.

The mandarins are watched with Argus eyes and the ears of Dionysius; an account of their merits and demerits is rigorously kept, and the examination of these merits and demerits is instituted every three years by the chamber of investigation.

In the provinces the governors and lieutenant governors examine into the conduct of officers personally. A select committee of great ministers and kings is at the same time established at the capital, where delinquent officials are summoned to appear. Their punishment is either dismissal, degradation, fine, or the bastinado. The vices which incapacitate mandarins from holding office are avarice, cruelty, remissness, idleness, disrespectfulness, levity, and general incapacity. Old age and incurable disease are also regarded as incapacitating "vices;" but the charge must be proven, and the accused has a right to defend himself.

Many refractory officers are transported to the banks of the Amoor, or the table land of Ele, to drag boats or become slaves to the soldiery. They are treated outrageously, and, like common convicts, are condemned to pine away their lives in those dreary regions. Meritorious actions are, on the other hand rewarded, not, however, as a matter of due, but as a special favor. The first vacancy which occurs in the scale of promotion is generally conferred upon the officer thus distinguished, who is also introduced into the imperial presence. The Emperor himself sends now and then a haunch of venison to a meritorious officer, or presents him with some tobacco pouches and other articles. His name is at the same time mentioned in the public gazette, and his merits are elaborately stated. An aged servant on retiring often obtains the favor of seeing his son promoted and his ancestors ennobled. The chamber of patents recommend meritorious officers for obtaining the rank of noblemen, and grants the necessary patent.

The chamber of records keeps an accurate and regular account of all the officers in the employ of the government, and publishes four times every year a list of all the civil and military functionaries, which is sent to the different functionaries. A mandarin asking leave of absence applies to this chamber. If one of his parents or relatives has died, he is obliged to retire from office and mourn their loss. Those neglectful of this duty are regarded as monsters. Even those who wish to return home and nurse their aged parents are honorably relieved from their duties for a certain time. But all must return at a stipulated period, at the risk of incurring fines or degradation.

THE TREASURY DEPARTMENTS AND REVENUE SERVICE.

There exist three distinct treasuries in China, namely, the imperial, the national, and the provincial. The first is hoarded up in the palace, and exceeds in riches and valuables any similar deposit in the world. The Emperor is the sole owner of this wealth and is responsible to none. The national treasury is under the special control of the board of revenue, while each province has its private treasury. There are, moreover, small funds in the possession of the different departments, all of which are under the control of the board of revenue, (Hoo-poo.)

The general control is in the hands of two presidents and four vice-presidents. The court itself is divided into 14 chambers, each having the superintendence over one or two provinces. This branch of the administration suffers from frauds and defalcations. The 14 chambers have each their respective jurisdiction, which comprise either one or two provinces. Each of these departments has its agents in the provinces, and the means of ascertaining whether the provincial accounts they receive are correct or not.

The treasure itself is under the immediate control of a great minister, a Mautchoo and a friend of the monarch. It contains three deposits; one treasure of silver, one of cotton and silk piece goods, and another of sundries, such as metals, wax, stationery, &c., and all such articles as are sent from the provinces as tribute. Attached to this office which comprises several deputy presidents and assistants, are a superintendent of the mint and for the manufacture of coin. A committee, consisting of two vice-presidents and other officers, examines into the annual receipts and expenditures, the provisions for the military, the transport of grain, and the state of the granaries. This court is again subdivided into four smaller departments; the first attends to the receipt of money and rice and the time of their delivery, the second to the transportation of the revenue, the third to the expenditure, and the fourth to the supplies furnished to the public servants and illustrious foreigners during their abode at the court.

The treasurer's department in the provinces stands in immediate connection with this board. This functionary is next in rank to the lieutenant governor, and has under him a number of inferior officers for the collection of revenue.

The lands of the peasantry are all rated, the longitude and latitude of the principal places determined, and a careful census of both the Chinese and Mantchoo population taken.

As the boards punish mandarins for embezzlements so it rewards officers who encourage the people to clear new lands and carry agriculture to the highest perfection. Parsimony is much recommended, since the population is rapidly increasing, and soon there will not be sufficient land to produce grain for so many millions of mouths.

For the collection of taxes every village is divided into five and ten families, and the grain is either received at the public offices or gathered by revenue servants.

This board also watches over the weights and measures. For all articles deposited in the treasury the high officers of the board are responsible.

The census of the Chinese is taken every tenth month by the governors and lieutenant governors. To effect it, a constable is appointed over 10 and a bailiff over 100 families. The constable always keeps a register of all the males, and hands the same to the magistrate, who again forwards it to the district magistrate, until the whole census arrives at the governor's office, and is from this forwarded to Pekin. This mode of enumerating the population is correct in principle but is carried out with great carelessness.

The revenue some thirty years ago was as follows, in round figures:

Land tax in money	54,000,000
Land tax in kind, value at	113,000,000
Salt tax	8,000,000
Duties on merchandise	4,500,000
Duties on foreign at Canton, value at	3,000,000
Duties upon shops and pawnbrokers	5,000,000
Sundries	4,500,000
Taels	192,000,000

Equivalent to about $286,000,000 (in gold at $1 40 the tael gold.)

The expenditures generally exceed the revenue, and the deficit is made up by new taxes and patriotic subscriptions.

Salaries to government officers vary from 250 to 15,000 taels ($350 to $21,000 gold) in cash or kind; besides which a certain sum of money, varying from 20 to 500 taels ($28 to $700 gold,) is paid as pocket money to the persons who are appointed to the civil or military service.

The military power in China is entirely at the command of civilians. The authority of military officers is so much abridged by slender pay and the absence of all prerogatives, that they are at the mercy of every literary mandarin.

The general control of the army is under the Ta-chin, or great minister. The governors and lieutenant governors, though generally civilians, are nevertheless intrusted with military command and often take the head of a whole army.

In China, it is taken for granted that whoever can rule a province, can also command an army. Lest, however, the governors should presume on their power, the government has given them, in the Tartar generals and Chinese commanders in-chief, coadjutors by whom their actions are regulated.

The law permits every private to rise to the highest honors. Whoever is deserving promotion may rise to the rank of general. Many officers have thus risen from the ranks, and in all respects, except archery, are very ignorant. With the exception of a peacock's feather to be worn in the cap, the Emperor does not grant any order. Whoever signalizes himself in battle, receives a pecuniary reward; and whoever falls in defence of his country has his name inscribed on the list of promotion in Hades.

The more impartial laws regarding the public officers are contained in the Book of Statutes. Responsibility and a commensurate punishment do not fall so heavily upon those who are of low estate as upon the highest functionaries.

APPENDIX G.

THE CIVIL SERVICE OF PRUSSIA.

The civil service of Prussia is indebted for its world-renowned efficiency and purity—

Firstly. To the common law of Prussia, which contains the provision that "*nobody shall be appointed to a public office unless he possesses the competent qualifications and has produced evidence of his fitness.*"

Secondly. To the universities, colleges, gymnasia, and schools of Prussia, from the graduates of which the bulk of the civil service employés are recruited.

Thirdly. To the stringent systems of examinations regulating the graduation of the students at these institutions, preliminary to the system of examinations enforced in the various branches of the administration.

Fourthly. To the measures taken for the enforcement of integrity and good behavior, and the prevention of frauds and negligence by imposing a severe oath of office in addition to securities to be furnished in cash by the greater number of civil-service officers, particularly by those employed in the financial, revenue, customs, and post office departments.

Fifthly. To the spirit of discipline peculiar to a military monarchy like Prussia, and pervading not only the military service, but all branches of public life.

Sixthly. To the superior moral and mental culture of the German people, which causes most holders of office to live within their means, however small they may be, and to make continuous exertions for the improvement of their capacities and opportunities.

Seventhly. To the measures taken by the government for promoting the worthy officers, for continuing to pay part of their salary to those who are temporarily out of employ, and finally for allowing a pension to those that are obliged to retire from ill health or old age.

Eighthly. To the comparative absence of restlessness of persons who live under military monarchies, and to their tendency of being contented to fill during a whole lifetime the positions, however unremunerative or painstaking, for which they happen to have been educated and to have secured from their earliest age.

Ninthly. To the impartiality of the appointing power, and to the general conviction that appointments are, on the whole, regulated upon consideration of the merit of the applicants, unbiased by political prejudices or by nepotism.

Tenthly. To the almost total absence of fraud in the Prussian service since its establishment, and to the care taken in combining economy with efficiency, integrity with competency.

Persons.

*The forces of the Prussian administration, exclusive of the provincial administration, comprises in the ministry of state and foreign affairs, about 110
Ministry of finance 260
Ministry of religion, education, and sanitary affairs 400
Ministry of commerce, industry, and public works 400
Ministry of interior 425
Ministry of justice 135
Ministry of war 165
Ministry of marine 90
Ministry of agriculture 15

About 2,000

persons all told, but not including the vast numbers of professors, teachers, and employés in universities, colleges, military academies, agricultural, forest, mining, scientific, and civil service training schools and other similar institutions under the control of the national government.

The paper annexed, and marked "Forces of the civil service," contains a detailed statement of the above-mentioned persons employed in the departments of the Prussian government in the capital, the slight discrepancy of numbers being accounted for by the adoption of round numbers in the above statement.

The public service of Prussia being open to all classes of the population, every Prussian subject may become a supernumerary, or, in other words, enter the service upon probation, under conditions and regulations which are stated in the annexed paper marked "supernumeraries."

The subordinate branches of the administration are chiefly recruited from the ranks of these supernumeraries.

---

* These forces do not comprise the increase in the number of public officers, probably appointed lately, consequent upon the recent additions of North German territory to the Prussian government.

The higher branches of the home civil service are selected from referendaries who have passed their examination as assessors.   See "referendaries."

The diplomatic service is recruited from referendaries who have passed their examination as secretary of legation.

The consular service is, according to a new act, to be recruited in future from referendaries who have passed their examination as chancellors of consulates.

The paper marked "on the appointment of civil officers in Prussia" contains the general laws and regulations relating thereto.

A stringent scrutiny of the competency and fitness of the candidates constitutes the most salient characteristic of the Prussian service, at the same time that rigorous measures are taken for the enforcement of integrity and good behavior, and the prevention of fraud and blunders, by exacting bonds from all the employés, as guarantees to that effect.

A paper marked " guarantees in the Prussian service against fraud," contains a statement of the regulations on this subject.

A paper marked "direct petitions to the King for subordinate offices," relates to the circumstances under which such petitions are entertained by the King.

A paper marked " examination of treasury clerks," gives a special account of this sort of examination.

A paper marked " probatory service of military men in the civil service," relates to the qualifications demanded of military men who are entitled to have a preference over civilians in the civil service.

A paper marked " land office," relates to the qualifications and examinations in that branch of the civil service.

A paper marked " post office," relates to the most numerous branch of that service, namely, the despatch clerks ; and annexed thereto is a brief explanation of the railway service.

FORCES OF THE PRUSSIAN ADMINISTRATION.

A.

The council of state, composed of the royal princes who have attained their eighteenth year, and of public functionaries who are members of it ex officio as the members of the cabinet, and many principal military, judicial, ecclesiastical, civil, and diplomatic officers of the state, including the historiographer of the Prussian state, the celebrated historian, Ranke.

The council of state is divided into the following six departments :
1. For foreign affairs.
2. For military affairs.
3. For the judiciary.
4. For finance, commerce, and industry.
5. For home affairs.
6. For religion and education.

Adjoined to the council of state is a tribunal to decide on contests which may may arise in regard to the credentials of the members nominated.

B.

The ministry of state, consisting :
1. President, (Premier) who.is at the same time minister of foreign affairs.
2. Minsiter of finance.
3. Minister of war and marine.
4. Minister of commerce, industry, and public works.
5. Minister of ecclesiastical, educational, and sanitary affairs.
6. Minister of justice.
7. Minister of agriculture.
8. Minister of the interior.

The following officers are employed in the ministry of state, besides two councillors and two clerks :

In the secretariat.. 2
Secret registry and journal... 4
Secret chancellory.. 1

The following officers are under the official control of the ministry of state :

1. The disciplinary tribunal for not judicial officers—president, 10 members, one clerk, and two bureau members........................ 14
2. The chief examination commission—president and four members...... 5
3. The literary bureau of the ministry of state—director and one secretary 2
4. The institute of the Prussian State Advertiser—director........... 1
5. The preparation of the collection of laws—two members............ 2
6. The secret principal court printing office—one.................... 1

Under the official control of the ministry of state are :

1. The general commission for affairs relating to royal orders—president, and five members and five officials............................ 11
2. The order for merit for sciences and arts—Cornelius, the painter, chancellor; and Boeckh, the Hellenist, vice-chancellor.................. 2
3. The state archives with a director, and consisting of the secret state archives, with three members, and the provincial archives, representing seven provinces, with a director and eight archivists........... 13

                                                                    ——
                                                                    62
                                                                    ══

The ministry of foreign affairs, vested in the minister of state, consists :

The minister himself.. 1
An under-secretary of state....................................... 1
A director of division.. 1
Seven active councillors.. 7
One honorary councillor... 1
Four clerks 4
Nine councillors in the secretariat............................... 9
Three councillors in the central and despatch bureau.............. 3
Seven councillors in the cipher bureau............................ 7
Four councillors in the secret registry and journal............... 4
Two councillors in the secret chancellory......................... 2
Two councillors in the pay department of the legation............. 2

                                                                    ——
                                                                    42
                                                                    ══

Under the official control of the minister of foreign affairs are the commissioners of examination for the qualification of diplomatic officers, consisting of a president (the under-secretary of state) and of two members who are professors and members of the judiciary.

The diplomatic and consular agents of Prussia are, of course, also under the official control of the minister of foreign affairs, while the foreign ministers and consuls representing foreign powers in Prussia obtain through him their exequaturs.

C.

The ministry of finance consists, besides its own office, of:

1. The principal stamp office 2
2. The administrator of stamp tax and of stamps on inheritances for the city of Berlin.. 1
3. Stamp-tax bureau for Potsdam, exclusive of Berlin............... 1

4. Principal tax bureau for indigenous articles in Berlin, including stamps
   on bills of exchange.................................   5
5. Principal tax bureau for foreign articles in Berlin.................   4
6. Principal tax bureau for direct taxes..........................   3
7. Commission of valuation for the classification of revenue tax........   1
8. Delegates of the states of the custom's association near the custom-
   house—one at Munich, one at Dresden, one at Hanover, one at
   Carlsruhe, one at Cassel, Wiesbaden and Frankfort, one at Thuringia   6
9. General direction of lotteries   10
10. Mint..   15
11. General direction of the general widow's asylum..................   6
12. Secret ministerial archives..................................   2
13. Administration of the superior forest academy at Neustadt-Eberswulde   7
14. Maritime association (Seehandlung)............................   17
15. Loan office   14
16. Principal administration of the public debt..   27
17. Printing offices of the government..............................   3
18. Commission of the public debt at Berlin........................   7

                                                              131
                                                            ======

The minister's office is divided as follows :

1. Division for the administration of taxes—1 director, 8 councillors, 1
   assessor..   10
2. Division for the civil list and for the treasury—1 director, 5 councillors,
   1 assessor   7
3. Division for domains and forests—2 directors, 10 councillors, 2 assessors   14
4. Division for ground tax—1 director, 4 councillors, 2 assessors........   7

                                                              38
                                                            ======

Minister himself   1
Secret secretaries and accountants in minister's office..................   2
Secret secretaries, administration of taxes   20
Secret secretaries, civil list and treasury   11
Secret secretaries, domains and forests............................   14
Secret secretaries, ground tax....................................   2
Secret registers, administration of taxes............................   11
Secret registers, civil list and treasury..............................   5
Secret registers, domains and forests...............................   7
President of chamber of charts....................................   1
Director secret chancellory.......................................   1
Treasurer's office—1 treasurer, 1 chief clerk, (bookkeeper,) 6 clerks, (book-
   keepers,) 2 cashiers, 1 bookkeeper of state treasury..................   11
Chief bookkeeping office—1 director, 5 bookkeepers..................   6

Total force in the office of the minister..............................   130
Total force in the offices under his official control....................   131

      Grand total..   261
                                                            ======

D.—*The Ministry of Religion, Education, and Sanitary Affairs.*

This ministry has the following offices under its official control :

1. Commission for the establishment and preservation of monuments of art.
2. Scientific deputation of sanitary affairs.

3. Directorium Montis Pietatis, (pawnbrokers' establishments.)
4. Cathedral of Berlin.
5. Institution at Berlin for the candidates to the pulpit of the cathedral.
6. Academy of sciences at Berlin.
7. Academy of fine arts at Berlin and the art and mining academies in the provinces.
8. Academy of fine arts at Königsberg.
9. Academy of fine arts at Düsseldorf.
10. Museums in Berlin.
11. Scientific institutions in Berlin.
12. Universisties, &c.
13. Preacher's seminaries in Wittenberg.
14. Seminary for learned schools, Berlin.
15. Seminary for learned schools, Breslau.
16. Seminary for learned schools, Königsberg.
17. Seminary for learned schools, (burghers,) and higher classes, Stettin.
18. Medical cure institutions of charité, Berlin.
19. Veterinary academy, Berlin.
20. Association for the advancement of practical knowledge, (Sachverständige Vereine.)
21. Examination commissioners for physicians and apothecaries.
22. Commission of court apothecaries.
  Total force about 400, exclusive of the universities.

E.—*The Ministry for Commerce, Industry, and Public Works.*

Central bureau, (inclusive of minister)	4
General post office department, (inclusive of director)	41
Telegraph directories................do	107
Chief post offices, (Berlin)..........do	12
Railway department ....do	
Land, water, and high road administrator do	225
Commerce and industry ....do	
Total force	389

F.—*The Ministry of the Interior.*

Minister's bureau, inclusive of minister and under secretary	43
Statistical bureau, inclusive of director	9
Meteorological institute, (Dr. Dove)	1
Police service, inclusive of chief of police	74
Miscellaneous, chiefly administratories of the estates of nobility, &c., about	300
Total force	427

G.—*Ministry of Justice.*

Minister's office, inclusive of minister and under secretary	36
Tribunes	53
Attorney General's office	32
Examining commission for judicial offices	11
Total force	132

H.—*War Ministry.*

Minister and adjutant	2
Central bureau	11
General war department	15
Artillery division	11
Engineer's division	11
Personal affairs	11
Military economy	55
Corollary offices, (remonte)	15
General auditor's office	8
General pay office	17
Examining office	7

Force, (exclusive of military academic administration, employing several hundred teachers, professors, directors, &c., and exclusive of military intendanture, and depots of provisions, &c., &c , lazaerrettoes, &c., &c.   163

I.—*Ministry of Agriculture.*

Minister's office, (exclusive of agricultural colleges, and employing hundreds of persons)   10

K.—*Marine Department.*

Minister's office	23
Examining of cadets	12
Marine administration and college forces at Dantzic, Stralsund, Berlin, Oldenburg, &c., about	50
Total, about	85

All this exclusive of provincial administration bureaus, and of course of the army, the navy, and police forces.

SUPERNUMERARIES IN THE CIVIL SERVICE OF PRUSSIA.

1. Academical studies or various evidences of intellectual qualification are required for all offices of the Prussian government.

2. The central government and the provincial authorities have the power to establish schools for the training and employment of a certain number of supernumeraries for various branches of the civil service, relieved military men having the precedence for the subordinate offices of the second class.

.3. The candidates for admission to the post of supernumerary must have fulfilled their military duties; they must produce evidence that they are able to support themselves for three years by their own means or with the assistance of their relatives, and they must have attended a gymnasium or a higher burgher's school, and produce a certificate from the first class of such institution testifying to their attainments and their moral character. These conditions are, however, dispensed with if the candidate shall have already been for several years in some public employment, and be able to give satisfactory evidence of his practical capacities. Those who are admitted as supernumeraries do not, however, receive thereby a claim to immediate official appointments.

They are, on the contrary, liable to be dismissed from the colleges and the offices in which they serve as supernumeraries, and can only depend upon a permanent admission to the civil service if they show a particular aptitude for its functions and if their conduct is in every way unobjectionable. Candidates for supernumeraryships in the revenue service must have successfully attended for at least one year the first class of a gymnasium, or have left one of the higher schools with a satisfactory certificate, or pass through an examination by the president of one of these institutions, testifying that they possess the attainments which are acquired after one year's study in the first class. They must further produce testimonials of a fair industry, good conduct, and good capacities; write a fine, legible hand, and be skilful accountants; they must have fulfilled their military duties in a satisfactory manner, possess a strong constitution, capable to bear fatigue, and possess the means of supporting themselves by their own means, without receiving any payment from the state, for at least three years, and in some cases for a longer period. Candidates who could not fulfil their military duties from feebleness of constitution or ill health, and who are yet strong enough for the civil service, may be admitted, though they will be called upon to serve in the army in the event of their health subsequently permitting it. Irrespective of the school testimonials and other requisite certificates, the examiners have to ascertain whether the candidates are persons of good address, of quick understanding, and of innate intelligence. This is ascertained by entering into conversation with them on various subjects, by calling upon them to write out without preparation their views upon any given subject, and to let them solve several mathematical and arithmetical problems.

The commission entitling the candidate to a post as supernumerary in the revenue service is preceded by a provision to the effect that in the event of a want of talent and progress, of insubordination and objectionable conduct, he will be liable to be dismissed forthwith.

The supernumeraries have to apply themselves to the study of laws and regulations in such a manner that gradually they may become conversant with the various branches of the service. To this effect they also have to serve successively in one of the frontier custom-houses and in one of the more extensive revenue offices. Those who show special talents for the civil service are provisionally to be employed in the provincial revenue offices, and only after having worked as assistants and in other similar capacities in such offices are they to be invested with permanent posts in the government departments. For some time they must also have first acted in the place of disabled or suspended officials, so as to familiarize themselves with the practical requirements of the respective offices.

The supernumerary, after one year of service, is either employed in the inspectors' service or in the bureaus. In the event of an altogether unfavorable report of his qualifications, he is then dismissed. If he is deemed fit to be employed in the bureau of the provincial revenue service, he receives a salary without the necessity of undergoing a further examination; but if his superior officers have not acquired a sufficient proof of his qualifications, another examination takes place, the result of which must establish the fact how far he is competent to fill the post of an assistant and to be promoted to the post of a chief comptroller. In case of an unsuccessful examination he cannot even receive a post as inspector.

The examination is conducted by one of the councillors of the provincial counsellors and by a treasury official, both verbally and by writing, the latter by the preparation of some work as it occurs in the regular course of business in the various branches of the revenue service.

Although supernumeraries must possess the means of serving for three years without remuneration, it does not follow that they are debarred from receiving a payment of their services, either by a salary or by fees, if the same should be offered to them by the chief of the office in which they are employed.

REFERENDARIES.

Admission to the higher administrative branches of the government is granted only to referendaries who passed their examination before the supreme court, or obtain from this court a certificate of qualification. They are further subjected to an oral examination conducted by three commissioners, the president of the government acting as chairman.

This examination relates to the political sciences, the leading principles of the national economy, financial science and matters relating to administrative sciences and to the general knowledge of all the auxiliary branches of political, international, and public-revenue science, particularly agricultural science.

The certificate of the commissioners relating to the result of such examination must specify the subjects to which it referred, as well as the extent of knowledge and judgment of the candidate, with a report of his general scientific culture.

The result of the examination is decided by a majority of votes of the commissioners, and the decision is conveyed in the following sentences: Either, the candidate passed the examination, (to which may be added, if expedient, "with distinction,") or, the candidate has not passed the examination. In the latter case he may pass a second examination, but not later than six months from the period of his first examination, the second examination being final.

The candidate who passed his examination is admitted as government referendary and may be assigned to one or the other public office, but is only eligible to the highest office after having passed an examination before the supreme board of examination, or having received a certificate from the president of the government under whom he passed his previous examination, testifying to his qualifications as equivalent with those requisite by the supreme board.

The examination before the supreme board of examination is both oral and by writing, and conducted as follows: The candidate is called upon to furnish, within one year from the period of examination, disquisitions on stated subjects relating to the services of the statesman, to administrative and to financial affairs, the last two subjects to be treated rather from a practical than a theoretical point of view. At least one of these disquisitions must be in the candidates own handwriting, and in regard to all of them he is bound to declare under oath that he prepared them himself and without any assistance excepting that which he found in the study of books. The board may select the theme for the disquisitions from transactions that have actually occurred in the public service, and may also call upon the various branches of the government to submit appropriate themes. The candidate is also permitted to submit any disquisition on administrative and financial subjects which he may have prepared for a branch of the service in which he was previously occupied.

On receipt of the disquisition, the board proceeds to consider the degree of knowledge, and of scientific power, of vigor and precision of judgment, of general ability, of clearness, cogency, and fluency and elegance of expression which the candidate brought to bear upon their elaboration, and if the board decides in his favor by a majority of votes the candidate is admitted to the oral examination within a period stipulated by the board, previous to which, however, all the evidences of qualification, as acquired in his previous occupations and examinations, must have been submitted to all the members of the board.

For the oral examination, the candidate must show himself competent to give a satisfactory account relating to all questions that may bear upon the duties of the branch of the service to which he aspires. It is not sufficient that he masters the theories of the requisite knowledge, but his whole individuality, his bearing, his manners, his natural ability, the extent of his judgment and practical skill, as well as the thoroughness and depth of his power in grappling with the scientific knowledge which he has acquired, are scrutinized with the utmost rigor.

He must further deliver before the board a speech on a stated theme which is selected on the day preceding the examination, and that may consist of one of his own written disquisitions, for the purpose of testing his power of expressing his views with terseness, clearness, thoroughness and logical power.

The number of candidates to be admitted to the same examination is not to exceed three.

The successful candidate is immediately appointed as *government assessor ;* and if he gives satisfaction in this official capacity and produces evidence of his progress in knowledge, of his zeal and industry, and of his aptitude, he is subsequently promoted by the king to the rank of councillor in the governmental office or in the provincial administration.

Candidates whose examination was not sufficiently satisfactory may undergo a second examination, but not later than six months from the period of the first, this second examination being final.

Candidates whose examination was "altogether unsatisfactory," are not permitted to pass a second examination. To this category belong those who, although they possess the requisite knowledge, are so destitute of natural ability and general culture as to unfit them for the higher branches of the service.

To the category of "sufficiently satisfactory" belong those who possess natural ability and general culture, but are deficient in one or the other requisite branches of knowledge.

"Entirely satisfactory" are only those who combine natural ability and general culture with a mastery of all the details of the various branches of knowledge.

The supreme board of examination constitutes a department of the government, which is under the official control of the ministry of state.

It is located in the capital, and consists of a permanent chairman and four members, who may be changed at any time and who are selected from the ministerial councillors of the various branches of the government and the bench. The appointments to this board are purely honorary.

The members of the ministry of state, the directors and councillors of all other ministries, and the presidents of national colleges, are at liberty to be present during the oral examination of candidates.

ON THE APPOINTMENT OF CIVIL OFFICERS IN PRUSSIA.

1. The King appoints to all offices in the army, and to other branches of the public service, unless otherwise decreed by the constitution.

2. The judges are appointed by the King for life. They can be only removed or suspended in due process of law.

3. Those only who possess the requisite qualifications, as prescribed by the laws, are eligible to the office of judge.

4. The presidents and counsels of the supreme court, and of the courts of appeal, the directors and counsels of district and city courts, are nominated by the King. Assessors, attorneys-at-law, notaries, and referendaries, are nominated by the minister of justice in behalf of the King.

Referendaries who have passed through the great state examination, fill the office of court assessor until they have received a permanent appointment. If this is not assigned to them either temporarily in the court of appeal, or in the ministry of justice, they are, like the unpaid assessors of the chief tribunal, adjoined as unpaid members to the bar of a district or city court.

5. As regards the qualifications for the judges, and the examinations in jurisprudence connected therewith, the regulations on the subject are subject to revision. A director of district courts must have passed the great state examination. The professional judges of the supreme court must have officiated at least for four years, as judges or chief government counsel at a court of

appeal, and the members of courts of appeal must have officiated at least four years at a chief tribunal, and subsequently at district or city courts, or definitively in the capacity of government counsel.

6. Subordinate officers of private tribunals are either appointed for life, or employed in other branches of the civil service, or permitted to officiate at the courts as civil supernumeraries.

7. The appointments in the administrative branches of the public service are made by the respective heads of the department, who have also the power to promote, dismiss, and pension their subordinates. This power, however, is liable to many limitations, particularly as regards the receivers of public moneys (*rendant*) and other responsible trusts, while in all appointments the candidates are subject to a severe test of examination, and preferred according to their superior fitness.

8. The common law of Prussia contains the following provision :

Nobody shall be appointed to a public office unless he possesses the competent qualifications and has given evidences of his fitness.

9. Officers who knowingly employ an unfit person, are held responsible to the state and to the individual citizens thereof, for all damages that may arise through the incompetency and unfitness of such employé.

10. Officers who intrust money to a treasury employé previous to his having furnished the requisite securities, are responsible for all damages that may accrue therefrom.

11. The oath of service imposes upon the civil officers the solemn duty to fulfil his functions with the utmost fidelity and strictness, not only as prescribed by the law, but also in obedience to the voice of his conscience. This oath will impel every honest man to discharge his responsibilities, not only satisfactorily to his King and official superiors, but also in such a manner as to give satisfaction to the highest judge.

In view of this oath, it is hoped that even in such cases where conscience is the only witness, this will be sufficient to resist all temptations and to act under all circumstances with inflexible integrity.

On taking the oath, God is invoked to punish perjury and to reward the faithful performance of duty.

The significance of the oath, from a religious and moral point of view, is further dwelt upon, so as to make it binding upon the conscience, while at the same time the sense of honor and ambition is appealed to, and promotion promised in reward of faithful and efficient services.

The following is the form of the oath of service :

I, N. N. make oath before God, the Almighty and Omniscient, that after having been appointed in the capacity of   *   *   *   *   *   I will be subject, faithful and obedient to his Royal Majesty of Prussia, my most gracious master, that I will perform the duties of my office according to my best knowledge and judgment, and that I will faithfully comply with the Constitution, so help me God, &c., &c.

12. Whosoever obtains an appointment by bribery or by other illicit means will be dismissed forthwith.

13. All contracts and agreements promising private advantages or actually conceding them for procuring a public office, are null and void.

14. Agreements between an out-going official and his successor securing to the former a portion of the salary of the respective office, are only valuable in so far as they have been expressly sanctioned by the superior authorities.

15. The acts of a public officer, in his official capacity, cannot be resented personal insults.

16. A blunder that might have been averted by proper attention and by the exercise of the qualifications which are required for the respective office, must be rectified at the expense of the employé who committed it.

17. Superior officers, who, by the exercise of the vigilance prescribed by the

regulations of the service, might have averted the commission of blunders on the part of their subordinate employés, are held responsible for the same to the state, as well as to private citizens who may suffer therefrom.

18. The superior officer or head of department has the power to suspend or dismiss his subordinates, the matter being subject to the decision of the council of state, and the respective employés having the right to be heard in explanation or in defence.

19. Drunkards in the civil service are. dismissed and forfeit their right to pension.

20. The heads of departments are liable to severe punishment, besides dismissal from the service and forfeiture of pension, for divulging the secrets of the administration.

21. Civil officers are admonished not to run into debt, and liable to be seriously prejudiced thereby and to be restricted in the mode of receiving their salaries.

22. The subordinate officers of the civil service are divided into four classes, viz:

First class.—Dispatching secretaries, journalists, calculators, registers, rendants, receivers of moneys, comptrollers, presidents of chancellories, and other similar functionaries.

Second class.—Referendaries and graduates of the national collegos. (gymnasia)

Third class.—The subordinate employés of national colleges, (occupying the functions designated under the first class,) the secretaries of chancellories and the chancellors of ministries. District secretaries are regarded as goverument subordinates of the first class.

Fourth class.—Secretaries of chancellories and chancellors of national colleges.

23. The higher officers of the ministries are divided into three classes, according to their rank :

Firt class.—The heads and directories of separate divisions in the ministries; the secret cabinet councillors; the Postmaster Geueral, (as long as he does not occupy a higher station in virtue of the title excellency ;) the president-in-chief of the chief court of accounts; the president-in-chief of the secret supreme court, (if he is not invested with the title "excellency" ;) the president in chief of the whole court of exchequer, (if this office has an incumbent ;) the chief mining officer; the secretary of state, (if he does not possess the title "excellency" ;) the presidents-in-chief and the provincial consistorial presidents.

All these officers have access to the royal court.

Second class. The effective councillors who have the titles of secret councillor of legation, secret chief councillor of justice, secret councillor of the chief tribunal, secret and councillor-in-chief of finance, actual secret councillor of war, secret chief councillor of the government, the actual governmental presidents, the presidents of the exchequer tribunal, and of the chief national tribunals, the directors of the chief chambers of accounts, the secret chief mining councillors, the secret chief medical councillors, (if they are at the same time effective councillors in the ministries,) the president of police of Berlin.

All these officers have likewise access to the royal court.

Third class.—Effective councillors with the title of actual councillor of legation, secret councillor of justice, secret councillor of finance, secret councillor of war, or actual councillor of war, secret councillor of government, the chief director of the mint, the directors of the bank and of the maritime association, the vice-presidents and directors of the provincial colleges, the chief commissioners for the relations of the peasantry, the secret councillors of the maritime association, secret chief councillors of architecture, secret councillors of accounts, secret chief councillors of account of the chief chamber of accounts, secret councillors of the post, secret chief medical councillors, (if they are not at the same time effective councillors in the ministries,) the chief councillors of architecture, the chief medical councillors, and the chief consistoral councillors at the ministries.

The foregoing officers are not accessible to the royal court.

24. The higher officers of the provincial colleges are divided into five classes, the specification of which, however, is omitted as unessential for the present purpose.

GUARANTEES IN THE PRUSSIAN CIVIL SERVICE AGAINST MISMANAGEMENT AND FRAUD.

Proper organization of the treasury departments, sufficient payment of the employés, and a stringent control may relieve the state from the imputation of having itself brought about the crime of fraud.—*Bülau.*

The persons employed in the civil service of Prussia are bound to take an oath by which they pledge themselves to a faithful, active and intelligent observance of their duties.

The moneys which are to be deposited by various officers are securities for the proper discharge of their duties, as well for the indemnification of the State for any damage or fraud arising in the administration of the regular functions.

a. The principal officers of the treasury department and the superintendent of mortgages in certain parts of the monarchy have to give bonds to the extent of 6,000 Prussian thalers.

b. Postmasters, custom-house directors, revenue directors, &c., &c., to the extent of 3,000 Prussian thalers, in all such cases where the annual salary of the officers is 900 Prussian thalers, or in excess of 900 thalers.

c. If the salary of these and similar officers is less than 900 thalers annually, the securities are to be to the extent of two years' salary, provided that this will exceed one-twelfth of the average annual amount of money passing through each of these respective offices.

d. Chief bookkeepers at a central and government treasury who act in the place of the chief officers and comptrollers, cashiers, and other officials who take an immediate part in the receipt of funds, or in the administration of depots of goods, have to furnish security to the extent of the amount of one year of their respective salaries.

e. Other subordinate and inferior employés, particularly those in the departments of justice and of the post, who handle valuable objects and money, have to furnish security equivalent to the amount of six months of their respective salaries.

f. The securities in the clauses C, D, and E are to be proportioned in rates of 25 thalers for each year during the duration of the service.

g. An officer who unites several functions which require the deposit of securities, has to furnish them only once and according to the total amount of his united salaries. If these securities fall under the different categories of C, D, and E, they are apportioned according to the highest rate.

Exempted from giving security are those officers who handle public money as an accessory occupation without remuneration; but from the moment they receive a remuneration for their services the double amount of the same is to be deposited as security.

The security must be deposited in cash, either by the office-holder or by a third party for his account.

The permission to custom-house and revenue officers to cover their securities by deductions from their salaries is granted only exceptionally.

The government pays four per centum annual interest upon these amounts, thus deposited as security, these interests being payable at the end of June and December.

On leaving the service the deposit of security is refunded without delay.

As regards these officials whose trusts do not fall within any of the aforementioned categories, the amount of the security is determined by analogy, and in such cases where the office-holders are not intrusted with the management of money, but with that of real estate or corporate interests, the security may be deposited either in cash or in public stocks, or railway shares or in mortgage bonds.

EXAMINATION OF TREASURY CLERKS.

Examination for the treasury departments, including all branches of the service that relate to accounts and calculation.

Supernumeraries who desire to devote themselves exclusively to the above-mentioned branches of the public service have to pass a special examination relating to the administration of deposit and specie banks, of the budget, of matters pertaining to calculation, of taxation and the regulations in respect to stamps. The examiners have to decide whether the candidate possesses the prescribed qualifications in a fair or superior degree for the independent administration of a treasury or calculator's office.

Supernumeraries are dismissed after five years of probatory or supernumerary service if, previous to the expiration of that period, they have not actually passed the abovesaid examination with a view of becoming officers in the various treasury departments, or the examination as actuary with a view of officiating in the judiciary departments the president of the court of appeals being bound by officers to call upon the supernumeraries within four years from the beginning of their supernumerary service, to submit to the treasury or judiciary examination at the risk of their being dismissed altogether, if they fail to subject themselves to meet an examination within the above-stated period.

PROBATORY SERVICE OF MILITARY MEN IN THE CIVIL SERVICE.

Under-officers of 12 years' service and military invalids entitled to public employment are preferred to the civil supernumeraries. Probatory service, however, is required of them in all offices relating to the treasury and to chancellory duties which do not imply merely mechanical labor further in all offices of the executive police in penitentiaries and reform institutions, in the post office, the *gensdarmerie*, the revenue, woods and forest and domain administration, inspectorships of public roads, &c., &c.

Messengers and other menial employés need not serve on probation, with exception, however, of the administration of woods and forests and of domains, where such offices imply a certain amount of intelligence beyond merely mechanical labor.

DIRECT PETITIONS TO THE KING FOR SUBORDINATE OFFICES.

Persons who are desirous of entering the subordinate civil service may petition the King directly; provided, however, that they have fulfilled their military duties to the state by actual service in the army, or that they have been released therefrom by law; and provided, further, that they possess such excellent qualifications for the office to which they aspire, that their appointment may hold out positive advantages to the state.

A petition for an office of the higher subordinate branches of the civil service falls to the ground, unless the applicant gives evidence of his qualifications by passing examination as first-class actuary.

Petitioners for employment in the judiciary must have officiated for at least eight years at royal tribunals, or in royal chambers—of royal justices, and not merely of commissaries of justice—or in colleges, corporations, and communes of the state, and produce evidence of their exemplary conduct and of their efficiency for the whole period of this official service.

Applicants who cannot comply with these regulations must serve as civil supernumeraries before they can expect to secure a permanent appointment.

Those whose petitions are favorably considered are yet in the same position with supernumeraries, as far as the preference is concerned, which is accorded to under-officers of 12 years' service and to military invalids.

LAND OFFICE.

Land offices—Commissioner of economy.

The qualifications for these offices embrace—

1. Practical and theoretical agricultural science.
2. Capacity to manage, superintend, and work a farm.
3. Familiarity with the best standard works on land, agriculture, farming, &c.
4. Knowledge of the laws and practices regulating the tenure and distribution of landed property, the laws of mortgage, the discrimination between the various descriptions of land, the processes of irrigation and improvement, the taxes on land, and of all other laws, regulations, practices, circumstances bearing upon the tenure, cultivation, distribution, improvement, or neglect of landed property.
5. Familiarity with all commercial and manufacturing establishments, as breweries, distilleries, &c., and which relate to the products of the soil; also with the science of woods and forests, of gardening, and other branches of knowledge that are cognate to agricultural studies.

A commissioner of a land office in Prussia, or of an agricultural department, must be a sound real estate lawyer, an accomplished scientific man, a practical farmer, a good business man, and an expert in public affairs.

It is not sufficient that applicants for such office pass a stringent oral and verbal examination, but they must actually have been either business men who have obtained the grade of actuary in the principal judiciary departments or have been practical farmers who must produce evidence of aptitude by preparing disquisitions on any stated subject relating to agricultural science for the purpose of displaying their power to discuss principles with cogency and precision as well as to carry them into practical effect. They must further produce evidence of having successfully worked, for at least three years, on one or two great estates, either as proprietors or as administrators, or at least six years in a subordinate capacity. In the event of their having attended a well-known agricultural academy, one year of such attendance will be deemed as equivalent to two years' work as administrator or subordinate employé.

After the compliance with the foregoing conditions, the first examination takes place in the principal branches of science and experience bearing upon land, and agriculture, and national economy, and resources of foreign nations—the examination being both written and oral, as prescribed for the higher civil offices.

The successful candidate is then attached as a writer of protocols to a commissioner, and after one or two years of such service, which includes also experience in surveying, accounts, reports, and other functions of the land offices, he may be promoted to the post of assistant, provided that the evidences of his aptitude, specimens of which have to be submitted to the government to that effect, prove in every respect satisfactory. After having served for several years as assistant and taken a part in the labor of the colleges of the general land commission and some further probationary occupations, he may receive a certificate from the commissioner under whom he is employed to the effect that he is fully prepared for the examination as commissioner.

Then comes the great state examination in all the branches of knowledge and experience to which we have referred, and it is only after satisfactorily passing through this ordeal, and after serving at first again as assistant, with a view of additional preparation for the discharge of the office of head of the department, that the appointment as commissioner is at last granted.

RAILWAY SERVICE.

The railway administration have the appointing power of all officers employed in the railway service, such appointment, however, to be notified to the minister of finance, with a view of ascertaining the qualifications of the respective applicants.

Persons employed in the police force of the railway service must not be younger than 21 years; they must be of irreproachable character, and able to read and to write, and possess all the other requisite qualifications for the service of police.

They have no claim to pay during such probationary service, but in the event of their giving satisfaction they may be remunerated, but not to an extent exceeding 20 thalers per month. In the event of their dismissal after the one year probation, the security of 200 thalers, which they are bound to deposit in public paper money or in public stocks on entering the service, is restored to them one year and one month subsequent to their removal from the service, provided that nothing has occurred which makes its retention necessary for the state.

Post office despatch clerks may be promoted to the rank of postmasters of the second class, liable to suspension, however, after three months' notice, and subject to an examination embracing all the regulations and taxes of the post office, all the branches of the despatch business, treaties and regulations relating to foreign post offices, articles liable to duty, the financial department of the post office, &c., &c., &c.

The despatch clerks may be transferred from one to the other post office district, according to the discretion of the respective chief postmastership.

EXAMINATION.

Post office despatch clerks constitute the third class of subordinate employés.

1. Applicants must not be older than 35 years.

2. They must furnish a medical certificate testifying to their health, particularly to the excellent condition of their organs of sight and of hearing.

3. Unless they have been military men, entitled as such to public offices, they must produce evidence of having served during the requisite three years in the army.

4. They must produce satisfactory evidence of their antecedents in respect to integrity, morality, and respectability; further, of their being free from debt, and of their sincere devotion to the king and the government.

After compliance with the foregoing conditions, the applicant is subjected to the following examination:

a. Penmanship, as a specimen of which he is called upon to write down a report of his past career.

b. Geography.

c. Arithmetic.

d. General composition, as a means of testing his knowledge and ability.

A special importance is attached to a clear, steady, legible handwriting and to efficiency and accuracy in arithmetic.

In the event of the applicant's familiarity with a foreign language, the examination is extended thereto.

This examination takes place in the general post office administration in which the applicant seeks employment. After passing a satisfactory examination, they are admitted to a probatory service of one year, after which they are either dismissed or permanently retained.

APPENDIX H.

THE ENGLISH CIVIL SERVICE.

The improvement of the English civil service since the establishment of the act for the better government of India, (1859,) recognizing the system of open competition and providing for the conduct of the examinations by the civil service commissioners and the superannuation act, passed in the same year, providing that no person appointed after its date shall, for its purposes, be considered as serving in the permanent civil service of the state, unless admitted with a certificate from the civil service commissioners, has been fully described in the report from the joint select committee of the two houses of Congress, appointed under concurrent resolution of July 19, 1866.

It may only be repeated here that according to the latest report of the civil service commissioners, dated 12th June, 1865, it appears that the total number of nominations since the commencement of their proceedings in May, 1855, amounts to 29,763.

The service has not only become more efficient under the system of qualified employés by competitive examination, but also more economical, as appears from the following table, which contains a comparative statement of the average expenditure in four of the principal departments during six years previous and six years subsequent to the adoption of the reformed system :

	1847.	1848.	1849.	1850.	1851.	1852.	Total.	Average.
Treasury...........	£60,300	£60,800	£57,200	£56,100	£53,700	£54,400	£342,500	£57,083
Home Office........	29,900	29,200	25,400	26,000	25,270	26,550	162,320	27,054
Foreign Office......	83,848	82,000	76,000	71,000	71,000	67,735	451,683	75,280
Colonial Office......	31,500	36,961	36,900	37,400	37,100	38,815	218,676	36,446
								195,863

	1861.	1862.	1863.	1864.	1865.	1866.	Total.	Average.	Decr'se.
Treasury	£53,173	£52,363	£51,730	£53,147	£53,488	£52,432	£316,333	£52,722	£4,361
Home Office	25,753	25,856	26,263	26,883	27,118	26,417	158,290	26,381	673
Foreign Office......	62,715	64,319	72,325	72,015	66,883	63,840	402,099	67,016	8,164
Colonial Office	30,449	30,748	31,047	31,421	31,658	32,124	187,447	31,241	5,205
Showing a decrease of expenditure of about 9¼ per cent., or................									18,403

A thorough insight into the present organization of the various branches of the home civil service in England is afforded by the annexed statements of the persons employed, together with their salaries, in the following departments of the service :

	Total forces.	Estimate of total cost in 1866.
A. Custom-house service.....................................	5,850	£798,493
B. Inland revenue service....................................	5,036	1,295,645
C. Post office..	25,142	2,436,016
D. Paymaster general's department...........................	83	21,000
E. Colonial office...	40	30,000
F. Foreign office...	64	40,000
G. Home office...	45	26,000
H. Treasury	92	50,000

It will be perceived from a careful perusal of these tables, that the bulk of the cost of these public offices goes towards the payment of clerical salaries exceeding the amount of £500 or about $3,000 in currency annually, thus securing competent men by offering adequate remuneration, while the whole cost of the service is diminished by the relief from the necessity of appointing thousands of £200 and £300 or $1,200 and $1,800 clerks. The system of annual increase until the maximum salary is reached is also an element of great public utility and of encouragement and advantage to the persons employed.

In analyzing for instance the treasury service, (not including, as in this country, all, but only a portion of the financial department,) it will be found that about four-tenths of the total cost is for salaries in excess of £500 and only one-tenth for salaries of smaller amounts.

The same applies more or less to the inland service, customs, and other important branches of the English service.

A.—Custom-house service, England.

LONDON CUSTOM-HOUSE.

	Minimum.	Gradual annual increase.	Maximum.
The board—			
1 chairman..........................	...	..	£2,000
1 deputy chairman	...	..	1,600
3 commissioners.....................	...	..	1,200
Secretary's office—			
1 secretary.			1,600
1 assistant secretary...............	£800	£25	1,000
3 committee clerks..................	600	20	700
1 London petition clerk.............	470	15	500
3 chief clerks	350	15	450
Clerks for general duty—			
6 first class.......................	260	15	320
7 second class......................	170	10	230
8 third class.......................	100	10	160
Additional to clerks for special duties..........	...	..	220
1 housekeeper and storekeeper.......	...	..	260
2 doorkeepers.......................	...	..	100
1 house porter......................	...	..	80
Solicitor's office—			
1 solicitor.........................	...	..	2,000
2 assistant solicitors..............	...	..	800
9 clerks, varying from £90 to £500....	...	..	500
2 surveyors general, £800; after 5 years..........	...	..	900
1 principal surveyor for tonnage....	...	..	500
1 draughtsman.......................	200	10	250
2 draughtsmen.......................	...	..	200
1 surveyor of buildings, £400, (£50 after 5 years' and £50 after 10 years' service)..............	...	..	500
1 professional clerk, £200, (£50 after 5 years and £50 after 10 years' service)................	...	..	300
1 clerk of the works................	...	..	150
Receiver general's office—			
1 receiver general..................	...	..	1,200
1 assistant receiver general........	...	..	600
4 principal clerks	350	20	450

	Minimum.	Gradual annual increase.	Maximum.
4 clerks, 1st class	£240	£15	£320
6 clerks, 2d class	160	10	220
9 clerks, 3d class	80	10	140
Comptroller general's office—			
1 comptroller general	700	20	800
1 assistant comptroller general	450	20	550
6 principal clerks	350	20	450
7 1st class clerks	260	15	320
14 2d class clerks	160	10	220
20 3d class clerks	80	10	140
Inspector general of imports and exports—			
1 inspector general, £800; after 5 years	...	..	900
1 assistant inspector general	450	25	550
4 principal clerks	320	15	400
8 1st class clerks	230	10	300
15 2d class clerks	150	10	220
20 3d class clerks	80	*5	160
Examiner's office—			
1 examiner and jerquer	650	25	†800
1 assistant examiner	450	25	556
9 principal clerks	320	15	400
27 1st class clerks	230	10	300
54 2d class clerks	150	10	220
80 3d class clerks	80	‡5	140
Pay to extra clerks	...	..	2,000
Travelling charges, &c.	...	..	1,000
Total number of persons employed	...	..	355
Total expenses	...	..	£91,660

	Persons employed.	Expenditures.
London custom-house	355	£91,660
Port of London, (docks, searcher's office, &c., &c.)	1,768	258,923
Port of Liverpool	824	107,040
Other ports, United Kingdom	2,561	314,570
Law charges, rewards for capture of smugglers, &c., &c.		16,300
	5,508	798,493

B.—*Inland revenue service system.*

INLAND REVENUE.

England	3,406	£617,441
Scotland	969	138,374
Ireland	661	100,732
Sundry expenses, (including £136,000 poundage to collectors and assessors		439,098
Total forces and cost	5,036	1,295,645

* And, by two years afterward, 10.   † Additional 50.
‡ And 10, two years afterwards.

The board—	Minimum.	Gradual annual increase.	Maximum.
Salary of chairman	...	..	£2,000
Deputy chairman	...	..	1,600
6 commissioners	...	..	1,200
Secretary's office—			
2 secretaries	...	..	1,200
2 assistant secretaries	...	..	800
4 committee clerks	£550	£20	650
8 clerks, 1st class	450	20	550
1 registrar of papers	450	20	550
1 assistant registrar of papers	350	10	450
9 clerks, 2d class	350	10	450
12 clerks, 3d class	250	10	350
14 clerks, 4th class	150	10	250
12 clerks, 5th class	90	10	150
Solicitor's office—			
1 solicitor	...	..	2,000
1 assistant solicitor's, (additional allowance of 200)	...	..	1,200
3 chief clerks	600	20	700
3 clerks, 1st class	450	20	550
4 clerks, 2d class	350	20	450
6 clerks, 3d class	200	10	300
10 clerks, 4th class	90	10	200
1 supplementary clerk for property tax	120	5	150
1 supplementary clerk for property tax	...	..	100
Receiver generals' office—			
1 receiver general	...	..	1,000
1 chief clerk	500	20	600
4 clerks, 1st class	350	20	450
4 clerks, 2d class	250	20	350
5 clerks, 3d class	150	10	250
6 clerks, 4th class	90	10	150
Comptroller of legacy and succession duty office—			
1 comptroller	...	..	1,500
1 assistant comptroller	900	..	*1,000
2 chief clerks	600	50	800
chief superintendents	500	20	600
2 superintendents, 1st class	450	10	500
3 superintendents, 1st class	32(	10	400
12 examiners	320	10	400
17 assistant examiners	250	10	300
7 superintendents, 2d class	200	10	240
28 clerks, 2d class	150	10	200
31 clerks, 3d class	90	10	140
1 senior keeper of wills	120	10	150
1 keeper of wills	90	5	110
4 keepers of wills	80	5	100
Accountant's office—			
3 chief accountants	...	..	800
6 clerks, 1st class	450	20	550
10 clerks, 1st class	400	15	450

* After three years.

	Minimum.	Gradual annual increase.	Maximum.
4 clerks, 2d class	£350	£10	£400
10 clerks, 2d class	300	10	350
14 clerks, 3d class	200	10	250
16 clerks, 4th class	150	10	200
19 clerks, 5th class	90	10	140
1 boy in warrant room	26	..	26
Inspector's office, (taxes)—			
1 chief inspector	800	..	800
1 assistant inspector	500	20	600
1 inspector, 1st class	600	20	650
6 inspectors 2d class	550	20	600
3 inspectors	450	10	500
Chief examiner	550	20	650
1 clerk, 1st class	450	20	550
1 clerk	400	20	500
4 clerks, 2d class	250	10	350
5 clerks, 3d class	150	10	250
6 clerks, 4th class	90	10	150
Surveying general examiners, (excise)—			
1 principal	600	20	700
3 1st class	550	10	600
1 2d class	400	..	400
14 2d second class	350	..	350
15 3d class	...	..	300
Laboratory—			
1 principal	700	20	750
1 assistant	300	10	400
Fire insurance office—			
1 registrar	400	20	500
1 chief clerk	300	15	350
3 clerks, 1st class	200	10	290
5 clerks, 2d class	150	10	190
6 clerks 3d class	90	5	140
Registrar of warrant's office—			
1 registrar	370	20	450
1 chief clerk	260	15	350
3 clerks, 1st class	150	10	240
4 clerks, 2d class	90	10	140
Spoiled stamps office—			
1 examiner	550	20	650
1 assistant examiner	450	15	500
1 chief clerk	350	10	450
1 clerk, 1st class	250	10	350
2 clerks, 2d class	150	10	250
2 clerks, 3d class	90	10	150
Registrars of licenses and distributors of stamps office—			
1 registrar	450	20	550
1 chief clerk	300	10	350
3 clerks, 1st class	220	10	270
3 clerks, 2d class	150	10	200
2 clerks, 3d class	90	10	140

	Minimum.	Gradual annual increase.	Maximum.
4 copying clerks, (per week) 36 shillings............	...	..	...
1 boy...	...	..	£26
Warehouse keeper's office—			
1 principal warehouse keeper	£450	£20	550
1 assistant warehouse keeper	350	10	400
1 chief clerk	280	10	330
1 diary clerk...................................	230	5	250
5 clerks, 1st class..............................	220	10	270
6 clerks, 2d class	150	10	200
6 clerks, 3d class	90	10	140
4 superintendents of warehouses..................	90	5	130
10 warehousemen, 1st class (additional allowance 20).	90	5	110
10 warehousemen, 2d class ....,..........	75	5	90
8 porters, 1 binder, and 3 sewers	...	..	...
Stamping department—			
1 controller of stamping.........................	...	..	750
1 deputy controller of stamping	...	..	500
1 chief superintendent	...	..	200
1 superintendent at Manchester	...	..	140
2 superintendents of stamping tables	130	5	150
1 superintendent of perforating stamps............	130	5	160
1 superintendent of stamping of newspapers (salary as stamper; additional allowance 20)	90	1	120
1 superintendent excise printing............	...	..	120
50 stampers......................	75	1	100
25 junior stampers...............................	40	5	75
Special commissioner of income tax office—			
3 special commissioners	...	..	600
First branch:			
1 chief examiner................................	300	20	550
1 assistant examiner.............................	300	15	350
6 clerks, 1st class..............................	250	10	290
12 clerks, 2d class	150	10	240
15 clerks, 3d class	90	5	140
1 clerk...	...	..	445
Second branch:			
1 chief clerk	350	15	400
1 clerk, 1st class............................. ..	200	10	250
2 clerks, 2d class	150	10	200
3 clerks, 3d class	90	10	150
Stage carriage duty office—			
1 assessor	400	20	500
2 clerks, 1st class..............................	150	10	250
3 clerks, 2d class	90	10	150
1 surveyor of buildings	...	..	400
1 medical officer...............................	...	..	400
Out-door establishment for taxes—			
3 inspectors of taxes, 1st class	600	20	650
3 inspectors of taxes, 2d class....................	550	20	600
25 surveyors, 1st class........................	420	20	500
30 surveyors, 2d class..........................	350	10	400

	Minimum.	Gradual annual increase.	Maximum.
40 surveyors, 3d class	300	10	350
45 surveyors, 4th class	250	10	300
100 surveyors, 5th class	200	10	250
60 assistant surveyors	90	10	150
Out-door establishment for excise—			
1 collector of excise and distributor of stamps at Liverpool	700	20	800
1 do......sea-policy stamps (London)	550	20	650
5 do......2d class	500	20	550
16 do......3d class	450	10	500
22 do......4th class	400	10	450
17 do......5th class	360	10	400
Additional allowances to collectors acting as distributors of stamps	...	..	300
8 clerks to collectors, 1st class	180	5	220
70 clerks to collectors, 2d class	140	5	180
64 clerks to collectors, 3d class	110	5	140
54 supervisors of foot-walk	230	5	250
222 supervisors of riding districts	200	5	230
40 examiners	...	..	170
396 officers of divisions	120	5	150
685 officers of rides	...	..	110
1 officer of diaries	120	5	150
Out-door establishment for excise—			
30 assistants, 1st class	...	..	95
255 assistants, 2d class	...	..	*60
1 preventive officer	...	..	100
1 surveyor (London)	...	..	350
1 office keeper	...	..	160
1 head messenger	...	..	120
2 messengers	...	..	100
9 messengers, 1st class	80	2	90
17 messengers, 2d class	70	2	80
61 menial officers	...	..	...
Total force inland revenue (England)			3,406
Total expenses			£617,441

C—Post office.

4,339 London, Dublin, Edinburg	£577,100
90 surveyors, &c.	41,925
5,012 provincial post office, England and Wales	523,245
2,604 provincial post office, Ireland	57,507
2,828 provincial post office, Scotland	79,516
93 provincial post office, colonies, &c.	13,209
134 conveyance of mails	763,462
..... buildings and repairs	348,432
42 manufacturers postage stamps	31,220
25,142	2,436,016

Salaries, highest, £2,500, £2,000, £1,500, £900, £1,200, £800, £600, £700, £500, £400, downward to the smallest amounts.

* And additional two shillings per diem when actively employed.

D.—*Paymaster General's Office.*

Paymaster receiving salary as vice-president board of trade.

	Minimum.	Increase.	Maximum.
Assistant paymaster general....................	£1,000	£50	£1,200
Deputy paymaster general (Dublin).............	820	20	950
2 first-class clerks, first section.................	670	20	950
5 first-class clerks, second section..............	520	20	650
10 second-class clerks, second section.............	520	20	650
16 second-class clerks	315	15	500
35 third-class clerks...........................	100	10	300
2 temporary clerks............................	100	5	150
1 office keeper...............................	...	..	150
9 messengers, { 3 at	100	5	110
{ 2 at	90	2½	100
{ 4 at	80	2½	90
83			**21,000**

E.—*Colonial Office.*

1 secretary of state...			£5,000
1 under secretary			2,000
1 under secretary			1,500
1 assistant secretary..			1,500
			10,000

	Minimum	Increase.	Maximum.
1 chief clerk....................................	£1,000	£50	£1,250
5 senior clerks.................................	700	25	1,000
7 assistant clerks...............................	350	20	600
6 junior clerks.................................	160	15	300
Private secretary to secretary of state...........	...	..	300
2 private secretaries to under secretary...........	...	..	150
1 private secretary to assistant secretary..........	...	..	150
1 librarian.....................................	600	20	800
1 assistant librarian	200	10	400
1 précis writer	...	..	1,000
1 registrar.....................................	...	..	400
1 first registry clerk...........................	...	10	250
1 second registry clerk..........................	...	..	150
1 clerk for parliamentary papers.................	...	..	200
1 clerk in department of ditto	...	10	250
1 clerk in chief clerk's department..............	200	15	305
1 compiler of indices...........................	...	..	150
Office keepers, &c., &c.			
40			**30,000**

F.—*Foreign Office.*

1 secretary of state	...	..	£5,000
1 under secretary	...	..	2,000
1 under secretary	...	..	1,500
1 assistant secretary............................	...	..	1,500
			10,000

	Minimum.	Increase.	Maximum.
1 chief clerk..	£1,000	£50	£1,250
8 senior clerks....................................	700	25	1,000
8 assistant clerks.................................	550	20	650
10 first-class junior clerks......................	350	15	415
9 second-class junior clerks.....................	150	10	300
6 third-class junior clerks.......................	100	10	150
1 librarian and keeper of the papers.............	600	25	800
3 library clerks...................................	250	15	360
2 library clerks...................................	100	10	240
1 superintendent treaty department...............	600	25	800
1 assistant ditto..................................	400	15	500
1 clerk ditto......................................	250	15	360
1 supplemental clerk consular department..........	250	15	360
1 clerk in chief clerk's department...............	400	15	500
2 clerks ditto, each..............................	100	10	240
1 translator......................................	500	..	500
Private secretary and précis writer, each.........	...	..	300
1 printer...	...	..	150
1 office keeper....................................	...	..	200
4 office keepers...................................	...	..	125
1 office porter....................................	...	..	230
1 office porter....................................	...	..	120
2 doorkeepers, each...............................	...	..	100
1 lamplighter and coal porter.....................	...	..	94
1 housekeeper.....................................	...	..	100

74   40,000

G.—Home Office.

1 secretary of state..............................			£5,000
1 under secretary of state			2,000
1 under secretary of state			1,500
1 counsel for drawing bills for parliament........			2,000

	Minimum.	Increase.	Maximum.
1 chief clerk	£1,000	£50	£1,200
3 senior clerks	700	25	1,000
2 senior clerks*	600	20	800
7 second-class clerks	350	20	600
5 third class	100	10	300
Librarian			600
1 clerk for signet and other business			300
1 private secretary to secretary of state			300
1 private secretary to parliamentary under secretary ...			150
9 extra clerks	300	15	400
	150	10	300
	100	5	150
2 clerks to the counsel for drawing parliamentary bills.	150	10	200
	100	5	150
1 chamber keeper			200
1 chamber keeper			190
5 office porters			£75 to 110
1 messenger to counsel for drawing bills for parliament			100

45   26,000

*To be abolished when vacant and additions made to third class clerks.

H.—Treasury.

		Salaries.
1	first lord	£5,000
1	chancellor of the exchequer	5,000
3	lords commissioners	1,000
2	secretaries	2,000
		'17,000

No.									Salaries.
1	assistant secretary..	minimum £2,000 (after 5 years 2,500)						£2,500	
1	auditor of ann'l list.	do	1,500		maximum	1,500			
4	principal clerks....	do	1,000	ann'l inc'e 50	max'm	1,200		£4,800	
7	first-class clerks....	do	700	do 25	do	900		6,300	
13	second-class clerks..	do	350	do 20	do	600		7,800	
7	third-class clerks...	do	100	do 15	do	250			
1	accountant.........	do	500	do 20	do	800		800	
1	assistant accountant.	do	350	do 15	do	500		500	
5	supplementary clk's, 1st class........	do	400	do 15	do	500		500	
5	supplementary clk's, 2d class.........	do	250	do 10	do	350		....	
8	supplementary clk's, 3d class.........	do	100	do 10	do	200		....	
2	private secretaries to first lord........	do	300	.. ..	do	300		....	
1	private secretary to chancellor.	do	300	.. ..	do	300		....	
2	to secretaries......	do	150	.. ..	do	150		....	
1	to ass't secretary...	do	150	.. ..	do	150		....	
1	office & house keeper	do	200	do 5	do	250		....	
1	superintending messenger of first lord	do	220	.. ..	do	220		....	
24	messengers........	do	85	to		150		....	
92								50,000	

APPENDIX I.

FRENCH CIVIL SERVICE.

A.—ON PUBLIC ADMINISTRATION, BY EMILE DE GIRARDIN.*—POLITICAL EDUCATION.—FUNCTIONARIES.

Public education should be established for the formation of statesmen by the study of history, living languages, public law, the interest of nations, and of all that can make them useful for public affairs. This would do away in empires with those ministers hastily appointed by patronage who only exhibit to the public supposed talents and who reveal their duties only by their blunders.—*Bacon.*

Considerations of classes and of fortunes—Government offices, public functions, of whatever order, have been for a long time, as they probably still are, dispensed by patronage in the interests of partisan politics. This is a great evil, the effect of which is felt in the very heart-life of the nation.

When governments select their officers according to their political opinions

---

* Since this disquisition was published by Mr. Girardin, the progress of reform in the French service has been remarkable.

or to narrow family considerations, they demoralize the nation, they revolution-
ize it, they increase the abuses, they squander the resources which are at their
disposal, and are only temporarily sustained by arbitrary power or by corruption.

We hope that the day will come when the interest of the nations is no longer
sacrificed to that of petty coteries, and when men of education and experience
are no longer wanting in the public service.

The number of capable officers is certainly not equal in France to that of
offices.

Diminish the number of offices and increase the number of good officers—this
is the progress which we still have to make.

There is a future for men who prepare themselves by serious studies for public functions. This future cannot be very remote, and we only suggest it to the
children of wealthy parents, but it must come sooner or later, the periodical
press and the parliamentary tribune affording two means to discriminate between
the mass of writers and politicians who discuss public affairs without study and
without experience.

Aptitude should imply the following qualities:

Comprehensiveness of ideas, soundness of judgment, a self-possessed mind,
a firm will, conciliatory character, and high integrity.

National instruction.—First and second degrees.

Professional instruction.—All that refers to the professional instruction of
young men destined for the public service is really provided for, but nothing
is harmonious, nothing obligatory.

Political economy, for instance, which all public functionaries ought to understand, is taught at the *Collége de France* and the *Conservatoire des arts et
métiers.* In the same manner the divers branches of political and administrative science are taught, but in a different manner. They are nowhere united in
one nucleus. They do not constitute a systematic and progressive method of
instruction; there is no royal school or special school of administration; there
is no faculty of economical, administrative, and political sciences where the
young men destined for the public service can obtain their certificates of
qualification and their degrees. Thus, while the faculties of letters, science,
law, medicine, and theology, offer extended resources to the various professions
and impose the safe check of examinations upon the public careers open to
intelligent men, the administrative career is the only one to which access is open
to the pretensions of ignorance and the presumption of incapacity.

It is well known from whence come the lawyers, the physicians, the teachers,
and by what studies they have prepared themselves for the exercise of their
profession and what guarantees they were obliged to furnish to society before
obtaining its confidence, but it is in vain to search the laws which have established these guarantees for regulations applicable to public administration, or, in
other words, it is in vain to look side by side with the various seats of learning
or a special civil service school, founded upon analogous bases and supported
by the state.

Such a serious want in our system of instruction has been recognized and
signalized by the illustrious Cuvier, who agrees on this subject with Bacon,
whose opinion we have quoted.

On this occasion we may cite what has been stated* by a distinguished professor, Mr. Macarel, councillor of state, on the necessity of establishing at Paris
a faculty of administrative and political sciences, or at least a special school: †

Superior instruction is taught in France in five orders of faculties; in the university of

---

* Elements of Political Law.   (*Eléments de Droit Politique*, page 510.)
† This note served for text to a letter addressed on December 24, 1832, to the minister of
public instruction, and ever since 1829 the same idea has been submitted to M. de Vatimesnil,
who then officiated in the same capacity.

France, the faculties of law, medicine, letters, physical and mathematical sciences, and theology.

The country is greatly benefited by these liberal institutions, but the University of France does not provide for the teaching of political and administrative sciences. In some of the academies there are courses of lectures on administrative law; formerly two courses of lectures on public economy were also given in Paris. But these lectures are evidently insufficient to form the class of men who devote themselves to the difficult conduct of general interests, and who are destined to occupy either the official posts in the various bureaus of the administration or the legislative chambers themselves. Such a separate institution seems to me necessary in France.

It is probable that at some future day the country will be endowed with a faculty of political and administrative sciences, and that degrees, and consequently certificates of qualification, will then be expected to be possessed at least by those who fill, under the supreme direction of the ministers, the functions of members of councils of state, civil officers of all grades, and the offices of chiefs of bureaus of divisions, &c.

The ministers will then have more enlightened auxiliaries. This sixth faculty might comprise the following branches of instruction, namely:

1. Natural law or moral philosophy.
2. International law.
3. Public, general, and positive law.
4. Political economy.
5. Statistics.
6. General administration.

Courses of lectures on the following subjects might be given in connection with the same institution, namely, on administrative law cases, parliamentary eloquence, history of French public law, and comparative administration.

These last-named subjects would crown, in a measure, for those who wish to study social science, the benefits conferred by the instruction of this sixth faculty.

The period of instruction might extend over three years. The first year to be devoted to natural law, (3 months;) to international law, (3 months;) and to public law, (4 months.) The second year to political economy, (3 months;) statistics, (3 months;) and to the first rudiments of general administration. (6 months.)

The third year to be altogether devoted to general administration, (10 months;) degrees would be conferred in this faculty according to the different grades of studies.

For that of *bachelier* the institution to be attended during two years, and the natural law, public law, and general administration to be studied.

For that of *licencié*, three years of study will be required.

Finally, the *doctorate* could not be obtained without having also attended the lectures on public law and comparative administration.

Moreover, on leaving this faculty the young supernumeraries entering the public service might find in the special administration for which they are destined a special course on legislation, on the regulations and customs of the service in which they are employed; this special instruction to be equal to that afforded to the youthful *élèves*—engineers of mining and public works in their respective bureaus.

Efficacious measures might be taken by government to that effect, and I have no doubt that each administrative branch could obtain an efficient special professor.

In this manner the theoretical instruction on the most extended scale possible would be perfected for the French service.

That of practical knowledge could be afterwards added thereto, and rectify by its actual applications erroneous or impracticable ideas.

Thus the complete framework of this excellent system of instruction might be established upon the foregoing basis.

In the University of France there are faculties which offer more extended means of instruction. The faculty of sciences, for instance, comprises the instruction of arithmetic, the various geometrical and mathematical sciences, algebra applied to geometry, differential and integral calculation, statics, mathematical science, astronomy, physical science, chemistry, and natural history.

These are the vast studies intended for the formation of learned mathematicians and physicists.

Is it not equally necessary to devise means for the creation of civil functionaries and statesmen?

The science of government, is it not too much neglected?

Should it not be taught in all its bearings?

Is it not possible to achieve this result successfully?

The rapid progress of civilization seems to call for such a system of instruction.

It would be honorable to France if she were to give the first example of systematic and perfect studies in that direction.

In proportion that men are enlightened in regard to their individual rights, is it not necessary that the civil officers of the country should better understand the rights of society, of which they are the organs and defenders?

The periodical press is incessantly engaged in the discussion of principles.

It is important for society that the doctrine really essential for its conservation, welfare, and perfection, should be taught publicly with the same incontestable authority which generally attends the sworn interpreters of other sciences.

It is easy, therefore, to anticipate the good which would result from the new creation which I invoke at present with all the force of my personal conviction.

We fully agree with the foregoing views expressed by Mr. Macarel, and are glad to join him in the task of speedily effecting the realization of ideas which have received the imposing sanction of two men like Bacon and Cuvier.

We will only refer on this occasion to the necessity of frequent rhetorical exercises. The bar has created for lawyers a species of monopoly of speechifying, which, in our electoral legislative assemblies, in our general and municipal councils, is often exercised in an unfortunate manner, detrimental to the men of specialities, of practical powers and experience, though these are more conversant with the routine of business than with rhetoric, and allow themselves to be too often intimidated by the pluck of lawyers in rushing into speech, by their coolness and the nonchalance in keeping the platform, and by their artfulness and talent in the manipulation of words.

Hence the narrow lawyer-like spirit which is generally perceptible in our laws and strips them of all grandeur and all stability; hence their meanness and weakness; hence a certain one-sided and deplorable tendency to discuss and regulate our greatest interests only from one point of view; hence the barrenness of the representative system in France.

In our opinion, an enlightened and far-seeing government could not too much encourage by all the means in its power the opening and the multiplication of courses of study of improvisation and of all exercises calculated to promote the art of public speaking. We have stated in our introductory the motives and the interests in behalf of which we demand that elementary education should cease to be the privilege of a few and become a duty for all. The same considerations of the welfare of society lead us to wish that those who know how to read should also learn how to speak, so that the talent of expressing one's thoughts should cease to be a general difficulty and a professional privilege, and simply become a free and easy exercise of a faculty of the mind.

Other not less important considerations also militate in favor of the prompt establishment of a faculty of economical administration and political sciences.

Is it not one of the saddest spectacles to see all avenues of the public service encumbered with office-seekers without legitimate claims, and generally with no other rights than their pretensions? *The only efficacious way to diminish their number, is it not, to subject them to severe tests of examination and competition?*

Public education, thoughtfully considered from an elevated point of view, presents the advantage of providing means of restraining and regulating the very ambitions which it stimulates. From the moment that all the resources of public education become manifest to statesmen of resolute will and powerful judgment, a new era would be inaugurated in the hierarchy of society; order would then take the place of the present deplorable chaos; the degree of education would then determine political right and administrative aptitudes, and place invincible obstacles in the way of exaggerated pretensions and improper applications for office; the speciality and variety of education would then maintain the balance between all professions; for the sake of its own preservation, the government would then be made to understand that it must impose upon itself the imperious duty of employing only the most capable and educated men, who have proven themselves to be so in the examination and competition to which they have been successively subjected. The public functionaries will then be necessarily composed of the *élite* of the nation, and ambitious mediocrities will be, as a matter of course, excluded and consigned to obscurity by the mere force of their ignorance. Thus will the government be elevated by the respect due to its agents. It will then achieve what it now fails to accomplish, namely : the goverument will govern and at length acquire that moral authority without which its precarious existence is ever jeopardized by the conflict of personal ambition.

How many mediocrities, even incapacities, are there not who only covet public offices because they seem to be open to whomsoever feels inclined to take them, and because they may be secured all in one bound without any test of qualification. This access to them without preliminary studies, without trial, without guarantees, must necessarily encourage the most shallow pretensions. Indeed there are not a few persons who, on seeing the candidates to the public service relieved from presenting any test of fitness, imagine that the law winks at these proceedings and that tests are not at all necessary. They will tell you that common sense is all that is required to become an efficient prefect, and that no special studies are needed; that administrative business consists only of constant intercourse with human nature, and that for its management nothing more is required than tact and prudence ; as regards the questions of facts and of material interests confided to the departmental administration, they will make very light of it, without entertaining the least doubt that several months of experience will be sufficient to initiate an intelligent and sagacious man into the management of all this public business. Hence the predilections in favor of the old routine, the subjection to routine, the too frequent incapability to deal with questions the examination of which would require a solid instruction ; hence, lastly, the little confidence in the application of the best-established principles of economical science and the prejudice which still prevails to such a great extent, against what is called *theories*, as if a theory worthy of that name were not the faithful embodiment and analysis of *facts*, upon which all issues depend.

It is not so in Germany. For a long time past political economy, or cameralistics (science of administration and finance) have been taught everywhere by special professorships, and the faithful attendance to the same, *the evidence of the knowledge there acquired* are demanded from all candidates to offices, in which such knowledge is required.

These candidates are subjected to examinations. Their admission to or exclusion from the public service is dependent upon the more or less favorable result of the same, in the same manner which with us (in France) determines the fitness to enter the professions of the pedagogue, the lawyer, and the physician.

In France, on the contrary, administrative science is little regarded. Its detractors are all those who find it more convenient to neglect than to cultivate it. Hence the constant struggles imposed upon the government against so many preposterous office-seekers, who, strong in their sense of the immunity of the laws, hope to find the minister as little able to baffle their pretensions as the law itself. Those guarantees of instruction, morality and experience which the laws fail to impose upon the candidates, must be frequently demanded by the government whenever it fears that its confidence may be abused by incapable or faithless persons ; its interest as well as its duty require it to make up by severe vigilance for the remissness of the law, but the most vigilant minister is not always proof against mistakes. Responsible for the conduct of their agent, the ministers need, no doubt, much latitude in their selections, but guarantees of qualification would not impose any impediment upon the freedom of selection, and certainly diminish ministerial responsibility by securing greater chances of infallibility for the secondary branches of the service.

The imperial decree of December 26, 1809, which regulates the instruction of auditors to the council of state, organized administrative grades. Forty auditors were attached to the different ministers ; 120 were distributed among the ministry of police ; the general direction of military reviews and of conscription; the administration of public works; of registry and domains; of asylums; of waters and forests; of the various taxes; of victuals; of the post; of the lottery; of powder; the board of maritime seizures; the board of mines; the redeeming fund; the prefecture of the department of the Seine, and the prefecture of voters.

One hundred and sixty auditors thus received in the various special administrations of Paris an instruction which fitted them to occupy, next to the supernumerary posts, more or less important situations in the different offices to which they had been attached.

The youthful auxiliaries of the provincial administration passed, under the direction of the prefects, a regular apprenticeship. They were at the disposal of this magistrate who could appoint them to officiate provisionally, in the case of death, vacancy, leave of absence, or other legitimate causes, as sub-prefects of the provinces. They could be, at the same time, intrusted with the management of all litigious business.

By the article 20 of this law, the fourth part of sub-prefectures that became vacant was to be allotted to auditors.

In combining the plan proposed by Mr. Macarel with the stipulations of the decree of 1809, the organization of tests of qualification for the public service might be fully effected, and to perfect it some faculties of economical, administrative, political, agricultural, industrial and commercial sciences should be established.

B.—FORCES OF THE FRENCH SERVICE.

The following are the principal members of the government:

1. The *secretary of state* and of the house of the Emperor.

In the latter capacity he is charged with the administration of the civil list; of the domains and forests; of the imperial palaces; of the museums; of the imperial manufactures; of the libraries belonging to the crown; the administration of the private domain, and the direction of the imperial theatre of the opera. He is the highest dignitary of the house of the Emperor, and presents the decrees of nominations to public functionaries of the house of the Emperor and of the princes and princesses of the imperial family.

As minister of state he has to attend to the relations between the government and the senate, the legislature and council of state; the correspondence of the Emperor with the different ministers; the certification of the decrees nominating ministers, president of the senate and legislature, senators and members of the council of state; decrees convening and closing the senate and legislature, and all those decrees which do not specially belong to any other ministerial department; the exclusive control over the official part of the Moniteur; the service of the fine arts, of the imperial archives; civil buildings and historical monuments.

The ministry of the house of the Emperor consists in a general secretariate, with three divisions of, respectively, three and two bureaus; and in a general administration of domains and forests, with four bureaus; in a general direction of imperial museums, with a general director and intendent of fine arts; in an administration of the effects of the Crown, (with a superintendent,) assisted by a chief of bureau, an inspector general and three adjoint inspectors, and in the imperial manufactories, (*Sèvres, Gobelins, Beauvoir,*) and under the charge of a director.

The same ministry is further assisted by three committees, namely: a committee for litigious affairs, a permanent superior board for the investigation of affairs relating to the imperial theatre of the opera, and a board for the verification and sifting of the accounts of the administration of the imperial civil list.

The ministry of state consists of a general secretariate, with four sections, namely: section of the secretariate and accounts, (with two bureaus;) section of civil buildings, (two bureaus ;) section of fine arts, including schools of fine arts; publication of works relating to the fine arts; orders and compensations to artists ; section of the theatres, comprising theatres of Paris and the provinces ; imperial conservatory of music and declamation : schools for music in the provinces ; compensations to authors and dramatic artists. Further, of the service of historical monuments, including the preservation of historical monuments and the distribution of credits granted to that effect to the general inspector attached to this service, and finally of the general direction of the archives of the empire, including three sections, viz., historical, administrative, and judiciary, in the personal and disbursing branches of the secretariate.

The ministry of state is also assisted by two committees, viz : a board of control relating to the public works connected with the Louvre, and a special service to that effect, and a permanent board relating to historical monuments.

2. The *minister of justice*, or keeper of the seal, is charged with the organization and the superintendence of all parts of the judiciary. He is in constant correspondence with the solicitor general concerning all matters which are subject to the action or pertaining to the administration of the public ministry. He attends to the nomination of ministerial officers and superintends the organization of notaries. He draws up reports to the Emperor on all subjects relative to the administration of justice; on the demands of dispensation of age and parentage in marriages ; on naturalization ; on the application for pardons and the commutation of penalties. He prosecutes in criminal cases and watches over the execution of verdicts. He promulgates the laws, and retains the original of the same. He has, finally, charge of the direction of the imperial printing establishment, and of the publication of the Journal des Savants.

The ministry of justice consists of a general secretariate, with three bureaus; of a direction of civil affairs and of the seal, with four bureaus; of a direction of criminal cases and pardons, with three bureaus ; of a direction of accounts and pensions, with two bureaus.

The minister is assisted by a council of administration, composed of directors, and presided over by the general secretary.

The imperial printing establishment is administered by a director, assisted by six chiefs of the service : 1st, for the administrative ; 2d, for all concerning typography, lithography, &c.; 3d, for the superintendence of the transmission of the Bulletin des Lois, and of all publications and works of the imperial printing establishment ; 4th, for accounts and comptrol ; 5th, for accountability in raw material and in money ; and 6th, for the superintendence of the interior service of the establishment.

The director is assisted by a committee for the examination of those works of which a gratuitous publication is demanded.

3. The *minister of foreign affairs* is charged with all that regards relations with foreign countries. He negotiates treaties of alliance and commerce, and attends to their execution; he is in correspondence with diplomatic and consular agents, and is in intercourse with the foreign agents accredited near the emperor.

This ministry consists of—

A. Bureau of protocol for the despatch of treaties or conventions, &c.

B. Direction of political affairs, divided into a sub-direction for the north and for America, and a sub-direction for the south and the Orient, charged with the correspondence and business relating to the respective countries in the respective divisions; and a sub-direction of litigious business, i. e., claims of Frenchmen against foreign governments, and *vice versa*.

C. Direction of consulates and commercial affairs, divided into sub-directions for the north, for the south and the Orient, and a bureau for America and the Indies.

D. Direction of the archives and the chancellary, consisting of a depot of correspondence and diplomatic documents, and of a bureau of passport; legalizations, viz., as of claims of individual citizens against foreign governments.

E. Direction of the funds and accounts allowed to general and particular business relating to the expenditures of the ministry.

4. The *minister of the interior* has under his control the bureau of prefects, sub-prefects, councillors, of prefects, and mayors. He superintends the execution of the laws relative to electoral assemblies and national guards, the general administration of the provinces and communes, of hospitals, charitable institutions, and the distribution of relief to the poor; the prisons, central police stations and penitentiaries, the telegraphic wires, and all that relates to public safety. The printing establishment, the library, the censure office, and that of colportage are annexed to his ministry.

The ministry of the interior consists of—

A. The office of the minister, with two bureaus.

B. General secretariate, with three bureaus.

C. Division of general and departmental administration, with three bureaus.

D. Division of commercial and hospital administration, with four bureaus.

E. Division of prisons and penitentiaries, with three bureaus.

F. Two divisions of general direction of public safety, with, respectively, four and two bureaus.

G. Two divisions of telegraphic service, with, respectively, two and three bureaus.

H. Direction of accounts, with four bureaus.

5. *Ministry of finance*, (Treasury,) charged with the administration of the national resources, namely, public revenues proceeding from direct and indirect duties and taxes, from domains, forests, tobacco, post, and all monopolies, (régies,) and enterprises which yield an income to the treasury. The finance minister pays all public expenditures decreed by the different ministers, in accordance with legislative appropriations, inscription on the *rentes*, (public securities,) pensions, and moneys serving as securities, the debts of the state, and all transactions of the treasury. He superintends the public treasuries and responsible accountants, all matters relating to the receipt and the appropriation of public moneys, takes proceedings against the bondsmen of reponsible accountants and against the debtors of the treasury, and verifies the coinage and fineness of money. Besides, he is bound to submit the general budget to the legislative body, and to attend to the definitive settlement of the public accounts. The ministry of finance is divided into two distinct parts: firstly, the central administration; and, secondly, the administrations which are under its control.

First. The central administration consists of—

A. The minister's office and inspector general's office, with one bureau each, respectively.

B. General secretariate, with two divisions, namely, central bureau with two bureaus, accounts of the ministers' expenses, &c., &c., and financial administration, with two bureaus, domains, forests, direct taxes and mints, custom-houses, indirect taxes, tobacco and mints.

C. Law officer of the treasury, attending to all litigation connected with the treasury, with three bureaus, and having sub-law offices in every principal division of the treasury.

D. Direction of the general distribution of public expenditures of home and foreign service, with four bureaus.

E. Direction of the inscribed public debt, with five bureaus.

F. Direction of the general comptrol of the finance department, with five bureaus.

G. Treasurer's office, with two bureaus.

H. Division of central comptrol of the daily receipts and expenditures of the treasury, three sections.

Secondly. The administrations under the control of the treasury—

A. General direction of direct taxes, with two divisions and, respectively, two and one bureaus.

B. General direction of registry and domains, with two bureaus, containing the director general's office and the office of litigious cases, and four divisions, consisting each of four bureaus.

C. General direction of customs and indirect taxes, consisting of the following three bureaus, namely, customs, indirect taxation, and direct taxation, and of six divisions :

1st division, (three bureaus.) Customs tariff; colonial and transatlantic, and commercial and merchants' navy statistics.

2d division, (4 bureaus) Land boundaries; ports and coasts; other limits; general liquidation and regulation of the expenditure of, the general direction.

3d division, (three bureaus.) Seizures and inspection of the custom-house laws; premiums on exports; general estimate of salt production, and fisheries.

4th division, (four bureaus.) Administration of laws regulating drinks and public carriages; direction of indirect taxation in 33 departments, (provinces;) direction of indirect taxation in 27 departments, (provinces)—the other departments included in the custom-house service ; legal documents relating to seizures and other litigious business.

5th division, (three bureaus.) Navigation on rivers, streams and canals; tariff and regulation of towns' dues, pension-list and bonds of all custom-house and indirect revenue officers.

6th division, (tobacco and powder—in four bureaus.) Direction of the service in the stores and manufactories of tobacco, culture of tobacco in France and Algeria, distribution of tobacco (in leaves) among the manufactories, and orders and distribution of powder, comptrol regarding tobacco and powder.

D. General direction of the post, (two bureaus,) namely : director general's office, and two divisions, namely, first division, (six bureaus and archives,) home correspondence, foreign correspondence, inspection and reclamations, franking privileges, infractions, verification of revenue, dead letters, &c.

Second division, (five bureaus.) Establishment and suspension of relay stations, (diligences,) transmission of despatches, budget, accounts, printed and various other matter, articles of money.

Active service, (six bureaus.) Arrival and departure of mails, distribution of letters in Paris, prepaid and registered letters, prepaid and registered journals and printed matter, poste restante letters, dead letters, and misaddressed letters.

E. General direction of forests, in three divisions :

First division, (two bureaus.) Budgets, accounts, works of improvements in regard to forests, purchase of real estate.

Second division, (two bureaus.) Clearing of forests, laws regarding forests, examination of general and particular functions.

Third division, (two bureaus.) Civil matters, questions of deportment and of menial service, police matters, appeals, &c., &c.

F. Board of merits and medals, consisting of a president and ten members, with the function to comptrol and superintend the coinage of moneys and medals in every part of France, and assisted by verifiers, assayers and engravers.

6. *Ministry of war*, intrusted with the defence of the state, recruiting and organization of the land forces, administration of arsenals and manufactories of fire-arms, and of powder and saltpetre ; provisions for the men and the horses ; clothing of the troops ; mounting of the cavalry ; quartermaster's department ; military equipages. These are among the principal and most important functions of the minister of war. Besides, he is charged with the preservation of the archives, the civil status of the army, &c., and the high administration of Algeria.

The minister's office consists of the service of despatches, particular and secret business, and business that does not come within the duties of any special bureau.

The ministry is composed of—

A. First directoriat, five bureaus; general correspondence and military operations; staffs; military schools; recruiting and military justice; infantry. (Special direction of cavalry and police force, two bureaus.)

B. Second directoriat—(artillery, two bureaus.)

C. Third directoriat—(engineer corps, two bureaus.)

D. Fourth directoriat administration—(five bureaus.) Military intendance, transports, quartermasters; military provisions, fuel; medical officers, military hospitals, invalids; equipment, encampment, harnesses; pay; accounts.

E. Fifth direction, Algerian affairs, (four bureaus.) General and municipal administration; colonization and domains; public works, mines, forests, diverse taxes; commerce, customs.

F. Sixth direction, war office, (two sections.) Geodesy, topography, drawing and engraving, historical archives, libraries, charts and plans.

G. Seventh direction, general accounts, (five bureaus.) Control of expenditure, litigation, budgets, funds, decrees, general accounts, subject-matter of accounts, pensions, relief, laws, archives, decorations.

The minister of war is assisted by seven consultation committees, namely: 1, staffs; 2, infantry; 3, cavalry; 4, police force; 5, artillery; 6, fortification, and 7. Algeria; and further, by a board of health for the armies, by a board of health for the horses, (*hygiène hippique*,) and by a mixed board for public works.

The following public offices are also under the control of the minister of war, namely: The central depot of artillery; the powders and saltpetres; and the Imperial Hospital of the Invalides.

7. *Ministry of the navy and the colonies* comprises the personal and material forces of the imperial navy, the impressment for the naval service, the direction of commercial navigation and maritime fisheries, maritime tribunals, naval constructions, arsenals, iron works, forges and worksteads of the marine hospitals, the support of naval ports, the administration and the superintendence of the convict establishment, the establishment for invalid naval officers, the military, civil and judiciary administration of the colonies.

The ministry consists of—

A. The minister's office, (two bureaus.)

B. Directoriat of the personal forces, (six bureaus.) Military and civil employés; organized corps of the department of the marine; impressment for the naval service; superintendence of navigation; fisheries and maritime public domain, maritime justice, pay and compensations of all kind.

C. Directoriat of the material forces, (four bureaus.) Naval construction and hydraulic works, stock of artillery in the arsenals and on board of men-of-war, general arrangements, provisions, hospitals, &c.

D. Directoriat of the colonies, (three bureaus.) Political and commercial system, legislation, justice, education, religion, civil, judiciary, ecclesiastical and military officers, finance, and supplies of provisions.

E. Directoriat of general accounts, (five bureaus.)

F. Treasury of the invalids of the maritime service, (three bureaus.)

The minister of the navy is assisted by—

1st. A board for seizures, (prizes.)

2d. A consultation committee for the colonies.

3d. A committee of surveillance of colonial banks.

4th. A superior commission for the treasury of the invalids of the maritime service, and

5th. A superior commission for the improvement of the system of training in the imperial naval school.

The following public offices are also under the control of the minister of the navy:

The general depot of maps and plans of the navy and the colonies, and the depot of fortifications of the colonies.

8. *Ministry of public education and of religion.*—In the former capacity the minister controls the whole educational system, the chief administration of superior, secondary and primary public schools, and of scientific and literary institutions, and has the surveillance of all institutions in France in which instruction is gratuitous. As minister of religion he attends to the execution of the laws connected therewith; he publishes the bulls, pastoral letters, and rescripts of the Holy See; he proposes to the Emperor nominations for archbishoprics and bishoprics, for the canons of St. Denis, and he submits for the Emperor's approval the nominations made by the bishops, as well as by the ministers, pastors, and rabbis; he regulates the boundaries of parishes, congregations, and synagogues; he provides for the temporary administration of diaconal establishments, authorizes the acceptance of donations made to religious bodies, attends to the preservation of religious buildings, and, finally, extends his surveillance over religious congregations.

A. The ministry consists of the secretariat of the ministry of education and religion, with three bureaus, namely: subscriptions, missions, historical labors, scientific bodies, literary and scientific institutions, public libraries, proceedings of the superior council; archives.

The academical administration and that of superior education is divided into three divisions: first, with two bureaus, academical administration; personal forces of superior education; second division, two bureaus, secondary schools; third division, two bureaus, primary schools.

B. The general directorate of the administration of religion is divided into: 1st division, (Catholic denomination,) two bureaus, clergy and ecclesiastical police, parish service, litigating religious congregations; 2d division, (Catholic denomination,) two bureaus, temporary administration of diocenal establishment, preservation of religious buildings.

Section of non-Catholic denomination, personal forces, organization and limits of congregational duties, oratorios and synagogues.

C. Division of central accountability, (three bureaus) The imperial council of public education, presided by the minister, is called upon to give its advice on all questions interesting to education. He also decides, in last appeal, on the verdict of the academical councils according to the 16th article of the statute of March 15, 1850. The ministry is attended by, first, a central committee of patrons of public asylums; second, a committee of the French languages, history, arts, divided into three sections, namely: philology, history, archaeology; third, a commission of the fine arts and religious buildings, divided into three sections, namely: architecture and sculpture, painted glass and religious ornaments, organs and sacred music.

9. *Minister of agriculture, commerce and public works.*—In regard to agriculture the minister has to attend to the improvement of agricultural labor, to the administration and the instruction in the various agricultural and veterinary schools, to the preparation of laws and regulations relating to agriculture, to the distribution of relief for losses proceeding from disastrous accidents and cattle diseases, to the study and the application of legislation to the question of food.

In regard to commerce, he prepares the laws and regulations concerning the domestic commerce, the industrial arts and manufactures; he controls the industrial schools, pension and savings banks, insurance companies, anonymous societies, the sanitary police, and that of weights and measures. Besides he is charged with the preparation of tariffs and custom-house laws, of the centralization and publication of documents relating to the commercial and maritime legislation of foreign countries, as well as all matters pertaining to the general movement of commerce and navigation.

As regards public works, he attends to the preservation and improvement of river, steam and canal navigation, of the great means of inter-communication, as railways, high roads, bridges, pontoons and ships. Further, he attends to the exploration and concession of mines, the administration of metallurgical worksteads and the construction of light-houses.

This department also comprises the service of harnasses and the general statistics of France.

The ministry is composed as follows :

General secretariat, (one bureau.)

Division for personal forces, (two bureaus,) nominations, promotions and changes, exponses, indemnities, relief, pensions, litigation.

Division of accounts, (three bureaus,) central operations and decrees, accounts relating to agriculture and commerce, to bridges, high roads and mines.

Depot of maps and plans, (archives,) presided over by an engineer.

Bureau of the general statistics of France: centralization, elaboration and publication of the documents relating to the continuation of the general statistics of France.

Division of agriculture, (three bureaus,) agriculture and veterinary instruction, encouragements to agriculture and relief, legislation relative to provisions.

Division of stables, (one bureau,) administration of the stables and depot of spurs, encouragement to hyppic industry, (relating to horses.)

Division of interior commerce, (three bureaus,) preparation of laws and regulations relative to interior commerce, authorization of anonymous societies, life insurances, &c., industrial arts and manufactures, sanitary and industrial police.

Division of foreign commerce, (three bureaus,) legislation and custom-house tariffs in France, commercial legislation and tariffs in foreign countries, general movement of commerce and navigation.

General directorat of bridges and high roads and railways.

Section of high roads and bridges, division of high roads and bridges, (two bureaus,) imperial high roads, departmental high roads, police of traffic.

Division of navigation, (two bureaus,) naval ports, navigable canals, navigable rivers and accessible to fleets.

Hydraulic bureau, water-courses, and various studies.

Section of railways, (two bureaus,) projects and concessions, works.

Section of railways, in exploration, (two bureaus,) commercial exploration, technical exploration, central statistical railway bureau, collection of statistics of engineers, inspectors and companies.

Mines, included in the general secretariat.

Division of mines and worksteads, (two bureaus.)

Bureau of mineralogical statistics.

The ministry is assisted by, first, a superior council of commerce and agriculture and industry; second, a general council of agriculture; third, a commission of registry of matriculation for the inscription of animals of pure race and of the bovine species; fourth, a commission for a bank for old people; fifth, a consultation committee on the public sanitary condition in France; sixth, a commission of stables; seventh, a central commission of races; eighth, a consultation committee on arts and manufactures; and 11 more committees, altogether 19. The ministry also controls a great number of imperial schools, &c., &c., &c.

The total number of persons more or less connected with the public service in France are estimated at about 250,000, exclusive of the army and the navy. Indeed the number is so great that, although a law passed in 1849 made it incumbent upon the government to render an account of all the persons employed, this law has not been acted upon, the government declaring that to carry it out would require the publication of at least 50 quarto volumes of 600 pages each, and entail an expenditure of upwards of 500,000 francs.

The following list gives a tabular statement of these 250,000 persons. Under the control of the minister of finance are:

Revenue assessors	1,000	
Revenue collectors	7,700	
Registry and stamps	3,600	
Forests	3,400	
Customs	30,000	
Indirect taxes	18,000	
Postal service	17,000	
Mint	200	
Court of accounts	100	
Bureaus of the ministry of finance	2,000	
		83,000
Bureaus of the ministry of justice	100	
Bureaus of the public instruction	150	
Bureaus of religious instruction	60	
Bureaus of the navy	250	
Bureaus of war	460	
		1,020
Bureaus of the interior	......	230
Bureaus of commerce and agriculture	......	140
Bureaus of public works	......	150
Bureau of foreign affairs	90	
Under the control of foreign affairs, viz: diplomatic and consular agents	310	
		400
Agents employed in the navy and arsenals	6,000	
Agents employed in the army	6,000	
		12,000
Commercial and departmental organization: 86 prefects, 7 secretaries general, 278 sub-prefects, 329 counsellors of prefecture, 4,000 mayors		4,700
Public works		2,700
Surveyors and naval officers		161
Inspectors of rivers and navigation		17
Agents of agricultural and industrial establishments		700
Ministers of religion, Roman Catholic	40,800	
Protestant	755	
Hebrew	114	
		41,669
Judiciary		14,872
Justices of the peace	2,847	
Deputies of justices of the peace	5,694	
		8,541
Education, viz: professors, teachers, &c., not including the special administrative schools		40,000
		210,300
Sundries, of which no official estimate is accessible, about		39,700
		250,000

C.—GENERAL PRINCIPLES RESPECTING ADMISSION TO THE FRENCH CIVIL
SERVICE.

The special schools are most fertile in supplying the state with able public officers.

These are the various polytechnic and military academies; the naval academy; the normal school, for teachers; the school of forests; of charts; of foreign languages (called *écoledes jeunes de langues*, school of languages for the young, because boys from 8 to 12 years are admitted there, languages being more easily learned at this early than at a more mature age;) the veterinary school, &c.

In most of the branches of the revenue, customs, and treasury services, the candidates are subjected to repeated examinations.

In many of the branches of the public service candidates must possess diplomas attesting to their proficiency in law or in literature.

The probationary system exists in many branches of the service, to which young men are, as it were, put in apprenticeship under the name of pupils, auditors, supernumeraries, attachés, aspirants, or auxiliaries.

The word "pupil" *(élève)* is employed in the consular, telegraph, and surgical service. That of auditor is applied to the young men attached to the council of state; in the central and treasury bureaus the probationers are styled supernumeraries, and aspirants to the supernumeraryship. In the ministry of interior they are called attachés, as well as in the ministry of foreign affairs and in the foreign legations. In the bureaus of public works, in the sanitary bureau, and in various branches of the war and army department, the probationers are called auxiliaries. In some cases these titles do not imply the possibility of promotion, but generally they do, and in almost all cases it would be next to impossible to obtain an office without having served in one or the other probationary capacity. Those who prove to lack in zeal or in capacity are dismissed. If not dismissed after three months in the postal service, after two years in the department of the interior and the direct revenue bureaus, and after six months in the bureaus of public works, the respective probationers are sure to be appointed to some permanent office. In other branches of the public service the term of probation varies according to circumstances, and in *all* cases it is subordinate to the relative merits of the candidates, and the number of vacations of which they have availed themselves. In the navy department no person is admitted to the bureaus of the minister who has not been previously employed three years in some other branch of the department. Persons who have been employed seven years in the civil service, or whose office happens to have been abolished, may be appointed collectors of revenue without serving as supernumerary in that branch of the service.

The system, however, of examination and competition is only fully perfected in those branches of the service which are recruited from the special schools and comprising the army, the navy, and several kindred avocations, and the educational bureaus. Although the admission to other branches of the services is hemmed in by various regulations, comprising probation and examination, they cannot be expected to attain the same perfection as in the military, naval, and pedagogical service, until a special school exists for each principal branch of the public service; and candidates for the treasury, interior, and judiciary and other departments are recruited from those that have been disciplined in special schools, whose aptitude for the service has been sedulously developed from their earliest infancy.

Singular anomalies continue to exist; so-called diplomats, for instance, may be appointed to important foreign missions without having passed through the ordeal of examination, or having given the evidence of possessing the first essentials of a qualification for their important duties, which they do not hesitate to exercise. The same applies to some extent to the magistrature and the judiciary.

The consular service is better perfected, the system of consular pupils having been in successful operation since the times of Louis XIV. The diplomatic service, on the other hand, is altogether chaotic, and the transfer of young attachés to the ministry of foreign affairs and attachéships of legations seems to be discretionary with the minister, and hence objectionable. Napoleon I charged the Count de Hauterive with the elaboration of an appropriate system for the diplomatic service, but nothing came of it. Polignac in 1830 established in the ministry of foreign affairs a course of public law and diplomatic instructions, destined for 24 pupils, but the July revolution crushed this establishment in its bud, and nothing has been done about it since.

It will be difficult, of course, to establish special schools for each separate branch of the public service; but no doubt that M. de Girardin's ideas on the subject, namely, the establishment of new professorships for teaching the principal branches of the public services, are entitled to serious consideration.

Promotions can take place in all the ministries after two years, excepting in those of the interior and public instruction, when employés may be promoted after one year's service. The mode of promotion varies in the different departments. The general rule is not to make any nominations, excepting among the titularies of the grade or the class immediately inferior to the vacant office. This rule is strictly adopted in the army, the public works and mines, the consulates, the university, and in the financial administration and the central war department, in the ministries of foreign affairs, of justice, of religion, of the navy; only a portion of the intermediate offices of writers, chief clerks, subchiefs, is reserved for the purpose of promotion.

No rule has been laid down for the still higher offices. In the war department the mode of promotion is defined by stringent regulations, from the smallest office up to the chiefs of bureau. In the ministries of the interior, of commerce, and of public instruction, the offices are accessible to all the functionaries without distinction, only that measures are taken to prevent promotion from being too rapid.

But the nominating power uses discretionary power in the conditions upon which promotion is contingent. The deputy inspector general of finance must have made two tours of inspection. The employés of the direct revenue bureau are called upon to execute certain labors for the central administration. Examination is resorted to for the inferior treasury and war office employés who still occupy probational positions. When there is no examination the intermediate chiefs of the respective bureaus are called upon to render accounts, at stated periods, of the capacity of their subordinates.

Promotion is dependent, therefore, in some cases, upon probation; in others upon examination; and in others upon the report of superior officers. However, in the army, in the public works, in the mining department, the university and the financial bureaus, the various offices are *reserved only for those who have commenced to serve from the lowest grade.*

Special examinations are held for verifiers of weights and measures and for several other public servants; and, on the whole, there are few persons occupying public offices in France, excepting the diplomatic service, who have not proven their competence by probation or by examination or by authoritative testimonials.

The members of the clergy, of the magistrature, of the army, and of the diplomatic service, must be native-born Frenchmen. In the other branches of the public service, the government may admit those who have declared their intention of becoming naturalized citizens.

The most stringent inquiries are made into the integrity, good morals, and upright character of the candidates for the public service.

Women are only employed in the postal service, and, strange to say, are not allowed to occupy posts the salary of which exceeds 2,000 francs annually. They may be also employed in the stamp and printing bureaus, but rather as mechanics than as functionaries. As regards opening the civil service to competent women. France is decidedly far behind the United States, superior as she is to this country in all the other principles regulating the civil service.

APPENDIX K.

EXTRACTS FROM HOUSE REPORT No. 8, 39th CONGRESS, 2d SESSION.

From the testimony of Abraham Wakeman, surveyor of customs for the port of New York:

The duty of an inspector of customs is one of the most important that can be assigned to the revenue officers. In the port they have charge of the landing of all the goods on board a vessel, comparing the cargo with the permits and the manifest, and therefore it requires a good deal of judgment and care and precision in the performance of this duty; and so much depends on it that I have been anxious that the grade of inspectors should be increased rather than diminished. I am sorry to say that many of our new incumbents are not quite up to what I should desire. We have had a list of very excellent officers, indeed. Their great experience and general faithfulness has enabled me to perform the duties of this part of the service with great success.

Question. How do you account for the fact that the new appointments are not up to the proper standard?

Answer. No man can come into the office of an inspector without experience and perform the duty well at once. It requires time to become acquainted with his duties; it requires time to learn the manner of performing the service, and experience is a great thing in it, to say nothing of the business tact and management that are essential.

Q. Then why do you change from experienced to inexperienced men?

A. I do not change. The changes are made, I suppose, on personal grounds by the collector. A collector coming into office has his own friends to serve; he has his own friends to put into place, and he feels that they must, to some extent, be provided for. Changes, therefore, have been made to a considerable extent.

Q. What effect would it have upon the public service if officers of this class were appointed for qualifications only, to be ascertained by personal examination, and by their previous conduct and character?

A. I am unhesitatingly of the opinion that, if it could be done, it would be a very advantageous arrangement for the public service.

Q. Would it not be an improvement, also, to have a term of office, or have the tenure of office more certain and fixed than it is now?

A. Unquestionably.

Q. Would it not also promote the service to have promotions made for merit?

A. Undoubtedly so. And I should say, in this connection, that those persons who are nominated by the collector for appointment to the Secretary of the Treasury are, by the regulations, required to be examined by the head of the department in which they are to serve. For example, if they are inspectors, it is necessary, before they are nominated—that is the phraseology of the regulation, but it is not carried out—they should be sent to my department to be examined. The practice is, that before a man enters upon his duty as inspector, he is sent down to my department to be examined as to his qualifications. In several instances, in quite a number recently, I have rejected men who were incompetent. The difficulty is that—I think more through inattention than anything else—these nominations are made to the Secretary of the Treasury, and the men are appointed and come down to my office to take their place and be assigned to duty before they are examined. I am asked to examine a man and the next minute to put him on duty, and frequently that has involved trouble; but I have not hesitated to reject a man where I found I could not conscientiously pass him. We have had repeated cases of that within the last few months.

Extract from the testimony of J. H. Stedwell, deputy collector of customs at New York:

I believe that the efficiency of the entire revenue service would be increased by making the tenure of office dependent entirely upon the good behavior of the incumbent, and not upon the caprice or political opinion of the appointing power. I say that from my observation of the comparative efficiency of tried and experienced officers to the new officers who are sent in—sent in, many of them, for political reasons—who feel that their office is more dependent on their political fidelity and services than upon their clerical ability.

Question. And that applies as strongly to the officers in your division, under your charge, as to any in the department?

Answer. It is a rule of general application, I think.

Extract of a letter addressed to the Secretary of the Treasury, April 19, 1864, by the Commissioner of Customs, proposing a plan for the prevention and suppression of smuggling:

I hold it to be sound policy for a government, as well as individuals, to pay such prices as will command the services of competent, faithful, and conscientious men, and then to exact of them the most rigid performance of their duties.

It is the experience of every business man that he who will not pay well will not be served well, and the rule is quite as applicable to governments as to individuals. In many instances heretofore men have been employed at small salaries, or per diem, with the understanding that their whole time would not be required, and that they might, when unemployed, attend to their own private affairs.

In such cases it generally happens that the government comes in for but a small share of their time, and is served with such indifference and carelessness as to render the service little better than none at all.

But the government has been victimized in times past by another most reprehensible, not to say fraudulent, practice. It is known that men have been appointed as custom-house inspectors, at compensations varying from $1 50 to $2 50 or $3 a day, who were never required to perform a single day's service, and whose only attendance at the custom-house was for the purpose of receiving and receipting for their pay. Such appointments were made as rewards for past or expected political labors or influence, and were so understood by the appointees, who felt under no obligations, not even a moral one, to render any service to the government whose money their consciences did not forbid them to take.

What the political morality of a community must be where such frauds can be practiced upon the government without calling forth a burst of popular censure and remonstrance I need not attempt to describe. Men thus appointed, and thus perpetrating a continuous fraud upon their country, could hardly be expected to exhibit any very extraordinary indignation should some one, desirous to evade the revenue laws, chance to tempt them with money to favor such evasions.

One of the obstacles in the way of bringing these custom-house employés to a proper sense of what is due from them to the government has been the idea that they were appointed to their positions in consequence, and perhaps in payment, of services rendered to the party having possession of the government, or of some friend to whose political influence they conceive themselves indebted for their positions, and who they imagine can alone displace them.

I need not say that such ideas, the natural product of practices in which they have their origin, are calculated to paralyze the public service and destroy its efficiency.

ORGANIZATION AND ADMINISTRATION OF THE REVENUE SYSTEM.

Under the terms of the act authorizing the commission they were required to consider the best and most efficient mode of raising the revenue, and were intrusted with power to "inquire into the manner and efficiency of the present and past methods of collecting the internal revenue."

In accordance with this provision the commission have devoted as much time as was at their command to the consideration of the above subject.

It must be obvious, in the outset, that however perfect may be the system of revenue law devised, unless an efficient and judicious administration of the same is also provided for, the results will be anything but satisfactory.

As the case now stands, there can hardly be said to be any general and efficient organization of that department of the revenue which relates to the customs. The system devised in the infancy of the nation has been gradually enlarged and modified to meet the requirements of an increasing and now enormous commerce; but so imperfectly and irregularly has this been done that the whole system at present seems wanting in method and centralization; and the government, in this department of its business, is obliged, as it were, to do the work of a giant with the toy instruments of a child. The commission believe, furthermore, that there is not, at this time, any individual connected with this branch of the revenue who possesses such an acquaintance with the relations of our customs system to the trade and commerce of the country as is possessed by the supervising official of the customs departments of either Great Britain or France; and, what is more, there probably never will be any such so long as appointment and continuance in office are made dependent on political considerations.

H. Rep. Com. 47——12

As regards the New York custom-house, the channel through which about two-thirds of the custom receipts of the whole country pass, want of time has prevented the commission from making extensive personal inquiry; but, judging from the numerous statements presented to them, and from the evidence elicited by the Committee on Public Expenditures, (H. of Rep., 38th Cong., 2d sess., Report No. 25, 1865,) they feel satisfied that the necessity of reform in the manner of doing business in this institution was never more urgent than at present.

Of the officers employed in the New York custom-house, it is believed that a majority of them have no special qualifications for their places, and little knowledge of the law under which they discharge their duties; while the estimates presented to the commission of the annual losses experienced by the government, through the frauds perpetrated in connection with this institution, range from $12,000,000 to $25,000,000.

*   *   *   *   *   *   *

It ought to be clearly understood by the people of the country that a continuance of this laxity in the management of the customs revenue is equivalent to increased taxation, and that every dollar taken from the revenue under various pretences in this department must, necessarily, be made up by an equivalent assessment.

In regard to the internal revenue department, the commission have no allegation of fraud to present, but at the same time are constrained to say that, in point of organization, it is very far from what it should be. In proof of this they have but to cite the opinion of the late Commissioner, before referred to as concurred in by the commission, that if the law, as it now stands, could be fully and effectually executed, the receipts from it would not fall short of $500,000,000 per annum; or, in other words, that a complete administration of the law would justify wiping out more than one-half of the excise tax from the statute-book.* If we admit the truth of this statement, even in an approximate degree, the commission might here rest their argument in favor of the necessity of reorganization. They will, however, briefly call attention to some of the leading imperfections of the present system.

One of the most prominent of these is a lack of power and authority in this department to control itself, especially in the matter of expenditures. In regard to this latter, the law itself allows but little discretion; and what little there is is vested in officers of the Treasury Department, who, although they may be the most faithful and vigilant guardians of the public moneys, have little or no experience in connection with the collection of internal revenue, or practical knowledge of its workings. It therefore, undoubtedly, often happens that in an honest desire to prevent the waste of public money, a small sum may be saved at an expense of one of much greater magnitude.

Thus, as illustrations of this character brought to the notice of the commission, they might cite cases where vigilant officers, who have devised plans at slight expense for simplifying returns or detecting fraud, have been obliged, after the government has adopted their recommendations and been benefited by their services, to have the small expenditures thus incurred deducted from their salaries—a course equivalent, in fact, to offering a premium for continued inefficiency and want of method. Again: officers who have been detailed on special service, and have performed such service, bringing back thousands of dollars to the treasury, have had their accounts for small expenditures, even when approved by the Commissioner, disallowed or reduced by the auditing officers. The commission would not be understood as intending to censure the auditing officers for the course pursued by them, as it was undoubtedly in strict accordance with the law; but they would say that they do not think it is for the interest of the government or the country to allow the revenue system to be curtailed of its usefulness, either by reason of such laws, or by any special interpretation placed upon them.

Another cause of imperfection in the internal revenue system is undoubtedly due to a limitation in the number of highly competent and responsible officers, and to the inadequacy of the salaries paid to them. Starting less than four years since with one Commissioner and one clerk, the business of the internal revenue has increased to such an extent that probably it now exceeds in magnitude the entire Treasury Department previous to the war, and is at present receiving more money every quarter than the whole annual revenue of the government prior to 1860. The amount of mailable matter which leaves the office is reported to average one and a half ton daily.

With all this labor and responsibility, the internal revenue is but a bureau of the Treasury Department, and, with the exception of the Commissioner, deputy commissioner, and cashier, no provision has been made for clerical assistance independent of the department.

With the present organization of the office, the commission believe that no one man can be found mentally or physically competent to faithfully discharge all the duties devolving upon and expected from the Commissioner; while the clerk in charge of the division of accounts is required to possess as high an order of qualifications, and to perform more intricate, responsible, and laborious duties than any employé of any private firm or corporation

---

* Thus a committee of the association of journeymen boot and shoe makers of the city of New York, in a return to the commission, estimate the value of the boot and shoe industry in that city as being $16,867,200 per annum. Deducting 50 per cent. from this to represent the exemptions of $1,000 each to each manufacturer, allowed by law, and for over-estimates, the amount of revenue which ought to have accrued to the government from this source, under the six per cent. manufacturing tax, would be $506,016, while the amount actually collected was less than $100,000.

in the country. The salary of the former of these officials is now fixed by law at four thousand dollars per annum, and that of the latter at eighteen hundred dollars.

The operations of the internal revenue, and also of the customs, affect the character of nearly every industrial and moneyed interest in the country; and all experience has shown that great numbers of designing persons are ever on the alert to take advantage of imperfections in the law, and of the inexperience of officials, to evade the law and defraud the government.

The only counter-check, therefore, for government to rely upon is the integrity, faithfulness, capacity, and experience of its agents; and for the government to endeavor to procure and retain the services of men competent to discharge responsible trusts at less salaries than are paid by leading banks or private mercantile firms or corporations, will not only, probably, be impossible, but will result in very poor economy.

The system under which drawbacks are allowed on products of American industry exported from the country which have previously been subjected to excise is also represented as being very imperfect and complicated, and as presenting an obstacle to the resuscitation and development of our trade with foreign nations, impaired by the events of the last four years.

With the adoption, however, of the policy recommended by the commission, viz., of removing the excise from nearly all products of industry, many of these difficulties will undoubtedly be obviated.

The present system of the allowance of moieties of forfeitures and penalties to informers is also undoubtedly exercising a very demoralizing influence. In a mere pecuniary point of view, however, no expenditures of the government probably produce so large a return, both direct and indirect, as flow from the distribution of these moieties, and so long as the present organization of the revenue is retained the commission find it difficult to devise a better arrangement.

Attention should also be called to the fact that the chief business of the office of the internal revenue at Washington, and the chief depository of its records and papers, are located in a building which is not fire-proof, and that at any moment the whole machinery of the department is liable to be thrown into great confusion, with the infliction of irreparable losses, by reason of circumstances against which there is now no adequate prevision.

But an imperfection in our whole revenue policy more serious and radical than any yet adverted to, and which affects alike both the customs and the excise, is that of making the appointment, retention, and promotion of officers of the revenue dependent on other circumstances than qualifications or good behavior. So long as this policy prevails—a policy never adopted by any private firm or corporation having a due regard to their own interests, and one entirely ignored by all the leading states of Europe—a thoroughly efficient and economical administration of the revenue, coupled with the education of a competent corps of officials, cannot reasonably be expected. Under the present system, inspectors of spirits have been appointed who were entirely ignorant of the hydrometer and disregarded its use; and inspectors of tobacco who require to be instructed as to the nature of the different varieties of this article when manufactured, previous to entering upon the discharge of their duties.

The commission are also informed that efforts for the removal of competent officers have, in some instances, undoubtedly been made for the sole reason that in the faithful discharge of their duties they have interfered with the private interests of wealthy and influential individuals.

The commission consider it imperative that some action should be speedily taken by Congress on this subject; and that the necessities of the country should override any advantages that now may accrue in the distribution of patronage in the revenue department of the government. Good men, honest, competent, and efficient, should be sought out and placed in all the positions requiring tact, skill, and judgment, and on such salaries as will enable them to live and continue honest; they should, moreover, hold their situations by such assured tenure as to induce application and faithfulness. Thus would the government have the benefit of experience, every year growing more and more valuable.

To remedy the imperfections of the existing revenue system, which the commission have thus briefly alluded to, an entire reorganization of the whole machinery and policy of its administration seems necessary; but, before offering any suggestions on the subject, they would call attention to some of the peculiarities of the administration of the British revenue.

The leading features of the British administrative system consist in placing the customs and excise under the charge of separate and distinct boards of commissioners, each consisting of five members and a secretary. To each is also attached a law officer of great ability and large salary,* which are respectively known as the solicitor of the customs and solicitor of the excise. To these separate boards of commissioners (which the commission understand it is now contemplated to unite) very large powers are intrusted to make and amend the regulations under which the revenues are to be assessed and collected, and in respect to the appointment of all subordinate officials, who, before receiving such appointments, are required to undergo strict examinations as to education, business qualifications, health, and moral character. No distribution of moieties of fines and forfeitures to informers

---

* The salary of the solicitor of customs is £2,000, ($10,000 in gold,) and the appointment is for life.

is allowed, but the boards of commissioners are empowered, at discretion, to pay for information, to distribute rewards, and to promote in office for good service.

Superannuated and faithful officers are also allowed pensions on retirement from office. To such an extent, moreover, is the British revenue, in all its departments, divorced from party and politics, that all officers and employés of the revenue are even deprived of the right of suffrage while in service, though otherwise qualified; while it is understood that no influence on the part of any member of Parliament, or even of the chancellor of the exchequer, will avail for the securement of an appointment under the revenue, unless the candidate receive, at the same time, the approval of a majority of the board of commissioners, under whose supervision his duties are to be discharged. The consequence of this is, that the administration of the British revenue law is constantly improving, while frauds and defalcations on the part of the officials are rarely, if ever, heard of.

The responsibility of the collection, preparation, and publication of statistics of British revenue, trade, and commerce, to the accuracy and clearness of which we would bear testimony, is divided between the respective boards of commissioners and the board of trade. The decision of all law points connected with the revenue, and the publication and legal enforcement of the same, appear to devolve upon the respective revenue solicitors.

Whether a plan analogous to the British system, as thus presented, could be advantageously carried out in detail in the United States, and whether the same would be in all respects in accordance with the spirit of our institutions, is a question upon which the commission are not prepared to express an opinion, but they have no doubt that some of its leading features must form the basis of any sound national revenue policy.

In proposing a plan of change, however, they would suggest that the work of a reorganization should commence in the office of the Secretary of the Treasury itself. This office, with the exception of that of the Executive, is now undoubtedly the most responsible and important of any under the government; and the position of its occupant, as respects the future condition of the country, is not unlike that sustained by the commander-in-chief of the army during the most critical period of the war—a position in which the nation cannot afford to allow any risks of mistakes in judgment. With far more power than is intrusted to the British chancellor of the exchequer, or the French minister of finance, the office of the Secretary of the Treasury is at the same time, by long usage and custom, in many respects merely clerical. He is called upon at one hour as a member of the cabinet to participate in the decisions of grave political questions, and in the next to decide upon the transactions of his lowest subordinate. Intrusted with the supervision of the expenditures of hundreds of millions annually, he is also the final arbiter for the settlement of the most insignificant disbursements. It is also the assumed privilege of nearly every individual in the country to address him all on subjects connected with either public or private interests; and courtesy and usage demand that, in all instances, a reply of some nature should be given. The demands thus made at present upon the time and attention of the Secretary of the Treasury are wholly inconsistent with a proper consideration of those great questions of finance submitted to his decision, upon the wise determination of which the future welfare of the nation is inevitably dependent. To impose, therefore, any subordinate and trivial duties on this great officer of state is both to degrade his office and to imperil the financial interests of the country.

EDUCATION AND THE ADMINISTRATIVE SYSTEM OF PROBATION IN GERMANY, BY EDOUARD LABOULAYE.

CHAPTER 1.—On the necessity of political and administrative instruction for citizens who receive a liberal education, and in particular for those who are destined to public functions.

1. In order to be truly worthy of its name, and to respond fully to the dignity of its mission, the university should embrace in its system of education the whole range of human knowledge, so completely that no superior education than that given by the state should be possible. This universality is the condition and also the justification of the monopoly with which the state is invested by the laws. Hence arises the obligation that the university should continually keep pace with scientific progress; hence springs the duty to appropriate to itself all new truths which appear, so soon as they have acquired the degree of consistency and perfection necessary to render them the objects of regular instruction. At the present day especially, when the government can lay claim to the direction of society only by summoning all knowledge to its aid, since its power is no longer anything but the force of opinion, it is absolutely necessary that the university should take possession of the intellectual movement, in order to place at the service of the state, from their first appearance, all those just and useful ideas which the progress of the human mind brings to light. It is in the chair of the professor that not only the doctrines which claim to take rank among scientific truths, but also the theories which profess to reform government and society, should be brought to the test of examination and proof; it is through the university and in the university that progress should be made, if we would not abandon opinion to the mercy of passion or of charlatanism, and transform a power into a danger. Thus the political interest and the interests of science impose upon the educational body the same duties. Every ac-

of negligence or of delay is a species of forfeiture, and the university cannot postpone any useful instruction without being derelict at once to science, of which it has the precious deposit, and to the country, which confides to it the new generation, its dearest possession.

2. Our ancient universities comprehended perfectly the grandeur of the function which was marked out for them by destiny; and, moreover, their organization, more free than the existing one, and more independent of the action of the government, lent itself with much less effort to the aid of scientific progress. Education, following the human mind in its march, was developed and enlarged along with it, chairs of professors and faculties were multiplied whenever there appeared any new light upon the horizon, and Bologna, and Salamanca, and Toulouse, and Paris, disputed between them the honor of inaugurating in public and elevating to the rank of its elders a science which was, as yet, but newly born. Medicine, jurisprudence, literature, have thus come to demand their place by the side of theology, and all the universities flew open to welcome those queens of the earth; then came philosophy, so long repulsed as a stranger; afterwards, in its train, the natural sciences, which have shed so vivid a light upon the close of the last century. Thus each age, according to its bent and its vocation, has impelled human thought in a particular direction, and at each epoch, the university, the faithful handmaid of science, has followed the march of the human mind, without abandoning the conquests already achieved; at each epoch a new education has come to complete existing studies, and to satisfy the wants which have revealed themselves for the first time. It is thus that science has been diffused and popularized; it is thus that truths discovered by certain advanced spirits have become the patrimony of the human race. This wise conduct of the elder daughter of our kings should now serve us as the rule and model for our new university, upon which, in a democratic state like our own, devolves a weight of responsibility immensely greater than upon its predecessor, since, through the education which it gives to the superior classes, it decides almost infallibly the destiny of the country.

3. The sciences, as we have said, are not contemporaries, and every age lends a new light to that torch of civilization which the generations of mankind pass from hand to hand: our fathers witnessed the birth of the natural sciences, while comparative anatomy and geology are younger than the present century. Now, a new progress is being realized, and the human mind throws itself into paths hitherto unexplored. On the one side, the historical and juridical sciences, left for a moment neglected, are regaining the ground which they had lost; they are borrowing from the physical sciences the severity of their method and the exactitude of their processes, so as to obtain, by a precise analysis, certain and immediately useful results. On the other hand, we have seen sciences unknown to antiquity and the middle ages appearing, sciences new and as yet imperfect, but which appear destined to form the glory of our epoch. I speak of the political sciences, and I understand by that name all the doctrines which the constitution and administration of modern societies embrace, that is to say, political economy, statistics, industrial legislation, comparative legislation, politics properly speaking, administration, diplomacy, the law of nations, &c.

4. To any one who has followed the progress of ideas for forty years past, it is evident that the political sciences have acquired a theoretical development and possess a practical importance sufficient to demand at this day the right of naturalization in the university. I might even say that we had delayed too long, and that their admission is now not only useful, but that it is indispensable, that it is obligatory. I invoke special attention upon this point.

In all ages there have been great minds who have preoccupied themselves with the organization of the state. Among the ancients Plato, Aristotle, Cicero, and among the moderns Machiavelli, Grotius, Hobbes, Fenelon, Locke, Montesquieu, Rousseau, have grappled with this difficult problem, and prepared by their labors for the solution of this delicate question; but, if I may venture to say so, it is in our days alone that science has discovered its true *point d'appui*, that it has emerged from the domain of the imagination to enter upon that of reality. In fact it is only in our day that there has taken place in Europe an immense revolution, which, while fully respecting the forms and exterior pomp of monarchy, has displaced the sovereignty, and transformed all governments into real democracies; the name is wanting, but the thing exists: the change is more apparent in France than elsewhere, but it is to be found throughout the continent, and it is this change which has rendered possible both political science and its instruction.

The state, in former days, was the patrimony of the prince; the King pretended to hold his monarchy as a freehold confided to him by God himself, and for the administration of which he was responsible to God alone. Now, the state is the patrimony of the people, and royalty is no longer a sovereign domain, but a magistracy instituted for the common benefit, and confided by the nation to the prince whom it places or whom it keeps hereditarily at its head. The interest of the governed has been substituted for the interest of the prince, and at the same time (so profound has been the revolution) that interest of subjects has become the avowed principle of the most absolute monarchies, even of those which struggle with the greatest energy against this dislodgment of the sovereign power.*

5. The very principle of government having been radically changed throughout Europe,

---

* See Maurenbrecher, *Grundsätze des Heutigen Deutschen Staatsrechts*, §59, Dahlmann, *Die Politik auf den Grund*, &c., § 354.

(and in France this revolution is consecrated by the national compact of 1830,) the science of government has been necessarily compelled to undergo an entire remodeling. Formerly, the constitution was a mystery which no one might penetrate, and a prompt and terrible punishment awaited the rash innovator who dared to lay his hand upon the sacred ark, were it even for the purpose of steadying it; now, thanks to God, and to the devotion of our fathers, it is no longer such; the constitution belongs to all, and should be for all a subject of earnest study, since there is no enlightened person who cannot, either by his actions, his words, or his writings, exercise an influence, more or less direct, upon the march of affairs. Moreover, we are no longer on the threshold of these grand and important studies; the philosophical researches of the eighteenth century, the oftentimes cruel proof which our fathers and ourselves have made of all that was visionary in the most attractive theories, history issuing from the domain of literature and of eloquence to raise itself to the rank of a positive science, political economy created for half a century, and, above all, the habit of public life, have given us lights upon the science of government which were wanting to our predecessors, and which permit us to-day to make of that science the object of regular instruction.[*] Thus, the interest of science alone would suffice to demand the extension of universal education to all the political sciences, it being ridiculous that instruction in the sciences most largely developed in the last half century should be found nowhere except in books and writings often dangerous by their doctrines, hostile to the state, or false; and thus that the science of government should be taught outside of the government, and oftentimes in hostility thereto. But, in addition, it should be carefully noted that at the present day, in our social situation, (and what I say of France is true of all Europe,) political education is an absolute necessity. Since 1789, of immortal memory, the state, and its organization, has been the grand and difficult problem which has occupied all the genius, all the life of the nations of Europe. What has been, during the past fifty years, the cause of all the agitations, of all the revolutions, of all the civil or external wars, which have agitated the continent, if it has not been political reform? Why have so many millions of men been slain, so many thousands of millions of money been spent, except to preserve or to destroy forms of government? It is no longer questions of religion, as in the sixteenth century, nor of the balance of power, as in the seventeenth, which agitate the continent; the question which dominates and absorbs all others is how to direct this vast democracy, whose tide is continually rising. The political and social organization of the democracy—it is this that preoccupies the most thoroughly monarchical states as well as our own; and Prussia, for example, although further from the goal than France, although having to struggle against greater difficulties—Prussia, with her diverse nationalities, a race of nobles, a soil fettered with primogenitures and entails, preoccupies herself far more than our legislators and our ministers with the means of solving that problem which each day renders more important and more difficult. In this situation, and in a country like France, where every man may be summoned at a critical moment to put his hand to the sail, as to the helm of affairs, what knowledge can be more immediately useful? What more necessary than the political sciences? And I do not intend by this name to characterize mere theoretical researches upon the origin of society and government; but, on the contrary, the positive and practical science of existing governments, that which comprehends the most profound studies upon the constitution of the state, upon its interior and exterior mechanism, upon the machinery of the administration, upon the grand scientific or historical laws according to which are developed the wealth, the power, and the liberty of nations. Such an education is indispensable, not only for those who, placed in seats of power, hold the destiny of the country in their hands, but for every functionary charged with any share in the administration, however small it may be, and for every citizen who, by his vote or his opinion, may be one day summoned to decide for his part the future of the country. In the sixteenth century every man was a theologian, as in the eighteenth every one was a philosopher—princes, nobles, merchants, priests, physicians, and the rest. Now the physician, the theologian, the philosopher, who desire to be anything more than mere tradesmen, and who remember that before all things they are citizens, ought to possess political knowledge—not alone that profound knowledge which demands an impossible sacrifice of time, but a sufficient knowledge to keep out of the control of opinion and of power that species of political *dilettanti* who, assured of the ignorance of others, and without faith or belief themselves, make of their audacity a stepping-stone to a political fortune, oftentimes scandalous, to the great detriment of the country.

7. Finally, and after these general considerations upon the utility of political instruction for all citizens who receive a liberal education, there is a particular consideration of the greatest weight, which should determine the government to establish such instruction, if not for all citizens whose intelligence will one day give them an influence more or less direct upon public affairs, at least for those who are called to the direct service of the state; for it is at once dangerous and absurd, that the only public functions which do not demand preparatory studies should be precisely those which the most directly concern the country. Let an engineer of highways miscarry, through ignorance, in the construction of a bridge or a

---

[*]France has profited by its long and costly experience. Healthy ideas have been diffused; intelligence becomes continually one of the best guarantees of order. Reason does itself honor in consolidating the foundations of the noblest beliefs of humanity, and the moral and political sciences will henceforth serve to reaffirm that which formerly they disturbed. (Report to the King upon the re-establishment of the Academy of Moral and Political Sciences, by M. Guizot, minister of public instruction, October 26, 1832.)

sluice-way, and there results only loss of time and of money, which is easily repaired ; but let the administration be exacting or vexatious—let the taxes be ill-imposed or collected with intolerable annoyance—and the result is inconvenience and vexation to the entire nation. In a country where the press diffuses, with the rapidity of lightning, the intelligence of the injustice or unskilfulness of the administration, upon the very first fault, an electric movement, as it were, agitates the public mind ; every man conceives an instant distrust of an unskilful government, and throws upon it the responsibility of the faults committed by its agents. How happens it that in a country so susceptible, so easily alarmed, the state does not assure itself in advance of the capacity of men whom it employs ? How happens it that we assure ourselves by rigorous tests of the qualifications of an engineer, of an officer, of a professor, even of a school-master, while we take no heed of the political or administrative education of a diplomatist and of a prefect ? Why is one part of our administration organized upon the democratic principle of capacity, while the other is regulated only by the caprice of a minister ? Why are 12 years' study required to command a battery, while to govern a department nothing more is oftentimes required than the recommendation of a deputy or the importunity of a favorite ?

Why this state of things prevailed formerly is easily comprehended. In the ancient monarchy, the administration, as well as the entire government, was under the control of the prince, and it was sought above all things to keep the subject in profound ignorance on that head. Men acted precisely as Austria acts at this day ; and God knows how great was the weakness of such an administration—weakness so extreme that it precipitated the ruin of the monarchy for a miserable *deficit* of a few millions. The management of the finances, for example, that vital element of the administration, was not the intelligent dispensation of the public revenue in the national interest, but a species of organized rapine for the benefit of the follies or debaucheries of the prince and of his favorites. The whole art of the financier then consisted in squeezing the utmost possible amount from the people, in what the Germans call *plus mackerey*, or, according to the French expression, in *the art of plucking the fowl without making it cry out.*

In our day we are no longer in such a case, and, thanks to the intelligent government of the restoration, and to the still more intelligent conduct of the government of July, 1830, we have recovered from our prejudices against the administration ; we are no longer forced to consider that great body which presides over the destinies of the country as an instrument of despotism and of oppression, which only profits by its power, and injures instead of promoting the development of the public wealth. We have recovered equally from the doctrine put forth by M. Say and his disciples, that government is an *ulcer on the body politic ;* and M. de Tocqueville has long since cured us of our admiration for the *self-government* of the Americans.

It is to the excellence of the administration that we may attribute a share of the prosperity of France, and of the greatness of Prussia ; it is owing to the power of that element that France has been able to resist, without too great a shock, two invasions and three changes of dynasty ; it is owing to the wisdom of its administration that Prussia has been able to artfully console its subjects for the absence of the constitutional guarantees promised in 1813, and to replace in some sort by administrative guarantees the political rights which it has to this day refused. And not only has governmental administration become, for half a century, the most important of arts, but at the same time, and thanks to the labors of the administrators and economists of all nations, it has become a science of the first rank, of which political economy, statistics, agriculture, technology, are, so to speak, so many fragments.

So great a change in the administration has necessarily modified the condition of the employés of the state. Under the ancient regime, they were clerks—that is to say, men in a subaltern position, enjoying no higher rank in public estimation than that which now attaches to the principal employés of our heavier financial houses. Strangers to the public, the public knew nothing of them. But at this day their functions have greatly risen in importance ; they are no longer mere agents of the treasury, they are its administrators ; *inserviunt, non serviunt.* Their function is as important and as honorable as that of the officer who defends his country, or of the magistrate who executes the laws. The administration has become a magistracy, which, in the importance of its functions, in the magnitude of the interests involved, in the influence of its decisions, is in nowise inferior to the civil magistracy. The resemblance is so much the more striking as the sphere of its action is the more closely approached. Since the administration has passed from the realm of caprice to that of the law and the ordinances, it has become in reality a tribunal whose function is the more elevated because, in the questions to be decided, the state is at once a judge and a party, and consequently the administrator must possess an impartiality and a capacity of the highest rank, in order not to be wanting either to his function of a judge or to the duties of his office, and in order to infringe neither upon the public interest which he defends nor the private interest which he decides upon.

The administration being once raised to the rank of the civil magistracy, the necessity of giving to it the same guarantees has been perceived. One step further, and it will appear equally indispensable to exact of the men who devote themselves to these honorable functions knowledge as extensive and as various as we require of our future magistrates.*

---

* See some excellent remarks upon this subject in Emile de Girardin : *De l'Instruction Publique en France*, p. 405.

Under the restoration, the principles of the old regime were too often followed in respect to administrative officers, in disposing of places with the greatest inconsiderateness, and in superseding an officer, as one would have done a clerk, toward whom, besides paying his salary, no sort of obligation existed. Since the revolution of July, this state of things has been reformed; the higher offices are bestowed, it is true, quite as badly as under the restoration, and electoral influence has succeeded to the patronage of the court and the congregation* without the country having gained anything; but at least these offices, once bestowed, are not withdrawn at the pleasure of ministerial caprice, and in fact, if not in law, administrative functions have become unremovable. This is true especially of the inferior employments, and we have no longer the sad example of those removals for opinion's sake so frequent under the restoration—removals frequently provoked by base denunciations. The administration of office is now a stable profession—a service of the state—not very brilliant, it is true, with small rewards, where advancement is slow, difficult, capricious, but a service to which one may devote himself at least without misgivings, without fear of seeing his future career broken up with each succeeding day.

However limited may be the administrative career, and however necessary it may be in entering upon it to renounce the hope of one day attaining a great fortune or a superior position, nevertheless this stability of employment, the first consideration which surrounds public functions, and a lingering aristocratic prejudice against trade—a prejudice from which our middle classes are not wholly free—all these motives, and others which it would be too tedious to enumerate, have sufficed to turn in this direction all the youth of the middle classes; for every place in the ministry of finance there are now twenty candidates, and the title of *supernumerary aspirant* is more warmly contested than that of an overseer.

In presence of this crowd of solicitors, drawing in their train friends, relatives, deputies, what should be the duty of a government which is more solicitous of the welfare of its administration than of the personal satisfaction of the intriguers who surround it? Evidently it should be to exact from the candidates presenting themselves conditions of capacity, and, since the number of aspirants is such that it is free to choose, to take only the most instructed, the best qualified by their attainments and their moral character to discharge the duties to which they are destined, and to honor the body to which they belong.

Is it thus that the affair is managed, and does the administration exact from the men whom it admits to its communion sufficient guarantees of capacity and of fitness? No; and while the army, the artillery, the engineer corps, the navy, the highways, the mines, the woods and waters, have all of them special schools and studies, while the public instruction has its examinations, the normal school, and the competitive admission, while the magistracy is guarded by the guarantee (a slight one, it is true) of the licentiate's diploma, yet the other branches of the government, on the contrary, and those not the least important, the exchequer office, the bureau of direct and indirect taxes, the land-registry office, the customs, the post office, have no other condition of admissibility except a trifling novitiate, since the appointment goes by favor, and, once admitted, it is through favor alone that one looks for his title and his promotion; finally—and this is the most singular of all—while a novitiate is required in order to obtain the place of a subaltern in the treasury service, it is not at all necessary in order to become a counsellor of finance, sub-prefect, prefect, referee, or counsellor-referee.

The capacity required is in the inverse ratio of the importance of the office, and its responsibility. How strange that the law should exact conditions of capacity for a lawyer, for an attorney, for a notary, in order that the private interests of citizens should not fall into unsafe hands, and should exact no guarantee whatever that the public interests should not be endangered by inexperienced or unskilful administrators.

Still more, and as if it were not already dangerous enough to subject the choice of public functionaries to the risks of chance, the government augments the chances of inexperience and incapacity by requiring no special studies of its officers after they have entered the service of the state. There is not even one public institution by whose instructions the well-disposed might profit, who desire to be anything more than mere routine officers. One chair of administrative law in each faculty, a chair in which the administrative disputes are exposed rather than the system of administration; a few chairs of political economy scattered over Paris and giving rare instructions—such are all the resources afforded by a great nation to those who devote themselves to public employments. So that it is no exaggeration to say that, from the counsellor of state down to the humblest functionary, there cannot be found 10 persons who, in their youth, have made a special study of administrative functions. All that our functionaries know they have learned by experience, or by individual labor performed after their entrance upon public affairs. The consequences of such a defect of public education are easily seen. The employés of the state are divided between the men of routine, who, by dint of continual practice in the bureaus, acquire a mechanical knowledge of the received forms, of the laws and ordinances most frequently employed, without ever elevating their minds to a solitary idea of reform or of progress, and another small class of superior men who owe their education to themselves alone. But the intelligence of these last is but a useless, and frequently even dangerous element; for they are not comprehended either by their official superiors or subordinates, and when they have in their minds an idea of reform,

---

*A political association in the days of the restoration.—TRANSLATOR.

they are sustained neither by the administration (at least if the reform be a financial one) nor by public opinion, directed by journalists to whom the first elements of political education are frequently wanting, and who have no experience in affairs, nor, finally, by the representatives of the country, who are neither better instructed nor more enlightened than the rest of the nation, being frequently ignorant of the simplest principles of political science. The disastrous consequences of such an order of things are apparent at a glance. It breeds rashness in designs, timidity in execution. In this common ignorance, all men walk on tiptoe and hesitate as in the dark. The administration holds fast to the existing order of things; every change appals it, since it is utterly unable to calculate its bearing, and it recoils, from sheer ignorance and inexperience, before innovations the most useful and frequently the most necessary.

How different would be the case if a thorough political instruction, if special studies of principles, were to give to the administration that superiority of intelligence which now forms the sole title to the respect and obedience of nations. A wise administration, having confidence in its power, sustained by public esteem, recruited from among the most enlightened men of each generation, would give to our government that point of stability—that anchor—which is wanting to it in the flux and reflux of parties, of opinions, and of events.

CHAPTER 2.—*On political and administrative instruction in Germany.*

While we are still occupied with asking ourselves if the system of administrative education and probation for official functions is useful and necessary, and more than one even of the more enlightened minds recoil before the boldness of such a reform, because we have upon that subject only confused and imperfect ideas, the different governments of Germany, which are certainly far enough removed from democracy or revolution, have entered freely upon this course, with that profusion of regulations, ordinances, and laws which has always distinguished the administrations beyond the Rhine. Far from being alarmed at a system of competition, the German governments have favored it to such a degree that it has become almost the only method of admission to public functions, whatever may be their nature and their character.   *   *   *

The most successful government in Germany, that of Prussia, has taken in the confederation that foremost rank to which neither its population, nor its wealth, nor its history would have entitled it; and when we look for the secret of its power, we find that its two grand supports are the university on the one side, and the administrative service on the other. The superiority of its system of education attracts to Prussia from all parts of Germany the flower of its industrious youth, and the administration, open to industry and to capacity, summons to public functions every man who has the ambition to serve his country.

At the same time, Prussia, in its essays toward administrative organization, seems to me inferior to Würtemberg, a country which is a model in respect of administration. This inferiority is attributable to two causes. In the first place, the system of competition has been more freely applied in Würtemberg than in Prussia, where the noblesse and the army are frequently invested with peculiar privileges. In the second place, the curriculum of studies required has not been determined with sufficient exactness. It has been thought unnecessary to found separate faculties of administration, and they have contented themselves with establishing in the faculty of philosophy a branch of instruction upon administrative affairs, as a complement of the juridical course of study required of the future functionaries. Too much influence has thus been left to the legal spirit. It has not been sufficiently recognized that administration is a new science, *sui generis*, although closely related to jurisprudence, and that it is needful to develop the administrative spirit, as in the other faculties are created the *esprit de corps* of the physician, the lawyer, and the theologian. In Würtemberg, on the contrary, this necessity has been thoroughly felt. A special faculty has been created, and the examinations have been better calculated than those of Prussia to prepare candidates for the various public services.   *   *   *

In Würtemberg, up to the year 1817, at which time a special faculty was established, the administration was recruited in a very similar manner to our own. In order to enter the public service, it was requisite to begin by being admitted in the capacity of supernumerary (*incipient*) in the bureau of some superior officer. For such an admission, no condition was required, either of age, of fortune, or of education, but the will of the chief of the bureau (*principal*) was the law. During this probation, which frequently lasted many years, the occupations of the candidates were purely mechanical, involving certain despatches, certain copies of letters, and the like. As to the instruction of the supernumerary, nobody looked after that; and the period of youth, that precious season in which the intellect and the capacity are formed, passed away in this degrading occupation. Some reflective, laborious minds drew instruction more or less solid from this commerce with affairs; but, if I may say so, these men shone out as a light in the midst of darkness, and, without reforming the administration, only rendered more visible and more deplorable the ignorance of those who surrounded them.

This routine was no less prejudicial to the sovereigns than to their subjects, for in this matter the interest of the people is often the same as that of the treasury.   Listen to a complaint made in 1776, by the landgrave Louis, of Hesse Darmstadt:

From the first day of our accession to the government, we saw with regret that the administration of our revenues, the care of the well-being and prosperity of our subjects, in a word, the whole administrative organization of the country, was very different from what we had a right to expect, from the number of laws and ordinances on that subject, the multitude of our employés, and the excellent example given by neighboring countries.   Our astonishment, but not our chagrin, was diminished when we found that the care of our revenues, as of the interests of our subjects, was in the hands of men who had devoted themselves to office only because they were too ignorant, too poor, or in too little favor to enter into any other public service. These persons have treated our domain and our subjects as an *anima vilis* at whose expense and risk they have acquired their experience.   *   *   *   These dull spirits have never conceived any of those liberal ideas which a zeal for the government, or a desire to rival countries whose administration is superior to our own, would produce.   On the contrary, we have seen with profound regret, that even those whose intelligence or experience acquired abroad placed them in a condition to introduce order and intelligence into any part of the administration, were blamed through the ignorance of others, envied, reviled, spit upon, persecuted, crushed, until they were discouraged and compelled to renounce those improvements and attempts at reform whose realization has been postponed by ill-will, and which, moreover, soon fall into the hands of ignorant and presumptuous subalterns.

Such was the situation of the Hessian administration; such, also, was that of Würtemberg toward the close of the last century.   *   *   *   In 1816, in consequence of the reiterated complaints of the two chambers, the government (of Würtemberg) perceived the necessity of seriously occupying itself with the education of its functionaries; moreover, as the separation of the administration from the courts of justice was about to be consummated, it began to be comprehended that it was necessary to exact from future officers of the administration knowledge of a special character, which was not communicated by the faculty of law.   The reigning sovereign, one of the wisest princes whom Germany ever possessed, yielded to the desire of his subjects and established a faculty of administration at Tubingen, the only university in the kingdom.

His Majesty, (as is recited in the act of 29th December, 1817, founding this institution,) convinced that it is necessary to enable all those who are destined to the service of the state to acquire a scientific education, has determined to establish a faculty of administration in the University of Tubingen.

And, moreover, in order to place this department of instruction on an equality with others, it is ordained:

1. That hereafter, in awarding such offices as require administrative knowledge, particular regard shall be had to persons who have pursued studies connected with government in the university, and who shall have passed the examinations of the faculty; and these persons shall be regularly preferred to those who have not acquired these special studies.

2. The students of administrative science shall pursue such a course of jurisprudence as may be most essential to them; as, for example, the philosophy of positive law; constitutional law; the private law of Würtemberg; administrative law, and the encyclopædia; and the law students shall, on their part, pursue the most important portion of the administrative course, such as the encyclopædia of political science, and the practice of the administrative service.

3. To encourage more especially those who devote themselves to administrative studies, there shall be bestowed in the two next succeeding years from four to six purses of 150 florins each.

Although the ordinance of 1817 has not produced all the results which might have been anticipated, yet, says M. Schütz, from whom I borrow these details, it is beyond question that these 20 years, during which more than 400 candidates for administrative office have pursued their studies at the university, have produced remarkable results, and the examinations for the public service have constantly demonstrated the superiority of the candidates possessing theoretical knowledge over the candidates who had only practical knowledge.

The year 1837 introduced a new period, and Würtemberg entered into the true pathway to success; from that day the results have been continually more and more satisfactory.

Two most important measures were introduced.

First, the course of instruction was enlarged.   The existing chairs were:
1. Political economy.
2. Agriculture and the allied sciences.
3. Technology.
4. Administrative law and administrative practice.

To these were now added two new chairs: one for the practice of administrative science, or rather a chair of administrative law applied; the other for political history and statistics.

Second, the system of examination was transferred to the departments of the interior and of finance.

The following are the principal dispositions of this ordinance of 22d February, 1837, concerning examinations:

1. For the department of the interior a distinction is made between the candidates who are destined for superior employments and those who are destined for the inferior; hence there is a superior and an inferior examination established.

Each of these examinations consists of a double test—the one written, the other oral.   The written test is an open competition between all the candidates. Assembled under the eye of the commission, they are required to prepare a composition upon a given subject, without any other assistance than the official collections. Those who are declared inadmissible can be entered as candidates only in the following year. The oral test is an individual examination, and follows the written one.

The inferior examination takes place before the *Kreis Regierung*, (the *Kreis* corresponds to our *department*,) a commission of officers in which the professors of the university do not participate. The candidates who are found capable can be employed as inferior administrators, directors in schools, prisons, orphan or insane asylums, and as assistant inspectors. There is required of these candidates:

1. A knowledge of the administration of communes and of districts.
2. A knowledge of the distribution of taxes, of accounts, and of the laws relating thereto.
3. A knowledge of the private laws of Würtemberg, especially in all that relates to contracts, as well as to the civil procedure.
4. An immediate solution of questions relative to the above-mentioned subjects, and especially to the most difficult calculations.

The superior examination is required of all candidates who desire to obtain other employments from the ministry of the government.

Each candidate is required to be at least 21 years of age, and to have undergone, at least three years antecedently, his preparatory academical examination.

This latter condition is the first important reform which the ordinance introduced. Previously, any one might enter into the public service without the exaction of this certificate of attainments. Hence ensued the inconvenience of those premature supernumeraries which brought into the discharge of public functions many young persons having scarcely the first elements of a liberal education.

The superior examination for government service is composed of two tests, separated by an interval of one year; in the first, theoretical knowledge is required; in the second, practical knowledge. It is thus necessary to prove successively, a thorough acquaintance with the laws and ordinances of the country, and a certain practical capacity. It is required that the claims of science and of the administration should be satisfied, the one after the other.

The first examination (the theoretical) takes place before a commission composed wholly of university professors; the jury of examination consists entirely of the professors of the administrative faculty, of two or three professors of the faculty of law, and of a counsellor chosen for that purpose. This examination being required as well of the students of administrative science as of the practical students—that is to say, of those who have entered the government bureaus by simple supernumerary service—it results that it is next to impossible now to pass that examination without having previously acquired the university studies, and that, consequently, in fact if not in law, the university is the only preparatory school for the future administrators. It is to be added that the government, in order to encourage universal studies, has decreed that the students of administrative science alone should have the right of exemption from military service as candidates for the civil service of the state.

The second examination, separated from the first by a long interval, is essentially practical; and as it concerns the interests of the administration, and those who are examined are no longer students, but functionaries, the examination takes place before a commission, presided over by the chief of the department, and composed of all the members of the council. This commission assembles at Stuttgart twice every year. The following are the subjects upon which the two examinations turn:

1. The public law of Würtemberg, considered by itself and in its relations with the public law of Germany. Candidates are to be interrogated specially upon the laws relative to the organization and administration of the communes, the district, the public domain, and the estates of the noblesse.

2. Private law, both the common and that of Würtemberg. The examination turns particularly upon matters, a knowledge of which closely concerns administrators, such as obligations, hypothecations, servitude, conditions of holding property, &c.

3. The canon law of Catholics and Protestants. Whatever relates to benefices, patronage, titles, the administration of church revenues, and whatever concerns the church and the state.

4. The elements of civil procedure, of law, and of criminal procedure.

5. National economy.

6 Administration.

7. The system of duties and accounts.

8. A summary knowledge of commerce and of agriculture.

After the first examination the candidates, in order to acquire practical knowledge, are subjected, in quality of counsellor-referee of the administration of the second class, to a supernumerary position or probation of one year, eight months of which are employed in a district office, and four months in a ministerial bureau. In the district offices they are exercised in the different branches of the administration, by having to treat the less important questions that arise, and they are familiarized with the practice by causing them to assist in all the deliberations and in all administrative measures. In the bureaus they are employed as copyists, revisers, and auditors.

The heads of bureaus and the district officers are required to devote special attention to the conduct of the probationers, and, upon the expiration of the term, to address to the ministry a report upon the zeal, the capacity, and the morality of the candidate, a report which remains in the hands of the ministry, and constitutes the commencement of the record of the future administrative officer. The candidate who has successfully passed this second examination is nominated a counsellor-referee of the first class, and placed upon a stipend. He becomes thenceforth an integral part of the administration.

The theoretical examination, the novitiate, the practical examination, such are the three guarantees which the state exacts from its functionaries. The first guarantee is, that the candidate has received an adequate special education; the second is the test of the moral fitness and administrative capacity of the probationer; and, finally, the practical examination secures to the government the certainty of not being deceived by the indulgence or connivance of the superior employés, and at the same time enables it to class, according to their different degrees of capacity, those functionaries who have already passed the probationary stage. These three tests, which are in practical use throughout almost all Germany, and form the condition of admission into the entire civil service of Prussia, as well for the administration of justice as of the civil service, form the vital portion of the whole system. * *

I return to Würtemberg: The examination for the treasury service much resembles the examination for the department of the interior. The principles are the same; the only difference consists in the object of the examination. Thus, there are for the treasury, as for the interior department, two classes of employés—one inferior, the other superior. Candidates arrive at the first by a special examination, which does not suppose an early education of the highest order; they arrive at the second by a course of university studies, followed by a double examination and a probationary period.

The inferior examination, which conducts to the positions of inspector and comptroller of customs, of finances, &c., turns upon the following points:

1. General knowledge of the principles of financial administration.
2. Financial accounts, and the laws relative thereto.
3. Principles of civil law, especially in what concerns contracts, and a summary knowledge of the civil procedure.
4. Practical acquaintance with accounts, and with the various administrative acts, such as the process-verbal, &c.

This examination is held at Stuttgart, once every year, before a commission composed of the principal members of the overseers of the treasury and the customs.

As to the superior examination which qualifies for the administrative grades above to that of comptroller, the special classes of knowledge required for the two tests, theoretical and practical, are the following:

1. The public law of Würtemburg, especially in all that relates to the organization and administration of districts and communes, the law of public domains, and the estates of the noblesse.
2. The private law of Würtemberg. The examination will lay especial stress upon such matters as concern the administration, contracts, mortgages, prescription, servitude, the property of the common people, tithes, &c.
3. The general principles of civil and criminal procedure.
4. National economy.
5. The science of finance, the financial legislation and institutions of Würtemberg.
6. Accounts.
7. Commercial, industrial, and agricultural knowledge.

The practical examination takes place before a commission of the ministry of finance; the pupils who pass the first as well as the second test bear the title of probationers of the finances, of the second or of the first class; and a period of one year separates equally the theoretical test from the practical.

Such is the system carried into effect by Würtemberg, and if it is sought to learn what has been the result of this innovation, we may cite the opinion of one of the men best fitted to pronounce upon that subject, Mr. Schutz, professor in the administrative faculty at Tubingen, and one of the examiners.

"This ordinance," says M. Schutz—"I say it with all the respect which I owe to the capable officers who have made themselves such by practical service—this ordinance has been the death blow of the ancient bureaucracy; it keeps at the lowest round of the ladder the mere ignorant copyist, and suffers only those who have achieved the consecration of knowledge to arrive at the superior degrees. The employés of the government administration and finance, whom public opinion formerly placed much below ecclesiastics and lawyers, precisely because of their inferior education, resume to-day the place which belongs to them. The moral power of the state is enlarged in proportion to the capacity of the men who consecrate themselves to the public service; and on the other hand, the more these functionaries rise in the public estimation, the more are such functions sought by men of character and talent."

An intelligent and considerate administration of his office constitutes the firmest and most secure support for a minister, and this is too frequently forgotten in a country which has twice owed its grandeur to the men of genius who conducted its administration—Colbert,

Napoleon—two men whose whole secret was to search everywhere and at any price for the man who was best fitted for the place to be filled. Their policy was very different from that of to-day, which consists in giving to the men of whom one has need the places which suit them, without regard to the country, which, nevertheless, it should seem, ought to be somewhat of a party to a contract in which its interests alone are at stake.

In Baden a similar experience has led to the same results as in Würtemberg. Thre is no special examination for the administration, properly speaking, since, in Baden, the civil service is not separate from that of justice; it is a judicial examination, consequently, which admits to the functions of civil office dependent upon the ministry of the interior.

But for the treasury service there appeared on the 26th of March, 1838, a remarkable ordinance, the principle ragulations of which are the following:

Whoever desires to enter into the treasury service, and does not wish to connect himself with the active service, or to remain in subordinate position, must go through a course of study as an administrative pupil, submit to an examination, and pass through a probationary period.

The studies required are, among the preparatory branches of knowledge—1, arithmetic, algebra, geometry, trigonometry, mechanics, bookkeeping; 2, zoology, botany, geology, geography, physics, chemistry.

Among the special sciences—1, agriculture, the science of woodlands, mines, technology, the science of trades and manufactures; 2, administration, financial science, administrative law, administrative practice.

Among the accessory sciences—the encyclopædia of jurisprudence; public law in general, private law, procedure, &c.

The students continue three years and a half—seven terms—and it must be admitted that this is none too long to instruct oneself in so many different sciences; there are twenty-seven to twenty-eight courses of study required, which is an average of about four courses per term, or about three hours and a half of instruction per day. The examinations take place annually, in the autumn, at Carlsruhe; they are presided over by a ministerial counsellor, assisted by counsellors of the college of finance, and by certain professors.

The examination is written and oral; the written exercises are performed under a severe scrutiny; the oral examination takes place in common for all the candidates, before the full commission united; the members of the ministry of finance may assist at it. It is this ministry which determines the admissions, upon advice of the commission and the report of the president. The candidates admitted as probationers must serve at least two years in a district, and are during this period subjected to a careful and rigid oversight. This period passed, they are entitled to be named *assistants*—that is to say, salaried employés.

A second ordinance, of the 28th of May, 1838, organizes the positions of the inferior employés; this ordinance has been rendered necessary, the candidates not having presented themselves for examination in sufficient number for the necessities of the service. Two orders, therefore, of probationers were distinguished—those who have entered into the government service by superior examination, the counsellor referees, and those who have entered it without examination; these last bear the name of *assistant counsellors*, and are nominated by the administration without examination; it is exacted, nevertheless, that they should have sufficient education, and one which corresponds nearly to the instruction which the title of bachelor carries with it among us.

When one has served three years in this position, and is more than twenty-one years of age, he may become a *probationary assistant* by an examination. This examination consists of the translation of the more simple Latin and French authors, the elements of arithmetic, algebra, and geometry, history, statistics, and the knowledge of that part of financial administration to which the candidate is admitted as supernumerary. The examination takes place orally and in writing, under the direction of the superintendent of the revenue, assisted by the counsellors of the bureau of public lands, customs, and taxes, and the professors of Carlsruhe. The candidate who, at the close of the examination, is named *probationary assistant*, (which is not an officer, but a title,) competes exclusively with the practical probationers for the posts of inspector and receiver, but he cannot become a counsellor of the finances.

This organization of a higher and a lower examination, establishing two degrees of capacity and two classes of employés, has been generally considered satisfactory. In effect it does not permit well educated and laborious men to linger in too subordinate positions, and it arrests the advancement of ignorance and mediocrity.

Moreover it is now a long time since the good effect of this system have been experienced in Baden, for the ordinance of 1838 simply confirms and ameliorates a state of things already long existing; and already for forty years previously there had been required of the employés of the treasury special qualifications, attested by an examination.

I will add but a single word: It is only necessary to have travelled in Baden, Würtemberg, or in Prussia, to be struck with the perfect arrangements of the administration. In no country has more been accomplished with a less wealth of resources. Würtemberg, especially, is admirable in its public roads and cultivation, and yet it is a country without wealth, and the population of which is only equal to two of our departments.

I should complete this report by a statement of what has been done in Prussia, but I will stop here for two reasons: the first is, that Prussia following almost precisely the same usage as Würtemberg, I should extend indefinitely an essay already very long; the second is, that I propose to give hereafter the organization of the judicial novitiate in Prussia; and, that organization being nearly the same for the judicial as for the civil administration, one can readily form an idea of the Prussian system. For the rest, I repeat, this system is the same as that of Würtemberg—a theoretical test by examination, a probation to assure the moral character and the capacity of the candidate, and a practical test by examination.* Prussia has even pushed this system of examinations further than any other of the German states, for, in order to advance more rapidly the youth of capacity, and to bring to the head of affairs men who are still full of zeal and activity, she has established a double examination in practical tests, so that, after having been auditor upon graduating at the university, and counsellor-reeferee after a preliminary practical examination, preceded by a probation, it is necessary then to pass a second probation, and submit to a second examination in practice, in order to attain the more important positions in the administration. Thus, while Baden and Würtemberg have established the system of competition only at the threshold of the political career, Prussia has made it in addition a means of advancement within the service of the administration. The claims of education and capacity thus become entirely preponderant, and rank even before length of service, for it is a recognized principle in Prussia† that length of service in an inferior function is not of itself any title to advancement. It is only a presumptive evidence of capacity which yields before those positive proofs of fitness which an examination furnishes. I think it would be difficult to favor industry more effectually, or to hold out to studious young men a more powerful attraction to the service of the state.

There is thus established, by the fact of competition, a most profitable emulation among the industrious youth, which secures to the service of the state men of profound knowledge, and continually higher standards of attainment. This is the case in Prussia. Far from the rigorous conditions of examination having diminished the number of candidates, it has augmented them; and, in fact, all the competitors having an equal chance of success, without distinction of birth or of fortune, there are few students who do not enter into the list of competition. Consequently, and to diminish somewhat the crowd of competitors, Prussia has multiplied the competitions, and added to the difficulties of the examination, so that the standard of attainment of which the candidates must make proof is far superior to the scientific maximum of the former competitions.

The competition established in France for certain departments of the government service has produced the same results. The army, the navy, public instruction, the service of highways, all exact long and laborious study, followed by a competitive examination, without there being, on that account, any deficiency of candidates for those important services. On the contrary, the number of competitors is every year augmented; and while, at the beginning, more than one-third of the candidates were admitted to the Polytechnic School, at the present time more than three-fourths are refused, although the conditions of admission are more difficult. Still further, since the public service must gain in consideration in proportion as the conditions of admission are made more difficult, this rigorous scrutiny, and the multiplicity of knowledge exacted, will augment the number of candidates, since a great number of young men occupying an elevated social rank will throw themselves into the public service from the moment that it comes into close relation to their position in the world. How much must the state be the gainer by a progress like this! And this progress, be it remembered, needs but a single word to be initiated. It needs but the will of a thoroughly enlightened minister to reform and elevate a whole generation of employés.

Mr. Bigelow to Mr. Seward.

No. 102.]   UNITED STATES CONSULATE,
                                              Paris, August 25, 1863.

SIR: I am in receipt of circular No. 30 of the State Department for 1862, requesting information of the means adopted, in the country of my official residence, for the protection of its revenues, the collection of duties in the passage of goods across the national frontiers,

---

* It is the glory and pride of Prussia to reckon among her civil functionaries so great a number of men well instructed in all departments; and, in order to maintain this distinction, scrupulous care is exercised that the standard of scientific education should not be lowered or relaxed. No one is admitted to the university who cannot exhibit sufficient preparatory knowledge. These examinations passed, one must then go through three years of study, devoted exclusively to science, and without the interference of business and its necessities, which would interrupt the student. Thus, armed at all points, the future functionary enters upon a new career. It is no longer to books and formularies, it is to the men with whom he must henceforth live, and to the affairs which he must one day conduct, that he must go to seek the complement of his education, and that, too, under the direction of men thoroughly versed in practical administration, and whose experience must be highly advantageous to him. The future professor labors under the surveillance of the oldest masters of his art; the future magistrate is sent to the tribunals; the future administrator is placed with the functionaries of the same order. Afterward follows a final examination, in order to ascertain that the superior has judged of the young probationer without favor, without partiality, and, if this last examination is favorable, the candidate is definitively adjudged capable of entering into the service of the state. (Perthes: Der Staatsdienst in Preussen, page 63.)

† An ordinance of the 23d October, 1817, expressly prescribes that more attention should be given to fidelity, to zeal, and to capacity than to the time of service of the employés, and that no preference shall be given to the oldest functionary, except in case of an equality of merit.

and in their transhipment in its ports for export to a foreign land; also the ferms that are used, the rules and regulations in force, the fees charged, and other expenses incurred in its foreign revenue service.

At the earliest convenient opportunity, after the receipt of this circular, I addressed to his excellency Mr. Fould, the minister of finance, a request that he would refer me to a person in the service to whom I could apply for the required information; and in a few days I was advised by a letter from the director general that Mr. Delmas, administrator of the second division of the direction general des douanes, was instructed to give me the information I sought. I immediately waited upon Mr. Delmas, who, after some conversation with me upon the subject of my inquiries, in the course of which he promised me the cordial co-operation of his department, referred me to Mr. Masseron, the head of one of the bureaus.

Mr. Masseron manifested a prompt alacrity in furthering the objects of my visit, and kindly informed me that I would save myself much trouble by procuring a book prepared expressly for government use by Mr. A. Delandre, head of one of the bureaus, entitled "Traité-pratique des douanes," which contains a full digest of all the revenue laws and regulations of France, and in which I would be likely to find nearly, if not quite, all the information I required.

I sent for Mr. Delandre's book, and found it fully to answer Mr. Masseron's description. It gives all the laws, decrees, and regulations of the revenue department of France now in force, digested and arranged conveniently for reference, and in so compact a form as almost to defy further condensation. I saw at once that, so far as the general organization of the revenue force was concerned, the definition of the duties and responsibilities of the respective officers, I could add nothing to the clearness or sufficiency of Mr. Delandre's statement.

If I knew precisely the points upon which information is most needed, I might, perhaps, have gleaned it from Mr. Delandre's pages and other sources, and submitted it to you in a more compact shape. But, in the absence of specific inquiries, I found that no digest or condensation would be a satisfactory substitute for this thorough and comprehensive work.

The French revenue system, like all other administrative organizations, is the fruit of nearly a century's profitable experience; it is singularly logical and systematic; it has been devised and usually operated under the direction of men of great administrative abilities, and with such singular skill that each part of it, like the features of the human countenance, seems to have such an adaptation one to the other that they must be seen all together to be properly appreciated. I have, therefore, concluded to send you the work of Mr. Delandre, in which will be found nearly everything that can be learned from the revenue experiences of France since the days of Colbert.

I also send you a complete set of forms used in the customs service, for which I am likewise indebted to the courtesy of Mr. Masseron. They are very necessary to the working of the French system, and may be studied with great advantage by those whose duty it is to provide the checks by which the accountability and responsibility of subordinates are insured. To comprehend them, however, it is first necessary to comprehend thoroughly the personal organization of the French douanerie, for which there is no shorter method than the study of the first 300 sections of Delandre.

I also send you a little work entitled *Guide théorique et pratique du contribuable en matiere des contributions indirectes renferment en ce qui concerne specialement les contribuables, le resumé des lois, des instructions, et de la jurisprudence, par I. S. Isoard, Controleur des Contributions Directes.* This is official, and contains all the practical information that can be required in regard to the collection of indirect taxes, not given in Delandre.

The French government collects about 2,000,000,000 francs, at an expense of about 350,000,000 of francs, annually. Of the sum thus collected, about 400,000,000 francs are realized from direct taxes, and the rest from indirect taxes, but the douanerie organization is auxiliary to the collection of the whole sum.

I do not think so large an amount of revenue is collected by any government in the world, with so small a loss from fraud, as in France, and I attribute the fact in a large degree to the method by which the agents of the customs are selected, and the terms upon which they hold their places, about which I will add a few words in addition to what a reader would be likely to gather from a perusal of these works. The whole revenue service of this empire is under direction of what is termed a director general, who alone, of all the officers of the customs, is in direct communication with the minister of finance. The labor of this general direction is shared by a central bureau, under the immediate orders of the director general, and six divisions, each having an administrator at its head. These administrators, with the director general, who presides, form an administrative council, and regulate what is termed the "central administration." Then there is a director in each department of the empire who superintends the department service. The director general, the administrators at the head of each division, and the directors at the head of each department, are the only officers connected with the customs department who receive their appointment directly from the head of the state. They, however, and all their subordinates, are appointed for life, or until their age entitles them to a pension and retreat. They never commence their career in any of the superior grades, but have to be promoted to them as the reward of continued faithful service through the lower grades.

All the officers below the minister of finance have to commence their career of service as clerk in a bureau, at a salary of from 800 to 1,000 francs, say $160 to $300 a year, according to the class they are found qualified to enter upon examination, or in the still lower grade of préposé, or overseer, on a salary of from $150 to $160. To this there are no exceptions. The present director general, Mr. Barbier, has passed through all the grades, commencing as simple préposé des brigades in the direction of Strasbourg, on a salary in those days of only 650 francs (about $130) a year.

From préposé de brigade of the 2d class he was advanced to the 1st class. He then became brigadier of the different classes successively; then lieutenant of the 3d, 2d, and 1st classes in succession; then captain of the 3d, 2d, and 1st classes respectively; then sub-inspector; then inspector; and so on up through every grade, remaining in each at least one year, until he finally, at 60 years of age, reached his present exalted position of director general, councillor of state, and commander of the legion of honor.

No political influence or favor, no revolution in the government, interferes with this law of promotion. Even in the revolution of 1848, no modifications whatever were made in the personnel of the douanes. Mr. Gréterin, who had risen from the position of a simple clerk in a bureau, to which he was appointed in 1830, was director general in 1848, and remained such until he retired in 1857, when he was succeeded by Mr. Barbier. The political vicissitudes of the government have no more appreciable influence upon the selection of the revenue agents than upon their promotion.

No candidate is received under 18 or over 25 years of age in the bureau service, nor in the out-door service, except in certain inferior employs, and upon terms which do not affect the general policy. On presenting himself, the postulant must produce proofs of his age; that he is a Frenchman; that his moral character is unexceptionable; that he is exempt from any physical deformity, and that he has the necessary means of supporting himself during the period that may elapse after he is accepted, before a vacancy occurs, till when he receives no pay. This period is termed his "supernumeriat," which is at least of one year's duration.

On producing these vouchers he is sent to a special committee, designated each year by the director general, for examination as to his education and other aptitudes for the service. The programme by which he is tested is as follows:

1. He writes a page from dictation, on unruled paper, without any external aid in correcting the orthography.

2. He copies the same page.

3. He is required to give a grammatical analysis of part of the text thus copied.

4. He is examined on the first four rules of arithmetic, the theory of proportions, and the solution of various problems of elementary arithmetic.

5. He is examined on the metrical system.

6. He is required to prepare inventories and tables after a given model.

7. To answer various questions in physical geography and politics.

8. To write a letter or note on a given subject.

After this is finished the postulant is further examined upon any matters to which he may have given special attention, especially on the living and dead languages, law, chemistry, natural history, drawing, &c., &c., &c.

The results of the examination of each postulant are reduced to writing, and all the trial papers produced during the session, which commences at eight in the morning and closes at four in the afternoon, are annexed to the report, which concludes with a written statement of the reasons for or against inscribing the name of the postulant on the list of candidates. This list, when completed, is sent to the director general, to assist him in preparing his list of candidates most deserving of promotion, which is submitted annually to the minister, accompanied with all the documents necessary to enlighten him as to their respective qualifications.

The number of supernumeraries never exceeds a twentieth of the whole number employed in the bureaus, and a preference is always given, other things being equal, to the sons of persons in good standing already in the service.

The supernumeriat never lasts less than a year, during which period the successful candidate is detailed for service either in the bureau of the central administration, in the bureaus of direction, or in the principal receiving bureaus to await a vacancy, when his services will begin to receive compensation.

The mode of examination which I have described is designed exclusively for candidates entering the bureau or sedentary service, whether in Paris or the departments.

For admission to the brigadier active service there is no supernumeriat, and the terms of admission are less rigorous, inasmuch as the service exacts a lower grade of accomplishments. The organization of brigades is based upon a general system of surveillance, to prevent fraud and contraband; it consists of a single line of posts or brigades, as they are termed, along the sea-coast, and a double line on the frontier.

To each brigade is assigned a determined tract to guard, called his penthieré, or beat. The brigades are composed of captains, lieutenants, brigadiers, sub-brigadiers, overseers, packers, weighers, storekeepers, boatmen, &c., &c.

To be admitted to the brigades it is necessary to be a Frenchman, 20 years of age at least, and not more than 25, except those who have been soldiers, who may be 29, if they apply the year of their leaving the army.

The sons of persons in the service are sometimes received as young as 18 in capacity of sailors and overseers, on half wages; but their service before 20 does not count towards their retirement, and the number of such can never exceed two per cent. of the effective force of the brigade. The postulants must produce certificates of good conduct, either from the mayor of the place where they usually reside, or from the regiment in which they have served, and a preference is given to persons who have served in the army or navy.

They are visited by a physician in the presence of a captain in the revenue service, who gives a certificate as to their physical condition, their instruction, and their intelligence, and such guarantees of their morality as are to be found in their social relations and past habits and position. They must know how to read and write, though in the case of simple marines the standard of clerical accomplishments is not very high; they must also be unmarried.

Persons entering the brigades or active service cannot compete for places in the bureau or sedentary service, which leads to the highest grades of the service, until they have reached the grade of sub-inspector; but any accomplishments they bring into the brigade service will count in their promotion to this point, as well as to their subsequent promotion, so that no person begins in so low a position that he cannot aspire to the highest; and he is encouraged constantly by the example and success of those who have preceded him, as in the case of the present director general, who, as I have already stated, entered the brigade service as a simple préposé or overseer.

The compensation, both in the active and sedentary service, is small for the first few years, never amounting to $200 a year; but the young officer knows that a respectable support is secured him for life if he is faithful and diligent, and whether he preserves or loses his health, and that his widow will be provided for if he dies a married man. He knows, also, that his promotion will depend upon his efficiency.

The hierarchical system of promotion in the French service is insisted upon with inflexible rigor. No one advances to a superior grade without having served at least two years in an inferior grade, nor to a superior class of the same grade without at least one year's service in the inferior class.

At the beginning of every six months the sedentary inspectors, or sub-inspectors, and the principal receivers, address to the division inspector an "etat," or list of the officers under their orders who seem to possess the necessary qualifications to pass into a more elevated class, or to be promoted to a superior grade. For a model of these "etats" see the blank hereto annexed, marked A, which is designated in the official series of blanks as Serié E, No. 82. I had it filled out with the "etat" of a single employé verificateur, in order to render it more intelligible In this list they state, in a precise though summary way, whether, in their opinion, the employé deserves promotion on account of the length or distinction of service. The division inspector, on the receipt of these lists, prepares a similar table for his arrondissement, which he addresses to his director, accompanied with the "etats" of the principal receivers and sub-inspectors, and his own observations and recommendations in regard to the officers under his order. Finally, the director transmits these "etats" to the administration, with what is termed an "etat general," containing his views of the merits and demerits of the candidates recommended for promotion, and a special "etat," to embrace the clerks in his bureau entitled to promotion. These "etats" relate exclusively to the bureau service. A similar system of reports is required through the proper hierarchy for the brigade service. At the end of each year the director general makes a list of vacancies which are expected to occur during the following year, and another one of all those who have been found to possess the qualifications for promotion. This list is sent to the minister, and when a vacancy occurs in any of those places, (very few in number,) the nomination to which is made by the Emperor or the minister of finance, the director general selects three candidates from the list referred to for promotion, and the minister selects one of the three for the vacancy. If, in an extraordinary case, there should seem to be occasion to make an exception in favor of some person not on the promotion list, whose services merited immediate recompense, the exception must be made the subject of a special decree, and the reasons for it assigned in writing by the minister. No nomination, however, is ever made by the director general, or by any one below him, of any person not on "Etats" No. 82. Thus, every man's promotion mainly depends upon the impression his official conduct leaves upon those superior officers with whom he is in immediate contact, and who have the best means of appreciating him.

As an additional precaution, and for the better enlightenment of the director general, on the 1st of January of each year the inspectors, sub-inspectors, and principal receivers, prepare what are termed "*signolements moraux*" in regard to all persons under their immediate orders who had received commissions from the director general, or from the minister. These reports are expected to state, with exactness and impartiality, whether the employé has received a liberal education; if he has initiative discernment, firmness, deliberation; the grade of classic and administrative instruction; as to his administrative conduct; if he is zealous, assiduous; if his private life is creditable to the administration; as to the position of his family: if he is married or single; if he has children, and what, if any, other charges; the extent of his personal resources; if he merits promotion; if he will accept it in any department of the service in Algeria and the colonies, for example, and to what grade he is equal; and, finally, for what sort of employ he possesses special aptitudes. It is expected that those should be specially named in this list toward whom the opinions of their superiors may have undergone a favorable change, in order that the previous records may not stand in the way of their future promotion, more especially if made from bad motives or without discrimination.

Further to assist the authorities in reaching accurate conclusions in regard to their agents, a system of annotations, or conduct record, has been adopted since 1802, which has been productive, it is said, of the happiest effects. A register is kept by every officer in command in the active or out-door service, who receives his appointment from the directors, of whom there are 31. In these registers an annotation is made of any grave negligence in the service, any want of subordination to superior officers or lack of respect to the public, any infraction of rules against passing the frontier, entering cabarets unnecessarily, drunkenness, or any scandalous conduct outside of those more serious offences which involve dismissal from the service, degradation, or surrender to the officers of justice. These annotations are transmitted hierarchically to the captain. The captain, after verifying the facts, sends it with his remarks to the inspector, who sends it back to him with authority to inscribe the annotation against the offender, if he finds the facts justify it; if not, he reserves his decision until he makes his next tour of inspection in that division.

If the annotation is inscribed, and while it remains, the subject of it is incapacitated for competing for promotion, and excluded from participation in certain gratifications, amounting to some 300,000 francs a year, which are divided among certain classes in the active service. A first annotation can only be removed by six months of unexceptionable conduct; a second, by a year; and a third, by 15 months.

The overseer who receives a fourth annotation for an offence similar to the one which provoked the preceding annotation, forfeits his commission; and for a second offence he is sent to a post of smaller pay, if there is any. The brigadier is degraded for the third annotation, on account of the same offence. Less offences are visited with reprimands, but the third reprimand in the course of the same year provokes an annotation.

Thus it happens that every six months from the day a young man enters the service until he leaves it, a careful record is made of every change in his conduct calculated to affect his value as a public servant. He is judged and reported upon every year or two by different persons, so that he never can be for any considerable period the victim of unjust prejudice or the object of an undeserved partiality. Officers who make these reports are rendered cautious in their judgments by the risk they run of having them received each successive year by officers of a higher grade and of more consideration, as the subject of them is promoted. These records remain as testimony not only for or against the officer reported upon, but for or against the fairness, the discrimination, and the vigilance of the officers reporting.

Thus every official phase of every man's career in the revenue service of France, for nearly a century, can be turned to and verified at a moment's notice, and the judgment of his superiors brought to a test which furnishes the highest possible guarantee against prejudice and favoritism. Thus the faithful servant of the government is secure, not only of a permanent position that cannot be seriously affected by any political vicissitudes, but he also has a prospect of promotion according to his merits, depending in the least possible degree upon political influence and personal favor. For this security he can afford to accept comparatively moderate compensation. The emoluments of a French revenue officer are scarcely half what are enjoyed by officers of the same grade in the United States; and yet, reckoning the cost of procuring the commission and the uncertainty of retaining it, the United States officer is not nearly as well paid as the French. Here is a list of the salaries paid to officers of the central administration in France. I give the amount in dollars, at the rate of five francs to the dollar.

Director general, $6,000 a year; administrators, $2,400; heads of bureaus, four classes, $1,800, $1,600, $1,400, $1,200; sub-heads, four classes, $1,100, $1,000, $900, $800; principal clerks, $700, $600, $540; expeditionaries, $480 to $240.

In the department service the salaries range as follows:

Directors, four classes, $2,400, $2,000, $1,800, $1,600; directors' clerks, divided into three grades of two classes each, receive from $600 down to $200, according to their rank. Inspectors, in three classes, receive, respectively, $1,200, $1,000, $900. The sub-inspectors, also composed of three classes, receive $700, $600, $500.

The receivers, divided into seven classes, receive salaries ranging from $1,200 to $500, and the assistant receives from $480 to $200. The controllers, consisting of four classes, receive from $600 to $480. The verifiers, in three classes, receive from $440 to $320 and less. The visitors, $200.

The captains receive from $480 to $400; the lieutenants from $320 to $240; brigadiers, $200 to $190; sub-brigadiers, from $180 to $170; overseers or préposés, sailors, &c., &c., $160 to $150; storekeepers, $200 to $180.

The receipt of any sort of present or gratuity in recompense for their services, except from the state, is strictly prohibited, and any person guilty of the offence is visited with a fine, and in some cases with imprisonment.

Besides these salaries the officers of the French customs and their widows are further secured against the contingencies of the future by retiring pensions.

At the age of 60, and after 30 years' service, a right to a retiring pension, *par ancienneté*, as it is called, is complete. Those who have been 15 years in the active, as distinguished from the sedentary, service, can retire at 55 years of age, after 25 years' service. In case of inability to discharge his duty from moral or physical causes, the full term of service is not required as a condition of being retired. The pension is based upon the average of regular emoluments received and enjoyed by the candidate for the six years preceding his application. The pension is the one-sixtieth of the average pay for each year of service, except in case of 25 years in the active service, when a small percentage is added. In no case can the pension exceed three-fourths of the average pay, nor the following maximums:

Pay	$200 and under	....	$150
"	202 to	$480, ⅓ of the the average pay, not to go below $150.	
"	480 to	640	320
"	640 to	1,600, half the average pay.	
"	1,600 to	1,800	800
"	1,800 to	2,100	900
"	2,100 to	2,400	1,000
"	above $2,400	....	1,200

As a partial indemnity to the state for these pensions, each officer bears a light tax every year upon his salary while he is in the service.

All the law and regulations upon this subject will be found in Delandre, pages 98 to 113 inclusive.

Such is the system by which France trains a class of picked men for her revenue service from their early manhood; profits by the labor of the best years of their lives, and by all the experience and skill which they possess and acquire during the 20 or 30 years they are in her employ, by a well-digested system of compensations and discipline; contrives to weed out all who prove unprofitable, and, at an expense far below what the same service coul l be procured for any private business, to provide herself with a corps of from 20,000 to 30,000 men remarkable in every respect for their intelligence, their efficiency, and their fidelity.

I have been at particular pains to inform myself in regard to the fidelity of the service, and what, if any, kind of corruption prevailed in any of its departments. I was assured by Mr. Masseron that such a thing as fraud or corruption of any kind was almost unknown. The system of inspection is so rigorous, the reports so frequent, and the consequences of fixing an act of corruption or even of neglect upon any one so fatal to him, that it is impossible for an evil-disposed officer to get up through the lower grades, where the opportunities for committing fraud are most limited, without being detected, degraded, or dismissed. Any man who has an imperfect appreciation of the value of a good character, even in matters of minor importance, will be constantly thrown back, and four annotations for the same offence dismiss him from the service. Under such a system advancement becomes impossible except upon ample proofs of good character and capacity.

I have confirmed this impression from other sources. An American gentleman, who has been largely engaged in commerce in Paris, assured me that in all the principal custom-houses of the world, of which he had a large experience, he had found a little money, judiciously bestowed, would hasten the delivery of goods and secure other important facilities in the transaction of custom-house business, but that in France he could do nothing with money; a polite and respectful appeal to those whose service he required was the only stimulant he had ever found of any avail. During my residence here I have never heard of a French custom-house officer being successfully approached with money or a bribe of any sort.

The French custom service is very numerous. The following is about the force now employed:

Administrative and collective service:		Active or brigadier service:	
Directors	31	Captains	279
Clerks of direction	167	Brigadiers and sub-brigadiers	5,087
Principal and subordinate receivers	790	Lieutenants	545
Clerks of all classes	644	Overseers of all classes	17,599
Inspectors	95	Mounted men	52
Sub-inspectors	82	Cockswains	394
Controllers	86	Sailors	1,420
Verifiers and visitors	714		25,374
	2,609		27,983

A large force is necessary for a service conducted with so much system, and where so much work is required; for about everything that is done by an officer in command is reported upon to some superior in writing. It is in this way that the supervision and accountability is rendered so perfect.

But there is another reason why a larger force is employed than the simple collection of the revenues absolutely requires. The revenue force of France is a military as well as civil organization. Every man in it is a soldier, and capable of taking the command to which his rank in the service entitles him. If he has not seen active service, he has, at least, been duly trained and disciplined to arms. The advantage of this is, that the force thus employed and scattered all along the frontiers, both by land and sea, and familiar with the country, constitutes a reserve of incalculable value in case of a foreign war. It can garrison all the frontiers by land and sea, and thus liberate the whole regular army for any service to which it may be called. This actually occurred during the Italian campaign of 1860. Paris, and many other parts of France, were exclusively garrisoned by the revenue force. This secondary duty does not interfere with the primary duties of the service, because till their beat is threatened with invasion they can attend to their regular business as usual, and when that is threatened, of course, all commerce across the threatened point is suspended, and the brigades are occupied in watching hostile soldiers instead of smugglers.

Permit me to conclude this report by stating my conviction, that there is much in the organization of the French revenue service by which the United States might profit, and I deeply regret that my ignorance of the details of our system does not permit me to point out more specifically the lessons to be derived from it. I may say, however, that in my judgment its greatest merits consist—

1st. In the perpetuity of the tenure of office, by virtue of which the country profits by the accumulated skill and experience of its servants.

2d. Its system of promotion secures the most competent and faithful men for the higher and more responsible grades of service.

3d. It takes only young men into service, and thus secures to the state the benefit of their service during the best years of their lives; and,

4th. It guarantees to them a constantly improving livelihood, and in case of accident, provision for their families, upon terms which furnish the incumbent a constant inducement to do his duty faithfully, and to render distinguished service when an opportunity is offered to him, and in turn secures that service to the state at very advantageous rates.

Unhappily, I fear, none of these advantages can be grafted upon our system of quadrennial changes in the administration. The whole value of the French system depends upon the permanent tenure of the service. The moment that is rendered insecure the whole fabric crumbles to pieces; and unless some method can be devised by which those who enter the subordinate departments of the United States government can be guaranteed a similar permanence, we must pay much higher salaries, get very inferior service, waste our experience, and, withal, fall a prey to the infinite brood of frauds which inevitably result from the constant conflict between interest and duty which our execrable practice of mutation in office engenders.

In confirmation of the high estimate I have formed of the douane organization of France, it is proper that I should state that the administration has been applied to by several foreign governments, including Italy, Russia, and Turkey, for working details of its operation, and for skilled officers of the French service to aid in transplanting it to their soil. One of these officers is now in Mexico, organizing a new revenue system for that country entirely upon the French model.

Yours, very respectfully,

JOHN BIGELOW,
United States Consul.

Hon. WILLIAM H. SEWARD,
Secretary of State.

Extract from Delandre, Traité Pratique des Douanes: Paris, 1858.—*Tome* 1, pp. 96–142.

ORGANIZATION.—FORCE EMPLOYED.

The general organization comprehends the graduated succession of offices, the prerogatives of the several agents, and the obligations imposed upon each within his individual responsibility, and the duties and the rights in respect of third parties.

Whatever may be the organization and the prerogatives, the obligations of each agent arise more especially out of the instructions he receives, varying, of course, with the relative force employed in each locality.

Theoretically, the corps employed in active labors must be distinguished from that whose duty is supervision and control; and it always is so in those great custom-houses where the value of the merchandise justifies great expense; but in many localities the departments will be combined, more or less.

Being compelled to provide for ever-pressing necessities and occurrences, varying to infinity, the administration must hold itself ready to employ men according to their real ability, while mindful of their acquired positions, without ever allowing these to interpose an obstacle to the rapid and continuous service of the establishment.

Higher administration.—The administration of custom-houses is directed and supervised, under the authority of the minister of finance, by a director general.

The minister of finance appoints, upon the recommendation of the director general, the heads of bureau in all the divisions of the central administration, inspectors, and principal receivers of the first, second, third, and fourth class.

The director general appoints, in virtue of his commission from the minister, the incumbents of all offices inferior to those designated above, except that the directors have the privilege of appointing to subordinate places in brigades, up to the rank of brigadier or patron, inclusively.

The director general, after advising with the administrative council, recalls the appointments, or dismisses the employés whose nomination is assigned to him.

He can also suspend the other employés, provided he immediately informs the minister, who decides the case.

Privileges of departments and bureaus of the central authority.—Central bureau and bureau of appointments.

1. Presentation of names for nomination to office by the supreme ruler, or by the minister.

2. Nomination to places in the bureau, and of officials for the management of custom-houses.

3. Nomination to all the employments, and to the duty of selling tobacco, (in the department of indirect taxation.)

4. Admission to the corps of supernumeraries; certificates of desert and lists of promotion; honorary badges; reception and transmission of despatches.

Every demand for the degradation or dismission of an employé should be the subject of a report drawn up by the proximate superior of the accused person. This report, backed by the opinion of the intermediate heads, is transmitted to the director by the inspector of divisions, who accepts their conclusions only after a thorough examination, and after having heard the defence of the accused. If the latter is to be degraded or dismissed, the notice conveying this decision sets forth the grounds of such action, in order that he may be well informed of the cause of the proceeding against him, through a duplicate remitted along with the notification. All documents important to the understanding of the affair, especially the interrogatories, (which must always be reduced to writing,) should be arranged in a file by themselves.

The director ought to be acquainted with the kind of work performed by each person under his control. His previous consent is necessary to any changes among employés of the same grade when their effect is the acquisition or loss of any advantage: and he may always rectify proceedings adopted by the heads, even within the limits of their legitimate authority.

When the director deems it necessary to reinforce the service at any locality by detaching to it, temporarily, an employé of bureau, he must inform the administration of it by a special letter. All detachment of an employé with a view to private advantage is strictly forbidden.

Inspectors.—The inspector of a division, being superior of the department at the head of which he is placed, extends his activity over the entire field of service committed to him, while he watches all its details of execution. He checks the accounts of the principal and subordinate receivers, whose cash it is his duty to verify; and he holds these accountants responsible for sums whose receipt may have been lost sight of by a train of material errors.

The different employés are installed by the divisionary inspector. It is the inspector who, in case of necessity, suspends from duty the employés whose action it is requisite to arrest. He designates temporary employés for duties below those of principal receiver or sub inspector, (subject to the approbation of the director,) and gives directions in all emergencies which may arise in the service, as in case of accident happening to employés.

To diminish the difficulties of inspection and collection through the assistance of employés, by means of facilities which they learn to create for themselves, and, above all, by striving that the intercourse between officials and those paying duty may be always agreeable; to watch over the former in their public and private conduct, as well as in the habits of expense existing in their families; to estimate their relative merit and their rectitude; to distribute among them, equitably, rewards and punishments: such are some of the principal duties of inspectors, duties the performance of which, if characterized by originality, by acuteness, by firmness, by moderation, and by a severe impartiality, has a most salutary influence upon the service.

As a whole, the inspectors should exercise their functions with a view to the interest of all, under the impulse of the director, to whom they are bound to render an exact report of the condition of the service under their control, and which, with this exception, is committed wholly to them.

Without prescribing the mode according to which the inspectors are to distribute their rounds, the administration rigidly insists that these shall be performed in a thorough and efficient manner, and that the examinations shall embrace only the number of stations that may be included without diminishing their efficiency.

It may be required, from the zeal of inspectors, that they give information, as speedily as possible, of the passage of contraband goods in considerable quantities; but it would be impossible, on such occasions, precisely to determine what are excusable delays, the value of an early discovery depending upon the nature of the circumstances and the results obtained. Such questions can only be referred to the decision of the director, who, with the report before him, must judge whether the inspector's examination was delayed too long, and address to him appropriate observations thereupon.

In those large ports where there exists a resident inspector as well as a general or divisionary inspector, the first, charged with the duty of giving orders and superintending their execution, presides at the daily distribution of the employés belonging to the residence, bureaus, and brigades; directs these officials, according to his single pleasure and at his own responsibility, in all the parts and all the details; decides directly on the daily exigencies which occur, in order to prevent delays, and inspects all the operations, except the money transactions, of the receiver general.

The local inspector is under the supervision of the principal inspector; but he owes him deference rather than obedience. Since both these heads are placed under the director, it is to the latter that the local inspector gives an account of the service, and applies for assistance in doubtful cases.

General and permanent decisions upon important points in all parts of the port service, or, otherwise, the code or series of directions which is most appropriate, must be determined by the director, with the concurrence of the local and principal inspectors.

Measures which, although general, are of minor importance, may be temporarily ordered by one or the other inspector, mutual consultation and finally gaining the consent of the director being supposed; but the initiative belongs to the principal director in matters relating to brigades, and to the local inspector in those which concern the bureaus, those of receipt excepted.

The local inspector regulates and follows out the daily application of the ordinances in all details, according to necessity.

The local inspector ought, by inspections as frequent as possible, to assure himself of the regularity of the different operations, accomplished or not.

The under-inspectors, assistants of the local inspector, watch and control, like him, not only the operations of the port but also the papers of the interior districts, and render to him each day an account of the result of their action. It should be remarked that in large custom-houses, examination of the sections can take place only on working days.

If the principal inspector should not consult with the local inspector upon any doubtful subject, he must refer it to the director.

On account of the importance of their work at the desk, the local inspectors alone can demand the services of an employé of bureau, or of a supernumerary, for the despatch of their manuscript labors.

Sub-inspectors.—Local sub-inspectors are attached to the most important custom-houses. The local sub-inspector, whatever may be his salary, is independent of the principal receiver, or subordinate, but is not his superior.

Being especially charged with the direction and control of the service of inspection, the sub-inspector has in other matters merely the power of oversight, without being able to extend it to the supervision of the receiver's cash. He assigns and distributes, according to his pleasure, the duties of inspectors of merchandise, whose immediate superior he is. He extends his oversight to all the other employés, and rectifies and regulates all branches of the service, (except the state of the cash,) the papers of the receiver, the registry of receipts, the notes and vouchers of expenses, extracts of statistics, &c. To repeat: while the receiver, chief or subordinate, directs, oversees, and controls the whole custom-house, except the inspecting department, it is the duty of the sub-inspector to oversee the examination of goods, and to superintend the whole custom-house, the papers of the several departments, except the actual condition of the cash. This simultaneous surveillance and control, which makes up the province of the inspector, cannot fail to be advantageous to the service.

At those places where the magnitude of business does not require the appointment of a separate official for the care of the papers of inspection, that custody devolves upon the sub-inspector, who ought to review all payments before transmission to the receiver, and that in such a manner that there shall be no delay in expediting business.

In every custom-house controlled by a principal or subordinate receiver, whatever may be his salary, and by an under-inspector, if the latter discovers any irregularities in the accounts of the receiver, he must limit himself to reporting them.

The sub-inspector designates the examiner, who shall look into the goods, assures himself that in the space of one or two months every employé shall examine a nearly equal number of ships or vehicles, and takes the precautions necessary to conceal the knowledge who shall be the examiner employed in any particular case. Whenever it is possible, he will be present at inspections. As soon as a vessel arrives he demands the manifest, clearance, &c., in order to compare them. He ascertains whether the manifest is signed by the captain. He takes care that the ships be discharged in the order of the numbers indicated on the list.

General reports of the service are made out every three months, and addressed in duplicate, to the director, by the divisionary or local inspectors, and by the sub-inspectors, local or divisionary.

The divisionary inspectors and sub-inspectors present for each month, in the first week following, a summary exposé, in simple duplicate, exhibiting, first, a chronological statement of the circuits performed, with the specification of the bureaus and stations visited each day, and, moreover, an enumeration of the portions of the residentiary service which have been examined. Second, a tabular view, recapitulating the circuits of the captains, lieutenants, and inferior officers, and the amount of their service.

Inspectors being required to oversee each month, and in an exhaustive manner, all parts of the service, all the bureaus and all the posts of their division, must declare if they have omitted any in their examination, and, when that case occurs, for what reason. These reports should enable the administration itself to judge what may have been the individual activity of the heads of service.

Bureau service.—The bureaus, according to their importance, are composed of principal or subordinate receivers, comptrollers, general agents, examiners, (in the principal bureaus,) searchers, (in the lower bureaus,) and clerks.

Whatever may be the graduation of salaries, the receiver is theoretically superior to the sub-inspector, although occasionally, in view of prerogative, the sub-inspector, when he supervises a division, or acts in virtue of a special order from the inspector, may be called to verify the transactions and the cash of the responsible party. In other circumstances these two are completely independent of each other.

The privileges of principal receivers vary according to the locality. In custom-houses of the first-class, when there is a local inspector, the general receiver being engrossed by the work of receipt, takes no part in the other operations of the bureau, while the inspector directs and oversees in his place.

In other custom-houses all the labor is under his direction, (except that of inspection when there is a sub-inspector,) superintendence, and control, and he can exert authority over all classes of employés without regard to their special duties. The functions of the receiver-general are, specifically, to report in condensed form the receipts and condition of all the bureaus of his principality, meet all its expenses, pay over all funds, prosecute all litigations in the courts, never proceeding, however, in such matter without the sanction of higher authority, nor neglecting, in case of necessity, the help of professional advocates. He has the direction and assistance of the officials in respect to giving or withholding credit, depositing in warehouses, giving certificates of deposit and other kinds, and he corresponds with the director on all matters appertaining thereto. His immediate superior is the divisionary inspector, who examines his work, but cannot give him orders, except for the execution of legislative or imperial ordinances, unless, indeed, some exceptional uncertainty should arise, for the solution of which the receiver-general requires the advice of the divisionary inspector. On the receiver-general devolves the duty of drawing up the list of appointments of bureau employés.

The receivers must ascertain whether the accounts of payments sent to them are well vouched; that is to say, if they are free from errors of computation, if the examiner has made a correct application of the tariff; if he has taken into view abatements on account of tare, advance of price, &c.

The receiver makes application of the statutes on his own responsibility. But he must report to the general or divisionary inspector, as if to the director, the exceptional decisions which he makes on his own responsibility.

In the prosecution of litigated cases he is the natural proxy of the administration, which always makes choice of his house for a residence.

Independently of the receipt of funds, responsibility for them, and the care of litigation, the receiver-general is intrusted with the correspondence on all matters of business, which, although instituted in great custom-houses under the supervision of the local inspector, may be considered as of the nature of liens on the treasury; for example, the recovery of duties, the exaction of certificates, warehousing, the payment of insurance.

The comptrollers, the chief clerks, the examiners in large custom-houses, the special agents who are associated with them, and the subordinate receivers whose salary is less than 2,000 francs, may be competitors for the offices of sub-inspector, and principal receiver of the fifth and sixth class.

Supernumeraries.—Every person who wishes a position in either of the bureaus must begin as a supernumerary.

The candidates for the situation of supernumerary must submit to a previous examination.

The decisions of the minister of finance, made at the suggestion of the general director, fix the standard of intelligence demanded from the candidates, the conditions of age and fitness required in order to be admitted to this examination, and designate the persons in whose presence it must take place.

The result of the examinations is transmitted to the central administration, who, each year, prepare the list of candidates recognized as admissible. This list is submitted to the minister of finance, who sanctions it, and decides the number of candidates called to fill vacancies which may occur during the year.

Admission to the supernumerariat in the management of custom-houses takes place according to the following rules:

Each competitor is required to certify:

1st. That he is at least 18 years old, and not more than 25; and to prove this, he must produce a certificate, in due form, of the time of his birth.

2d. That he is a native of France.

3d. That he is exempt from all constitutional weakness, and from all physical deformity.

4th. That his character and mode of life are unexceptionable.

5th. That he possesses, either personally or by inheritance, the means of securing his livelihood during the period of his supernumeraryship.

6th. That he has the knowledge and ability requisite for the position.

This last requirement must be determined by an examination before a special committee.

The committee for examination of candidates is composed (in the central administration) of a comptroller, three heads of bureaus, and an under head. At the headquarters of each directorship, of a director, an inspector, a receiver-general, a sub-inspector, and of the head clerks of the bureaus of that directorship.

The presence of three members of the committee is sufficient for it to proceed to business.

The presidency belongs to the employé highest in rank among those present.

This rule has been introduced in view of an event which might happen, namely, the absence from some unforeseen cause of one or two members of the committee; but, generally, in the directorships the three highest members conduct the examination, the two lower members being retained to supply a deficiency.

It is very expressly urged upon the higher officers who are required to participate in these examinations, to make it a most serious duty to be present always, except in case of absolute inability, and to take an active part in examining candidates. An interest of great importance attaches to this duty being well performed, that of possessing a good corps of successors to the administrative body.

The members of the examining committees are appointed each year by the director-general, who fixes also the periods for the assembling of the committees.

In mixed directorships, the committee of examination is composed of a director, an inspector of customs, an inspector of indirect taxes, the chief receivers of the two sorts of service done at the residence, of a manager or superior agent for tobacco, at those stations where there exists a bureau of cultivation or of manufacture.

The first condition of admission to examination is, that every candidate express himself willing, if he should be received, to make his residence wherever the administration shall judge best to designate him. The only exception is in favor of the sons of employés, and for reasons which must be previously referred to the director-general.

Before proceeding to the examination, the director shall make known to the candidates that, if any among them are willing to take their station in the department of indirect taxation, this concession shall make their admission as candidates twice as easy, and their appointment as supernumeraries more prompt.

The programme of questions is narrow and simple. The questions are short and of easy solution. The trial, once begun, proceeds from the first moment continuously, and without interruption. Therefore, the session opens at 8 o'clock in the morning, and closes at 4 o'clock in the afternoon. Only, the next day, the candidates may be examined beyond the specifications of the programme, upon other subjects on which they may be prepared.

A distinct and separate report is drawn up by the examining committee upon each of the three branches of service, customs, indirect taxes, and tobacco.

The candidates who, having been notified of the time, do not directly appear, are held to have forfeited their right to examination.

The programme of subjects at the examination for admission is as follows:

1. A page of writing, under dictation, on paper not ruled; the candidate not being allowed to correct his orthography by means of any book or foreign aid.

2. The same page recopied in a neat hand.

3. Grammatical analysis of a part of the text of this page.

4. Computations in the first four rules, theory of proportions, solution of many problems in elementary arithmetic.

5. Knowledge and system of measures.

6. Drawing up notes and accounts according to given model.

7. Solution of various questions upon physical and political geography.

8. Composition of a letter or a note upon a given subject.

The candidate can be examined, besides, upon other subjects, indicated by himself as being objects of his past study, as the living and dead languages, law, chemistry, natural history, linear drawing, &c.

The results of the examination of each candidate are stated in a report, to which are annexed the written answers presented during the continuance of the session.

If the candidate is a bachelor of letters, a copy of his diploma, certified to by the president of the examining committee, is annexed to the report.

The report ought to contain an opinion whether the candidate is or is not worthy to be admitted as a supernumerary. In cases of equal merit, preference is given to sons of employés of known desert. Each committee should draw up, besides, a list of the candidates it has examined, classing them in order of merit. These lists and reports, addressed to the director general, are used to form a general list of the candidates, which is submitted annually to the minister.

This general list is accompanied by all the information and documents necessary to inform the minister respecting the fitness of each of the candidates.

As an exception to the previous rules, the conditions of examination and supernumeraryship are not imposed upon officers and brigadiers of the active service who, disabled by wounds or physical infirmities from the discharge of their duties, are fit to be usefully employed in the administrative branch, or as collectors, and have been designated for this purpose in the lists of promotion.

The number of supernumeraries in the custom-houses is fixed at the twentieth part of all the employés of bureaus.

Each supernumerary must hold his place a year at least.

Supernumeraries are attached to the bureau of central administration, the bureaus of direction, or of principal receipts.

It is for the heads of the service a duty to which they are in honor bound to watch over supernumeraries with solicitude, both as regards their work and their conduct.

Admission to the corps of supernumeraryship is secured by order from the director general. The director in whose division any person is nominated for admission should address to the administration (personal division) a sheet of recommendations relative to him.

No person can be permitted to work in the bureaus, of whatever kind, unless an employé or a supernumerary.

It is not allowable to permit persons not employed in the service to mark a despatch, or any part of it. The employés must therefore transcribe the authenticating marks, and the weights in gross of the packages, upon the certificates of transit, or of exchange of warehouse, as well as upon the supplementary sheets attached to their despatches.

THE CIVIL SERVICE.

The term "civil service" is a phrase popularly used for general convenience, and represents the large body of men by whose labors the executive business of the country is carried on. It has been officially stated that the civil service includes more than 50,000 officers, which would make it a class more than twice as numerous as the clergy. Deducting, however, 4,000 as office-keepers, messengers, &c., 17,000 as inferior revenue officers, postmen, &c., and 15,000 artificers and laborers employed in the various government dock-yards, we may calculate that there are, in round numbers 17,000 civil servants of the higher class who are engaged in the various public offices of the United Kingdom. It must, however, be remembered that the higher and the lower, the intellectual and the mechanical, departments under the crown, are all branches of the civil service. A secretary to the treasury and a tidewaiter in the customs, for instance, are equally component parts of the civil service; yet it would be difficult to quote two members of the community who have less in common, or to imagine two situations in life imposing duties and exacting requirements more thoroughly dissimilar on all essential points. The discrepancies and minor distinctions of the civil service are innumerable. Each office has its specialty, and every department is governed by its own rules and traditions, as its members are remunerated by distinct rates of pay. The term "civil service," therefore, represents a thing heterogeneous in its nature, embracing posts of a very different *status* and widely varying value. The object of this work is so to classify these situations as to enable the aspirant for government employment to ascertain at a glance the respective advantages held out to him by each department of the state, the indispensable qualifications he must himself possess before he is eligible for admission into such department, and the particular channel of patronage through which he may best hope to obtain a nomination.

In estimating the advantages of the civil service, and particularly if we compare its attractions with those offered by the professions, it is necessary to remember that, though the remuneration may not be high as compared with the law, it is, in the superior offices at least, high as compared with that of the army and navy, and even of the church; but, practically speaking, the money to be earned is the solitary attraction. A clerk in a public office may not even dream of fame to be acquired in that capacity. He labors in an obscurity as profound as it is unavoidable. His official character is absorbed in that of his superior. He must devote his talents and his skill to measures, some of which he may probably disapprove, without having the slightest power to prevent them; and to some of which he will most essentially contribute, without having any share whatever in the credit of them. He must listen silently to praises bestowed on others, which his pen may have earned for him; and if any accident should make him notorious enough to become the suspected author of any unpopular act, he must submit silently to the reproach, even though it be totally unmerited by him. These are, indeed, the indispensable disadvantages of a clerk in a public office, and no man of sense or temper will complain of them. On the other hand it must be remembered that a person is eligible for admission into the civil service at an early age. He is not required to have taken an university degree, or to have gone through a professional course of education. No outfit is required; he is not compelled to procure uniforms or horses, to hire chambers, or to buy books. He avoids the vicissitudes and uncertainties of an open profession; his advancement, if his conduct is good and his attendance regular, is a matter of course. His position may be obscure, but if he is not praised for his acts, neither is he blamed for them; if he does not enjoy personal distinction, he avoids personal responsibility with respect to the public at large. The income of the civil servant may be more moderate than that of the successful mercantile man, but it is fixed and certain; and when declining health or waning powers warn him of the necessity for rest and quiet, he has the prospect, nay the certainty, of a provision for the close of life, and this is perhaps the strongest motive offered by the state for the fidelity of its servants.

The leading members of the civil service consist of two classes; the one strictly civil, and the other political; the one permanent, the other changing with the change of ministry. Some departments and offices are presided over by persons who have won their way to their present high position by struggles in the House of Commons, and who hold their offices only as long as the party to which they have attached themselves remains in power. Other offices are presided over by persons who are virtually appointed for life, and some of whom owe their elevation to a similar political career; others there are (and it speaks well for the country that this is an increasing class) who, having worked their way up from the inferior classes, now preside over the office in which they commenced early in life at the drudgery of the desk. It is scarcely to be expected, and perhaps not to be wished, that the pressure of the political party which is in the ascendant should not make itself felt in the first choice of candidates for government appointments. The nominations to clerkships in the public offices are accordingly made in the two following manners: Where the office is under a political head, the appointment is in general made by the head of the department; where it is not under a political head, the appointment is in general made by the prime minister, who acts through one of the parliamentary secretaries of the treasury. The numerous appointments of the subordinate officers of the customs and inland revenue departments are made in the latter manner. With regard to the post office, which revenue department is under a political head, a portion of the officers are appointed by the postmaster general himself, and a portion upon the nomination of the secretary to the treasury.*

Government situations are ordinarily obtained this wise: A member of Parliament, whose political opinions coincide with those held by the party in power, is asked by an influential constituent to get a place in a government office for a relation or a friend. The member of Parliament applies to the parliamentary secretary of the treasury, who has the distribution of patronage, or to the political head of some department. The secretary to the treasury, or the head of the department, willing to gratify a parliamentary supporter, accedes to the request, and presents the member's *protégé* with a *nomination* to one of the junior clerk-ships in his gift. The person nominated does not, however, as a matter of course, enter the public service, for *no interest, however powerful*, can confirm an appointment unless the nominee is able to obtain a certificate of fitness from the commissioners of the civil service appointed by the crown.† Before granting their certificate the commissioners ascertain—

First. That the nominee is within the limits of the age prescribed for the department to which he desires to be admitted.

Secondly. That he is free from any physical defect or disease which would be likely to interfere with the proper discharge of his duties.

Thirdly. That his character is such as to qualify him for public employment, and

Fourthly. That he possesses the necessary knowledge and ability for the proper discharge of his official duties.

Different requirements are needed in different, and even in cognate offices, although certain standard every-day qualifications are equally demanded in all. These indispensable qualifications have been established by the various heads of departments, and are rigidly enforced by the examiners of the civil service commission. The examiners are men of indisputable learning and integrity, and there can be no doubt that they impartially admit into the service every nominee possessing the necessary skill and knowledge prescribed for the particular branch to which he may be appointed, and peremptorily reject every candidate who falls below that standard. The functions of the civil service commissioners end, however, with the examination of the candidate and the report on his fitness. When the person nominated has proved, by certificates, that he is within the prescribed limit of age, and is reported to have the requisite degree of constitutional vigor, and the necessary intellectual and educational endowments, he enters upon a period of probation, during which his conduct and capacity for the transaction of business is subjected to such tests as the chief of his department may think fit. If found competent, his appointment, which has been hitherto conditional, is now confirmed, and the responsibility of governing his conduct, and of his subsequent promotions, rests exclusively with the head of his office. Even the annual increase of salary is dependent on the certificate of the chief of the department that his conduct during the past year has been satisfactory. Each clerk is thus left to work his way freely on under the hourly observation of his colleagues and superiors, and by officially educating himself as he progresses from one stage to another, he is fitted, should he be called upon, to undertake the higher duties of the department.

It is hardly necessary to state that the primary appointments to the civil service are to junior clerkships; that in nearly every office an annual increase of salary is usually accorded to each official until he arrives at the maximum of his class; and that when this is reached, it is only as vacancies occur, through the death or retirement of his seniors, that any further augmentation of income can be attained.

---

* See Treasury.   † See Civil Service Commission.

HER MAJESTY'S CIVIL SERVICE COMMISSIONERS.

RIGHT HON. SIR EDWARD RYAN.
SIR JOHN GEORGE SHAW LEFEVRE, K. C. B.

SECRETARY: John G. Maitland, esq.
REGISTRAR: Horace Mann, esq., Barrister-at-law.

The examinations are conducted by the assistant examiners to the commission, with the occasional aid of other gentlemen, when the number of simultaneous candidates or subjects renders such aid necessary.

ASSISTANT EXAMINERS.

Theodore Walrond, esq., M. A., late Fellow of Baliol College, Oxford.
Edward Headlam, esq., M. A., Fellow of St. John's College, Cambridge.

EMPLOYED OCCASIONALLY IN GENERAL SUBJECTS.

G. Brodrick, esq., M. A., Fellow of Merton College, Oxford.
S. Butler, esq., M. A., late Scholar of Trinity College, Cambridge.
G. W. Dasent, esq., D. C. L., of Magdalen Hall, Oxford.
W. F. Edwards, esq., M. A., Fellow of Trinity College, Cambridge.
F. Headlam, esq., M. A., Fellow of University College, Oxford.
G. D. Liveing, esq., M. A., Fellow of St. John's College, Cambridge.
E. Poste, esq., M. A., Fellow of Oriel College, Oxford.
G. Roberts, esq., M. A., Fellow of Magdalen College, Cambridge.

EMPLOYED FOR SPECIAL SUBJECTS.

Dutch.—Rev. Dr. Gehle.
Eastern Languages.—Colonel Ouseley; C. B. Eastwick, esq.; J. W. Redhouse, esq.
French.—M. Dupont.
German.—Max Muller, esq., M. A., Fellow of All Souls' College, and Professor of Modern European Languages, Oxford; Rev. Dr. Walbaum, Chaplain to the Prussian Legation; Herr Fontaine.
Italian.—Count Arrivabeue, Professor of Italian at University College, London.
Polish.—Major Czulczewski; M. Sosnowski.
Russian.—Rev. E. Popoff, Chaplain to the Russian Embassy.
Civil Engineering, &c.—Captain Galton, R. E., late Assistant Secretary to the Board of Trade.
Law.—H. S. Maine, esq., LL. D., Reader in Jurisprudence to the Hon. Society of the Middle Temple.
Physical Science.—M. H. N. Story-Maskelyne, esq., M. A., Deputy Reader in Mineralogy, Oxford.
Physiology.—Dr. W. B. Carpenter, F. R. S., Professor of Medical Jurisprudence in University College.

FOR EXAMINATIONS IN SCOTLAND.

A. C. Longmore, esq.

FOR EXAMINATIONS IN IRELAND.

G. Johnstone Stoney, esq., Secretary to the Queen's University in Ireland.

GOVERNMENT EXAMINATIONS.

Government situations are not in the gift of her Majesty's civil service commissioners. The functions of these commissioners, as regards first appointments to the civil service, are never exercised until after a nomination has been made to some vacant situation. It has been imagined that the power of making appointments is now taken away from the Crown and its officers and transferred to a body of examiners. This is not the fact. The conferring of certificates of eligibility is not patronage, but a judicial act. The examiners for honors at the universities of Oxford, Cambridge, or London have not the patronage of honors any more than the lord chancellor, when he decrees an estate to one person instead of another, has the patronage of the estate. The distinguishing feature of the present system of nominating to the civil service is merely that appointments are no longer bestowed by the independent exercise of unrestricted patronage, but are received subject to the limitations and conditions specified in the following extract from an order in counsel, dated 21st May, 1855:

And it is hereby ordered, that all such young men as may be proposed to be appointed to any junior situation in any department of the civil service shall, before they are admitted to probation, be examined by or under the directions of the said commissioners, and shall receive from them a certificate of qualifications for such situation.

And it shall be the duty of the commissioners in respect of every such candidate, before granting any such certificate aforesaid—

1st. To ascertain that the candidate is within the limits of age prescribed for the department to which he desires to be admitted.

2d. To ascertain that the candidate is free from any physical defect or disease which would be likely to interfere with the proper discharge of his duties.

3d. To ascertain that the character of the candidate is such as to fit him for public employment; and

4th. To ascertain that the candidate possesses the requisite knowledge and ability for the proper discharge of his official duties.

The standards of qualification are fixed by the various heads of departments, acting in co-operation with the civil service commissioners, and the list of prescribed subjects is in every instance liable to alteration. In all cases, whether of success or failure of candidates, the commissioners reserve to themselves alone the duty of granting or refusing a certificate; and for all acts done under their authority they hold themselves exclusively responsible.

There are two sorts of examinations in use at the civil service commission. The one of these is the competitive or maximum examination, which has been twice approved by resolutions of the House of Commons, and the object of which is to select the best of a given number of candidates; the other is the standard or minimum examination, the object of which is to ascertain that every candidate possesses, at the least, a certain prescribed amount of knowledge. The first of these, for example, is such an examination as determines who is senior wrangler at Cambridge; the second is such an examination as that of a candidate for a common pass degree at Oxford. By which of these two methods a candidate's fitness is tested is not determined by the commissioners, but depends solely upon the nomination he receives from the authorities. Competitive examinations are not open to all comers, able to fulfil the requisite conditions as to age, health, and character, but are limited to such persons as are nominated by the authorities, who have the duty of appointing to the vacant situations.* A competitive examination being fixed, the commissioners, instead of, as in the case of a simple nomination, conferring a certain guarantee of efficiency, are required to select the best among the candidates nominated to compete. The examiners receive from the commissioner clear and precise instructions, and carry them into execution with rigid fidelity. As far, therefore, as the matter can be settled by answers to questions, the comparative intellectual proportions of the candidates are determined with unerring precision, and their selection reduced to the simplicity and certainty of an arithmetical problem. Marks are given for each subject, and the successful candidate is the one who obtains the greatest number of marks in the aggregate, provided he has done sufficiently well in all the prescribed subjects. The last report of the commissioners shows that this is not always the case, and it sometimes happens that the candidate at the top of the list does not obtain the appointment, because he has failed to exhibit a minimum of proficiency in some one of the subjects.

The ordinary examinations are instituted for a double purpose :

First. To ascertain the candidate's fitness for the actual duties which he will be called upon to perform upon his first admission into office.

Secondly. To test his education and general intelligence.

For the first of these purposes he is almost invariably tested in writing, orthography, and arithmetic, a lower or higher degree of proficiency being required according to the situation to which he is appointed. In this class of subjects may also be included, in certain departments, book-keeping; in others, the power of making a précis of correspondence and official papers, or some acquaintance with English composition. For the second purpose of the examinations, various subjects have been selected by the different heads of departments; among them are the outlines of history, geography, Latin, or, as an alternative, some foreign language, either previously defined or left to the option of the candidate. Some of these prescribed subjects have not a direct relation to the business to be transacted, but are intended as tests of education and intellect. The commissioners consider them extremely useful, both in determining the positive merits of a nominated candidate and in ascertaining the relative merits of candidates in a competitive examination.

In all examinations, whether competitive or otherwise, the marks of merit are so arranged as to give due weight to excellence in strictly practical acquirements, as contradistinguished from the subjects denoting intellectual cultivation; and it may be added that, apart from actual information or the knowledge of particular facts, the general intelligence, good sense, and good taste of the candidate, as manifested in this manner of treating the subjects proposed to him, are not without weight in the assignment of marks.

The examination in extra subjects is an important item in the existing arrangements. The commissioners consider it of advantage, both to the public service and to the candidates themselves, that in addition to the subjects prescribed by the departments to which they are appointed, opportunity should be afforded them of showing their ability and acquirements in other branches of knowledge. Candidates are therefore allowed and encouraged to offer themselves voluntarily to be examined on subjects with which they may believe themselves to be well acquainted, and a statement of the result of such examinations, if satisfactory, is added to their certificate of competency.

There is scarcely any limit to this permission; even in the case of a candidate professing purely professional knowledge, such as an acquaintance with the principles of civil engineering, provision has been made by the commissioners to duly test his proficiency, and the result has been recorded on his certificate; but it must be remembered that these are merely honorary subjects, and neither compensate for failure in a prescribed subject, nor to receive marks in a competiton.

---

* See "Under Government."

HINTS TO CANDIDATES.

It is now proposed to give a brief general notice of the principal subjects in which candidates are examined. The various standards of qualification prescribed for admission into each department will be found in the table of contents. which is so arranged as to enable the reader to turn at once to any specimen of the examination papers to which he may have occasion to refer.

Writing.—Good handwriting is officially defined as "consisting in the clear formation of the letters of the alphabet;" it should also be rapid, neat, and of that even stroke which allows legible copies to be taken by pressing. The candidate's fitness in this subject is tested by his writing from dictation, and by the degree of proficiency he displays in copying his orthographical exercise. As this qualification is of great practical importance in the business of an office, no candidate should neglect to take means to insure competency.

Spelling is tested by dictation, (which in examinations for the lower offices is invariably short and easy,) and by the submission of a paper purposely misspelt, which candidates are expected to correct. This paper is adapted to the eye of the candidate much in the same manner as that which is dictated addresses itself to the ear, and the commissioners consider that, far from adding to the risk of failure in the case of a candidate moderately conversant with the rules of orthography, it diminishes that risk by giving him the opportunity of showing what he can do when his attention is expressly called to the matter, and when he is free from the nervousness which may sometimes be occasioned by dictation. The orthographical exercises set to candidates for clerkships and similar positions frequently consist of from 20 to 30 lines of misspelt English or general history, which they are requested to copy clearly and legibly, correcting mistakes of spelling and grammar, but not otherwise altering either the words or their order.

Dictation.—The course pursued to test the candidate's proficiency in this subject is, to select a passage of average difficulty, to read it through in the first instance with ordinary rapidity, in order that its general purport may be understood, afterwards to read it more slowly, so as to allow of its being taken down, and then either to read it once more, or to give the candidate time to correct his performance. The exercise for the lower offices consists of about a dozen lines of the simplest English, and in the case of letter-carriers is restricted to three or four lines. For clerkships and similar offices, from 12 to 20 lines are read by the examiner from some English classic. Candidates are cautioned, by a notice printed at the top of the paper on which they write, that attention must be paid to clear and legible handwriting, to correct spelling, and to proper punctuation.

Arithmetic.—This is regarded as one of the most important of the prescribed subjects, and a considerable preponderance is assigned to it in the distribution of the marks of merit. In the examination for the lower offices the arithmetical questions are of the very simplest character, and in no case do those prescribed reach beyond vulgar and decimal fractions; further, as will be seen from the examples hereafter given, the examination papers are so framed as to present nothing to the candidate of a puzzling character, being merely sufficient to ascertain whether he understands the principle, and is acquainted with the practice in the portion of arithmetic to which the questions belong. In the lower offices the examination is restricted to addition, multiplication, subtraction, and division, (in money, weights, or measures;) and in the case of letter carriers it is confined to addition and subtraction. In the examination of candidates for clerkships and similar offices, compound addition is made a special subject, for which separate marks of merit are assigned; the other questions, where a "knowledge of arithmetic, including vulgar and decimal fractions" is required, commence at reduction, and extend as far as decimal fractions.

Bookkeeping.—In some departments "bookkeeping" simply, in others "bookkeeping by double entry," and in others again a "knowledge of the principles of bookkeeping" is required. The various papers are adapted, as far as possible, to these distinctions of phraseology; and in decisions on doubtful cases regard is had to the degree of proficiency which the departmental authorities require. From candidates for situations in the inland revenue department, for example, a higher degree of proficiency is exacted than in some other cases is deemed sufficient. In some instances the questions include the ruling of a set of books. No erasures are permitted, but if any entries are thought to be wrong, they may be cancelled by drawing a pen through them, so as to leave the original clearly visible. The candidate is not allowed to make a fair copy of his answers, and if in answering his paper (when "double entry" is prescribed) he finds that so long has been taken by the first part as to render it unlikely that the whole can be finished in the time allowed, so much only must be proceeded with as can be completed, it being important that at least a portion of the paper should be carried through all the books.

English composition.—The candidate is not, in general, required to write anything in the nature of a formal theme or essay; but some very familiar and simple subject is selected, such as the Great Eastern steamship or the Crystal Palace, upon which he is to write an imaginary letter to a friend. In other cases the candidate is required to give his written opinion on some book, place, or subject with which he may happen to be familiar. A short sketch of the life and character of any one of the kings of England, and a notice of the life and writings of the author of any well-known and standard work, are among the subjects which have been set to candidates in an ordinary examination. The exercise is intended to test the power of writing correct and grammatical English, and not less than two folio pages should be written.

Précis writing is the art of presenting a succinct, faithful, and intelligent abridgment of documents or correspondence. This subject tests several very important intellectual qualities, and the commissioners value it highly in the relative distribution of marks. It will be seen that the candidate receives "instructions" from the examiners, along with the correspondence of which a précis is required. The making a short abstract of several letters, and the drawing up of a memorandum or précis stating briefly their contents, the indexing correspondence for easy reference, and the making a summary of parliamentary evidence, are the several methods adopted to test the candidate's ability in précis writing.

History and geography.—The examination papers on these subjects are so framed as to defeat the practice familiarly known as "cramming," and at the same time to give opportunities to those who know but little to show some degree of information, and to those who have been well instructed to display a greater amount of knowledge. To give an account of the leading statesmen of a particular reign; to mention the names of the commanders on each side, and the general result of some of our most famous battles; to state the principal events of a certain epoch in history, in all cases with dates, are fair specimens of the kind of questions of which an historical examination paper is composed. In geography the candidate may be called upon to mark the position of the principal towns, and to trace the course of the chief rivers, on an outline map of some European country; to explain fully the meaning of the geographical terms commonly in use; to enumerate the independent states of Europe and their capital towns; and to make a list describing the position of the most important foreign seaports with which England has commercial dealings, stating the country to which each belongs, and the principal articles of its trade with Great Britain. These, with other questions of a like nature, form an ordinary examination in geography. Unpaid attachés are specially examined in the geography and statistics of the country to which they are about to proceed.

Latin, modern languages, and extra subjects.—Examinations in languages, literature, and science are instituted for the purpose of ascertaining the relative ability, industry, and general education of the candidate. It is as an evidence of these, rather than in reference to the value of the attainments themselves, (except when from the nature of the appointment they fall into the class of practical subjects, as French and modern history, in the foreign office,) that the commissioners regard the display of merit in these branches of knowledge. In offices where Greek or Latin are prescribed, a passage of from twenty to thirty lines of some well-known author, such as Homer or Tacitus, is given to be translated into English. Translation into Greek or Latin is not prescribed for any office, but is introduced into those competitive examinations of which these languages form a part. When French, German, Italian, Spanish, or Russian is either prescribed or selected by the candidate as a branch of his examination, a page of a foreign author, such as Voltaire, Goëthe, Ariosto, Quintana, or Ystrjaloff, is given to be translated into English. Translation into these languages is not prescribed, except in the examination of candidates for the diplomatic and consular services, but it is, except in the case of candidates for the admiralty, introduced into all competitive examinations of which these languages form a part. Equity, common law, political economy, Euclid, algebra, trigonometry, geology, chemistry, and natural science, are all subjects which have been set, either in competitive examinations or when voluntarily chosen by candidates with a view of displaying their industry and intelligence.

Time and place of Examination.—After obtaining a nomination in the manner indicated in "Under Government," the candidate receives instructions from the civil service commissioners. Generally speaking not more than a fortnight elapses between nomination and examination. The commissioners hold examinations weekly throughout the year, commencing on the Tuesday, and their usual practice is to examine candidates at the next weekly examination after they receive notice of the nomination. Sometimes, however, there is a longer interval.

Competitions are occasionally held in Edinburg and Dublin for situations in Scotland and Ireland; but the examinations for situations in London are always held at the offices of the commissioners, Dean's Yard, Westminister, S. W.

The commissioners sometimes despatch one of their staff to provincial towns to conduct competitions for clerkships in such places.

The time occupied by the examination varies, according to the extent of the prescribed course, from two days to four or five.

Order of examination.—Candidates for competition, nominated by the treasury, usually receive from that department a notice of the day appointed for their examination, and subsequently receive from the civil service commissioners the following formal order, which is their passport to the examination room, and which explains the nature of their examination:

CIVIL SERVICE COMMISSION,
Dean's Yard, Westminister.

Mr. —— ——, having been nominated to [compete* with —— other candidates for] ——,

It is ordered that he be examined at ——, on Tuesday, the ——, 185-, at — o'clock precisely, in the following prescribed subjects: †

1. Writing from dictation.
2. Arithmetic, including vulgar and decimal fractions.
3. English composition.
4. Geography.
5. English history.
6. ——.

It is also ordered, at his own request, that he be examined in the following extra subjects:
* * * * *

[*This order must be produced on the day of examination.*]

Rules of examination.—Each candidate receives the following code of instructions:

1. Every candidate is required to present himself punctually at the time specified in his order.

2. The examination will commence every morning at —— and close at 5 p. m. An interval of about an hour will be allowed in the middle of the day.

3. Each candidate is required to sign his name every morning, before proceeding to his examination, in a book kept for that purpose.

4 Candidates will be permitted to leave the examination room for a short time, after having given up each paper, before proceeding to the next; but no candidate can be allowed to quit the room until he has given up the paper on which he is engaged.

5. No candidate will, on any account, be permitted to exceed the time allowed for each paper. Candidates are warned to pay attention to any instructions on this subject which may appear on the papers given to them.

6. Candidates are required to write their answers on the paper which will be given them, and to write their names at the top of every sheet of paper which they use.

7 Any candidate who is dissatisfied with the pens, ink, or paper supplied to him, is requested to apply to one of the examiners; but those who are accustomed to use any particular kind of pen are recommended to bring it with them.

8. Copy of notice given to candidates:

"Cases having occurred in which candidates under examination have been detected in attempting to use books and manuscripts which they had brought with them for their assistance, the civil service commissioners think it right to give notice that they will regard any offence of this description, committed either in the examination room or elsewhere, during the hours of examination, as affecting the moral character of the candidate, and as rendering it necessary that his certificate should be refused.

"Any candidate copying from the papers of another, or permitting his own papers to be copied, or receiving or giving assistance of any description, will expose himself to the same penalty."

9. Each candidate is informed by letter from this office of the results of his examination as soon as his case is disposed of.

10. The commissioners usually return the baptismal certificates, &c., of candidates who have failed in their examinations and apply for those documents; but it must be understood that no candidate is, under any circumstances, entitled to claim the return of any certificate deposited by him in their office, and that official forms are not in any case parted with.

Limit of age.‡—The following particulars show the evidence of age required from candidates:

1. Every candidate born in England or Wales after the 30th of June, 1837, should produce a certificate from the registrar general of births, marriages, and deaths, or his provincial officers. These certificates may be obtained at Somerset House, or from the superintendent registrar of the district in which the birth took place.

II. Every candidate not producing the above certificate must prove his age by statutory declaration, and should also, if possible, produce a baptismal certificate, or an official extract from a non-parochial register, deposited at Somerset House, under the act 3 and 4 Vict., cap. 92. This regulation applies—

1. To all candidates not born in England or Wales.
2. To candidates born in England or Wales on or before the 30th of June, 1837.
3. To candidates who, though born in England or Wales after the 30th of June, 1837, cannot produce the registrar general's certificate.

---

* If the examination is not competitive these words are omitted in the order.
† These subjects vary according to the office for which the candidate is nominated. (See List of Departments.
‡ For limit of age prescribed for admission into each department, see "Under Government."

The civil service commissioners reserve to themselves the right of deciding, in each case, upon the sufficiency of the evidence produced, but they subjoin the following general rules for the guidance of candidates:

(*a*) The declaration should specify precisely the date and place of birth, and should, if possible, be made by the father or mother of the candidate. If made by any other person it should state the circumstances which enable the declarant to speak to the fact. If an entry in a Bible or other family record be referred to, the Bible or other record must be produced at the time of making the declaration, and must be mentioned in the declaration as having been so produced.

(*b*) If the candidate was born in England or Wales after the 30th of June, 1837, the declaration must contain a statement that after due inquiry no entry has been found in the books of the registrar general, or a separate declaration containing that statement must be made.

(*c*) If no extract from a parochial or non-parochial register is produced, the declaration must contain a statement that after careful inquiry no such record has been found, and that none is believed to exist, or a separate declaration containing that statement must be made.

(*d*) Statutory declarations must be exactly in the form prescribed by the act of 5 and 6 William IV, c. 62. The eighteenth section of that act is as follows:

"And whereas it may be necessary and proper in many cases, not herein specified, to require confirmation of written instruments or allegations, or proof of debts, or of the execution of deeds or other matters: Be it therefore further enacted. That it shall and may be lawful for any justice of the peace, notary public, or other officer now by law authorized to administer an oath, to take and receive the declaration of any person voluntarily making the same before him, in the form in the schedule to this act annexed; and if any declaration so made shall be false or untrue in any material particular, the person wilfully making such false declaration shall be deemed guilty of a misdemeanor."

The prescribed form is the following:

"I, A. B., of ——, do solemnly and sincerely declare, &c., * * * and I make this solemn declaration conscientiously believing the same to be true, and by virtue of the provisions of an act made and passed in the sixth year of the reign of his late majesty, entitled 'An act to repeal an act of the present session of Parliament, for the more effectual abolition of oaths and affirmations taken and made in the various departments of the state, and to substitute declarations in lieu thereof, and for the more entire suppression of voluntary and extra judicial oaths and affidavits, and to make other provisions for the abolition of unnecessary oaths.'"

Instructions.—Candidates resident in the metropolis, or its vicinity, receive their order and instructions on their personal attendance on days specified in letters sent to them; but competitors resident in the country receive the following letter. enclosing their order and instructions through the post:

CIVIL SERVICE COMMISSION, DEAN'S YARD,
Westminster, S. W.

SIR: In consequence of a communication which has been received, acquainting the civil service commissioners that you have been nominated to compete for ——, I am to enclose an order for your examination, with other papers, and at the same time to request your attention to the following particulars:

1. The paper marked "Form A" should be filled up by you, and sent to this office by return of post, in the enclosed envelope, together with the other half of this sheet.

2. The evidence of age required by the enclosed instructions should be sent at your earliest convenience, as also the certificate as to your health, filled up and signed by a duly qualified medical practitioner.

I am, sir, your obedient servant,

———— ————.

[*This portion of the form to be torn off, signed, and sent with* "*Form A.*"]

Received:
1. An order of examination dated for the *——— day of ———.*
2. "Form A."
3. Instructions as to evidence required.
4. A form of medical certificate.

(Signature.) ———— ————.

* The date to be filled up by the candidate.

Antecedents.—Candidates are required to insert in the following form particulars of their age, education, and previous employment.

FORM A.

[To be filled up by the candidate himself.]

It is important that this form should contain a full account of the employment of your time since leaving school, whether passed in business, or however otherwise occupied.

Christian name and surname (in full)............................ Usual signature, and date........................	
Usual address....................... [If two addresses, state also that to which you wish the result of your examination to be sent.]	
Day and year of birth.. Age on last birthday............................... Place of birth....................................	
Father's name .... Father's residence............................. Father's profession or trade................................ [If deceased, give the last residence, profession, &c.]	
Schools .... [Mention the school or schools at which you were educated, stating the kind of schools, whether public or private, collegiate, national, British, &c. Mention the length of your stay in each, and the name of the master of the school last attended.] Age on finally quitting school	
Referees as to character............................... [Mention the names and addresses of two responsible persons who are well acquainted with you in private life.]	
Medical referee................................... [Give the name and address of the medical practitioner who has generally attended you or your family.]	
Are you free from pecuniary embarrassments?..................	
Have you been on any former occasion examined by the civil service commissioners?................................ [If so, state when, and for what situation.]	

First situation.	
1. Name and address of employer, &c................... 2. Business, &c., of employer............................. 3. Position held by you................................... 4. Salary or wages...................................... 5. Length of stay (giving dates)........................ 6. Cause of leaving .... Occupation in interval between first and second situation......	From —— to ——
Second situation.	
1. Name and address of employer, &c................... 2. Business, &c., of employer............................. 3. Position held by you................................... 4. Salary or wages...................................... 5. Length of stay (giving dates)........................ 6. Cause of leaving .... Occupation in interval between second and third situation.....	From —— to ——

H. Rep. Com. 47——14

FORM A—Continued.

Third situation.	
1. Name and address of employer, &c.......................	
2. Business, &c., of employer...........................	
3. Position held by you................................	
4. Salary·or wages....................................	
5. Length of stay (giving dates).......................	From —— to ——
6. Cause of leaving	
Occupation in interval between third and fourth situation......	
Fourth situation.	
1. Name and address of employer, &c.......................	
2. Business, &c., of employer...........................	
3. Position held by you................................	
4. Salary or wages....................................	
5. Length of stay (giving dates).......................	From —— to ——
6. Cause of leaving...................................	
Occupation in interval between fourth and fifth situation.......	
Fifth situation.	
1. Name and address of employer, &c.......................	
2. Business, &c., of employer...........................	
3. Position held by you................................	
4. Salary or wages....................................	
5. Length of stay (giving dates).......................	From —— to ——
6. Cause of leaving	

Character.—The following letter and list of questions is sent to each person whose name and address is given by the candidate as having employed him subsequent to his leaving school; a similar form is sent, omitting the fourth question, to the referees, whose names and addresses are given by the candidate as responsible persons well acquainted with him in private life:

CIVIL SERVICE COMMISSION, S. W.

SIR : Mr. —— ——, a candidate for the junior situation of ——, having stated that he was employed by ——, I am directed by the civil service commissioners to request that you will oblige them by filling up and returning to me, in the enclosed envelope, the "statement" hereto annexed.   The postage need not be paid.

I am to add that your answer will, if you desire it, be regarded as confidential, and that the word "confidential" should in that case be written on the envelope.

The favor of an early answer is requested.

I am, sir, your obedient servant,

—— ——.

This portion of the form to be torn off, filled up, and returned in the envelope sent therewith.]

Statement respecting —— ——, a candidate for the junior situation of ——.

QUESTIONS.

1. Are you related to the candidate ?   If so, what is the relationship ?
2. Are you well acquainted with the candidate ?
3. From what circumstances does your knowledge of him arise ?
4. Will you have the goodness to mention the dates of his entering and quitting your employment, and his reasons for leaving ?
5. How long have you known him ?
6. Is he strictly honest and sober, intelligent and diligent ?
7. Do you believe him to be free from pecuniary embarrassments ?
8. What do you know of his education and acquirements ?
9. Has he ever been in the service of the government ? and if so, in what situation ?
10. What has been the state of his health since you have known him ?
11. Are you aware of any circumstance tending to disqualify him for the situation which he now seeks ?

[Signature.]　—— ——

[Address.]　—— ——.

[Date.] —— —, ——.

Unsuccessful candidates.

In cases where the commissioners are obliged to refuse their certificate, the candidates receive the following circular, apprising them in which of the prescribed subjects they have failed:

CIVIL SERVICE COMMISSION,
Westminster, S. W.

SIR: I am directed by the civil service commissioners to acquaint you that the results of your recent examination have not been such as to justify them in granting their certificate of qualification.

The subject in which you failed ———— specified below, but it is desirable you should understand that if you are again nominated to the same or a different situation, you will be examined in all the prescribed subjects, and will not receive your certificate unless you pass to the satisfaction of the commissioners in all.

I am, sir, your obedient servant,

———— ————.

```
*    *    *    *    *    *
*    *    *    *    *    *
```

The commissioners consider that the only serious evil to be apprehended from this course of proceeding is, that the information of details of failure may lead to the second nomination of those who have failed, and that a system of cramming in respect of the particular deficiency may be resorted to. In such cases, however, this evil is obviated by an examination carefully adapted to test the reality of such knowledge. Any candidate, therefore, expecting a second nomination, should strenuously apply himself to the thorough mastery of the subject or subjects in which he previously failed.

GUIDE TO THE CIVIL SERVICE.

1. *History and proceedings of the civil service commission.*—For many years the unsatisfactory condition of the permanent civil service had attracted considerable attention, as well out of Parliament as in, until, in 1853, a commission was appointed with a view to the improvement and reorganization of that body. In November of the same year Sir Stafford Northcote and Sir Charles Trevelyan addressed a report to the lords of the treasury, stating their opinion that "the right of competing for appointment in the civil service should be open to all persons of a given age, subject only to the necessity of giving satisfactory references to persons able to speak to their moral conduct and character." Her Majesty's speech at the opening of Parliament in 1854 contained the following passage: "The establishment required for the conduct of the civil service, and the arrangements bearing upon its condition, have recently been under review, and I shall direct a plan to be laid before you which will have for its object to improve the system of admission, and thereby to increase the efficiency of the service." No such plan was laid before Parliament, but on the 21st May, 1855, her Majesty issued an order in council, appointing Sir E. Ryan, J. G. Shaw Lefevre, esq., C. B., and E. Romily, esq., commissioners for conducting the examination of young men proposed to be appointed to any of the junior situations in the civil establishments, and authorizing them to give certificates of qualification before such young men entered on their duties. After due consultation with the heads of the several departments of the civil service, a scheme of examinations was prepared, and the first examination took place on the 30th June, 1855, since which time examinations have been held nearly every week.

The principle of examination has not only been twice affirmed by resolutions of the House of Commons, but has been more formally sanctioned by two acts of Parliament. The "Act for the better government of India," (1859,) by its thirty-second section, recognizes the system of open competition, which had previously been established for appointments in the Indian civil service, and provides for the conduct of the examinations by the civil service commissioners, enacting that without their certificate no candidate shall be admitted to service in India. The superannuation act, passed in the same year, provides that, with certain exceptions, no person appointed after its date shall, for its purposes, be considered as serving in the permanent civil service of the state, unless admitted with a certificate from the civil service commissioners. In February, 1860, a select committee was appointed by the House of Commons "to inquire into the present mode of nominating and examining candidates for junior appointments in the civil service, with a view to ascertaining whether greater facility may not be afforded for the admission of properly qualified persons." In the report of this committee, dated 9th July following, the competitive principle is very strongly affirmed, and private patronage condemned. The committee do not, however, propose any sweeping change, but think that "an important step in advance will have been taken if, for the system now generally prevailing of simple nomination, there be substituted one of lim ited, but of real, competition;" and they recommend, accordingly, "that from henceforth every vacancy occurring among clerks in the civil service be competed for by not less than three candidates, to be nominated as at present, each of whom, in the first instance, shall have passed the preliminary test examination, except in the case of a single vacancy which shall not be competed for by less than five. The committee also recommend that several vacancies should be competed for at once, and that the present objectionable course of the commissioners, who inquire into the moral and physical qualifications of the candidates after examination, should be immediately altered. They further observe that "success in obtaining qualified candidates for the civil service must depend quite as much on the prospects and opportunities of promotion subsequently held out to the clerk in his official career, as on the immediate pecuniary advantages offered, or the judicious selection of young men in the first instance."

Ten reports have already been presented by the commissioners; from the latest of which, dated 12th June, 1865, it appears that the total number of nominations since the commencement of their proceedings in May, 1855, amounts to 29,763. The number of competitors for the superior situations in 1864 was 790 for 251 places, out of which 517 received nominations. Of the remaining 273, 241 fell below the standard of competence; 19 failed in respect of age; 5 in respect of health; and 8 in respect of character. For the inferior offices—letter-carriers, &c.—out of 2,384, 1,931 certificates were granted.

2. *Mode of examination.*—The mode in which the examinations are conducted in London is usually as follows: The candidates meet at the office of the civil service commission, Dean's Yard, or else at Great George street, Westminster. The arithmetic paper is given on the first morning, and the time allowed is about three hours; the afternoon is generally occupied with six or more long sums in compound addition (to be cast up without an error,) with dictation, exercises in orthography, and composition.

From many classes of candidates, as will be seen further on, no other test of proficiency is required. Others, whose examinations include a greater variety of subjects, are engaged for two or three days according to circumstances. On Wednesday morning the history paper is given, and in the afternoon the précis; on Thursday, geography and composition; and on Friday, languages and mathematics. This order depends, however, entirely upon the pleasure of the examiners, and may be changed at any time. The examination in voluntary subjects for honorary certificates never takes place until after the candidates have received notice that they have passed in the required subjects.

To insure uniformity of standard, the provincial examinations are all under the control of the central commission. The necessary papers are issued from the metropolitan office, to which the candidates' answers, with specimens of handwriting, and certificates, are returned for inspection, the commissioners deciding absolutely upon the documents then laid before them.

There is in "pass" examinations no fixed minimum, nor are marks assigned. The candidates are reported upon by epithets applied to the work they have done, the use of which is so far constant as to supply a fixed test. The commissioners, not the examiners, decide in all cases whether the candidate has passed or not. In competitive examinations marks are employed; and there are no *viva voce* questions, except in those cases where a *conversational* knowledge of a modern language is specified.

Candidates to be examined in London are generally required to attend at Dean's Yard on some day preceding that fixed for their examination, when they fill up a form containing particulars as to age, education, former employment, &c., and also give references as to character. Each then receives instruction as to the evidence of age and health required in his particular case; and, from the information thus given, the secretary writes to his referees, and also to any recent employer; to the education department, if he has been a pupil teacher; or to any of the government offices in which he has been employed. If he has served in the army or navy, or mercantile marine, he is required to produce his discharge. In all cases the commissioners refer to his former situation as to his general character; but whatever the inquiries may be, they do not delay the examination, though no certificate is granted unless the result of the inquiries is satisfactory.

As a general rule every paper is looked over twice, each of the two permanent examiners going over the other's work. In some cases, where it is perfectly clear to one of them, this is not necessary; both, however, make themselves jointly responsible for all that they do. They next report to the commissioners, who revise the papers and marks, and pronounce their decision; the successful candidates being selected as the result of such revision. Their decision is then announced to the treasury or other department, when the successful candidates are written to and requested to attend at the treasury or other office (as the case may be) on a day named, to choose their place, if there is a choice. The commissioners sometimes write to the candidates within about eight days after the close of the examination, though very often a fortnight elapses, sending them a list of marks, informing them of the place they each obtained in the competition; and, of course, whether successful or the contrary. The form of proceeding is pretty much the same in the case of "pass" examinations. The practice of renominating unsuccessful candidates within a short time after their failure having led to abuses, the lords of the treasury have fixed three months as the shortest period after which they will grant a second nomination, and in the admiralty and war office an interval of six months is required. A third chance is rarely offered to the unsuccessful candidate.

In a competitive examination each candidate is required to obtain a certain amount of marks in all the prescribed subjects.

3. *Preliminary examinations.*—Shortly after the publication of the report of the House of Commons committee of 1860, the whole character of the examinations was changed by the establishment of a preliminary or test examination, which all candidates are required to pass before going up for any competition. The subjects in this "little go" are generally limited to handwriting, orthography, arithmetic, and English composition, with Latin and book-keeping, where the departmental regulations require a knowledge of these subjects. The names of the successful candidates are returned to the treasury, where they are entered in the "qualified" list, from which all competitors for vacancies are chosen. In the year 1864, of the candidates nominated for preliminary examination, 204 passed the test and 160 failed.

In the preliminary examination, handwriting and arithmetic are the most important subjects.

(*a*) *Handwriting.*—Good writing consists in the "clear formation of the letters of the alphabet;" it should be "rapid, neat, and of that even stroke which allows of legible copies to be taken by pressing." With a moderate degree of perseverance and industry, this kind of handwriting is attainable by almost every educated person, and yet a slight acquaintance with official life shows that this most useful accomplishment is somewhat exceptional. Complaints are constantly made by the commissioners regarding the very unsatisfactory condition of the handwriting that comes before them. Great stress should be laid upon this subject No particular style is required, provided the writing possesses the main characteristic of legibility.

(*b*) *Spelling.*—The ability of the candidates in this most necessary branch of education is tested by their writing from dictation a passage of average difficulty. One of the examiners first reads aloud some passage from a book or extract from a newspaper, that the candidates may catch its general scope; he then reads it more deliberately, so that it may be written down; and lastly, he goes over it once more, that candidates may have an opportunity of correcting their errors and inserting the stops.

When an additional test of orthography is required, (as it is in all but the foreign office,) the somewhat objectionable plan is adopted of requiring the candidate to correct the erroneous spelling in a printed paper altered for the purpose. Earl Russell and Mr. Hammond, under-secretary in the foreign office, recommended as the best way of overcoming the difficulties of this "bad spelling paper," "to learn your line by heart, and shut your paper up and write from your head, not from the paper." There is no rule as to the number of faults in spelling that will "pluck" a man, as they are of such different quantity. "Some of them," says one of the examiners, "are really almost such that one of them would prove very great ignorance in a man, while others are so slight that you hardly know how to compare one with the other." No candidate has ever been rejected for less than *eight* or *ten* distinct errors in spelling; and there was a well-known case in which a candidate was not rejected until after much consideration, although his orthographical blunders amounted to *thirty-one*. The weight given to spelling is very great in competitive and pass examinations. The column in the reports of the competitive examinations headed "General Intelligence," has reference solely to the intelligence shown in the dictation and in correcting the orthography paper, including also the copying paper, where that is used.

(*c*) *Arithmetic.*—The examination under this head includes two sets of papers—the elementary, given to tidewaiters, weighers, doorkeepers, messengers, &c., and to candidates for temporary employment and in certain offices; the higher, commencing with reduction and ending with decimal fractions, given to candidates for permanent clerkships. The "test" does not extend the limits previously assigned, but the examiners require "the correct execution of a certain proportion of the sums set, especially in the addition of money." The difficulty of the long addition sums may be best overcome by dividing them into portions of five or six lines each, and then adding these partial totals. The number of questions set in the "test" paper is usually under forty.

(*d*) *Composition.*—The aptness of a candidate in English composition is not in general tested by requiring him to compose a formal theme or essay; but some familiar subject is selected as the topic on which he is to write. The subjects usually bear upon the events of the day or of recent occurrence, as "the Fenian insurrection," "the volunteer review," "the advantages and disadvantages derived from works of fiction," or some book or place with which the candidate may happen to be familiar. The commissioners "have found but few instances in which a candidate has shown great facility in composing even an ordinary letter." In assigning marks under this head, they have regard only to the exercise, strictly so called, and not at all to the style in which the questions are answered in the other papers on geography, history, or any other subject.

An important change was made in 1863 by the war office in the mode of admission to the department. Candidates who pass the test examination are appointed "temporary" clerks and in order to become "established" clerks they have to compete—five for a single vacancy and four each if several vacancies are to be filled up. Those who fail to pass the test examination cannot be nominated again until after the expiration of six months, and upon a second failure they are struck off the list. No candidate who fails in three competitive examinations will be sent up again.

4. *Final or competitive examination.*—Examination by competition is now almost entirely the plan adopted through which a government situation can be obtained. The mere *pass* is rarely resorted to, except in examinations for attachéships and offices in the consulate. The system of competition has been twice affirmed by resolutions of the House of Commons:

Resolution of 24th April, 1856.—"An address to thank her Majesty for having caused to be laid before this house the report of the civil service commissioners; to state humbly to her Majesty that the house has observed with great satisfaction the zeal and prudence with which the commission has proceeded in applying a remedy to evils of a serious character, the previous existence of which has now been placed beyond dispute; and also the degree of progress which has been made, with the sanction of the heads of various departments of the states towards the establishment of *a system of competition* among candidates for admission to the civil service; to assure her Majesty of the steady support of this house in the prosecution of the salutary measures which she has been graciously pleased to adopt; and humbly to make known to her Majesty that if she shall think fit further to extend them, and to make trial in the civil service of the method of *open competition* as a condition of entrance, this house will cheerfully provide for any charges which the adoption of that system may entail." (*Lord Goderich.*)

Resolution of 14th July, 1857.—"That in the opinion of this house the experience acquired since the issuing of the order in council of the 21st day of May, 1855, is in favor of the adoption of *the principle of competition* as a condition of entrance to the civil service; and that *the application of that principle ought to be extended,* in conformity with the resolution of the house agreed to on the 24th day of April, 1856." (*Lord Goderich.*)

The usual plan was (and to a great extent still is) to nominate three persons to one vacancy, when the candidate who obtains the greatest number of marks in the examination is appointed. But it was soon found that this was a very uncertain mode of filling up vacancies, and to some extent unfair to the competitors. In their third report, the civil service commissioners entered into the question at some length:

"With regard to the cases in which three candidates have been examined for one situation, we must notice an unsatisfactory result which is likely to arise, and which in fact has arisen, from the number of candidates who are to compete together being so frequently limited to three. In such cases it may and does happen, from time to time, that one or two of the competing candidates fail to reach the positive minimum which would entitle them to a certificate, so that the actual competition is either reduced to two, or virtually ends in a simple pass examination. Thus, out of 22 competitions for situations in the customs, there were ten cases in which only two, and eight in which only one of the candidates examined were capable of passing. In the inland revenue also, in 16 competitions, there were two in which two, and ten in which only one, of the candidates examined could have passed, while in others three capable candidates competed for two situations, and four for three situations.

"In noticing these anomalies, we must admit that under any conceivable arrangement there will still remain differences in the average merits of one set of competitors and another set, and candidates may gain or lose by being accidentally placed in a weak or strong body of competitors; but, at all events, this evil would be very much diminished by having one large instead of several small competitions."

They took up the subject again in the fourth report, and, to enforce their views, quoted two recent competitions for junior situations, of the same nature and in the same office, in which the marks given were as follows:

FIRST COMPETITION.	Total marks.	SECOND COMPETITION.	Total marks.
Candidate No. 1	3,685	Candidate No. 1	1,355
" No. 2	2,530	" No. 2	1,256
" No. 3	1,365	" No. 3	865

"It will be perceived that No. 2 in the first competition had much higher marks than No. 1 in the second, and that even No. 3 in the first examination just surpassed No. 1 in the second, although the subjects of examination and the examination papers were the same in both, and the examination took place simultaneously."

The practical conclusion to which the commissioners arrived was, that the number of candidates should be increased, so as to bear a larger proportion to the vacancies, three to one being insufficient. As yet they have not succeeded, to any great extent, in altering the number of competitors; but large competitions are more frequent and with the most satisfactory results. It is evident that the chance of obtaining the best men must be greater in one large competition than in several small ones, even when the same number of prizes and competitors is maintained. Thus, if 60 men go in to compete for 20 situations, the 20 successful competitors in one contest of the whole number would be almost certainly superior to the 20 victors in 20 separate competitions of three each, because the second and even the third man in one of the small competitions would occasionally be found superior to the first man in another.

In consequence of the proved failure of the competitive system when thus worked, the House of Commons committee of 1860 recommended (as we have mentioned before) that no candidate should be allowed to compete for any vacancy, unless he had passed a preliminary "test" examination. This at once excluded the incompetent, put the competitors more on a level, and also increased the severity of the examinations.

The following table will show the progress made by the competitive system during the last seven years:

	1858.	1859.	1860.	1861.	1862.	1863.	1864.
Number of examinations..................	122	96	80	94	118	133	131
Situations competed for....................	230	286	236	266	289	278	251
Number of competitors....................	745	1,260	688	812	994	920	859
Number examined......	647	1,107	603	715	864	813	784

The most important competitive examination that has taken place since the establishment of the commission was that for eight vacancies in the office of the secretary of state for India. It was thrown open to all comers; and, out of 789 applicants, no less than 339 actually presented themselves for examination at Willis's rooms, on the 18th January, 1859. The examination lasted three days, six hours each day, interrupted only by a break for refreshment; and, on the 11th February the names of the successful competitors were declared. The third and fourth and the seventh and eighth were bracketed as equal; but as the eighth had failed in history and the ninth in handwriting, the tenth received the required certificate. Seven of the successful candidates offered themselves for a voluntary examination in extra subjects, and obtained honorary additions to their certificates for proficiency in Greek, Latin, German, French, political economy, Euclid, algebra, &c. The total of marks was 1,550, but the highest only reached 1,130, while the lowest was 84. Of the successful competitors, one was a sub-editor of a newspaper, one a school-assistant, two were schoolmasters, and three clerks.

The object of the final examination is to ascertain whether the candidate has received a liberal education, and, with this view, he will have papers set before him on the following subjects:

(a) *Arithmetic.*—In addition to the arithmetic paper given in the "preliminary," the candidate is now required to solve a number of miscellaneous questions or problems, which occasionally tax his ingenuity very sorely.

(b) *History and geography.*—In pass examinations an amount of knowledge in these subjects, rarely exceeding what may be acquired at good schools, has been received as sufficient. In competitions a much more extensive acquaintance with them is required.

(c) *Bookkeeping.*—The specimens given further on will enable a candidate to form some idea of what will be required of him, though the nature of some of the questions will make an experienced and practical bookkeeper smile. The paper given in the final examination is generally more difficult than that in the preliminary, and sometimes consists of problems only.

(d) *English composition.*—If the candidate passes this in the "preliminary," he will probably not be called upon for another essay.

(e) *Latin and modern languages.*—The candidate is required to translate into English, except where the department specially requires in addition a version from English into other languages. Latin and modern languages are mostly ranked among the voluntary subjects, except in the record office and a few others, where they are absolutely required.

(f) *Euclid and algebra.*—In Euclid a knowledge of the first three books would suffice for an ordinary examination; but the addition of the fourth and sixth, with some practice in working problems, would not be too much for a stiff competition. The algebra papers are usually "tough customers," and require a thorough knowledge of quadratic equations and of progression, arithmetical and geometrical.

(g) *Précis.*—In some offices, especially in the foreign and record offices, very great weight is attached to *précis* writing. Mr. Hammond considers it "the only test of a candidate's ability." The exercises given in the following pages will show the nature of the examination to be passed, and in what manner the candidate may best prepare himself for it. It is one of those studies, however, that can hardly be followed successfully without a tutor.

[From the London Times, May 18, 1868.]

INDIA CIVIL SERVICE.

The following are the successful candidates at the recent open competition for the civil service of India, provided they pass a medical examination to be held in London in the course of this week :

Numbers.		Name.	Total number of marks.
In order of merit.	In examination.		
1	207	Bowie, Robert Wylie	2,523
2	46	Beaven, Alfred Beaven	2,151
3	154	Ibbetson, Denzil Charles Jelf	2,129
4	157	Jenkyns, William	1,989
5	182	Clarke, Robert	1,978
6	217	Campbell, John Colin	1,976
7	127	Deas, Joseph	1,878
8	293	Buckland, Charles Edward	1,865
9	83	Morrison, William Hudson	1,838
10	103	Burgess, George Douglas	1,825
11	190	Channing, Francis Chorley	1,820
12	161	Thomson, John Brown	1,788
13	167	Fisher, Frederic Henry	1,738
14	79	Wallace, James	1,722
15	252	Redfern, Thomas Robert	1,694
16	128	Thomas, Henry Dealtry	1,631
17	135	Graves, Arnold Felix	1,666
18	117	Bullock, Frederick Shore	1,660
19	234	Dames, Mansel Longworth	1,642
20	221	Horan, Thomas	1,608
21	187	Rivaz, George Wilmot	1,600
22	118	James, Stephen Harvey	1,596
23	70	Weidemann, George Lever	1,590
24	248	Henderson, Henry Philipse	1,584
25	282	Monteath, James	1,554
26	276	Bourdillon, James	1,544
27	37	Brown, Arthur Ormsby	1,528
28	15	Paul, Alfred Wallis	1,521
29	172	Baines, Jervoise Athelstane	1,520
30	{ 215	Abbott, Leonard Charles	1,494
	230	Bird, George Emilius	1,494
32	{ 20	Macaulay, Colman Patrick Louis	1,486
	211	Marsden, Delabene Weston	1,486
34	263	Cornish, Robert	1,476
35	5	Skrine, Francis Henry Bennet	1,464
36	188	Meiklejohn, David Ogilvy	1,457
37	206	Cuningham, William John	1,454
38	208	Ommanney, Henry Travers	1,434
39	140	Elliot, Frederick Augustus Hugh	1,427
40	35	Batty, Herbert	1,414
41	175	M'Cullum, Edwin	1,405
42	96	Brown, Robert Shelton	1,401
43	163	MacCartie, Charles Falkiner	1,392
44	56	Acworth, Henry Arbuthnot	1,385
45	133	Oliver, Arthur Knapp	1,379
46	113	Underwood, Walter Gregory	1,373
47	42	Frost, Charles Evitt	1,365
48	227	Jacob, Philip	1,338
49	151	Fitz Gerald, James Richard	1,331
50	201	Horsley, William Henry	1,325

The number of candidates examined was 268. A table showing the marks obtained in each subject is being printed, and a copy will be sent to each candidate in a few days.

A BILL to regulate the civil service of the United States and promote the efficiency thereof.

Be it enacted by the Senate and House of Representatives of the United States of America in Congress assembled, That from and after the passage of this act there shall be created a new department of the government of the United States, to be called the Department of the Civil Service; that the head of said department shall be the Vice-President of the United States, or in case of a vacancy in said office, the President of the Senate for the time being, who shall be a member and president of the board of commissioners hereinafter created, and shall perform all the duties pertaining thereto.

SEC. 2. *And be it further enacted,* That hereafter all appointments of civil officers in the several departments of the service of the United States, except postmasters and such officers as are by law required to be appointed by the President by and with the advice and consent of the Senate, shall be made from those persons who shall have been found best qualified for the performance of the duties of the offices to which such appointments are to be made, in [an] open and competitive examinations, to be conducted as herein prescribed.

SEC. 3. *And be it further enacted,* That there shall be appointed by the President, by and with the advice and consent of the Senate, a board of four commissioners, who shall hold their offices for the term of five years, to be called the civil service examination board, among whose duties shall be the following:

First. To prescribe the qualifications requisite for an appointment into each branch and grade of the civil service of the United States, having regard to the fitness of each candidate in respect to age, health, character, knowledge, and ability for the branch of service into which he seeks to enter.

Second. To provide for the examinations and periods and conditions of probation of all persons eligible under this act who may present themselves for admission into the civil service.

Third. To establish rules governing the applications of such persons, the times and places of their examinations, the subjects upon which such examinations shall be had, with other incidents thereof, and the mode of conducting the same, and the manner of keeping and preserving the records thereof, and of perpetuating the evidence of such applications, qualifications, examinations, probations, and their result, as they shall think expedient. Such rules shall be so framed as to keep the branches of the civil service and the different grades of each branch, as also the records applicable to each branch, distinct and separate. The said board shall divide the country into territorial districts for the purpose of holding examinations of applicants resident therein and others, and shall designate some convenient and accessible place in each district where examinations shall be held.

Fourth. To examine personally, or by persons by them specially designated, the applicants for appointment into the civil service of the United States.

Fifth. To make report of all rules and regulations established by them, and of a summary of their proceedings, including an abstract of their examinations for the different branches of the service, annually, to Congress at the opening of each session.

SEC. 4. *And be it further enacted,* That all appointments to the civil service provided for in this act shall be made from those who have passed the required examinations and probations in the following order and manner:

First. The applicant who stands highest in order of merit on the list of those who have passed the examination and probation for any particular branch and grade of the civil service shall have the preference in appointment to that branch and grade, and so on, in the order of precedence in examinations and merit during probation to the minimum degree of merit fixed by the board for such grade.

Second. Whenever any vacancy shall occur in any grade of the civil service above the lowest, in any branch, the senior in the next lower grade may be appointed to fill the same, or a new examination for that particular vacancy may be ordered, under the direction of the department, of those in the next lower grade, and the person found best qualified shall be entitled to the appointment to fill such vacancy : *Provided,* That no person now in office shall be promoted or transferred from a lower to a higher grade, unless he shall have passed at least one examination under this act.

Third. The right of seniority shall be determined by the rank of merit assigned by the board upon the examinations, having regard also to seniority in service; but it shall at all times be in the power of the heads of departments to order new examinations, which shall be conducted by the board, upon due notice, and according to fixed rules, and which shall determine seniority with regard to the persons ordered to be examined, or in the particular branch and grade of the service to which such examinations shall apply.

Fourth. Said board shall have power to establish rules for such special examinations, and also rules by which any persons exhibiting particular merit in any branch of the civil service may be advanced one or more points in their respective grades ; and one-fourth of the promotions may be made on account of merit, irrespective of seniority in service, such merit to be ascertained by special examinations, or by advancement for meritorious services and special fitness for the particular branch of service, according to rules to be established as aforesaid.

SEC. 5. *And be it further enacted,* That said board shall also have power to prescribe a fee, not exceeding five dollars, to be paid by each applicant for examination, and also a fee, not exceeding ten dollars, to be paid by each person who shall receive a certificate of recommendation for appointment or for promotion, or of seniority, which fees shall be first paid to the collector of internal revenue in the district where the applicant or officer resides or may be examined, to be accounted for and paid into the treasury of the United States by such collector ; and the certificates of payment of fees to collectors shall be forwarded quarterly by the commissioners to the Treasury Department.

SEC. 6. *And be it further enacted,* That said board shall have power to prescribe, by general rules, what misconduct or inefficiency shall be sufficient for the removal or suspension of all officers who come within the provisions of this act, and also to establish rules for the manner of preferring charges for such misconduct or inefficiency, and for the trial of the accused, and for determining his position pending such trial.

SEC. 7. *And be it further enacted,* That any one of said commissioners may conduct or superintend any examinations, and the board may call to their assistance in such examinations such men of learning and high character as they may think fit, or, in their discretion, such officers in the civil, military, or naval service of the United States, as may be designated from time to time, on application of the board, as assistants to said board, by the President or heads of departments ; and in special cases, to be fixed by rules or by resolutions of the board, they may delegate examinations to such persons, to be attended and presided over by one member of said board, or by some persons specially designated to preside.

SEC. 8. *And be it further enacted,* That the said board may also, upon reasonable notice to the person accused, hear and determine any case of alleged misconduct or inefficiency, under the general rules herein provided for, and in such case shall report to the head of the proper department their finding in the matter, and may recommend the suspension or dismissal from office of any person found guilty of such misconduct or inefficiency ; and such person shall be forthwith suspended or dismissed by the head of such department pursuant to such recommendation, and from the filing of such report shall receive no compensation for official service except from and after the expiration of any term of suspension recommended by such report.

SEC. 9. *And be it further enacted,* (That the salary of each of said commissioners, and the additional salary of the Vice-President for performing the duties required of him by this act, shall be five thousand dollars a year, and the said board may appoint a clerk at a salary of two thousand five hundred dollars a year, and a messenger at a salary of nine hundred dollars a year, and these sums and the necessary travelling expenses of the commissioners, clerk, and messenger, to be accounted for in detail and verified by affidavit, shall be paid from any money in the treasury not otherwise appropriated. The necessary expenses of any person employed by said commissioners, as assistants, to be accounted for and verified in like manner, and certified by the board, shall also be paid in like manner.

SEC. 10. *And be it further enacted,* That any officer in the civil service of the United States, at the date of the passage of this act, other than those excepted in the [first] *second* section of this act, may be required by the head of the department in which he serves to appear before said board, and if found not qualified for the place he occupies he shall be reported for dismissal, and be dismissed in the manner hereinbefore provided, and the vacancy shall be filled in manner aforesaid from those who may be found qualified for such grade of office after such examination.

SEC. 11. *And be it further enacted,* That all citizens of the United States shall be eligible to examination and appointment under the provisions of this act, and the heads of the several departments may, in their discretion, designate the offices in the several branches of the civil service the duties of which may be performed by females as well as males, and for all such offices females as well as males shall be eligible, and may make application therefor and be examined, recommended, appointed, tried, suspended, and dismissed, in manner aforesaid; and the names of those recommended by the examiners shall be placed upon the lists for appointment and promotion in the order of their merit and seniority, and without distinction, other than as aforesaid, from those of male applicants or officers.

SEC. 12. *And be it further enacted,* That the President, and also the Senate, may require any person applying for or recommended for any office which requires confirmation by the Senate to appear before said board and be examined as to his qualifications, either before or after being commissioned; and the result of such examination shall be reported to the President and to the Senate.

SEC. 13. *And be it further enacted,* That until the confirmation by the Senate of the commissioners authorized to be appointed by this act, the head of said department is hereby authorized to appoint persons to perform the duties of commissioners temporarily, with the same powers and at the same rate of compensation as hereinbefore provided.

www.ingramcontent.com/pod-product-compliance
Lightning Source LLC
Chambersburg PA
CBHW021437020726
47499CB00006BA/2041